G A Y L E   A N D   S T E P H E N

P O R T E R

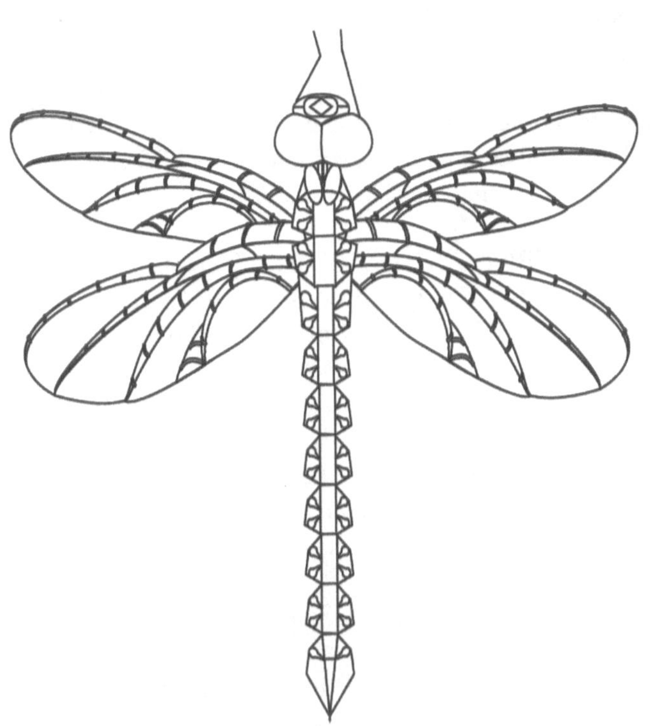

EX MAGICA

DIKAIÓ: Book I

ISBN: 978-1-957907-00-0 (Paperback)
ISBN: 978-1-957907-01-7 (Hardcover)
ISBN: 978-1-957907-02-4 (Ebook)

Library of Congress Control Number: 2022904475

Any references to historical events, real people, or real places are used fictitiously. Names, characters, and places are products of the authors' imagination.

Book design by Stephen Porter.

First printing edition 2022. Printed in the United States of America.

Porter Creative
3647 Oviedo
Brownsville TX 78520

www.portercreatives.com

To our children, Nathaniel and Elizabeth,

Your enthusiasm to see the work completed, and your polite begging to hear each new chapter, kept us going. We started this book with the desire to provide a good story for you—something that would inspire you to learn and do hard things, face failure with creativity, and pull together in faithful friendship when times are difficult. We finished this book because you lived out these qualities. Thanks for your patience, hard work, and diligence—in both homework and chores—so that we would have time to write this story for you.

THE CITY

Hospital
Rookery
PASTURELAND
PASTURELAND
MATRIARCH'S
HOUSE
ADMINISTRATOR'S
HOUSE
MAIN ST
GOVERNOR'S
SILVER ST
DISTRICT
GOVERNOR'S
HOUSE
City Hall

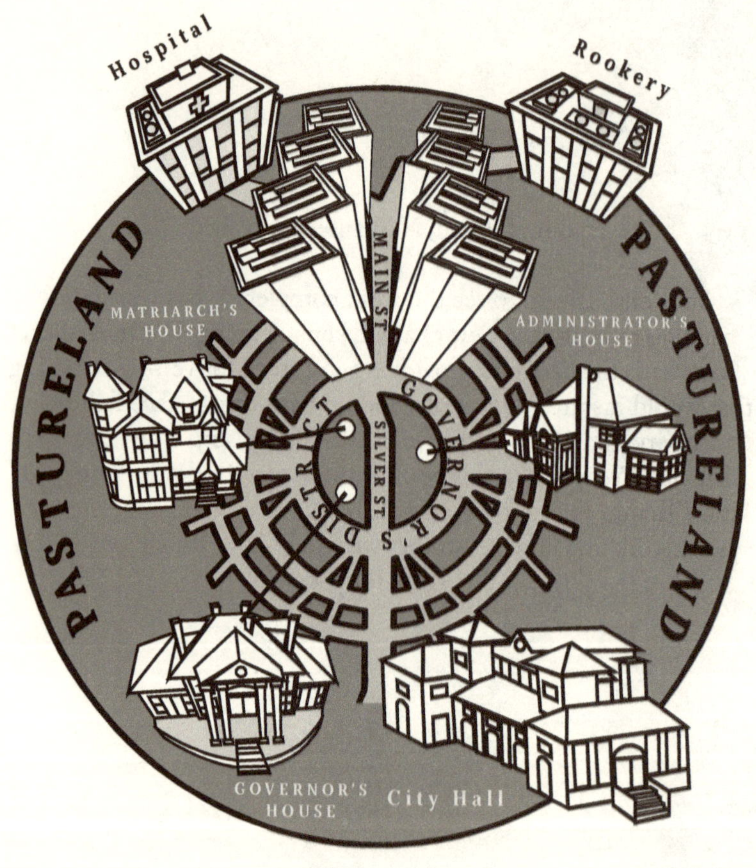

CONTENTS

In the garden, the dragonfly and the child regarded one another with wary curiosity. The one was perched on a stalk of purple sage, the other on a white stone bench. If it were possible to know one another's thoughts, they would have been amused to know that they were not all that different, each wondering whether the other was likely to bite. It was the child who decided to move first, reasoning, as well as a one-year-old might, that a bite from such a small creature was worth the risk of touching the dragonfly's stained-glass-like wings, and she might even try a taste should the opportunity present itself. Sensing the child's intention, the dragonfly tamped back its fear and leapt from the sage, flying straight at the girl, ready to fight if the need arose, but mostly hoping to catch its opponent off guard and escape. Startled, the child fell backwards and sat down hard on the garden path, her billowy white dress filling with air as she fell and landing about her like a white chrysanthemum.

The child's mother had brown hair nearly as curly as her daughter's but straightened into submission and stylishly imprisoned with bobby pins below her half-veiled derby hat. She had been watching the encounter and smiled softly at her confused little girl. The woman picked the girl up off the ground and placed her back atop the stone bench beside her. Their white dresses brushed lazily against one another in the breeze. The girl's father, dressed in his best suit, had not even noticed the dragonfly or his daughter's fall as he paced nervously behind them. The girl had his eyes, which were blue but had so little pigment that they looked gray and flashed with reflected light with every turn of his head. The girl's mother looked past her husband down the long cobblestone boulevard toward the garden's entrance. It was not quite noon, and she was trying to be patient.

She inclined her head toward her daughter, eyes twinkling with love and pride. "Your grandmother is almost here, Mallory. Do you remember the words?"

Mallory smiled. She had been playing this game since she first learned to walk and talk. "I want ball," she said with confidence.

"That's right, little one. Mallory wants to play with her ball." As soon as the words were out of her mother's mouth, a small red ball fell from her pocket and rolled across the bench to Mallory. Mallory picked up the ball and shouted, "My ball!

My ball!"

Mallory's father stopped pacing and touched his daughter's head tenderly, and her mother felt the pools of pride and love in her eyes spill over a bit. She dabbed at her pride with the humble handkerchief tucked in her white glove. Then her husband's head cocked to the left slightly. "Do you hear that?"

Just audible beyond the wind in the trees and the songbirds flirting in the branches above, faint music grew steadily louder. "They're coming," she said and stood up wrapping her gloved, trembling hand in her husband's. They turned toward the hedged entrance in anticipation. Mallory looked at her parents then at the entrance and back again, confused. Soon, the music pulsed through the garden, a symphony of strings, horns, and the intoxicating beat of a drumline. Mallory and her parents felt their hearts begin to beat in sync to the bass that pounded the air around them. Unconsciously, their hips began to sway, and their heads to nod in time with the rhythm.

Then Mallory's grandmother turned past the hedges onto the pathway. Her carved cane slapped the cobblestones of the path on every downbeat of the drums as she walked. The old woman was dressed in her official robes as the City Matriarch and strode down the lane with all the pomp and circumstance that a Dikaió christening of this magnitude deserved. Mallory's grandfather followed just behind his wife. He was also dressed in his official robes, but the joy of the occasion had overcome him. He danced rapturously. The musicians followed behind him. There were ten of them in the line, but each had three or four instruments that they were playing.

4 - EX MAGICA

The instruments flew around the musicians, and like electric songbirds, they swooped and swirled, blazing with vibrant hues of neon light as the notes played.

The musicians never physically touched their instruments, but every motion of their dance moved through the instruments' lights and pulled musical intonations from the swirling orchestra. The string musicians flowed in a line like ballerinas, using pirouettes and jetés to glide among the lights; their hands beckoning chords and vibrato from the guitars, violins, cellos, and basses flying around them. The woodwinds waltzed in tight circles around their flutes, clarinets, and bassoons. They bowed and tickled the light near the translucent sticks, twirling them about like dance partners at a ball. The brass musicians bopped and swung through the midst of their trumpets, French horns, trombones, and tubas; the musicians chests filling and expulsing just the right amount of breath while their mouths formed the necessary embouchures to sound their notes within the lights. They looked a bit like fish out of water, mouthing O's and U's, and it would have been comical if not for the overwhelming blasts from the hovering horns. Finally, the frenetic percussion line drove seventeen drums floating in a line before them. "Boom, t-t-tch hiss BOOM BOOM," their instruments pulsated as the drummers' arms popped, locked, and waved, intricately pounding the lights with precision. The individual motions of the musicians might have caused an onlooker to expect some discordancy in the music, but every note was tuned in perfect harmony with its neighbor.

All of the non-essential citizens of the city followed

behind the musicians, and like the music they expressed themselves both individually and in concert. Some were imitating the seriousness of the Matriarch and some the joy of her husband and musicians in their dance. But all seemed to be caught in the thrall of the music as their feet landed in unison on the down beat of the Matriarch's cane, and their heads nodded in sync, as if the entire community were one living organism drifting in a melodic wave of light and sound: a neon dance parade.

Despite the evidence of her cane's motion, the Matriarch seemed mostly unaffected by the music. Her gaze was aimed at Mallory and her parents in an "all-business" sort of way. Every now and then, when he danced too close, she gave her husband disparaging sidelong glances, but the tics of amusement at the corner of her mouth betrayed her desire to join him if not for her official role in the ceremony. Clearly, she was torn between the formality of her duty and the celebration of her granddaughter's Dikaió.

As the procession approached, Mallory dropped her ball, took her parent's hands, and tried to pull them toward her grandparents and the musical lights swirling down the boulevard. Her father knelt down and pointed toward the fountain at the center of the park. "We're going there," he tried to say, but his words were drowned out by the music.

Mallory shook her head and pointed toward the procession. The music stole her "NO!" as well, but her set jaw and squared hips carried the message.

Her mother laughed, shrugged, and weaved her hips in a figure eight: an invitation to her husband. Her father laughed in answer, leaned backward, and awkwardly began dancing toward the celebration, circling his fists in the air in front of him like he was spooling rope to the beat. Mallory squealed with delight, sprinting toward the musicians. Her mother's squeal trailed after her, as she chasséd after her husband like a ballerina, all of them joining the city as it danced.

The Matriarch stopped when she reached the fountain at the center of the gardens. She stood before the monument, taking a moment to trace the ancient reliefs sculpted into the fountain's center ring and appreciate the traditions of their people. In the center of the ring an old woman stooped to pick up a toddling girl, to the right of that image, a young girl ran after a kite without strings, to the right of that a preadolescent dancing among the flowers, and so the images aged through the life cycle of the woman until she was an old woman stooping to pick up a toddler. Men of all ages were sculpted into the twelve pillars between the scenes of the aging woman, their bodies forever straining to hold the massive basin where the fountain waters performed their choreographed acrobatics. At the very top of the highest arch of water, there was a small unadorned pedestal.

The Matriarch turned and loudly said, "Listen!" Her cane struck the cobblestones emitting trails of blue flame that swirled up its shaft and into the air in random directions like lightning arcs. The music stopped. The crowd stopped. Even the songbirds in the trees that no one had noticed stopped. The City Council walked silently to the fountain, flanking the Matriarch, six men on one side, and six women on the other. Every citizen was solemn.

The Matriarch spoke: "For generations we have lived in the mystery of the Dikaió. From birth to death, its magic sustains us. And today we bestow the mystery to Mallory Knenne." She turned to Mallory's mother and father. "Do you have the object of endearment?"

Mallory's mother looked down at Mallory who was standing wide eyed at her hip. Mallory did not have her red ball. "Mallory wants to play with her ball," her mother said, and after a moment the little red ball rolled from wherever it had been discarded to her daughter's feet. Her mother knelt gently down and looked her daughter in the eyes. "Your grandmother would like to see your ball, Mallory. Let's show everyone how well you know the words."

Mallory stooped to pick up her ball, and rather than take it to her grandmother, she clutched it tightly to her chest. "It's mine." She eyed her mother and then her grandmother defiantly, daring them to take it.

Every toddler made this part difficult, but the Matriarch had hoped for better from her own granddaughter. No matter: She turned and smiled broadly to the crowd. "As Dikaió Syntec, I christen Mallory Knenne-Dikaió Chorus." Her husband winced as a murmur erupted in the crowd. The City Council members turned in disbelief toward the Matriarch.

The City Administrator, an older man roughly the same age as the Matriarch, stepped forward from the line of council members smoothing back his peppered gray hair and stammered, "Sarah, we discussed this, and agreed . . ."

The Matriarch turned to him with fire in her eyes, "No,

you agreed! I speak only for the Dikaió!"

"You old witch! I hope you--"

The words were cut off when the Governor, young and newly appointed, leapt forward and clamped his hands over the Administrator's mouth. The Administrator struggled to free himself from the younger man's grip. The Governor held him soundly and shouted, "Even the Administrator of Justice is not above the law, James. Watch your tongue." In a world of magic, words could be dangerous, and the Administrator stopped struggling and stood still, signaling acquiescence.

The Governor pulled his hand away, and the Administrator looked at him, then back to the Matriarch, and hissed, "You'll both be the ruin of this city. I can only hope your daughter has better sense as a Matriarch than you, Sarah."

The Matriarch retorted, "We're all aware of your ambition for rule, James! You cannot control me, nor my daughter, nor my granddaughter. The Matriarchs speak for the Dikaió!"

A councilwoman stepped forward and touched her shoulder, "Sarah, the Matriarch is always a Syntec. Like you, like your daughter . . . he's just worried. We're all worried."

"I speak for the Dikaió," the Matriarch repeated firmly.

"But it was just a dream. How do you know it was the Dikaió?"

"We've been through this, Celeste," the Matriarch hissed. Then, she whispered urgently to all the council members, nodding toward the staring crowd, "This isn't the time."

The council members fell back in line. A mix of emotions ranging from shock to anger played across their collective faces. The crowd continued to murmur and pockets of agitation began to form. Questions floated in the air: "What's a Chorus?" "Why not a Syntec?" "Who will christen our grandchildren's children?" The Matriarch again stamped her cane on the cobblestone and spoke loudly, "Listen!"

The crowd settled and stood in nervous anticipation.

The Matriarch looked to Mallory and held out her hand for the little red ball. Mallory turned and held the ball away, looking back into her grandmother's eyes with her jaw set. She was ready to take this as far as her grandmother was willing to go. The Matriarch rolled her eyes. The city was already on edge and tangling with a toddler over a ball was not going to do much to improve the situation. She took a deep breath and firmly ordered, "Mallory's ball to the fountain pedestal!" The ball wrenched itself from Mallory's hands and leapt 20 feet in the air to alight gently onto the pedestal at the top of the fountain.

Mallory's mother braced for the toddler to break into tears, but the girl just stood looking after her ball determinedly, her little teeth biting her lip and her head cocked to the side. "The words, Mallory," she prompted.

"I want my ball!" Mallory yelled.

All eyes looked to the little red ball that sat motionless atop the fountain's pedestal then back to Mallory.

"Try again, sweetie," her mother prompted.

"I want my ball." Mallory said, quieter this time. Tears were nearer now.

Nothing happened.

The crowd erupted: "Why doesn't the ball move?" "Maybe,

she wasn't clear?" "I've heard toddlers less clear and the magic worked. Something's wrong!" "She doesn't have the Dikaió!" "What does it mean?" "What will we do?"

The entire council circled in fury around the Matriarch: "What have you done?" "We warned you about such foolishness!" "Try again! Give her a different christening."

The Matriarch, not usually one to admit a mistake, uttered quietly: "I christen Mallory Knenne-Dikaió Syntec."

The Administrator curled his lip in disgust, turning away from the Matriarch and shaking his head, "You can't change a christening once it's given. How many times did we warn you? You and your family are disgraced."

Then a small voice shouted above the din: "I got my ball!"

The whole city looked in hope toward the sound of the voice, but their hopes became confusion as they beheld, not a girl who had called her beloved ball to her with the magic of her voice, but a dripping wet toddler standing twenty feet in the air atop a small pedestal holding a little red ball triumphantly in the air like a torch bearer about to light the eternal flame.

An anonymous citizen voiced the whole city's question: "How did she do that?"

Red-and-white checkered awnings lined both sides of Main Street, providing shade to the countless tables, which were full of unnaturally large produce of every conceivable variety from every climate known to grow edible plants: carrots, cucumbers, tomatoes, potatoes, mangos, pineapple, coffee, cocoa. The Dikaió Culture citizens grew the crops that fed the city in their fields atop the glass towers downtown—each skyscraper roof grew an abundance of seasonal produce to fill the market each week. Some of the stalls displayed animal products like milk, cheese, and honey. Animals were precious, so meat was reserved for special occasions and could not be found at the market. It would not be safe to keep the animals atop the skyscrapers where the crops were grown, so the livestock were kept in the prairie lands just outside the city, but not outside the protection of the city's light.

On Saturdays, the Farmer's Market was usually full of the bustling noises of the city's citizens shopping for the week, but that day the crowds were silently staring at a seventeen-year-old girl with stormy gray eyes, olive skin, and wild, curly brown hair flowing behind her as she ran down the center lane carrying her groceries home.

A woman's voice broke the silence: "How did she do that?"

The question was familiar enough that it did not interrupt Mallory's concentration. She moved with wicked speed, pushing a one-wheeled wooden cart full of produce and using two long poles in the back to steer. Her chin jutted out with determination, as she deftly maneuvered the cart around the stunned crowd, including a magistrate in his pristine blue uniform and cap, who blew his whistle and called for her to stop. His calls were largely irrelevant, as everyone knew that he would never chase her down or bring her before the Administrator given her family's status. Besides, the cart was so heavy at this point that it was almost impossible to stop, and the slight slope of Main Street meant that Mallory was picking up speed. Two companions, roughly her age, were running after her. Her friends were transporting their groceries in the usual fashion, in their families' grocery boxes. The boxes, white with silver stripes, flew via six spinning propellers. Loaded with their families' allotted groceries, the boxes were struggling to keep up with the three teenagers.

The boy, Caleb, was tall with short-cropped sandy, blond

hair. His eyes were every bit as bright and piercing as the girl with the cart's were gray and stormy. The sky reflected in them seemed to laugh as he ran. The other girl, who went by Alex instead of Alexandria, had emerald-green eyes, and she was breathing heavily. Her straight, black hair bobbed harshly as she stumbled along. She wore a simple dark blue uniform, nearly identical to the magistrate's except for the insignia and holstered weapon. She was slightly shorter than the girl with the cart, but her demeaner demanded attention, which was saying something given the spectacle racing down the street.

"Mallory," Alex huffed, "would you please just let us help you? All we have to do is say the word."

"Whatever for, my dear?" Mallory laughed merrily as she turned a corner on the left, nearly spilling all the contents of her cart. "I think this new invention is working quite well, and it's so much faster than your silly old Dikaió boxes anyway. What do you think, Caleb?"

Caleb nodded, "Oh yes! It's one of your best ideas yet, Mal."

Mallory smiled genuinely this time; the flush in her cheeks from running, growing more crimson.

Alex teasingly threw her shoulder into Caleb as they rounded the corner behind Mallory, and he would have fallen into a table full of honey jars if the owner had not yelled, "Cloth, protect!" The tablecloth reached up and caught the boy just before he destroyed months of the bees' labor.

"Thanks!" Caleb smiled awkwardly. The stall owner glared at him but nodded an acknowledgment all the same. Then Caleb raced away to catch up with his friends.

The road Mallory had turned onto led to Silver Street. It was lined by some of the oldest buildings in the city, constructed by the founding families. Unlike the ten-to-twelve story buildings that were made of steel and glass along Main Street and some of the newer parts of the city, the houses on Silver Street were made of cobblestone, thick wooden beams, and stucco. Every home was immaculately kept up with beautiful yards of manicured grass and flower gardens. The wealthiest families of the Dikaió guilds lived in these houses. The wealthy homes of Silver Street were just downhill from Mallory's own house in the Governor's District where the leaders of the city lived.

The hill was not steep, but she was hoping the cart's momentum would keep her from having to strain too hard to push it the final few yards home. Nearing the crest, she did not quite make it to the top before her momentum ran out, and the cart began to push her back down the hill. She braced her feet, but the small stones in the road kept her feet from fully contacting the pavement, as they rolled out from under the treads of her shoes. Not being able to gain any friction to stop her descent, she slid backwards past Alex, who paused and watched sadly as her friend lost ground. About midway down the hill Mallory bumped into something solid in the middle of the road and stopped sliding backwards.

She looked over her shoulder to find herself wedged between the heavy cart and Caleb, who had finally caught up to his two friends. He was grinning and breathing heavily.

"Troubles?" He asked.

Mallory tried to move around him or push back up the

hill, but the weight of the cart kept her pinned against him. "Okay, move!" She ordered.

Caleb laughed, "If I move, you're going to end up all the way at the bottom of the hill and then what?"

Mallory bit her lip. She hated it when he was right, and she hated feeling powerless. "There has to be a way to get this thing up the hill."

"I can help," Alex yelled from the top of the hill, "I just need to say the word."

"I hope you fall in a lake!" Mallory yelled back at her.

Alex winced then yelled back, "If you had magic, you'd be in trouble for that you know."

Caleb laughed at the exchange as he always did, "And you'd be all wet, Alex!" Then he looked down at Mallory who was still struggling to push off of him, "But on the other hand, if you had magic, we wouldn't be in this position in the first place, would we?"

His breath tickled her ear, and Mallory's temperature, which was already elevated from running across the city with her cart, increased uncomfortably. Only last year, Caleb had been as awkward and spindly as she and Alex were, but overnight his tall frame had broadened. Now he looked more like her dad than her childhood friend, and Mallory was not sure how she felt about it. However, his increase in size and muscle was the only thing keeping her from embarrassingly sprawling at the bottom of the hill, so there were certainly perks to be considered—which gave her an idea.

"Here, hold these," she said, handing Caleb the poles she had been using to steer the cart. He took them and rather effortlessly supported the weight of the cart. Mallory ducked down under the pole, and she popped back up on the other side free of the weight of the cart. She giggled and smiled demurely at Caleb, "Would you mind?"

"Oh, I don't think so!" Caleb motioned to set the cart down, which would have almost certainly sent carrots, cabbages, and potatoes tumbling down the hill behind him.

"C'mon," Mallory said, "we're so close to the top. It wouldn't be much for you."

Alex had walked back down to the pair. "We could just use magic. Cart, up the hill," she ordered. The cart sat motionless in Caleb's hands.

Mallory's smile faded. "It's not that kind of cart, Alex. Now, Caleb, what do you say?"

Caleb looked from Mallory to the cart and back again, frowning. Then his face brightened. "What would be the difference between me doing the work for you and Alex using magic to help you? She could call a couple of sprites to lift the handles and push."

Mallory's eyebrows leaned in toward her brow, and the corners of her mouth sucked in slightly. He had her, and she knew it, and even worse, the smirking expression on her face showed that Alex knew it too. The three stood there in a standoff between the immaculate buildings on either side of Silver Street. The downwash of air between the buildings had created a gale of wind, and Mallory's curly hair whipped wildly around while she thought about how she was going to get that cart up the hill. Just then Alex and Caleb's grocery boxes finally turned the corner and caught up with them.

Mallory watched as the boxes fought the wind to climb the hill. They both leaned to one side, and began to zig zag, sluicing through the wind in a parallel two-step dance through the air until they reached the group. Mallory cocked her head to the side and bit her lip.

"Oh no!" Caleb muttered. "She's thinking."

Alex's eyes widened, "Mallory?"

Mallory smiled broadly, "Excuse me," she said, ducking below Caleb's hand holding the cart handle. She pressed herself back between Caleb and the cart. Caleb blushed slightly in the awkwardness of it all, but he could not help but laugh. Mallory took hold of the handles. "Okay, you can let go now. I've got this." Caleb let go, and Mallory began to push the cart, not directly up the hill, but imitating the grocery boxes, zigging and zagging from one side of the street to the other. The incline was much easier to manage as she was only climbing the hill a few feet at a time at an angle rather than trying to assault it head on. Caleb and Alex were waiting for her at the top of the hill when she finally made it, slightly winded but beaming with accomplishment. Both were silent at her victory, but that was how these sorts of things usually went, and so without a word they continued on toward Mallory's house.

The Matriarch's house was a picturesque shingle-style cottage with open-air verandas on the second floor that wrapped nearly all the way around, punctuated by four triangular walls inlaid with picture windows, one on each side of the home, and four turrets on each corner. Gray-and-brown cut cobblestones were intricately stacked about midway up the house, and brightly-painted periwinkle wooden siding ran from midway up to the deep-black shingles covering the roof. The door to the house was painted an inviting royal red, and matching roses were immaculately displayed throughout the landscaping, drawing the eye from every perspective. Two centuries-old oaks stood on the corners of the grounds; their branches hospitably bidding every passerby to come and be welcome in their shade. The house faced the public square, opposite the Governor's house—which was every bit as uninviting in its white colonial formality as the Matriarch's house was calm and cozy.

Mallory and her friends headed past the stone steps leading toward the red front door, past the waving oak, and turned in down a side path that led to the back door. Mallory stopped short and looked for a place to set her cart down. Right now, the cart was supported by a wheel and her two legs, but if she just dropped the handles then the only thing supporting it would be the wheel, and all the fruits and vegetables from the Farmer's Market would tumble out. "I think on the next iteration of this cart, I'll add a couple of legs for support under the handles. Would you two mind holding the handles while I unload the cart?"

Caleb reached down and took a handle, but Alex stepped back firmly. "No!"

"C'mon, Alex. It'll just take a minute," Mallory assured.

"No. I've put up with your experiment long enough, Mallory Knenne. You've had your fun with your 'girl-powered' grocery box.'" Alex made quotation marks with her fingers for emphasis. "Emptying this thing by hand is going to take a lot longer than a minute, and you know it. Let me unload the box, so we can do something fun with the rest of our day."

"She's right," Caleb nodded and put his free hand on Mallory's shoulder. "What d'ya say, Mal? Want to have some fun with your friends today?"

Mallory thought this had been fun, but after the fight up the hill with the cart, she didn't have the energy to argue: "Fine! Go ahead!"

Alex smiled and bounded up the stoop to the backdoor. She leaned inside and called with confident authority, "Pantry sprites, collect, sort, and store the groceries." Four silver wheels, each about two feet tall with neon white lights flashing near their centers, burst out of the door and rushed toward Alex and Caleb's grocery boxes, still hovering near them. "No, no! Pantry sprites, wrong boxes!" Alex yelled. The wheels stopped and sat, quivering in place, waiting for the right words. "Pantry sprites, collect groceries from this wooden cart." Flustered, Alex pointed toward Mallory's cart. Three of the silver wheels shot nylon cords from their centers, which spread into a net. The fourth wheel rolled into the cart, began quickly levering itself under the produce, and pitching it over the side into the net. Within a minute all the produce had been unloaded into the woven net, and the wheels scurried back into the house to unload their bounty.

Mallory dropped her handle, "I'm going to go find some wood to make legs for this cart. Who's with me?"

Caleb dropped his handle, tipping the cart on its side, "Another time, Mal. You agreed to have some fun with your friends."

"Caleb, you've always said helping me with my projects is fun."

"Have I?" Caleb scratched the back of his head, grinning awkwardly.

Alex stomped her foot. "Knock it off, you two! I already know what we're going to do for the rest of our day. I have a new book."

Mallory's jaw dropped. "Why didn't you start with that when we met this morning?"

Alex shrugged. "It was market day. You would have wanted to go look right away, and my mother would have lost her mind if I didn't get the edamame this week. That stuff disappears faster than Caleb when cleaning duty is being assigned at school."

"Well, let's go look at it now!"

Caleb ignored the jab at his aversion to cleaning, "I'm in. I'll go drop off my groceries and meet you both at Book Club."

In short order, the three teens were standing outside Alex's grandparents' house, static excitement charging the air around them. The Tudor house was dark even in the full light of the sun. Large pines stood at every corner. Moss covered, natural stone cladding rose up the first story of the house and the chimney above the roof. The half-story just below the roof was lined with dark brown, cedar-shake siding. The trim of the windows and doors were all hunter green, nearly the same color as the pines and the moss. The current Administrator, her grandfather, occupied the main house with her grandmother, and she and her parents lived in the Chief Magistrate's coach house in the rear.

As the apprentice to the Administrator, Alex's father led the magistrates in maintaining justice throughout the city. Soon though, they would be moving into the main house. Her father would take the master's position as soon as Alex turned eighteen, and Alex would become the Chief Magistrate administrating justice to the city like her ancestors before her. She had been trained as an expert marksman, knew martial arts, and all the laws and the words with which to enforce them with the Dikaió. One day the main house would be hers.

Alex checked the door; it was locked. Her grandparents and parents must all still be at the market, but the house knew Alex, and she unlocked the main door with a word: "Open." Mallory and Caleb followed her into a dark foyer. Normally, they would have made themselves at home, being frequent guests at the Administrator's home, but this was a clandestine visit. Alex lit no lights as the they crept to the back stairs that led to the attic. The attic door was sealed with old magic; there were no words that could open it, so no one in Alex's family had been in the room for generations, but while hunting for invention supplies in the old buildings on the estate, Mallory had found the secret. Alex pulled a golden key on a chain from under her shirt and inserted it in a small hole below a brass knob. The lock clicked as she turned it, and then she twisted the knob. The three teens burst into a dusty room full of bookshelves.

Books were a rarity in the city. Everyday life's Dikaió

magic was passed by word of mouth, and books were not only unnecessary, but had come to be seen as dangerous. Before the three teens were born, in their parents' youth, two young boys had turned up a book full of old magic. They had fiddled with a particular section of words and ended up creating a sprite that projected an intense arc of fire extruding from silver funnels on top of a spinning turret. Nearly as soon as they had used the Dikaió to birth the fire sprite, they had lost control of it and the boys were the sprite's first victims. Then it had started several houses on fire, and no one could turn it off or stop its advance down the street. The charred remains of the houses still stood on Manuel Ave. Caleb's grandfather, who had just become the acting governor that year, had confronted the sprite as it rolled mercilessly down the street. No one was sure if he could control the old magic, but when he yelled, "Dikaió fire cease!" the sprite went dark. It was quickly dismantled and destroyed. The City Council had issued the decree at that point that the ability to read would be reserved for the ruling Dikaió class, and it was only to be used in emergencies. All other magic for everyday life would be memorized; nothing was written down, and all other books were confiscated and destroyed by the Governor's Office.

Mallory had found the first unconfiscated book in her grandmother's study when she was ten-years old, playing hide and seek with Alex and Caleb. The book was behind a door under the oak shelves. All three had learned the basics of reading by that point, given their class, but none had actually seen a book that was not conjured in the light of the Dikaió.

It was large, about the size of a small painting in a frame, and heavy. It was titled Basics of Woodworking and had informed many of Mallory's earliest inventions, granting her a semblance of magic—some even called it old magic—that allowed her to do everyday things without using the Dikaió. Ever since, the three friends had been collecting books and squirreling them away in a secret room in Alex's grandfather's attic, which they called the "Book Club." Caleb had even smuggled out the book that had created the fire sprite from a shelf in the basement of city hall, but not even Mallory dared to touch that one on its perch at the top of the highest attic shelf. Mallory often wondered if this room contained all that was left of the old magic. If it did, and anyone found out about Book Club, it would surely be destroyed. They were the sacred protectors.

Alex closed the door and turned the ancient lock. The girls sat down in two armchairs that had bits of fluff protruding from their worn blue-and-red plaid fabric coverings. Caleb plopped lengthwise on an old couch that they'd covered with a sheet, so that a desert dust storm would not form every time the young man decided to get comfortable. Mallory started the process of lighting the oil lamp. Alex had wanted to outfit the Book Club with some Dikaió lamps, but Mallory insisted that the lighting should fit the atmosphere of having physical books, and by using one of their book finds as a guide, she had managed to convert two Dikaió lamps into old-magic lamps that used a flaming fabric wick hanging in a pool of paraffin to provide light by fire. The fire was easy enough to produce with a bit of magnesium they had taken from the Smith Guild, which could be sparked by striking it on metal. The paraffin had been a trick to find, but the book said that one of paraffin's uses was as an ingredient in pesticide, and it turned out that the Dikaió Culture Co-op still used it for that purpose in the rooftop gardens atop the skyscrapers and had readily parted with a gallon, completely unaware of its flammable nature.

As Mallory lit the lamps, a warm glow spread across the room. Shadows paired with the light in a chaotic but oddly soothing dance, recalling some primitive feeling of safety around the firelight. Awash in the amber light, Mallory leaned back in her chair, crossed her legs, and folded her hands in her lap. "I call this meeting of the Book Club to order. Alexandria Nelson, future Dikaió Administrator, you have summoned us here with news of an unread volume. Is this so?"

Alex sat up straight and smoothed the wrinkles from her navy-blue pants, always happy to take a more formal tone. "That is correct, future Madame Matriarch." She pulled a large, leatherbound book from behind her chair. "It's a peculiar volume with no title."

Caleb sat up and reached across, pulling the book from her hands.

"Hey," Alex yelled. "Give it back!"

He smiled, holding the book away. "As the future Dikaió Governor, it is my duty to inspect this volume to ensure the safety of the city," he replied smugly.

Mallory laughed, "C'mon, Caleb. Put it on the coffee table where we can all see." Caleb shrugged and laid the book on the table.

Alex carefully opened the cover, "As I was saying, there's no title, but it has a very curious table of contents."

Mallory's eyes widened as she quickly scanned the words. "What does it mean?"

"It means we shouldn't be messing with it," Caleb slammed the cover shut and picked it up again. He pushed off the couch with the book and started walking to the tallest bookshelf. "I'm putting it up top with the fire-sprite book."

"Caleb, wait!" Alex cried standing from her chair and moving after him. "C'mon, give it back!" Mallory followed after her, both girls trying to take the book back, but this time he held it above their heads.

"No!" Caleb's voice was low and threatening, and the girls stepped back. "I'm not joking around about this. These are the sorts of things that could really hurt people in this city, and even though I'm not the Governor yet, I am training to be. It's my christened duty to protect you and everyone else here. You invited me to be part of the Book Club because the three of us will one day be in charge of the city, and knowing when to take the knowledge from these old books and when to leave them alone is part of our legacy. You know as well as I do that this is one of those 'leave-it-alone moments.'"

"Well, there's no harm in me looking at it," Mallory whispered. "I can't use magic anyway."

"I'm sorry, Mal. We still don't know what a Dikaió Chorus is capable of. What if you start trying out some of the phrases in this book, and it turns out you can use the dangerous kind of magic after all?"

Alex pleaded, "And what if there's something in there that could help Mallory use the good and helpful magic like the rest of us?"

"It's not worth the risk to everyone else, Alex. We have to agree not to mess with this book."

Alex nearly spat, "I'm not agreeing to anything of the sort."

"You'll agree, or I'll tell my father about Book Club," Caleb retorted.

Mallory stepped back. "Caleb, no! You can't!"

"I can, and I will. I walk past those burned-out houses on Manuel every day on the way to my duties in the city, and every time I do, I wonder if we're going to end up like those two boys that created the fire sprite. People were in those houses, Mal. Do you want that on your conscience, Alex?"

"Of course not. But how do you know there's a fire sprite in that book?" Alex pointed.

"I don't, but I don't know there isn't one in here either, or something worse, and I'm not willing to risk it. Now promise me you'll leave it alone!"

"Fine!" Alex sank back into her chair.

Mallory also sat down and nodded slightly.

Caleb placed the large volume on top of the fire-sprite shelf. They sat for a time in awkward silence: the two girls brooding, and Caleb not willing to face their ire but drawing a blank on how to lighten the mood or change the subject. The joy of the Book Club was lost, at least for today. Finally, Mallory leaned over and blew out the lamps. The three friends did not say another word to each other as they slipped down the stairs and out of the house, heading for their respective homes.

When Mallory got home, her parents were still not home from the market either. They had moved into the Matriarch's home two years ago on her mother's thirty-fifth birthday, when she inherited the role of Matriarch. There had been a constant stream of Dikaió christenings that her mother had to attend after that, and Mallory was required to attend all of them as the Matriarch in training. Her mother drilled her daily on the magic words that the Matriarch was required to use in her various duties. Her mother gave her the same pitying look every time Mallory tried to use magic and nothing happened. It was maddening.

Mallory collapsed on a plush chaise in the living room. She did not want to think about her loss right now. There was a new variable at play, and she had not had time to process what it meant. She looked out the large bay window toward the Governor's house just past the large oak. She tilted her head and bit the corner of her lip. Mallory had never seen Caleb so upset about a book before, not even the fire-sprite book. He was the one who had brought it to the Book Club and placed it like a trophy on top of the tallest shelf. If he were so worried about them messing with hurtful magic, why would he make that book accessible to them? And was what Alex said possible? Could there be something in the new volume that would make her Dikaió useful, that would give her the same abilities with magic that everyone else in the city enjoyed? It seemed impossible, but she couldn't shake the small ember of feeling that the new book had fanned up inside her, a feeling she had not felt since she was a little girl: hope.

In the afternoon, the Matriarch's kitchen overflowed with the smoky bouquets of cumin and coriander on potatoes; the peppery woodiness of cinnamon and cloves in currant rice; the earthy lemon, mint, and licorice mixed with cilantro, basil, and fenugreek in lentil soup; and perhaps Mallory's favorite smell with any meal, the full smell of flatbread baking, soon to be coated in clear butter. There was also the bright aroma of fruits and chopped vegetables, which brought to mind images of brightly colored charcuterie boards complete with sweet and savory yogurt for dipping. While Mallory and her family usually just ate at the small table in the kitchen on most nights, the kitchen sprites were setting the large table in the dining hall for company.

Mallory's mother sat in her tall-backed chair at the foot of the table. Even though she was not currently employed in government duties, her curly brown hair had been immaculately straightened and pinned up for business. Mallory almost never saw her mother with a hair out of place; a trait she seemed not to have inherited. Her wild curls refused to be tamed, despite her mother's constant endeavoring to domesticate them. Her mother barked orders for this or that decoration or garnish to be moved or set just so. The sprites, ever-attentive to the Dikaió at her command, whizzed about busily, moving the flower arrangement to the left and that pesky table setting a smidge closer to the edge. Mallory's father sat at his position at the head of the table smiling across the expanse at his busy wife.

"This seems like a lot of trouble for an 'informal get-together' among friends, Sarai," he shouted above the din of preparations.

She smiled condescendingly back at him. "Roger, you know very well that a formal get-together at the Matriarch's home would entail much more pomp and circumstance than this."

He leaned back in his chair and waved his hands in circles in the air: "Weeks of planning. I know; I know."

She smiled, "If you want to be upset about the delay in dinner, perhaps you should discuss all the extra groceries with your daughter. The poor sprites couldn't find a place to store them all—it was a choice of either having a dinner party or throwing them out when they rot in a week." She turned toward a four-armed sprite that had arrived holding spoons with samples of tonight's selections. Mallory's mother tried the potatoes first. "Oh, these are just lovely, but add some cilantro leaves for garnish."

Mallory's father looked over his shoulder at Mallory who was leaning against the door post, biting the corner of her lip, and staring absently toward the kitchen and the line of sprites carrying glasses and saucers down the hallway. She felt useless at events like this, unable to even hang up a coat for their guests. She would sit idly by while her mother showed effortless hospitality. Today, Mallory had finally managed to help with getting groceries, but she still felt like she didn't belong in her own family.

"Mallory," her father called. "Mallory?"

She startled and turned her attention away from the bustle. "Yes, father?"

"Well, what about it then?"

"What about what, father?"

"Your mother says I should ask you why we need all this fuss over a few extra groceries."

Mallory smiled and looked toward her mother who was pretending not to hear. "Well, I suppose it's a celebration, father."

"A celebration?"

"Sure, it's not every day that the incompetent heir of the Matriarchy provides the groceries for her family." She regretted her words as soon as she said them, though they felt true.

A glass crashed to the floor on the other side of the room, having just fallen from her mother's grip. Both her parents stared at her, mouths opening and closing like the fish in the aquariums below the skyscraper gardens. A kitchen sprite weaved in and out of the line of helper sprites and quickly vacuumed the glass shards off the floor. Her mother composed herself first after the whirring of the vacuum ended, "Mallory, why do you have to be this way?"

Mallory squared her shoulders, "Grandmother always said it's because I was special, but we all know that's just a euphemism for 'less than.' There's no point in denying my place in life, Mother."

A sprite bumped past her leg then, and Mallory yelled at it, "Drop that carafe! Spill it on the floor! Jump up and down!" The sprite considered her for a moment and then continued down the length of the table to place the carafe in its designated place. "Why don't you just explode?" Still nothing.

"Mallory," her father whispered, trying to look her in the eyes.

Mallory forced back tears trying to escape her ducts as she turned away from him. Who would host the parties when she was grown? Her husband? "Maybe I just want to be normal, fit in like everyone else."

Mallory's mother held up a hand to the next sprite vying for her attention. "That's normal for a teenage girl, dear. When I was your age, I worried about fitting in as well."

"Really?!?"

Mallory's mother began to look around the table like she was searching for something. She pulled the wrinkles out of the tablecloth in front of her and then said, "Well, of course, it's not quite the same, but it's not all that different either. Your father and I are very proud of your independence, Mallory. I, for one, love having dinner parties. Yes, it's quite a lovely thing you've done for us Mallory. Thank you!"

Mallory's father looked from his wife to his daughter and back again, his gray eyes flashing as he nodded nervously. "Oh yes, I can wait for dinner. Company is always welcome. Thank you, Mallory."

Mallory was not in the mood for playful patronization. "What if I could be normal? What if there were words in the Dikaió that could make me like everyone else?"

"Oh, Mallory," her mother's face drooped. There it was; there was the pity Mallory hated. "It's too late for that. Even if I could change it, which is impossible, I'm not sure the Council . . . the Governor . . . No, they would never allow it. Your Dikaió is part of the records now. We can't just rewrite history."

Mallory growled and kicked the nearest sprite. It nearly dropped the butter dish it was carrying as it spun backwards down the hall, but it righted itself and restarted its inane march toward dinner prep. Her parents were mimicking fish again, this time gasping for air as if they had been pulled up in the Dikaió Culture's nets. Mallory could feel them sucking up the air and fled up the stairs to her room. The tears had fought their way through the guards in her eyes, and they were making a break for it down the trenches of her cheeks, flowing freer and freer, until their uprising was quashed by smashing her face into the synthetic-down of her pillow. Sobs racked her body for a time until she got enough control to roll over and stare at the barren whiteness of her ceiling.

She lay there on top the cool silk of her duvet cover, absently tracing the lines of the sateen weave with the tips of her fingers. As the sun began to set, the stained glass of her window filled the room with its image: an Art Deco dragonfly sitting on a lily leaf. The sun's orange and red hues swirled through the veins of the wing panes, while the hunter green and deep purple of the dragonfly's body floated in the room, waiting as dragonflies do, silent and motionless.

When she was younger, this room used to be her grandmother's study. She thought back to the days when she would sit and trace the veins of the dragonfly in the carpet while her grandmother repeated and rehearsed the necessary Dikaió christenings for the children who were coming of age in the city. Oftentimes, her mother was there, and the two older women would sit and rehearse the words together as a means of training the next Dikaió Syntec, always purposefully using alternative filler words in the phrasing, lest a mistake curse a child for life: "As Dikaió (Salamander), I christen Zachary Jons, Dikaió Technic." When they messed up the words, Mallory would often laugh and say the phrase correctly: "No, no, you sillies! It's 'As Dikaió Syntec, I christen Zachary Jons, Dikaió Technic." The older women would tense every time, and Mallory used to think the game was great fun, but then as she got older, she started to notice the tears in her grandmother's eyes and the pity in her mother's face when she would correct them and nothing would happen, so the game lost its luster.

Once when her mother did not join them, Mallory

demanded that her grandmother explain why she had not christened her a Dikaió Syntec. The old woman paused from rehearsing and told Mallory a story from her childhood:

"I can't quite remember how old I was, not much older than you, my sweet Mallory, when the last Dikaió Chorus passed into the life after life. He was quite old: a hundred and seven years since his birth, if you can imagine it. He hobbled about town with the use of a walking stick, but no one ever noticed him. I remember asking my mother, the Matriarch before me, about the Dikaió Chorus and how he served the city, but she only shrugged and said, 'My mother never taught me that christening.' And as my grandmother had passed away before I was born, that knowledge was nearly forever lost from the Matriarchs."

And then Mallory's grandmother leaned in close as if she were about to reveal a great secret, "But one day, I took matters into my own hands. I started following the Dikaió Chorus around town. He had a magic like I've never seen. Rather than using words to command magic, things just seemed to happen for him. For example, when he walked up to his house on Manuel Avenue, the door would unlock without him uttering one word, the lights in his house turned on just because he was there, and shopping sprites came and delivered whatever he needed to his home without him calling them or taking them to market. One day, as he was hobbling home from a walk in the park, I stepped into his path and blocked his door. 'How do you use magic without words? What is your purpose?'

"He looked down his nose at me long enough for me to

notice the overflowing billows of white hair puffing out from his nostrils, which was quite contrasted against his wrinkled dark skin. Then he laughed, and laughed, and laughed. 'My, aren't you a feisty little Matriarch! Does your mother know that you're running about accosting old men on their doorsteps, little one?'

"'My mother doesn't know what your purpose is either. So, what is it?'

"The old man looked a little sad at that. 'Much has been lost over the generations. Too much.' Then he shrugged. 'But life was never meant to be permanent. Change is the only way to advance. Still, conserving the things that were can help us not repeat the mistakes of the past. Come in and have a cup of tea with me, little one, and I will answer your questions as best I can.'

"He stepped past me, and I heard the bolt of his lock draw aside. The door opened like a dog recognizing its beloved master. He stepped briskly through, then paused and looked back: 'Coming, child?'

"I hesitated. The Chorus was a stranger, and while no one in the city was dangerous, adults can be mysterious to a child, and the unknown frightens even adults, but I was determined to know what the Chorus did in the city, so I stepped across his threshold. It was as if I had entered another world: books were piled on shelves, on tables, on seats, on the floor—if there was space for a book in the man's home, there were ten crammed there, balanced precariously one atop the other.

"'S'cuse the mess, child. I haven't had visitors in . . . well come to think of it, I don't know that I've ever had visitors in my own home. My parents used to entertain, but that was before—'

"He hobbled through a doorway and disappeared into another room. I assumed he had gone to make tea for us. He may have still been talking in the other room, as us older people do, but I was captivated by the books in the house and walked through the piles, turning my head sideways trying to read all their titles. They were coated with such a film of dust, I was certain that if I picked one up I might sneeze and bring the whole collection falling down about me. It would have taken the rescuers days to find me, and I would have only survived eating sheaves of dusty paper." Mallory's grandmother mimicked eating her journal on the desk for effect. "This was years before the fire sprite revealed how dangerous books could be, but still I had never seen so many books in the whole city, and the draw of the information that must have been contained in their pages cast a lazy, curious spell over my imagination.

"I don't know how long the Chorus was gone, but he must have been talking the whole time he was out of the room because he was still talking when he re-entered.

"'—and of course, we Choruses didn't have much say in the whole matter. And after that, our purpose was discarded and forgotten by the city, though you can well imagine that without us the city would have never been built in the first place.'

"I felt like I had missed something important, but I think children are trained in their lessons to never admit when they're not paying attention, both by the consternation of the teacher and the laughter of the other children. So, rather than asking the old man to repeat himself, I looked up at him from behind a tall stack of books like a curious neighbor peeking over a fence and said, 'Yes, I see. But what is your purpose in the city now?'

"He tossed his head back and laughed uproariously. 'Nothing like the honesty of a child. Yes, sir. One can always count on a child to shoot straight with you. Well, child, to be honest, in my opinion, the Chorus is still the most important role in the city. Without a Dikaió Chorus, the city has no purpose. It's just a soul-less machine perpetuating its own existence, like a shop owner with no customers, or a bakery with no one to eat its baked goods. Do you understand?'

"I didn't, but I nodded in earnest, eager to keep the company of that curious human being from another time for as long as he would have me. 'What should happen to the city without a Dikaió Chorus then?'

"The old man slowly lowered himself to sit atop a wobbly stack of books and looked thoughtfully down at me. 'Well, that's a question that many, some much older and wiser than you, have never thought to ask. To be honest, I hadn't quite thought about it myself since it means I would no longer be here, doesn't it?'

"'Well, you are quite old.'

"'There's that youthful honesty again.' He smiled gently. 'But you're right. No one should live forever, else what good is living—at least that's what my parents used to say before they left the city . . . so long ago . . .' His eyes started to glaze over a bit traveling back to some distant memory."

Mallory interrupted at that point: "His parents left the city? How?"

Her grandmother shrugged, "There were stories that before the city's light was stoked to protect it, people could leave whenever they wished, but that also meant that things in the wild beyond the borders could come in. That's why things like the fire sprite existed—they were tools used to fight the wilds and keep the city safe, but no one I have ever met other than the Chorus could remember a time before the light."

Mallory cocked her head to the side as though reading the titles of ancient texts like her grandmother's story and bit her lip, thinking silently about the wilds no longer seen.

Her grandmother continued: "Eventually, I began to wonder if he was reliving a memory, or if he fell asleep, so I half-shouted, 'Well, what do you think?'

"He started back to the present: 'What do I think about what!?'

"'What would happen to the city without a Dikaió Chorus?'

"'Oh, I suppose the same thing that would happen to the shop or the bakery without anyone to serve; it would close.'

"'Close?'

"'Yes, cease to be. Life is more than getting anything you want with a word. Do you understand, child?'

"'No, not really,' I said, and he threw his head back and laughed nearly falling off his stack of books.

"A shrill whistle sounded from the other room, and he haphazardly pushed off his makeshift seat. 'Well, if we're going to discuss the philosophy of existence, we ought to at least have our tea whilst we pontificate. Come along, child.' I followed him through the doorway into a cozy little kitchen with a tiny wooden dinette and two chairs. Books were piled chaotically in this room as well, leaving only a small trail in the kitchen. He pulled two mismatched mugs out of the cupboard and poured hot water into them then added teabags. 'Sugar? Milk?'

"'Yes, please . . . but why do you pour the tea yourself? Where are your kitchen sprites?'

"He again threw his head back and laughed his guttural guffaw causing tea water to slosh over the brims of the mugs. 'Oops!' He righted the mugs and carried them more solemnly to the table, and slowly lowered himself into one of the seats. 'Not all of us have the same luxuries as the Matriarch, dear child, but we make do as best we can with what we're given.'

"I had never considered that there might be differences among the classes in the city. 'So, you don't have much because you can't use the Dikaió like we can?' I asked.

"He grew suddenly serious. 'People were never meant to live by the Dikaió, child. He waved to the books piled in the kitchen. 'These are only a tiny bit of humanity's progress through the ages. There is so much more to life than just existing.'

"'I don't understand.'

"He sighed and shook his head. 'It's not my place to help you understand, child.' He reached over the tea and took my hands in his. 'But the world needs a Chorus. The Chorus is what enables humanity to continue, to accept things as they are and overcome the trials and tribulations of life. The Chorus is able to learn and adapt, to become more than what they began as. I'm old now, and my body has limited my usefulness, and the city has forgotten the Chorus—but when you are Matriarch, you can change that, child. Yes, you can save the city.'

"This old man who seemed to have so much less than our family, possessed something I did not. He understood the world, and I readily agreed to the idea. If the Dikaió Chorus could possess the wisdom of the ages, then that was something worth holding onto. I determined that I would learn everything I could from him about what a Chorus was, and how to help future Dikaió Choruses fulfill their purpose in the city. When I left that day, I decided I would come back as often as I could to talk with him and read as many of his books as I could . . .

" . . . But then those boys conjured up the fire sprite." Mallory's grandmother looked down at her with wide eyes, reliving the memory. "Oh child, I remember when the smoke filled the sky; it billowed up to the city's light. It swirled and billowed like mud settling in a stream when you toss a dirt clump into the water. I ran, like a lot of people, to see where the smoke was coming from. The sprite was terrible. It glowed like molten bronze, and when the fire spewed out, it shrieked with a voice that sounded like scraping metal on metal. The air was hot and acrid, and the smoke burned my lungs, but I couldn't move. I was transfixed by the fire, dancing atop the houses and in the streets, an otherworldly spirit summoned for destruction. Someone was screaming, maybe it was me; it's all so jumbled now.

"But I do remember the Governor. He stepped into the street like a knight in a fairytale facing down a dragon. His robes blew in the wind amidst the glowing embers and ash floating through the air. He seemed to be running slowly, though it probably was all happening much faster than I see it in my mind's eye. He stepped into the path of the fire sprite, standing defiantly there in the street, and it turned its deadly attention toward him. The screeching metal sound began, and its glow intensified. It was going to incinerate him. I covered my eyes not wanting to see what came next. But then I heard the Governor speak: 'Dikaió Fire Cease!'

"When I looked up, the fire sprite had gone dark, but the house fires were still burning. That's when I realized the first one in the line was the Dikaió Chorus's house. It turned out that the boys had snuck into his house through an open window and stole the book that contained instructions for birthing the fire sprite. When they loosed that thing, the Chorus, he, . . ." Her grandmother paused and turned to stare out the window, her words catching.

Mallory got up off the floor and climbed into her grandmother's lap, wrapping her arms around her neck. She laid her head on her grandmother's bosom and just sat there quietly while her grandmother absently stroked her hair, staring out the window with distant sadness.

Abruptly, her grandmother started speaking again, "In some ways, I was sorely disappointed that he went into the life after life without divulging all of his secrets and passing on the generations of learning he held, but in other ways I was glad to have learned anything about the Dikiaó Chorus at all, especially after all his books were lost in the fire, and the city's leadership started getting rid of the books that were left. Still, after time passed, I began to wonder if the city really was worse off without a Chorus, or his knowledge in general, as nothing changed after he died. The Dikaió still provided all we needed. Children were born. The old passed into the life after life. The city continued.

"But then just before you were conceived, I dreamt of a Matriarch. A Matriarch who was also a Dikaió Chorus who would save the city. When you were born, I knew that the dream was about you, little Mallory, and I knew that there was purpose in my having known the Chorus; it was not just a chance encounter of youth. I wish I could tell you more about your destiny. More about your heritage than strange magic, fire, and the knowledge of the ages, but life's mysteries are often left for us to discover on our own, my dear girl, and the mystery of the Dikaió Chorus will be yours to solve, but I know that you can."

The light shining through the stained glass had all but faded, along with the image of her grandmother holding her, and the Dikaió lights drained all the color from the dragonfly and left it shrouded in darkness. Mallory's thoughts shifted from the hallowed memories of her childhood to her current situation. Mallory did not want to disappoint her grandmother's vision for her, but so far it seemed that a Dikaió Chorus was the most useless role a person could have in the city. She had long ago figured out the secrets to the wordless magic the old man her grandmother knew had used.

It was just the same Dikaió magic as always: When Mallory's mother became the Matriarch, she ordered the house sprites to serve Mallory. For example, her mother had told the door, "Door, this is Mallory. Unlock for her when she comes in and out." And ever since then, the door locked and unlocked for her when she was near. Someone must have done the same for the older Chorus. It was embarrassing to have everyone have to order sprites and magic items to serve her and not be able to do anything herself.

Mallory wished that she could talk with her grandmother about the book Alex found, but her grandmother had gotten sick . . . and so early in her retirement, she hardly had a chance to enjoy the time without the duty that came with being elderly. Life was not fair. But now! Now, there might be a possibility to undo the curse of the Chorus and be the Matriarch the city needed. Mallory sat up, leaning on her elbow as she imagined it. Now, she could have a purpose like the other citizens and not be a burden. Now, perhaps she could be normal.

She was startled out of her thoughts by a tap at her window. She looked out just as a small pebble struck the window again. Alex was standing behind one of the twin oaks with her arm drawn back, getting ready to launch another projectile. She dropped the pebble when Mallory opened the window.

"Mallory!" Alex's voice hissed in nigh hysterical excitement. "I found it!"

Mallory's heart climbed into her throat, but she was trying hard not to get her hopes up too high. "Are you sure?"

"Yes," Alex motioned for her to come with her. "Hurry! The words look simple. We can end the curse tonight!"

Mallory closed the window. The red ball from her childhood, once an object of endearment and now a reminder of her limitations, was sitting on a shelf with some other heirlooms. She grabbed it and pushed it into her pocket. She looked back at the dark dragonfly, closed her eyes slowly, held the lids tightly for a moment, and then decidedly turned away from the window toward a more hopeful future.

With a stiff wind chilling the night air, both girls pulled their light jackets closer around their bodies, and the large oaks in the yard waved their branches wildly at the two straying figures. Alex paused uncertainly before the rustle of their admonishment, but the atmosphere of danger and excitement galvanized Mallory's determination. She quietly pushed Alex toward the Administrator's house. Alex nodded, and then took the lead.

They kept to the shadows, avoiding the steady stream of important city leaders heading to the Matriarch's home in answer to her informal dinner invite. Mallory doubted anyone would question the children of two of the most powerful families in the city. Anyone they encountered would be more likely to assume they were running a last-minute errand for dinner and not up to something that was, if not illegal, then at least highly irregular.

But for Mallory, there was too much riding on this late-night mission to chance being caught on the way to their destination before they had even tried to remove the curse of the Chorus. Several times one or other of the girls would stop like a frightened rabbit and scan the street for move-ment. Determining to be extra careful, they crouched behind bushes, pressed themselves against trees, even laid flat in the Dikaió Architect's lawn just before Caleb appeared with his hands in his pockets, walking quickly behind his parents and Alex's family. The whole triad of governmental power was going to be at the Matriarch's tonight, and the girls needed to hurry, or they would be missed; someone, probably Caleb, would be sent to find them.

Despite their best efforts at avoiding detection, at one point the girls turned a corner without checking around it and very nearly ran right into the head of the Dikaió Smith Guild, a short, fat man with short-cropped hair and a well-quaffed mustache, and his tall, thin wife with her fiery red curls. They were both dressed to the nines with a tailored tuxedo and a form-fitting black dress, respectively. They were covered in jewelry: platinum earrings, diamond necklaces, feather broaches, gold medallions, silver bracelets, and a ring on every finger, sporting every type of precious stone known to the city—each piece was the workmanship of a different guild master. Mallory had heard the Smith Leader say that they wore the jewelry while socializing with the other leaders of the city to advertise the expertise of the Dikaió masters and drum up potential customers, but it certainly did not hurt that they looked so, so lovely while wearing their finery either. As it happened, they also sounded quite lovely while wearing their jewelry because when the girls turned the corner their surprised shrieks were nearly auto-tuned into a delicate vibrato by the tinkling of their trinkets while they swayed, clasped their chests, and then hugged each other in terror and surprise.

Mallory and Alex both smiled, bowed slightly, and said, "Excuse us." They rushed by before the startled couple could catch their breath, though the jingling sounds of their movements carried on the wind, chasing the girls all the way to the Administrator's house. Mallory kept looking over her shoulder half expecting to see a small fat man and tall thin woman lurking in the shadows, only noticeable by the glints of outrageously priced metal reflecting the glint of the moon and the sizzle of the light of the city, but no one was there.

The light could be beautiful at night. It was dimmed to let the citizens sleep, and just noticeable by the irregular crackling and spitting of purple lightning when a stray bug or piece of dirt tried to cross the barrier. On a windy night like this, the lightning was even more active, and Mallory was arrested by a particular violent patch of electric brilliance when a slipstream of leaves hit the light. Even the light seemed to be calling them to stop and turn back before it was too late. Alex tugged on Mallory's sleeve, and she turned to find herself standing for the second time that day at the Administrator's giant back door.

Alex ordered the door open, and they both stood on the threshold looking into the dark, echoing entryway. Mallory turned to her friend, "You don't have to, you know."

Alex looked stung. "It's all I've ever wanted for you, Mallory. You're my best friend. Every time I see you struggle, my heart breaks. If we don't do this, they'll have a different Matriarch, and we won't be able to stay friends."

"What!?" Mallory stepped back, hurt and confused.

"Well, I mean I'd like to stay friends anyway, but you've seen what's happened to our parents. The only friends they have are the other leaders."

Mallory shook her head. "No, no—the part about another Matriarch. What are you talking about?"

"Mallory, you have to know. My grandfather, the Governor, and your mother have discussed it several times. Has she never told you?"

"Told me that I won't be the next Matriarch? No, never! Where are they going to find a new Matriarch in the family line? I'm the only daughter of the governing families besides you, and then who would be the Administrator?"

"Mallory, your mother is pregnant. The baby is a girl, and they have decided that she will be the Matriarch when she comes of age."

Mallory was shocked and fell awkwardly backwards off the stoop. Her ankle twisted just enough to register pain, and she reeled back, barely maintaining her footing while trampling the Administrator's lovely flowerbed full of summer bounty, daffodils, and tulips. It felt like Alex had punched her in the stomach.

Her vision was suddenly blurry with tears. But all of that physical discomfort was multiplied exponentially by the questions that filled her mind. Her mother was having another daughter to replace her? Why hadn't she said anything? Why hadn't her father said anything if he knew? If she wasn't going to be Matriarch, what was she going to be? What purpose did a Chorus have? She imagined herself an old woman, hobbling down the street on her cane, alone, dejected, cast out by the city she loved. Children avoided her on the streets, casting fearful glances at the crazed Dikaió Chorus. Who was that old woman that only existed to exist? What was her purpose? Would anyone remember that she was part of the Matriarchal leaders of the city, or would she have only a few books to comfort her? Would Alex reject her too? Would Caleb even see her after this, or would he look through her like an invisible wraith?

"Mallory? Mallory!" Mallory gradually climbed out of the pit of anxious uncertainty to find Alex standing in the flower garden shaking her. "It's not too late. They haven't announced anything, so it's not part of the records yet. That's why we have to change your Dikaió, tonight!"

Mallory's eyes focused as hope began to bloom once more in her chest, burning back the marauding self-doubts and depression. Yes, there was still a chance to claim her birthright. She would let her usurping unborn sister taste the misery of a life without purpose in the city. Let her join the ranks of the lower Dikaió. Mallory checked herself. That's not quite the spirit a Matriarch ought to have. Every citizen should be treated respectfully as the city could not function if they did not provide their service. Maybe she'd hire the girl as an assistant. She would be family after all, and without the threat of having her title stolen, it might be nice to have a sister to help out while managing the affairs of the Matriarchy. But first she needed to be a Dikaió Syntec.

Mallory reached up and took hold of Alex's hand. Fresh tears filled her eyes. "Thank you, Alex."

Alex inhaled deeply and wiped a tear away. "Let's just try it and make sure it works before we get all emotional."

"Of course, but even if it doesn't, Alex. You're the only one who has even been willing to try. Whatever happens, you will always be my best friend."

"Raw!" Alex shook loose from Mallory's hand and wiped tears from both cheeks. "Okay Mallory, seriously. Let's go do this."

Mallory nodded, and the two girls embraced quickly before turning in to the dark house. Alex thought it would be better not to order the lights of the house to turn on and attract attention. Despite the urgency of the situation, their plan for the night was still a clandestine operation, which could result in disciplinary repercussions. Alex's grandfather was the Dikaió Administrator of Justice for the city, and her father as heir to the Administrator was the Chief Magistrate who oversaw the Order of the Magistrates: officers that were tasked with upholding the laws of the city, but on a day-to-day basis they mostly decided disputes between citizens. However, for extreme cases, the magistrates were armed with old-magic projectile weapons, which were quite deadly—though only the magistrates had ever seen one in use, and then only in training. The city was a peaceful place, not perfect by any means, but no one saw any reason to break its laws and ruin a good thing.

As far as Mallory was aware, the Administrator himself had not issued judgment on a case in which a citizen had disobeyed the city's laws in the girls' entire lifetime. The consequences of getting caught were impossible to know, but the trouble that would come after the fact seemed relatively slim: Mallory would be the only other Dikaió Syntec and would have a rightful claim to the Matriarchy of the city, and up until now they always went easy on her because of her mother's position. Still, the risk was palpable in the air as they dodged furniture in the darkness of the night.

Shadows seemed to reach out for them, barring their way. Foreboding stared down at them from the portraits of Alex's ancestors lining the hallway, beginning with Daniel Nelson the first Administrator, who had always mesmerized Mallory. He had the most piercing blue eyes, perhaps exaggerated by the artist, but they seemed as if they could look past all a person's pretensions and see what was within. His eyes looked more like Caleb's crystalline blue eyes than Alex's, but that was expected, since the three families often married within their ranks if there was more than one child born to a house, so it was likely Daniel Nelson was related to all three of them in some distant past.

It had been at least three generations since one of the ruling families sired more than one child, and that was about to change. The House of the Matriarchy would have two girls, so whichever one was not Matriarch could be betrothed to

Caleb. Mallory had not considered that until this moment and felt her stomach turn with the thought of her little sister marrying Caleb—for an instant, she thought about turning and running home, but her duty was to the city, and what use would she be as the Governor's wife with no Dikaió? She could not even help her mother with the dinner party this evening, she would not even make a decent housewife. Any man who married her would have to leave his duties. Imagine a Governess calling on the Governor to leave the city's needs to help her in the cooking and cleaning, ordering around the sprites every night: the very thought was scandalous. The entire city would look at her as a person of inconvenience. Besides, the city needed a Matriarch, and that was the role she had been born for, until her grandmother cursed her. She glanced back at the painting, and Daniel Nelson's eyes danced warily in the reflection of a streetlamp shining in through the living room window, questioning her true intentions across the years.

Mallory turned away from the judgmental portraits to focus on Alex as they rushed down the hall. Alex had always been there for her. While Mallory had been busy trying to figure out how to make her way without magic, Alex had walked beside her making sure that the Dikaió would be there to bail her out of trouble if she needed it. It was Alex that first figured out that some magic items would respond to Mallory's presence if they were told to, which made getting through doors much easier. Even though Alex's interventions were always helpful, at times Mallory felt exhausted by her friend's charity, of which Alex seemed to have an inexhaustible well. Tonight was different though. Tonight, Alex was offering help that would grant Mallory independence and freedom.

The night closed in around the girls as they entered the staircase to the attic. Mallory realized she had never been to the Book Club in the dark before, and while the staircase was always somewhat dim and gloomy in the daytime, at night, it was pitch black. She moved her hand in front of her face and could see nothing. Alex pulled a tiny Dikaió torch from her jacket pocket. "Dikaió on," she whispered, and the stairway lit up in a dim white light that seemed blinding to their eyes, previously adjusted to the dark. Shadows crawled up the walls, undulating around them as they climbed the stairs.

Mallory briefly felt they must be the shadows of the Administrators in the hall come to put an end to their rebellion, but then she realized that they belonged to her and her friend, brought to life by the torch movement of Alex's hand. The realization did not relieve the feeling of foreboding as she trudged up the stairs.

Alex fumbled with balancing the key and the torch while trying to work the old lock at the top of the attic stairs, so Mallory reached up and took the small torch from her. "Thanks," Alex said without looking around. Even without the torch, Alex had trouble with the lock as her hands were trembling wildly. Mallory could not tell if it was excitement or fear that caused the tremors, but she assumed both as the two feelings were chasing each other in the pit of her stomach. She felt both profoundly sick and purposefully alive simultaneously.

The door swung open into more darkness. The torch's light barely passed the doorway of the inner sanctity of their Book Club. Alex froze, and Mallory took her turn to nudge her friend forward. The world is full of significant events that would never be realized if not for friends spurring each other onward into history. Alex walked quickly after Mallory's nudge, and Mallory followed close behind her, trying to stay within the torch's circle of light. The two girls rushed to the old lamp and struck the spark necessary to ignite the fabric wick. As they trimmed the lamp, the room settled into its familiar state of illuminated existence, and both girls visibly relaxed.

The book was sitting open on a large wooden crate between the seats and the couch that the group used for a coffee table, and Alex reached for it with the awe and reverence a priestess might display in touching a holy instrument. The girls' eyes were wide with reflected fire from the old lamp as they looked at the book: Alex's green eyes sparkling like the green gems in the Smith Guild jewelry; Mallory's grey eyes swirled red and yellow, becoming the fire of the old magic itself as she watched Alex open the book and turn to the page she had dogeared. Alex began to read, "Assume Dikaió re—"

"Wait!" Mallory grabbed her arm.

Alex screamed. "Oh my!" She breathed hard and held her chest. "Oh my, you scared me! What?!"

"I'm sorry. I just . . . I just, I'm scared."

Alex raised her eyebrows which caused her black-bobbed hair to rise visibly. "You're scared? What's there to be scared of Mallory?"

Mallory laughed. "Says the girl that just screamed and said, 'you scared me.'"

Alex softened at that retort. "Well, I guess this is all a little scary. I mean what will our parents think . . . the city . . . well, everything? But isn't it worth it, Mallory? To be able to live your purpose, I mean. Isn't it worth it?"

Mallory tilted her head to the side and bit her lip, considering. "Of course. But I can't help thinking about how everything will be different."

"Yes, but in a good way!"

"My life isn't so awful, you know." Mallory thought about her parents and wondered if they would be ashamed of her for breaking the rules, or proud of her for solving her problem independently. If they didn't have a reason to pity her, how would they look at her?

Alex interrupted her thoughts, "I've been there for all of it, Mallory. It's not great either. Building your death-trap contraptions to survive not having the Dikaió—it's not great, Mallory. You've nearly killed yourself . . . you've nearly killed me a dozen times or more."

Mallory laughed at that. "See, we've had some good times even without the Dikaió. Imagine how boring your life would be if I were just like everyone else."

"Boring, yes, but we both know that eventually we'll have to grow up. We'll have to take over our parents' roles. I'll be Administrator, Caleb will be Governor, and you could be . . . you will be Matriarch. Isn't that what you want?"

"I do, more than anything. I do. It's just that I keep

thinking about my grandmother's dream."

"More like, your grandmother's curse."

Mallory ignored that comment and continued, "Well, she said a Chorus would save the city. What if someone needs me to be what I am, and I just don't know it yet?"

"I believe it was 'a Matriarch who was a Chorus' that saved the city. Right? If we change your Dikaió, you will be 'a Matriarch who *WAS* a Chorus,' past tense, Mallory."

"Hmmm . . . I hadn't thought of it like that." Mallory stood up and walked over to look at the books on the shelves.

"Mallory? Are you ready?" Alex held up the book. "Can we do this?"

"Mmmm . . . ?" Mallory said absently, not looking at Alex.

"Mallory, can you just let me help you for once? Please? It's just a short phrase; I swear."

Mallory took a deep breath. "I've thought about using the Dikaió my whole life, Alex. I've thought about how nice it would be to just say something and have it happen like everyone else, but now that it comes to it, there's a part of me that enjoys the struggle of having to do things on my own; to say whatever I want, whenever I want, without worrying about hurting someone. And what about that, Alex? What if I say something with the Dikaió and hurt someone? You've seen my temper."

Alex set the book down on the coffee table and leaned back in her chair. She pulled her feet up and crossed her legs. "It seems like you're making excuses to not go through with this. You say you enjoy struggling. Why can't you enjoy the struggle of learning to control your tongue? I would welcome that change," she teased.

Mallory laughed. "I'm sure my parents would as well."

"To say nothing of Mrs. Alberts in culturing class. You've had her almost in tears worrying whether your curses would destroy the class's crops."

Mallory laughed louder at that, but Alex just looked exasperated, which made Mallory laugh even more. Eventually, she took deep gasping breaths between laughter and regained control. Alex was leaning forward, her elbows resting on her crossed legs, her hands dangling toward the floor. She was silent. Her eyes were like mirrors, and Mallory did not like the caginess of the girl standing at the bookshelf being reflected in them. Mallory sighed and turned back to the bookcase and pulled out a book titled *Understanding Body Language* from the shelf. She flipped through it to a page she knew well. It showed a drawing of a person with their arms crossed with a caption that read, "Crossing the arms is a sign of closing off conversation." There was another image a few pages ahead that said that leaning forward was a sign of engagement. However, the book did not say what crossing one's legs while leaning forward indicated. When Alex took that position, was she interested in what Mallory was saying or was she closing off conversation? She had never been able to figure that out, so she changed the subject.

"Do you suppose my sister will marry Caleb?"

Alex nearly fell forward off the chair and had to uncross her legs to pull herself up: "What?!"

"Well, she'll be the second child of the Matriarch. It's the way things used to be done, right?"

"Maybe, but it's better than her being the Matriarch."

"I suppose, but it's just that . . ." Mallory set the book gently back into its place and shook her head.

"Mallory?" Alex looked uncomfortable and now her arms were crossed as well.

"Never mind, it's silly. I'm ready." Mallory walked over and again sat in the chair beside her friend.

Alex quickly picked up the book off the coffee table and began to read before Mallory could change her mind, "Assume Dikaió readdress from Dikaió Administrator Alexandria Nelson. Dikaiós reset to Dikaió Chorus. Okay the book says that will clear your Dikaió class. Now, we'll reassign it." Alex turned to another page that she had marked. "Restart Dikaió for Mallory Knenne as Dikaió Syntec. That's it. How do you feel?"

Mallory stretched out her hands and looked down at them inquisitively. "I don't feel any different at all. Should I?"

"I guess I don't know. The book doesn't really say so. It just has the words. Try the ball."

"Oh, right." Mallory pulled the little red ball from her pocket and rolled it onto the floor. It rolled under the coffee table, and then lodged under Caleb's couch. Mallory leaned forward and thought about the ball. "Okay, ball, come to me."

Nothing happened.

Mallory tried again. "Mallory wants her ball."

Nothing happened.

"Mallory wants her red ball to come to her hand."
Still nothing.

Both girls sighed and heaved themselves back into their

chairs, exhausted by the disappointment. Mallory turned her face to Alex, "I don't think it worked."

"I can see that. I thought for sure it would. Maybe I missed something?" Alex opened the book again and began to read.

"Well, you're not going to find it tonight, Alex; besides, I'm starving. My mother's dinner party is probably just getting started. Let's go eat!"

Alex sighed again. "Yes, okay. Don't forget your ball."

Mallory turned and looked at Caleb's old couch. The filth was several layers deep: food, dirt, cobwebs. "There's no way I'm touching that couch. Who knows what's living in there— Would you mind?"

Alex visibly relaxed and laughed. "Oh, now you want my help? I don't mind at all. Ball, go to Mallory."

Nothing happened.

"Ball, go to Mallory."

Nothing happened.

Panic tinged Alex's voice. "Ball, come to me."

Still nothing.

Alex pulled the small Dikaió torch from her pocket. "Dikaió, on." The torch remained dark. Alex began to breathe hard, shallow breaths; her eyes were wild. "Dikaió Torch, turn on! Turn on! Turn on!" The torch remained dark.

Alex began to scream.

Alex ran out of the attic without bothering to close the door. Mallory quickly turned and blew out the flame of the old lamp, and the room went black. As an afterthought, she grabbed the book Alex had read from, and then Mallory was chasing her friend in the dark, moving slowly trying to piece together the layout of the attic from memory and her touch. Her shin rammed into the makeshift coffee table, and then she fell onto Caleb's couch. She inhaled the dust plume as she tried to free herself from the stench of the teenage boy's domain and coughed uncontrollably for a time. Her eyes burned and watered, and she held them tightly closed. The attic was too dark to see anything anyway. When her breathing had calmed and her eyes had stopped burning so much, she slowly pulled herself to her feet. She could hear Alex still shouting downstairs, and there was the sound of breaking glass and splintering wood.

Mallory called down to her as she felt her way to the staircase, "Alex, are you okay? Stay still; I'm coming." She pulled the door closed behind her, and the door's lock clicked into place. There was a faint reflection from the lights outside that made it so Mallory could make out the outlines of the stairs as she descended. "Alex? Alex? Talk to me, Alex!"

Alex was still screaming, but Mallory could hear her were words now: "Dikaió lights on, Dikaió music play, Dikaió vacuum sprite clean, Dikaió kitchen sprites cook, Dikaió water pump, Dikaió door open." The house remained silent and indifferent to her voice.

Mallory stepped gingerly over the pictures of the Administrators that Alex had pulled down from the hallway walls and picked her way carefully toward her friend—then she heard glass shattering in the kitchen. She turned the corner to find Alex standing on the counter throwing dishes at the kitchen sprites hurrying to clean up the broken bits of glass. "Listen to me! I am the Dikaió Administrator Alex Nelson. Stop cleaning up! Stop!" The sprites busily ignored her, vacuuming up each plate or cup as soon as it was thrown.

"Alex!" Mallory yelled.

Alex paused and looked at Mallory; there was no recognition in her eyes, just an emptiness that unnerved Mallory. Then Alex seemed to come to her senses, and her face contorted in grief. She sat down on the counter, crossed her legs, buried her face in her hands, and wept deep anguishing sobs. "What did I do? Oh, Mallory, what did I do?"

Mallory weaved through the kitchen sprites as they dumped glass shards in the waste receptacle. "Alex . . . Alex . . ." Mallory wanted desperately to comfort her friend, tell her that everything was going to be okay, but she had always been the one being comforted by others; it seemed to her such a worthless exercise because no matter how hard anyone tried, no one's words ever made her feel any better: Emotions could not be ordered by the Dikaió. Most of the time people's attempts at comfort just intensified whatever passion had control of her at the moment. The only thing that had ever been of any use was when her parents would hug her and stroke her hair. Sometimes they would hum the melodies of old hymns whose lyrics had long been lost, and that would at least calm the storm inside her.

Mallory climbed up on the counter and sat next to Alex. She set the book down and enveloped her friend in her arms and hummed a wordless song to the rhythm of Alex's breath, quickly at first and then slower and slower. Alex's breath kept time with Mallory's song, and soon, Alex was breathing normally, just weeping softly into Mallory's shoulder.

"Alex, we need help. We need to get our parents." She picked up the book and waved it.

Alex nodded into Mallory's shirt, wiping at her tears as she did. "I know . . . but what if they can't do anything? What if they won't do anything? Oh, Mallory . . . what if I? What if I?" Alex's breath was growing shallower as she spoke.

Mallory pressed Alex's shoulder warmly. "No," she said. "We're not going there until we know. Do you understand?"

Alex's eyes were starting to dart wildly around the room as the kitchen sprites whirred in the dark. But she nodded in silent agreement, and both girls climbed down from the counter. Alex immediately laid her head back on Mallory's shoulder and stood there for a moment, as if she were on a ship amidst the waves, and she was unsure her feet would hold her. "It's okay," Mallory said. "I've got you." Mallory tried to link her arm with Alex's, but Alex clutched tightly to her waist, so they stumbled haphazardly to the door.

Alex called out, "Dikaió door unlock." Nothing happened, and Alex looked helplessly at Mallory, "What do we do?"

"It's okay, Alex. This door knows you. Let's try walking up to it and see what happens." The girls took a step forward, and when they got near, the door unlocked and opened. The girls stumbled awkwardly over the threshold and down the back stoop because Alex was still leaning her head on Mallory's shoulder and wiping her nose on her shirt.

"Listen, Alex. I love you like a sister, but you're going to have to walk. I don't think we'll make it to my house like this. And honestly, that's just gross," Mallory said as she edged away gently.

Alex laughed a little mouse laugh, sniffled hard, and pulled herself up. She gestured confidently and said, "Right, sorry," but her voice was quavering. She looked ready to burst into tears again.

Mallory handed her the book and said, "Here, put this under your jacket, so it doesn't get too wet out here." Then she smiled and held out her hand, which Alex took and squeezed tight.

The way back to the Matriarch's home was filled with as much dread as the way to the Administrator's house had been filled with excitement and intrigue. Heavy rain pelted the light above, and pink lightning shone like a spider's web over the entire city. Some of the rain was immediately vaporized by the light, but much of it was dripping through, dampening them with warm droplets. The rain had not soaked into the ground enough to turn the dirt on the road into mud, so the wind was whipping sand and bits of debris into their eyes and mouths. On the way to the Administrator's house the wind had been at their back pushing them onward, but now it was pushing hard against them like a defender repelling invading hordes from the castle walls. If the girls had not had a tight hold of each other's hands, they would have fallen several times.

A blue shard of lightning struck hard against the light of the city; the entire light flashed bright blue. For an instant the city was lit up like it was the middle of the day. Mallory could see the green of the Dikaió Secretariat's hedges, and the red shutters of her house just as vividly as the brightest day. There were two small rabbits crouching below them, and when the flash lit the city, they both stood up and stared in wonder around the city. Mallory wondered how much the tiny creatures really understood about what had caused the night to become day without a sunrise, and she realized that she probably did not know much more than they did. The light had been constructed long before anyone who was currently living could remember, and every record of its construction had been lost. In that moment of ignorance, Mallory felt a deep connection to the rabbits below the hedge. She felt like a helpless creature living in a world impossible to understand, just trying to survive, and now Alex may be just like her with no Dikaió to rely on to make that life any easier. They did not know anymore than a rabbit what the future was going to bring for them, but here they were standing in the brilliance of the night; all their troubles momentarily suspended by fear and awe.

No more than a fraction of a moment later, thunder chased away the light, and darkness hit the city with a wall of sound. The ground shook, the trees wobbled, birds flushed from their nests into the sky, screaming in protest. Both Mallory and Alex dropped down, their hands remaining tightly bound, their voices too terrified to do more than mirror the birds with sharp chirps mostly stuck in their throats. Mallory had felt the sound in her chest; her heart trembled with its power. When her head cleared enough to think again, Mallory wondered if the lightning had done something to the Dikaió lights in the city because everything was pitch black, but then she realized that her eyes were still tightly closed. She opened them and found the city much the way it had been before the lightning strike, except that the rabbits were no longer beneath the Secretariat's hedges. They had vanished back to wherever it was that rabbits lived within the city.

Mallory wished she were home already, too: cozy and close to her mother and father. This was not the first time that lightning had struck the light above the city, and ever since she was little, her parents would surround her in their embrace when it did. When she was little, she thought that it was for her comfort, but now that she was older, she could recognize the fear in their eyes and feel their rapid heartbeats next to hers. She knew now that being a grownup did not take away the fear as much as help you become familiar with it, but in moments of extreme fright, everyone becomes a child that needs a hug. And she relished being with her parents in those moments to give each other mutual support. However, as she pulled Alex up and started walking, she knew that now her parents would have noticed that she was not at home, and she wondered if they would ever embrace her again once they found out what she and Alex had done.

The dust on the sidewalks and the roadways was turning to mud now, and Alex's feet were starting to drag as they got closer to the Matriarch's house, leaving long streaks behind the girls as they shuffled slowly forward. Mallory was all but dragging her by the hand.

"Mallory, stop! I don't want to go any farther," Alex said, bringing her feet to an immovable station on the sidewalk. Mallory slowed and turned slightly to look at her. Alex was soaked, her black bob now discombobulated and hanging in wet strands down her face. She was absently blowing at her hair, trying to clear it away, but it clung to her skin like wet wisps of misery.

"We're almost there, Alex. Just a little farther." Mallory tugged on her friend's hand, but Alex stood firm.

"No, I don't want to go. Let's just go back to the attic."

"Alex, they might be able to help."

"Like they helped you? I doubt it. Besides in all the

crazy schemes you've dragged us through, I've managed to never get into trouble. My father was just saying that he was proud of me for avoiding trouble my whole life, like a good Administrator ought to. This will kill him, Mallory, and then what? Would the city be stuck with a Dikaió Chorus for a Matriarch and an Administrator who can't administrate? No, I can't bear to see the look on his face when he finds out. I just can't. Not tonight."

Mallory had not considered how Alex would feel about getting into trouble. That was the place where she spent most of her waking hours, causing trouble and disappointing those she loved with her actions. And Alex was right—for their whole lives, Mallory had been the receiver of discipline, and Alex had been the practice of discipline: the perfect example of city civic-mindedness. She was always ready if there was ever a call for help when one of the citizens was in trouble. For example, when the Dikaió Piper had gotten himself and his plumbing sprite wedged in the crawl space under City Hall, Alex had jumped right in with her father, Mallory's mother, and the Governor, passing along orders and calling for the City Services Manager to bring earth-moving equipment to dig him out. Even Caleb had been interested enough to join in the work of a high-profile rescue, using the city's construction sprites to add concrete block piers along the back of the building as support while the machines dug. It was slow going for fear that too much excavation would cause irreparable damage to the old building, which had relied on old magic to construct it. Thus, the knowledge of how to repair a major problem in the old structure was, much like the knowledge of how the light worked, lost generations ago.

Being the useless citizen she was, Mallory stood back, watching and pacing. She wondered why they didn't just open the small door behind the second shelf in the City Hall basement to let the Piper into the building—but when she tried to suggest that alternative, she was promptly shushed and told to go home and let the leaders work. As the sun began to set, and it looked like they were not going to be able to get the Piper out before nightfall, Mallory went inside. She tiptoed down the stairs into the dark and slightly musty basement where the records of the city were stored.

The second shelf was not really all that remarkable on its own, just an oak shelf stuffed full of old binders. However, when Mallory was young, she had brought her ball into the basement to play, while the adults were upstairs handling city business. When she rolled the ball straight, it kept running off course directly into the corner of the shelf. She laid down flat on the floor to examine the stones and was surprised to find a curved rut that looked like it was carved into the floor. Then she began to examine the shelf and found that there was a tiny metal lever on the side. It seemed perfectly obvious to her that if someone had taken the time and effort to construct a tiny metal lever on the side of a shelf, that whoever had done such a crafty thing intended that the lever ought to be pressed and would probably be horribly disappointed if the finder had not pressed it, so she decided to make that creator happy and pressed the lever firmly. There was a small click, and the shelf pulled away from the wall. She slid her fingers behind it and pulled. The bookcase did not move at first, but then with a tiny creak it swung out from the wall: its corner tracing the curve in the floor.

Behind the shelf, there was a doorway that opened into a small empty room full of benches set along the walls. When Mallory walked through the doorway to explore the room, Dikaió torches sprang to life, lighting up the space. The only other thing in the room beyond the benches and the torches was another small wooden door at the far end that was bolted shut. Of course, Mallory had a similar thought about the small wooden door as she did about the lever behind the bookcase, if someone had built a door in a hidden room then it was intended to be opened.

Behind the small wooden door was a dark space with dirt floors and a mess of cobwebs. As her eyes adjusted to the darkness, she could make out brick pillars about two feet high, and there were wooden beams crisscrossing over them, acting as a foundation for the old building. She realized she was in the crawlspace under City Hall. She got down on her hands and knees and explored under the building for a time, but it was quite dark, and she could swear that she saw pairs of small red eyes peering out at her from the shadows, so she got out quickly, closed the doors tightly, and pretty much forgot about the room until the Piper got stuck.

Now, she did not really look forward to crawling under the dark space again, but if she could conquer her fears, she could at least provide some usefulness to the city. She made her way through the doors and crawled into the maze of pillars and beams. She could see the setting sun shining down through the small hole the excavation crew had made some ways away. The silhouette of the Dikaió Piper was kneeling in the pool of light, yelling up at the digging crew, pleading with them not to leave him there overnight.

Mallory dropped to her hands and knees and began crawling in the direction of the light. Suddenly a movement to her left made her freeze in panic. She tried to track whatever it was as it darted between the piers. It was heading toward the Piper. Mallory tried to call out but found herself frozen in fear. The light hit the moving object then, and she saw a glint of silver. It was the plumbing sprite going about its tasks servicing the pipes. She sighed and began to crawl toward the Piper again. Just as she was about to call out, the Piper turned and fell back against the collapsed dirt with a heavy sigh. He closed his eyes, covered them with his hand, and lowered his head. "Well, that's that. I guess we're stuck down here."

"Sir?" Mallory called.

The Piper startled and fell over in the dirt. "What, what? Who's there?"

"It's me, sir. Mallory Knenne. I've come to rescue you."

"What? Knenne? The Matriarch's daughter? But how are you here?" The piper picked himself up onto one elbow.

"I found a door, sir. It's just behind me." Mallory motioned with her head as best she could, indicating the direction of the door.

The Piper strained his neck and looked past her. He did not say anything but nodded. "C'mon, plumber; we're leaving." The plumbing sprite rushed up beside its master, and they slowly followed Mallory back to the door. They crawled into the room with the benches and walked out through the door behind the shelf. The Piper examined the mechanism that opened the door, and then ducked back into the bench room. He called out, "Dikaió torches off." The lights in the room immediately went dark. Then he pushed the shelf closed and started up the stairs with Mallory and the plumber sprite climbing behind him.

When they exited City Hall, they could see the workers cleaning up a bit and the city's leaders were standing in a circle busily discussing something—probably what would need to be done tomorrow to get the Piper out. Mallory started to walk toward the group to let them know that the Piper was free, but the Piper caught her arm. "Wait a moment, child. I'm still angry that they were just going to leave me there overnight. They wanted to go home and sleep in their nice, cozy beds, while I slept on the cold, hard earth. I'd hate to say something I ought not. You know how dangerous words can be."

Mallory nodded, "Well, if you'd like, I could say the words for you."

The Piper bobbed his head back and forth, looking up at the sky. He moved his cupped hands up and down as if they were a balancing scale, weighing her words. Finally, he said, "No, I think it's better to let this wait until tomorrow. Maybe the day after? Let them dig as long as they have the heart to. I'm tired. I think I'd just like to go home, shower, get some supper, and go to bed."

"But what will happen when they get under City Hall and find you gone?"

The Piper smiled wide and shrugged his shoulders. "I'd like to be in my nice, cozy bed by that time." Then he winked and turned around, walking away wearily. Mallory looked back at her mother and the other leaders, and for a moment thought about walking over and telling them anyway, but they would probably just dismiss her as a useless Chorus anyway, and so she raised her hands like a scale in imitation of the Piper, shrugged, and then walked home.

The day the crew finally got into the crawl space safely, her mother had burst into the house brimming with rage; her lips were so tight and narrow they became invisible on her face. She ripped open the kitchen cupboards and slammed them closed again, looking for nothing in particular. When Mallory's father asked what had happened, her mother just said, "the Piper got out three days ago and didn't bother to tell anyone."

Her father laughed uneasily the way he always did when he sensed danger was imminent but still foolishly asked, "but however did he do that?"

Her mother groaned, "I don't know. He won't tell anyone how."

Mallory looked up from her homework and said, "Oh, I let him out."

Both her parents' heads whipped her direction like a stretched rubber band let loose. Her mother looked like steam was going to boil her brain, and her father looked perplexed. "But how, Mallory?"

"I tried to tell them three days ago. There's a door behind the second shelf in the basement that leads to the crawlspace, but no one would listen to me, so I just went and let him out myself." Her mother grounded her for three days to her room for that, and even after she got out, Alex and Caleb had refused to talk to her for a week, and the other city leaders still gave her dirty looks whenever they passed by her. They had even banned her from City Hall until she came of age. The Council members would literally bar her path into the building and physically force her out if she slipped by them, although she'd found she could still slip through the hole they'd dug for the Piper and down into the secret room behind the shelf. It was not much of a victory, but she did enjoy spiting the leaders, so she would often sneak into City Hall and sit in the secret room, relishing in rebellion. She'd even brought Alex down into the room once, but Alex was so uncomfortable breaking rules that she barely lasted thirty seconds in the space before fleeing back out into the open.

But now Alex had lost her Dikaió, and the city leaders would feel more than spited by Mallory's rebellious spirit. What she and Alex had done made the Piper incident seem mild, and Mallory could completely understand why Alex would be hesitant to face off with the city leaders. However, this was also a problem far outside their ability to address, and they needed the experience of adults to help them. "What should we do then, Alex? Run? Hide? Where would we go that they wouldn't find us? The city's just not that big."

Alex was trembling and tears were threatening again. "I don't know, Mallory. I don't know. I don't like not knowing what to do next. Maybe we should go back and look at the book again—we could see if there's a way to undo what I did?"

"Well, maybe there is? But we should let the leaders look and see. We're in over our heads!"

"Oh, no! When you say that, it always gets worse."

Mallory chose to ignore the insult and said, "I'm not sure it can get worse, Alex. C'mon. We're getting soaked standing here arguing about it. Let's go face the music . . . together."

Alex shook her head, "It can get worse, Mallory. According to the laws of the city, if we did harm to another citizen even accidently, we could be . . . .." She hesitated to finish the sentence, but Mallory had been training as a city leader her whole life as well. She knew very well that harming another citizen in any way could lead to the ultimate punishment, death.

Mallory threw up her hands. "That's all the more reason to go in and get control over the situation before someone gets hurt. Don't you think?"

Alex looked uncertain, but then she nodded. The two girls began to move forward again.

The Matriarch's house was well lit, and despite the trouble looming inside, Mallory felt an incredible sense of peace when she got into her own yard. The familiar old house was always a place of refuge, and at times inside its walls when no one else was around to remind her, she forgot that she lacked the basic abilities of magic that the rest of the city enjoyed. Surrounded by the walls of her youth, she could escape into her imagination where her grandmother's prophecies were true, and she was the most powerful Matriarch the city had ever known, and she was able to save the city from danger using the old magic that she had learned in books.

Tonight, there was not going to be any escape from reality, and Mallory knew as they trudged slowly up the brick stairs to the front door that she and Alex would be in the biggest trouble of their lives. Mallory turned to her friend when they reached the front door: "Okay, whatever happens after this point, we stay friends, right?"

Alex started crying and nearly toppled Mallory backwards down the stairs in an embrace. They stood there for a long while, and then Alex sighed deeply and said, "I'm ready." She called out, "Dikaió open."

Nothing happened, and Alex's shoulders drooped.

Mallory smiled soothingly, "Here, let me." She reached up and touched the door. Recognizing her as an occupant of the house, the door unlatched and swung open.

When Mallory opened the door, she expected to find her mother's dinner party in full swing, with adults talking loudly about politics and gossip. They would be eating daintily, picking at the selections of food, so that their mouth would be ready to engage in a question or call for explanation. In the city's high society, it would be considered rude to have one's mouth full when asked a question, and the adults seemed to take great delight in trying to catch the other adults with a full mouth by asking them questions mid-bite. It was also considered impolite to address a question to an heir to a Dikaió when the master was at the table, so those lucky few heirs that got dragged along on these sorts of get-togethers would be stuffing their faces or sitting sullenly, waiting for the masters to finish, so they could escape the doldrum social engagement. However, that expectation was not what Mallory and Alex found on the other side of the door to the Matriarch's house.

Instead, they found the dinner party's guests standing on the table swinging knives and throwing the Matriarch's fine china at a pack of kitchen sprites that were busily whirring around the table, trying desperately to collect the silverware and china from the guests' hands. Mallory's mother and the other city leaders were calling over the din, "Stop! I command you to stop!" But the sprites kept on moving as if the most powerful leaders of the city were just as ordinary as Mallory had always been. Then, while trying desperately to hold on to her fork with a kitchen sprite pulling at it, the tall lanky wife of the Dikaió Smith Guild lost her balance and fell from the table with a grand tinkling of jewelry on top of the sprite. The woman rolled off the sprite onto her back. She reached up, clutched her chest, and groaned. Then she pulled her hand away and stared at it with confusion.

Whether it was the cutlery or the precious stones and sharp pins of her jewelry, the woman was bleeding. She sat there, blinking at the red stain on her hand, and her husband looked down at her, gaping with sweat dripping from the corners of his mustache. The sprite she landed on picked itself up and promptly grabbed the fork from her hand, which made the woman shriek in fright. The whole dinner party turned and saw the sprite holding a bloody fork, hovering over the injured woman.

Mallory looked at Caleb, who was staring at the bleeding woman in shock. She felt a twinge of some emotion that she could not quite name: guilt, fear, shame? It felt like a crushing tightness in her chest and made her want to cry, especially when Caleb's expression of shock morphed into rage. He looked to his father, who also looked angry, and in unison the pair grabbed the silver candelabras from the table and leapt in twin arcs of destruction upon the sprite as it wheeled away to continue its kitchen duties. Metal crashed down on the silvery sprite in heavy blows as the two warriors meted out vengeance. The sprite wheeled back from the onslaught and tried to circumvent the pair of attackers into the kitchen, but the two men blocked its path with strike after strike.

The rest of the dinner party stood motionless on top of the table watching the Governor and his son pound on the kitchen sprite. Even Mallory and Alex stood transfixed in the doorway watching the mêlée transpire. But despite the combined strength of the two men, the sprite seemed relatively indifferent to their strikes, its shiny silver surface not registering so much as a scratch. It just kept trying to make its way past its adversaries so that it could continue its duties in cleaning up the party. Eventually, the two men slumped in exhaustion, and whatever spell had overcome the room was broken.

Mallory looked at the table and found that the other sprites had taken advantage of the distraction and cleared away every trace of the dinner party, except the guests standing on the table. Mallory's mother looked down at the injured woman on her floor and jumped down to attend to her wounds, which were gory but seemed to be superficial. The other guests began to cautiously disembark from the perch, and it was at that point that the Smith Guild leader saw Mallory.

"You! You did this. I'm not sure how, but you did it." His arms and jaw were tense as he glared at her across the room.

Every eye in the room turned to Mallory. The Smith Guild leader turned to Alex's father and yelled, "Chief Magistrate Nelson, I demand that you summon the magistrates and take this girl into custody!" Mallory was used to this sort of attention, but her thoughts were immediately directed with worry toward her friend. She reached back to take Alex's hand and found empty air. Her head whipped back, and Mallory found that she was standing in the doorway alone.

Alex had disappeared.

The rest of the dinner guests began to dismount from the table, and they formed a small mob, moving intently toward Mallory. There was something different about the way they were looking at her this time—their eyes reminded Mallory of Alex's when she was standing on her kitchen counter, twitching slightly. Fear, panic, anxiety, negativity oozed from the group, and Mallory felt real fear for her safety. She tensed her muscles, preparing to flee back out the door.

The Matriarch suddenly pushed her way to the front of the crowd and turned to address them. She was covered with blood from the woman still lying on the ground moaning, so the crowd stood back from her, visibly aghast. She wiped her bloody hands on a napkin while she spoke: "Now, everyone stop! Let's find out what's going on before we do something that cannot be undone." For Mallory, having the Matriarch for a mother was like watching two different people living inside one person. One kissed her knee when she skinned it as a child; the other commanded the citizens into action and demanded respect, but it was not always easy to know who Mallory was dealing with in the moment. With the crowd aroused against her, Mallory was happy that these two roles her mother inhabited could coexist at times.

The crowd halted before the Matriarch's rebuke, and Mallory's fear dissipated a little when her mother turned to her and asked, "Mallory, what is going on? Did you do something tonight? Something that might have caused the Dikaió not to work the way it ought?"

Mallory fidgeted at the sight of her mother looking like a butcher just come from the slaughterhouse. Her hands were now clean, and Mallory watched her mother reach up and pin a few stray hairs, which had broken loose and curled, back into place. Her mother's ability to know when even one of those brown locks strayed always perplexed Mallory. Could she feel them break free from her control? Her mother looked intently at Mallory with her piercing blue eyes, waiting for an answer. Mallory provided her standard answer with more confidence than she felt, "Well, I didn't do anything per se. Alex was the one who—"

Her mother did not blink. They had had this conversation countless times over the years. "But you know what happened?"

"I don't know . . . maybe . . ."

The leader of the Smith Guild yelled from behind the Matriarch, "I knew it. That girl has been a bane to the city from the day that old witch of a Matriarch cursed her."

Mallory's mother moved like a viper strike. In an instant, she was standing over the fat little man, glaring with powerful intent, "Watch your tongue, Jules. That is my family you're speaking of with so much carelessness." He shrunk away from her but looked ready to answer back until she added, "We have no idea what the state of the Dikaió is. Your words might very well still cause irreparable damage."

The Governor stepped up then and added, "Quite right, Sarai! Until we investigate and figure out exactly what has happened, we must continue to live as if nothing has changed. But if this girl has done something to the Dikaió, we need to figure it out tonight. The city is vulnerable without the Dikaió."

The Administrator spoke then, "And we must also consider justice and assess damages that have occurred. We'll have to see if anyone has been hurt, and who is at fault."

The Matriarch acquiesced, "Of course, we have much to investigate and discuss, but becoming a mob is hardly going to accomplish any of those things, will it? Neither will justice be served by rushing to administer punishments before the facts have been investigated; don't you agree that could also do harm, James?"

The old Administrator smoothed the collar of his uniform and said, "Of course, Sarai. You sound so much like your mother when you're acting the mother hen. You know very well the city's court is fair."

"Thank you, James." The Matriarch waved away his comment about her mother. It was no secret the Administrator and Mallory's grandmother had been political rivals ever since the old woman gave Mallory the wrong christening. Her mother did not give him an opportunity to respond either way. "I suggest we convene the Council."

The head of the Smith Guild muttered, "I don't see what the Council has to do with it—the girl admitted she's behind it." He turned to the Administrator, "We demand justice!"

The Administrator looked down at the man, "You heard the Matriarch. We don't even know what has happened. How can justice be served without the facts? Should the facts reveal the heir of the Matriarchy is at fault, then we shall have justice."

Other voices began to chime in from the group, offering suggestions and demanding solutions.

Mallory was edging backward toward the door while they argued amongst themselves. Then she felt a strong arm wrap around her shoulders; she startled and turned to see her father pulling her into an embrace. She briefly saw the stretched lines of worry she had chiseled into his face with her adventures over the years, but he still smiled his infectious smile only dads seem to manage in difficult situations—the sort of look that dads seem to get even in the midst of the most pernicious danger; like if they were dangling over a pit of spears waiting to impale them, they would offer some silly pun like, "Why is grass dangerous? Because it's full of blades." There were no silly jokes tonight though, and Mallory's father just smiled gently and hugged her knowingly. When she was close, he whispered in her ear, "Oh, my girl. My girl."

Mallory just cried. What else could she do?

The din of the crowd was becoming feverish, and finally the Governor shouted, "Enough! We will convene the Council and investigate before any decisions will be made. This conversation is over." He turned to Alex's father and said, "Daniel, Mallory said Alex was involved in this. We'll need her here for the investigation. You and Charisse go home and round her up." The Chief Magistrate nodded and took his wife's arm heading out the door. The crowd mulled around a bit in silence after the Chief Magistrate left, but then those not on the Council noticed the Governor's stern glare and began to collect their belongings to leave.

The Matriarch turned away from the chaos of the dinner guests' exit to her husband and daughter; she seemed surprised by the scene of fatherly tenderness, and for a moment the Matriarch retreated before the mother. Her face contorted in concern, but she shook her head and stammered, "Mallory, you're a mess. Why don't you go change out of those clothes, and then we'll talk about what happened?"

Mallory looked up at her father with a bid for help and saw in his helpless expression there was nothing he could do. She did not wait to be asked twice and raced past her mother, the assembly, and up the stairs, taking them two at a time lest anyone below should change their mind and call her back. She got to her room and shut the door as quickly as she could. She leaned back up against the door. It was ice cold. It clung to her, freezing her skin at every point of contact, and only then did she realize how truly soaked the storm had left her. She looked down and saw a puddle of water spreading on the polished wooden planks below her feet. She wondered if her father was now as soaked as she was? He had not even seemed to notice that she was a sodden mess when he embraced her, nor seemed to care once he had her in his arms. Her heart swelled first with love then guilt and regret. What they had done would hurt her father. It would hurt her mother as well. Maybe the whole city. They had never considered there might be consequences for anyone other than themselves.

She pried herself free from the door and began to pull off her inundated clothing. The wet clothes had a mind of their own though, and they were determined to stay on her. She fought and struggled, releasing one side of clinging cloth from her body only to have the other side suck up against her skin again. Eventually she zigged and zagged and tugged each article of clothing off, dropping them into the puddle on the floor. She dressed quickly, and even the dry clothes rebelled somewhat against the dampness of her skin, but once she powered past the friction, she panted from cold and exertion.

The warm coziness of dry clothes seemed to sap every ounce of energy from her body, and she collapsed onto her bed in exhaustion. Laying there staring at the ceiling, her eyelids were lead anchors pulling a fishing line below the waves of the comforter she was sinking into. The gravity of comfort and exhaustion pulled her down further and further. Her arms and legs were dead weights, and her breathing was becoming more and more even as she lay there. The ceiling lights, barely seen through slits in her eyelids, were surrounded by fading rainbows, spiraling around them like moths flying too close to their flames. What was happening was more important than sleep, but she thought if she just closed her eyes, rested for a moment, she would be better prepared to face her mother's interrogation. So, Mallory curled into a fetal position, and sleep embraced her as fully as her father's arm had earlier. In her unconscious escape, she felt safe. And she enjoyed that feeling because exhaustion kept dreams at bay for a time. But as rest alleviated the exhaustion, there was a stirring of a quiescent fancy in her slumber: nothing substantial like images or actions, just a sensation of a conflicting urgent peace. Soon a voice emanated from the sensation. It was unintelligible at first, but as she strained her dormant self to hear, she could make out a familiar word:

"Mallory!"

Someone far away was calling her name now.

"Mallory!"

The tinny voice sounded like it was coming from deep in a tunnel, but it was drawing nearer.

"Mallory!"

She recognized it now. It was her mother, and she was coming closer, but it was so dark, Mallory could not find her, and she wasn't sure she wanted to.

"Mallory!"

The ground shifted, and Mallory felt a twinge of fear. Her eyes blinked open to find her mother standing over her, tugging on her pillow. Mallory recoiled and tried to scoot away. Her mother looked at her with a tenderness that

Mallory had not seen since she was a small child, sat down on the bed beside her, and stroked her hair, looking thoughtfully into Mallory's eyes. She began to hum a wordless hymn, and Mallory felt the fear subside. She snuggled up into her mother's lap and let herself be petted. After a while, Mallory began to think she must have been having a nightmare about Alex and the Dikaió, and she had called out, and her mother was there to calm her down. "I'll be okay, Mom. Good night." She slowly began to drift back to sleep, but then her mother stopped stroking her hair.

"Mallory, my dear girl, I know it's late, but the Council is downstairs waiting. I need you to come with me and tell them what you know about what happened to the Dikaió."

It was not a dream then. Mallory sighed deeply into her mother's lap then raised herself, straightened her clothes, and headed toward the door. She briefly noted that a sprite was holding her wet clothes while drying the floor with towels from the bathroom. Her mother gave the servant a wide berth, looking at it with a mixture of disgust and perhaps a hint of fear. Seeing her mother's expression started Mallory's stomach churning again, only this time it was fear and trep-idation chasing each other through the gurgling pit in her abdomen. If her mother was afraid, how much worse would the City Council be? What would they do to her when they found out that all of this was her fault? What would they do to Alex? Mallory walked slowly down the stairs holding firmly to the handrail lest her emotions best her and she fall. Her mother followed closely behind, gripping the handrail as firmly as Mallory.

The City Council sat around the Knenne family table. Apparently, this business was too urgent to convene in the assembly room at City Hall where they usually met, and Mallory supposed since they had all been there already for the dinner party, there was little reason to leave. Mallory looked to her right and saw Caleb sitting in one of the high wing-backed chairs with his mother in the living area. They were likely waiting for the Governor to finish before daring to walk home on a night as unpredictable as this one. Caleb looked at Mallory as she walked by, and she could tell he knew exactly what had happened. His silent, "Why?" took an emotional toll larger than anything else Mallory had experienced that night, and she stumbled slightly on the corner of a rug and would have fallen if her mother was not holding tightly to her arm.

There were two empty seats at the long table on each end. The Matriarch led her daughter to the nearest one and indicated that her daughter should sit, then she moved around the table and took her seat between the Governor and the Administrator, representing the familial Triad of Leadership. The Council was made up of the four Dikaió Elect, who were elected officials that represented the will of the people and rotated every four years; they looked very self-important, worried but also excited to be part of such important business as what was happening tonight. The rest of the Council included the representatives of the six Dikaió guilds of the city: the head of the Dikaió Mercantile Guild (and she was meticulously groomed and dressed in the finest, latest fashion); her older sister, the Head of the Dikaió Science

Guild, who had gray hair pulled back in a tight bun and wore thick glasses, as she scribbled busily in a ragged red notebook; the Manager of the Dikaió City Services Guild, a large, muscular man dressed in clean overalls (a rarity in his line of work); the Head of the Co-op of the Dikaió Culture Guild sat picking dirt from his fingernails, looking quite amused at all the commotion; the Sprite Master of the Dikaió Sprite Guild, a middle-aged woman with bright red hair, fidgeting endlessly with a fork that the sprites had failed to collect from her; and finally, of course, there was the decorated head of the Dikaió Smith Guild, who was watching Mallory with cold, buggy eyes. In fact, he was the only Council Member that had even acknowledged Mallory as she sat down, and he was like an old lion raging inside a cage, ready to tear her limb-from-limb if he could just be given the chance. She looked quickly away from him and focused her attention on the Matriarch who was firmly in her leadership persona, peering across the table at Mallory with severity.

The Matriarch nodded toward Mallory, "Okay, Mallory. Tells us what happened."

Mallory hesitated. She did not want to betray the secret of Book Club and have these adults destroy the treasure trove of books they had collected, even if they might be able to find answers to the current situation in those very books. She decided to test the waters of telling her story by starting with, "Well, Alex and I found a book."

Immediately, the table erupted in angry chatter. Books! Will there be no end to their danger?! I thought they were destroyed! This is what comes from letting anyone learn to read! Meddlesome children always finding books; it will be the death of us all!

That cinched Mallory's resolve. She would not be telling anyone about Book Club tonight. She'd focus on the one book that caused the trouble. If they destroyed it, then it would be just as well given the trouble it had caused so far. But she could not bear the loss of losing all their books. She waited to continue until murmuring died down, and Mallory could tell that her mother across the table had been watching her very closely during the excitement. She sensed that she was biting the corner of her lip. Her mother would see that she was planning something, so she would know if she were lying or concealing something. Mallory decided to stick as closely to the truth as possible to throw her off the scent. Hopefully, she would think the planning was just nerves. "Yes, well actually, Alex found the book. She said it had the words to undo the curse of my Dikaió, and she wanted to help me become the Matriarch."

The Matriarch stopped her, "Mallory, doesn't Alex know that you are in line to be the Matriarch already?"

"Well, yes." Mallory began to bite her lip again on purpose this time, "but she said that I would lose my title to my sister."

The Matriarch squirmed as the attention shifted across the table to her, and she would not meet Mallory's eye across the span. The murmuring had begun again and was growing louder. Clearly not all the Council Members were aware of her mother's pregnancy and the chance for a functioning Matriarch to hold the position. Is it true? Will we have a true

Matriarch? One that can bestow the Dikaió in the christening? How long have you known? When were you going to inform the Council? When is the future Matriarch to be born?

"Ladies and Gentleman," the Governor shouted over the commotion. "This all seems irrelevant with the current state of the Dikaió, doesn't it? Please, let's continue our investigation. We will discuss news of the Matriarch's second daughter at another time. Miss Knenne, continue."

Mallory stopped trying to catch her mother's eye, when it became evident that she could not look at her daughter. Satisfied that the search for concealment was over, Mallory began talking again: "Well, Alex said that unless I become a Dikaió Syntec tonight, my sister would become the Matriarch . . . and I didn't know where that would leave me. She thought she had found the answer in this book: a way to end my Dikaió as a Chorus and reinstate it as a Syntec. I was hesitant, but I'm barely acknowledged as a person in this city as it is, so I figured what did I have to lose? Alex said the words. Nothing happened. I didn't feel any different. My object of affection did not come when I called, nothing." Mallory paused and looked at the Council.

Then the Science Guild leader said, "So the experiment was a failure?"

Mallory sagged, "Well, I don't know. It depends if we understood the words right or not."

The Head of the Smiths yelled, "And what does that mean? What happened that you're not saying?"

"Well, nothing happened to me, but when Alex called

my object of affection, tried to turn on the Dikaió torch, or command the kitchen sprites, nothing happened for her either. It was like she was a Chorus like me. We were on our way here to find help, but then when we got here, we found all of you were the same as Alex."

There was silence as the implications began to settle over the Council.

Alex's grandfather, the Administrator spoke first, "And where is Alex, now?"

"I don't know. We walked in, saw the mess here, and when I turned around, she was gone."

"And the book?"

"I don't know. Alex had it."

Thunder crashed then, the lights flared bright, and the room was swallowed in darkness. In the unrelenting black, the murmuring Council shifted from anger and outrage to fear. Someone in the room was shouting, "Dikaió torch, on," but the room remained in darkness only briefly illuminated by flashes of lightning shining through the living area windows. Bodies bumped ungraciously into one another, as they all stumbled toward the living area. Mallory tried to stay upright amongst the throng of City Council members, but she nearly fell several times.

When they made it to the living area, there was still no light save the flashes of lightning. The streetlights were all out, so even the outdoors was nearly black.

"What's that sound?" Someone in the darkness spoke. The room went silent, and then Mallory heard it. It sounded like someone had opened a bag of marbles and dropped them all down a metal shoot. Or like a bunch of rocks being shaken in a tin can. Or like water sprinkling, mostly like water sprinkling, and that's when she pressed through the crowd to the window. She pressed her face up to the glass and looked up toward the sky. Darkness. The rain was no longer causing the pink arcs of lightning in the skies above the city, and all of it was now pouring through unhindered. The light over the city had gone out when the houselights did.

The Governor's voice sounded above the commotion, "The generators for the light and the city are below City Hall. We need to get there in order to get the light back up."

"How?" A voice asked. "Without the Dikaió, how do we reactivate the generators?"

The Governor did not respond. Instead, he called out, "C'mon, Jacob. Let's go see what we can do." Jacob Carpenter, the large City Services Manager grunted an acknowledgement, and the Governor yelled, "Caleb! Come with us, son. We may need your help."

Caleb shoved his way through the crowd, and Mallory briefly felt him push by her, and even in the midst of the crisis and trouble she found herself in, she still felt the hair on her arms raise at his touch. The Governor, the City Services Manager, and Caleb felt their way to the door and then flung it open, inviting the wind and rain into the house. The whole crowd then began to shuffle out into the storm and follow behind the Governor toward City Hall. Mallory was drawn along with them, as much by curiosity about what could be done to resurrect the light as by not wanting to be left alone in the dark house. The Governor did not dissuade the crowd from following them. Mallory figured he was used to the attention.

The water that hit Mallory as they exited the house was not the gentle mist of raindrops a storm usually passed through the light. This was a deluge of water. They were all instantly soaked. The streets had streams of water rushing through them, and more than one Council Member was pulled off their feet into the current and had to be rescued by the others, groping for them in the dark, their eyes still barely able to make out anything in the darkness. The floods made it slow going to City Hall, but the group trudged on.

Then lightning flashed down to the Earth, instantly followed by a clap of thunder so loud, that Mallory felt her heart skip a beat. As if by a miracle, when she opened her eyes, there was a soft glow of light, and she could make out some details of the people and the city around her. The light was weak and flickering, but at least it was light, and the group seemed to pick up speed now that they could see where they were going. In fact, soon they were all running. Then they were shouting as well. Panicked, Mallory saw what had excited the group and what had brought the light in the darkness: Lightning had struck City Hall, and the building was a black silhouette outlined by a small pillar of fire extending toward the heavens from its roof. Despite the heavy rains, the fire was spreading quickly through the wood-framed building.

For a moment, the crowd of city leaders stood transfixed by the blaze. Flames in the attic poked out of crevices in the white-wood shingles of the roof and were beat back by the rain when it tried to escape. Billows of smoke rose in pillars, blending into the dark cloud cover above. In the flickering second-floor windows, Mallory could see glowing soldiers of flame marching down the hallways of the civil servants' offices. Some of the fiery soldiers caught hold of the red curtains, and they burned quickly, leaving a lace of ashes before falling away in orange floating embers. The red brick of the interior and the white-columned porch seemed relatively unscathed, but the fire was spreading fast, and it would not be long before the entire interior of the building would be in flames, and then the fire would consume what it could outside the building. Suddenly a window burst from the intense heat, and the pop was louder than the deafening noise of the rain and thunder. The crowd winced in unison, and the spell the fire had them under was broken. The Governor turned to the City Services Manager and shouted, "Jake, without the Dikaió and with the generators offline, the fire department may not have received the emergency signal. Go, and make sure they're coming!"

"Yeah, but without the Dikaió, who knows if they can help?"

"We need to try! Go, quickly!"

The large man, looking more comfortable in his usual state, overalls caked in mud and grime from the storm, ran off swiftly toward the north side, giving the burning building a large berth.

The Governor yelled at the other city leaders: "If the fire department's sprites cannot be roused to put this fire out, we're going to have to do it ourselves. We need barrels, buckets, bowls, urns, anything that will hold water, and we need it now!" The rest of the crowd exploded into action, zig-zagging this way and that as they weaved around each other in different directions: everyone heading home to see what they could find to help. The Governor grabbed Caleb's and Mallory's arms before they could run away with the rest and shouted, "You two, wait! We need that book if we're going to have a chance of getting the Dikaió back. Go, find Alex!"

Caleb shouted back, "I can help with the fire, Dad! I want

to help!"

"The Dikaió is more important than a silly building. Find that book!"

Caleb nodded and turned toward Mallory and yelled, "Where do you think she would go?"

"I don't know. Maybe she went home?"

"Her father probably went there to look for her, but let's start there anyway. It couldn't hurt." Caleb took off at a sprint, which Mallory would normally have had a hard time keeping up with, except that the storm had turned City Hall's lawn into a mud pit, and Caleb's heavier frame caused his feet to sink further into the muck than hers. While the mud evened out their race with one another, it also held them both back considerably in their race against time.

The Governor needed the Dikaió to rekindle the light. The viciousness of the storm without the light to mitigate its effects was just one potential hazard the city faced without the light's protection. Since the passing of the last Chorus, no one in the city really knew what lay beyond the light, but parents told their children fantasies of beasts that hunted with claws and teeth, and a dangerous breed of humanity that had chosen to live in darkness rather than embrace life—all of whom would happily drag any stray child off into the darkness with them if not for the protection of the light. Thinking about childhood horror stories told round a Dikaió torch in the dark made Mallory's hair stand up on the back of her neck.

Maybe it was the terrors the memories carried, but she felt as if someone was watching them while they ran. She desperately wanted to call out to Caleb to stop, but her breathing was so heavy from their run that she could not catch hold of the air to speak. Her eyes darted left and right, looking for the invisible watcher when she saw movement in one of the tall townhomes on the street they were crossing. Mallory focused through the rain, and she could see vague shapes of people in the dark windows of the houses. The citizens of the city were looking out of their windows, wide-eyed with terror; every house they passed was the same. At this hour, it was mostly adults, but in some houses, there were children clinging to their parents' clothes for comfort. They knew the light had gone dark, they had likely figured out that the Dikaió was gone, and they were most likely remembering all the same wild stories Mallory was thinking about as she ran.

But then Mallory saw the citizens' terror transformed as they recognized the runners: When they saw that the Matriarch's daughter and the Governor's son were going somewhere, doing something about the light, their fear became hope. Mallory wondered how misplaced that hope was. She knew the city leaders and the limits of their ability to fix problems. City Hall might be burning to the ground even as they ran. The light might never come back. The Dikaió might never come back. Their old life might never come back. As if bidden by the city's crisis, her childhood memories, and the citizens' faith, her grandmother's voice spoke to her through the storm: "You will be the Matriarch who is a Dikaió Chorus, and you will save the city."

Mallory had little time to process that thought as they

rounded the corner to the Administrator's house, but she felt herself brimming with confidence: This was the moment for which she had been born. Caleb slowed down and ran up to the back door of the big house, but somehow Mallory knew that Alex would not have gone back to the place that started it all, so she ducked down the path that led to the Chief Magistrate's home in the back, just beyond the muddied gardens. Normally, the gardens were quite beautiful this time of the year, full of every color of flower one could imagine, but in the dark and the rain, they looked like a forbidding bog; all the color drowned in the downpour into mud and darkness. Lightning flashed through the shadows of broken plant stems waving wildly in the wind like beasts chained to the Earth, trying desperately to escape. Mallory ran gingerly along the path as the bare, wet plants lashed at her legs. Finally, she reached the door.

Alex had instructed the door to know Mallory and open to her when she knocked, but for some reason, tonight the door ignored her percussive presence. She rapped louder, but still the door did not budge. She moved to the small window and found herself looking into a pale, ghostly reflection that was not her own. Mallory shrieked and stumbled backward in terror. The apparition knocked on the window and seemed to be yelling something. It was hard to make out, but it sounded like, "Go to the back!"

Mallory took a second look at the face and realized it was Alex's mother looking out at her. "Go to the back! The door is open," Alex's mother yelled.

The backdoor was open, and both of Alex's parents were

standing in the doorway when Mallory got around the house. Chief Magistrate Daniel Nelson was in partial undress. He clearly had been changing out of his casual dining attire into his Magistrate's uniform, as he was wearing a white under-shirt and his uniform slacks. His wife was already wearing a nightgown as if she had given up on the excitement of the night.

"Mallory, what is happening—Why are the lights out? Has the Council come to a decision so soon?" Alex's parents peppered her with questions, one after another not allowing Mallory to answer. They had left in search of Alex at the Governor's direction, so there was no way they could know what was happening, and they were understandably fright-ened. Then the question came that hit at the heart of their fear: "Where is Alex?"

"I had hoped she would be here." Mallory's shoulders sagged.

The Chief Magistrate shook his head. "No, we searched the house from top to bottom. The Administrator's house, too. I was just getting dressed to call the magistrates to help with the search."

"Oh, Daniel! Is she okay?" Mrs. Nelson asked, concern rising in her voice.

"I don't know." He hugged his wife tenderly. "If she comes home, tell her to meet us at the Matriarch's."

Mallory interrupted: "No, everyone is at City Hall. The Governor sent us to get the book from Alex."

"What book?" Mr. Nelson demanded. "What is going on, Mallory?"

Mallory shook her head. "It might be able to fix the Dikaió and the light, but I don't have time to explain. You should call the magistrates out for another reason than finding Alex though. City Hall is on fire. They're asking people to bring containers of water."

Mr. Nelson's eyes widened, but as he turned to his wife, he seemed to stifle any worry or emotion that he was feeling and steeled himself for the work ahead of them. "Okay. Ellie, you stay here and wait for Alex. I'll get dressed and load water to help with the fire. Mallory, you might check my father's house. You children have spent a lot of time there. Maybe there's a place we haven't checked?"

Mallory looked blank, and then realized he was talking about the Administrator, Alex's grandfather. It always seemed strange to think of parents having parents. She nodded an affirmation. "Caleb was checking the big house while I ran down here."

Alex's father nodded and said, "Okay, when you find her, let us know that she's safe, please."

"Of course, Mr. Nelson."

The Chief Magistrate turned and dashed back into the house to finish dressing. Eyes brimming with worry, Mrs. Nelson touched Mallory's arm and held her other hand to her mouth to stifle whatever tearful words were fighting to escape. Mallory could see that she desperately wanted to steel herself like her husband, but the emotions were too strong. Tears traced down her cheeks. She nodded, touched Mallory's arm again, and then also turned back into the house.

Mallory stood still for a moment, wanting to go and

comfort Alex's mother. The thought of leaving her in this state was more than she could bear, but then her grandmother's words sounded in her mind again: "Save the city." The best thing she could do to help Mrs. Nelson would be to find Alex and get things back to normal. Mallory turned around and ran back through the dark garden. She found Caleb waiting on the Administrator's back porch. The door was standing wide open just like the Chief Magistrate's house. "She's not home," Mallory called.

"She's not here either."

"You checked the Book Club?"

"Yes, the door's still locked, and we can't lock it from the inside."

Mallory tried to think of where Alex might have gone to hide. She did not have any other friends that Mallory knew. Most buildings were locked for the night, and in this rain, Alex would have to find shelter of some sort. Then it hit her, and she shuddered: the secret room beneath City Hall. The only other people that knew it could be accessed through the hole in the back and crawling under the building were Alex and the Dikaió Piper. No one would ever think to look for her there. And right now, the building was on fire.

"I know where she is," Mallory began running back along the route they had just taken with Caleb following behind her. They passed the menagerie of silent onlookers behind their windows, cheering them on with their hopeful eyes, and then they ran slowly back uphill through the muck of City Hall's lawn, which seemed to be more of a shallow lake at this point.

The fire at City Hall showed no signs of dissipating. The City Services Manager was there with several of the Firefighting guild, and they had formed a human chain with the City Council members and several citizens that had been roused to help. They were passing small containers of water up and down the chain, then up a couple of rickety ladders, and were, rather ineffectively, dumping the water through the shattered windows of the second story of the building. The Firefighting guild must have been able to activate their hydrant sprites somehow because they were lined up with their large tanks full of water, but their hoses were spraying water haphazardly at the roof of the building. One of the firefighters was yelling desperately at them to aim at this or that point, but without the Dikaió, it seemed like the sprites were performing their basic duties without a mind to guide them. None of the efforts seemed to be doing anything to stop the fire, which was quite a bit larger than when Mallory had last seen it. Not even the rain seemed to be doing much to tamp it back.

Mallory ran past the commotion to the back of the building. She was about to do something incredibly dangerous, but she knew that Alex was in the secret room. She was absolutely convinced of it, and she was going in to get her out. She had read enough about fires to know that the smoke was the most dangerous part of a fire, so she tore a wet sleeve off her shirt and wrapped it around her face to protect her lungs. The hole that had been excavated under City Hall was full of mud and water, so she took a deep breath through her wet shirt sleeve and jumped into the puddle. She tried to squeeze under the building, but rain had washed too much of the excavated dirt back into the hole, and she could not get further than her waist under the building; the water was rising too quickly. She flipped over and tried to pull herself up but found that there was nothing stable to grab onto to leverage herself against the water and the mud. Water was pouring into the hole, and it splashed into the cloth covering her face, flooding her nose and mouth. She choked on the sudden inhalation of muddy water. Her hands slipped, and she found herself underwater again. Then a vice gripped her wrist, and she was yanked up above the water's surface. Caleb struggled and pulled until they were both laying in the puddle-strewn lawn of City Hall breathing hard.

Mallory could not allow herself to rest or to take time to thank Caleb, though she badly wanted both. She pulled herself quickly to her feet. There was no longer any way to get into the secret room from this point, which meant there was only one way to get there. Mallory jogged, coughing and wiping her face, to the front side of City Hall with Caleb following.

The adults were so preoccupied with the fire that they did not see her dash up the front steps. She checked her makeshift mask and then pushed on the double French doors. They were locked for the night. Yellow smoke puffed through the cracks of the doors, and the handles were hot. Peering through the smokey glass, Mallory could see only small pockets of fire in the hallway past the doors. It looked relatively safe, but she wondered how she would get in.

Without warning, Caleb's shoulder pushed past her, and

the bulk of his frame smashed into the doors, shattering glass and buckling the locks. He barely had time to step back because the instant the fire inside the building was introduced to the oxygen outside, a gigantic ball of smoke coalesced in the hallways and raced toward the open air. The doors catapulted outwards, flinging the two teenagers off the steps before they had a chance to move. They hit the ground with a thud.

Mallory's vision swayed, but Caleb barely seemed phased as he rolled over in the grass toward her and threw his heavy frame over her body to protect her from the flames, now hovering over them like the fingers of a hideous, burning monster. He put his hands over her head and although her arm bent the wrong way beneath his weight, she barely noticed. She was hidden there below her protector, watching the cannon of flame chase the smoke just above their prone forms. Caleb's bright blue eyes hovered over her own, his head haloed by flames as City Hall spewed deadly fire: a dragon woken from slumber. He looked surprised, but it was hard to tell since his eyebrows were almost completely singed off. Then his face faded into shadow almost as suddenly as it had started, the dragon calmed down, and the propulsion of fire receded quickly back into the building. The backdraft had balanced the oxygen levels in the building, but the flames were now raging along the walls and columns inside, heading back towards the open front door.

Caleb rolled off her and sat up, looking toward the open doorway. With Caleb off her, Mallory did a quick mental check of her body. She registered some abrasions from being hit by the door and hitting the ground, there was some burning pain on the exposed skin of her uncovered arm, but for the most part her water-logged clothes absorbed the brunt of the heat. She sat up and looked toward Caleb. He started coughing violently because his taller frame put his face directly in the path of the smoke escaping the building. Mallory crawled over to him and tore off his sleeve, which was warm but still wet. She pointed to the sleeved mask she was wearing, and he covered his face. He was still coughing from the smoke that had already been inhaled, but he gave her a thumbs up.

Mallory looked toward the adults, who had noticed them now after the violent explosion, and were moving toward them rapidly with pale, fatigued faces. There was not much time, and she pushed herself to her feet. Her clothes were still wet, and she did not know how long that protection would last inside. The stairs to the basement were only a few feet to the left of the front entrance, and it looked like the fire had left a small opening there if she hurried. Mallory heard her name being called, but there was no time to stop and explain as she dashed into the building to find Alex.

The heat inside felt like an oven just after opening the door. It roiled around her in waves. She could feel the water in her clothing begin to heat up, but not as quickly as the skin on her forehead and exposed arm. She ignored the pain and dashed down the stairs. The fire had not reached the basement, and the farther down the staircase she went, the cooler it got, but it was darker as well: There were no windows in the basement, and the only light was the fire at the top of the staircase. Mallory stepped off the final stair, and her foot landed in water. The water from the storm, flowing to the lowest point, had found the basement and was about six inches deep. She swished through the pools heading in the general direction of the record shelves. She felt blindly along the dark wall searching for the second stack with the secret lever.

Mallory felt along the shelf trying to make out where the lever was. It was very difficult to find anything in the dark, and she still felt somewhat disoriented from the explosion and heat. Then she saw a dim light in the dark space, and she could make out a small indentation where the lever was. She glanced behind her to find the source of the light and inhaled sharply. Small pockets of flame had clawed their way through the floor and were licking at the rafters in the basement overhead. Mallory reached down and pressed the lever. It was harder to push than she remembered but with some effort she heard the click of the secret mechanism. The shelf swung open of its own accord, and for the second time in so many minutes, Mallory found herself being knocked off her feet: This time it was a rush of water rather than a fireball.

She sputtered and spat as she tried to stand back up. The current was too strong, and she fell over and over again. Finally, she managed to get hold of one of the shelves and steady herself against the water. The secret door had been holding back enough water and mud that the basement was now flooded almost to Mallory's waist. She waded back to the door and found Alex clinging desperately to a post by the secret door, dripping wet and breathing hard.

"Oh, Mallory! Thank goodness! I thought I was going to drown in there."

"No time, Alex!" Mallory's throat burned when she shouted, and her shout came out as little more than a forceful rasp. Apparently, the smoke had gotten through her mask, and she hadn't noticed. She pointed at the burning rafters as the building creaked and groaned above them.

Alex's eyes grew wide with fear, and she made to bolt up the stairs, but Mallory grabbed her arm.

"Smoke," Mallory rasped indicating her masked face.

Alex signaled understanding and opened her jacket. Despite all the circumstances of the night, Mallory was relieved to see she still had the book tucked away under her jacket. It was wet, but if they could make it out of this building, there was hope.

Alex tore a strip of fabric from her wet shirt and then zipped her jacket back up, positioning the book safely near her arm. She tucked the torn fabric quickly behind her ears, stretching it over her nose and mouth. When it was tied securely, the two girls started to climb out of the flood toward the fire.

Mallory was dismayed to see the hallway entrance she had used to access the basement staircase was already engulfed in flames above them. With the back door caved in with mud, there was no option but to go into the fire and try to get through it.

Mallory took off at a run up the last few stairs and leaped through the flames. She was thankful for the floodwater below giving her clothing a fresh soak to protect her from the fire, but the heat was still nearly unbearable. Her shoes began to melt on the floor, making it difficult to run, but she kept pressing forward, heading toward the doorway, out of the inferno. Then there was a crash and a scream behind her.

Mallory turned to see the frame of the doorway to the basement had collapsed, and Alex was on the floor, her arm trapped under burning rubble. Mallory turned back, forgetting the heat and the pain and rushing back toward her terrified friend. Alex was screaming and trying desperately to get away from the flames. Her arm was caught beneath a heavy wooden beam and would not budge, and her jacket and her hair were both on fire.

Mallory unzipped Alex's jacket, burning her fingers on the zipper pull. Alex managed to wiggle out of it, except for Alex's arm, which was still caught under the rubble and while Mallory pulled hard at her panicked friend, she was not strong enough to free her. The fire was spreading over Alex as the water dried out of her clothing, and for a moment all Mallory could think of was the story of the old Governor and the fire sprite. Her grandmother was so sure she was going to watch him get burned to death, but he had trium- phantly rescued the city instead. Now, she was supposed to be rescuing the city but was instead about to watch her friend burn to death, and she may even burn to death beside her with no Dikaió to save them. If her tears were not instantly vaporized in the heat, she would have cried; she lowered her head in defeat.

She winced then as strong hands took hold of her and dragged her away from Alex. She screamed and tried to pull back to her friend, but she had no strength left to fight. Two men brushed past her toward Alex. She thought one of them was the City Services Manager and he was carrying a metal pole. He used the pole as a lever to pry the rubble off Alex's arm, and the other man scooped her up tenderly. Alex was going to be okay. They were both going to be okay.

Suddenly, Mallory was in the open air and out of the fire. She registered that she was being carried, cradled in someone's arms, though how she had transitioned from vertical to horizontal seemed to escape her. She looked around and saw the aghast faces of her parents and the City Council members as she floated toward them. Then she was falling and hit the ground with a thump—whoever was carrying her had dropped her and began to slap her.

She tried to fight back, but again found herself too weak to move. The slapping continued starting on her head, and then around her body. She looked down to see the hands slapping her and understood what was happening. She was on fire—or at least bits of her clothing were—and someone was trying to put it out. She looked up into her rescuer's face and saw Caleb's eyes just above a cloth mask: strong, blue, determined; but the longer she looked, the more she realized that these eyes were different than Caleb's somehow—older, wiser, indomitable in their determination.

It was Caleb's father, the Governor. Even without the Dikaió, the Governor had rescued her from the fire.

When the Governor got the fire on her clothes put
out, Mallory tried to sit up and see if Alex was okay, but her
body refused to acknowledge her wishes, choosing instead
to succumb to the exhaustion of the night. The Governor
did not stand by her side long. He went back to resume the
fight against the fire; a fight Mallory could tell that they were
destined to lose. Without the Dikaió, there was no way to
direct the hydrant sprites effectively to put out that fire, and
the city just wasn't equipped to fight a fire without the sprites.
She lay there in the wet grass staring up into the heavens. The
storm had passed, and the clouds had dissipated far enough
that she saw naked sky. She blinked at the brilliance of the
Milky Way, which she was seeing for the first time without

the lens of the city's light obscuring it from view. There were points of brilliance where single stars stood out, but the beautiful part was the purples and blues that swirled together in subtle harmony. It was beyond anything she had ever imagined.

While she admired the galaxy spread out above her, the adrenaline that had been driving her all night passed out of her system. Unlike the gentle calmness that nature was experiencing after the chaos of the storm, Mallory was suddenly aware of the injuries of the night. Her forehead and exposed skin were searing with burns. Her arm felt like it was broken, either from being hit by the explosion at the door or the rush of water in the basement. Her eyes were so dry that it hurt to blink, and her throat felt like she had swallowed gravel and a lot of it was still stuck there. Every breath was agony, and when she coughed, all her various aches and pains sent desperate electric signals into her brain, begging her not to move. Yet she could not stop coughing.

A motion to her right momentarily distracted her from her pain. Two men laid a figure in the grass next to her. It was Alex. Mallory saw that her arm was very burned, black and red streaks with spots of white swirled around her forearm, a horrible mimicry of the galaxy above them. Alex's eyes were rolling in her head, and she was moaning softly, writhing in the grass. The two men stood above her, shaking their heads.

Mallory recognized one of the men as the City Services Manager. He said, "We can't contact the hospital, and even if we could, there's no way to get there without the medic sprites. It's too far to carry her on foot."

The other man, one of the Dikaió elect, replied, "We have to do something. She's horribly hurt. The other one too," he nodded toward Mallory. "What kind of leaders are we if we don't take care of our people?"

"We're the kind that take care of our city—all of it—and our first duty is to preserve the government and order, and even more importantly the Dikaió. We need to get the fire out and see if we can reignite the light. Everyone in the city is at risk until those issues are resolved. When we're finished, we'll form relay teams and carry these two to the hospital."

"I'm not sure the Administrator's granddaughter will make it until then."

"She's going to have to. Now c'mon, let's get this fire out."

The two men ran back to help the efforts at City Hall. Mallory forced herself up onto her good arm. "Alex!" She called, but it came out as little more than a hoarse whisper, and Alex just moaned. There had to be something she could do. She forced herself up onto her hands and knees, biting her lip in thought and to keep herself from screaming from the pain. As she became more determined to get Alex to the hospital—even if she had to carry her the whole way there— the adrenaline began to pump again. Yes, she would carry her friend the whole way, with a broken arm, through the dark night, across the city, whatever it took. She stood to her feet and stumbled to Alex's side.

It was hard to decide where to grab hold of her to pick her up. The arm that had been trapped under the burning rubble was definitely not an option, as that would be the most painful, but even where Alex had had some protection from the fire with her wet clothes, there were burns where the fire had clawed through the water, then the fabric, and then her friend's flesh. Her face was remarkably unscathed by the flames but looked even paler than usual. Mallory could imagine what her own face felt like considering the painful heat she still felt on her forehead. Mallory picked what seemed to be the best places to leverage her friend off the ground and then up onto her back like a child playing piggyback with their father. She bent down and grabbed hold and started to pull. Alex moaned but did not offer resistance. It made little difference though, her friend was too heavy, and Mallory was too exhausted to pull off the rescue. She stumbled backward and bit her lip in consternation.

"Let me help." A raspy but familiar voice offered from a short distance away. It was Caleb, and he was pushing Mallory's grocery cart. "When I saw you carried out, I figured you'd need a ride to the hospital . . ." He gasped when he saw how extensive Alex's burns were. "I should take her first, though."

Mallory wanted to hug him, but instead she stuck to the business of the moment. The cart was still too unstable to sit upright without someone holding the poles, so Mallory reached out and took them from Caleb. Mallory tried to speak again and found her voice improving to a gurgling growl instead of just a whisper. "I'll hold the cart, and you lift her in. Be careful of her arm though." Caleb looked at Alex's arm and grimaced, but he squared his shoulders and gently picked up the injured girl. He lowered her carefully into the cart, her legs hanging out over the edge, and her arms folded in across her chest. As Caleb let go, Alex's weight pressed down hard on the cart, up its handles, and yanked on Mallory's injured arm. She hollered but forced her hands to clamp down harder on the poles, managing to keep the cart from tipping over.

"Are you, okay?" Caleb asked.

"I think my arm's broken, but I'll survive," she replied with a grimace. Caleb walked around behind Mallory and took the handles. She ducked out from under them just like she had done after the market. Mallory did not feel the same playful awkwardness brushing against Caleb this time. Too much had changed, and yet it was only that morning that the three of them had climbed the hill to the Matriarch's house with Mallory's Dikaió-free groceries. If one day could change so much, what would a week or a month from now look like if they could not restore the Dikaió?

Caleb pushed the cart forward with ease and moved in the direction of the hospital. "You stay here, Mal. I'll be back for you."

"No, I'm coming with you, Caleb. I can walk, and it's too far for a round trip. Besides, Alex might need help on the way." Almost as if on cue, Alex shifted in the cart and her injured arm spilled out, banging against the wooden panels. Alex screamed loudly but could not seem to pull her arm back up. Mallory rushed forward and gently placed Alex's arm back onto her chest. Alex calmed somewhat when her arm was moved, but her groans were louder than they were at first, and she was growing more fitful as the cart bumped and careened along the mud-strewn streets of the Governor's

District. Beads of sweat were standing out on her forehead and face.

Then Alex began to murmur almost inaudibly. "The book. Mal, I dropped the book! It's in the fire!" Her eyes sprung open, and she started trying to climb out of the cart.

"Alex! Please!" Caleb yelled, struggling to keep the cart upright. He had to stop walking to counterbalance all the motion rocking about in its bed.

Alex paused and looked around her, eyes wild. "Where am I? What are you doing to me? I've got to go back for the book!" She threw a leg up to swing out of the cart.

Without thinking, Mallory reached out and grabbed Alex's burned arm to restrain her. Alex shrieked and fell back into the cart breathing hard. Mallory let go of her arm and jumped back. "Alex, I'm sorry!"

Alex did not respond. She just sat there in the cart looking at her arm in confusion and pain. Slowly, she reached out and touched the red and black streaks blanketing her forearm. Pain and shock spread over her face. Her eyes rolled back in her head, and she slumped back into the cart shivering. Caleb looked at Mallory, "What should we do?"

"Get her to the hospital, Caleb. What else can we do?" Caleb did not respond, he just put one foot in front of the other, and the trio set off again. They came to the same hill on Silver Street they had climbed that morning and began to descend into the market district of the city. Caleb leaned back, straining against the weight of the cart as gravity threatened to pull Alex loose from his grip. "Back and forth, remember?" Mallory made a zigzagging motion with her good hand. Caleb followed her direction, angled the cart one way, and then another, working his way slowly but safely down the hill.

The market booths were all put away for the night. Dikaió cloths and crates stacked up neatly along the street. The steel and glass skyscrapers lined the road; their windows streaked with droplets still slowly dripping from the overhanging crops of the Dikaió Cultures on the tops of the buildings. There were bits of fruits, vegetables, and piles of leaves lying here and there along the gutters of the street, cast down from the heavenly fields by the fury of the storm.

It was still at least two miles to the hospital, but at least it was a straight line up Main Street to get there. The gentle slope that had made Mallory's grocery trip so quick was taking its toll on Caleb. He never complained though; he just gritted his teeth and kept pressing forward. At least the street was relatively clean. Ignoring the leaves and produce, the only mud was that which had stuck to their shoes from the Governor's District, so their feet at least had traction here. Still, Mallory could see that he was struggling pushing Alex along. Alex's murmuring had given way to a rhythmic but raspy breathing. She was asleep. Mallory walked slowly, nursing her arm, which was sending stabbing jabs up her shoulder with every step, and she wished she could help her friends more than walk limply along behind them. Caleb grunted occasionally when the mud on his shoes made his foot slip, or a rock or pothole made the cart bump. But overall, it was a quiet walk.

Caleb broke the silence with the question she knew he'd

been wanting to ask since she caught his eye in the sitting room of the Matriarch's house: "Why did you do it, Mal? I told you both not to. Why did you do it?"

"You were there. You heard what I told the Council."

"Because you're going to have a sister? You're not going to be Matriarch?" Caleb glanced over his shoulder, "And how would you be Matriarch without the Dikaió for a christening?"

"We'll fix it!" She answered, trying to hide the desperation in her voice.

Caleb's shoulders slumped as he looked forward again and asked quietly, "Where's the book, Mal?"

Mallory did not answer.

"Mallory, is what Alex said true? Was the book in City Hall? Is it gone?"

"Her jacket was on fire. That's where she had it . . . I took it off when I was trying to get her out of the fire."

Caleb did not answer.

"The Council will be able to figure it out, Caleb. They have to."

"They never figured out how to help you, Mal. Why do you think they'll do any better fixing this?"

"I don't know. But if they don't, then I will."

"You did a great job of fixing things, Mal. A great job!"

"Well, at least we tried. Like you just said, that's more than anyone else has ever done!"

She was always trying. Everyone around her had the luxury of not needing to try, but Mallory knew what it meant to struggle with hard problems—she tried to help at home, to be a good friend and not a nuisance, to study and become useful, to help others, and she even tried to rescue Alex when the city leaders walked away. Without her trying, Alex would have no stretcher tonight. But then without her trying, Alex wouldn't need a stretcher tonight. Tears formed in her eyes and her face felt hot. She almost knelt down on the street under the weight of guilt she felt for her friend; she seemed to always cause harm when she was only trying to help. And right now, her friend needed even more help, and here she was trudging along uselessly behind Caleb. She wished she could start this whole day over.

They walked on for a long time before either spoke again, and then Caleb said, "It wouldn't have been so bad having your sister be Matriarch, you know."

Mallory felt her blood boil; her guilt flipped to self-defense. "She's not even born—how do you know that? She could have been the worst Matriarch ever. She could have destroyed the city! How do you know anything about what kind of Matriarch she would be?"

Caleb chuckled. "I meant for you . . . for us, Mal. It wouldn't have been so bad . . . we could have been happy." He looked straight ahead at the street, and she wished she knew what he really thought of her now, walking in the darkness with their injured friend laying in front of them. He was talking about what could have been—and now that it was impossible, she realized it was the first time she had heard it out loud.

Mallory's boiling blood shot straight into her cheeks. Guilt and embarrassment mixed together, and her face was nearly as hot as the inner inferno of City Hall. They had always flirted, but neither had ever made their feelings known. As the only children in the Triad, they could not have married; what good would it have been to talk about whether either loved the other?

But now that he had made his intentions known, there was not any point in avoiding the topic anymore. Mallory's inner turmoil grew. After a long pause, she spoke haltingly without looking at him, "Do you think I didn't think of that, Caleb? But what good would I have been to you as a Chorus? With no magic, we'd have had to hire people to keep the house, prepare city events, ceremonies . . . your mother does more than anyone gives her credit for. How could I have done any of those things?"

"We would have made it work. We could still make it work, Mal." He looked back at her, gripping the cart and setting his jaw with determination. "You don't have to be the Matriarch. You've got a way out."

"What if I don't want a way out?" She didn't know why she said it—perhaps guilt or the trauma of the night—or the feeling that every time she touched something it broke. She didn't want to break Caleb.

Caleb inhaled deeply as if ready to question her answer—perhaps to demand something more of her—but instead he hung his head and continued wearily pushing the cart.

Mallory stared at him defiantly now, willing him to answer. She desperately wanted to know what he was thinking. Maybe he knew something she didn't know or had some idea to make it all work. Or was he angry? Sad?

Confused?

She began to be afraid that he might think she had rejected him. The Matriarchy was not hers for certain, and she did not want to close this door with Caleb. The thought stunned her in its selfishness. Had she been toying with Caleb's emotions, keeping him hooked like a live fish on a stringer until she found out if her dreams would be fulfilled? What kind of monster was she? But she was not just stringing him along; she truly did want to be with him. Her heart ached at the thought of not being together. That had to be more than selfishness, right? She reached out and touched his arm.

"Caleb, I'm sorry."

"Sorry for what? You should be Matriarch. It's your right. I've no right to ask anything of you—certainly not to give up your right to rule."

"Yes, but . . . that's not the point. That's not why I said what I said. I do want to be with you. . ." She felt over-whelmed saying it out loud now. "It's just that . . . that if my grandmother had made me Syntec, we wouldn't even be thinking about this. I'd be Matriarch and that would be that. But she didn't. She made me a Chorus, and she did it because of the prophecy."

Caleb sighed deeply.

"What was that for?" Mallory demanded.

"My father says that your grandmother made up the prophecy to cover over her mistake of making you a Dikaió Chorus instead of a Syntec."

His words hit her like a hard fall sucking the wind out of

her lungs. "You don't believe that do you?"

"I don't know what to believe, Mal. He's my father. He's the Governor. I think he'd know what happened."

"But my grandmother christened me after the dream . . . because of the dream."

Caleb's eyes narrowed as he considered that idea, and then shook his head. "In the end, what does it matter? What happened is in the past. That's what I always tell him when we talk about it anyway."

"But it does matter, Caleb!" Mallory pointed around them at the darkened city. "All of this is why I was born; why I am a Chorus. My grandmother saw it. Somehow, I'm supposed to save the city."

Caleb looked back at her, eyes wide. "Mallory, all this happened because your grandmother made you a Chorus. If she'd just made you a Syntec, the light would be up. City Hall wouldn't be burning." He nodded his head toward the cart, "Alex wouldn't be hurt. You wouldn't be hurt. Things would still be okay."

"And we could never be together."

Caleb got quiet again, but after a time said, "Yes. And maybe it would have been better without that possibility. Now, we are all living in your grandmother's nightmare."

"That's why I asked? I can't tell if it's better to live for a prophecy about tomorrow or to live in the present with you." That was the answer Mallory was struggling to find in her tightrope between the Matriarchy and Caleb and both options seemed to be full of risk; being Matriarch would solve so many problems, but it would take away the one thing she really wanted as a Chorus that she could never have as a Matriarch.

Ever the pragmatist, Caleb laughed dryly: "Well, that's neither here nor there I suppose. You are a Chorus, and maybe we all are now, so maybe we could still be happy?" He winked at her, and she smiled for the first time since their morning grocery trip.

Mallory's tension loosened. "You might have to work harder than you ever have. Being a Chorus isn't easy."

"I'm the definition of hard work. Look at me! I've hauled this cart across the city, haven't I? Look at all this sweat." He moved his arms up to show the sweat stains under his armpits. His movement jostled Alex, and she began to shiver and moan. "Oops!" Caleb evened out his arms and his gait, lulling Alex back to sleep.

Mallory smiled and touched his shoulder tenderly. "Well, if this is our future, we'll have to add legs to this cart like I wanted to this morning, so you can set it down and rest occasionally."

Caleb smiled his lop-sided grin and looked over at her out of the corners of his eyes. "You think I'm going to be pushing a cart forever? Who's going to govern the city?"

Mallory smiled back and attempted to push some of her curly brown hair behind her ear, only to have it spring back into place. "I'm sure they'll find someone less suited for manual labor. No sense wasting a hard worker like you," she teased.

"I'll show you. After this is over, I'm done working hard. Next time you see me, I'll be lounging on a dusty couch reading dangerous books."

Mallory laughed, "And maybe one day your belly will rival the leader of the Smith Guild."

"Rival?!" Caleb roared with mock indignation. "My belly will have no rival. They'll have to widen the doors of City Hall just for me . . ." Caleb's face darkened at the mention of City Hall, and they both went quiet again, walking for a time in silence; the fire still too fresh to joke about.

Mallory looked up the street and saw the glow of Dikaió lights in the distance. She looked back and saw that the city was still dark. But there were definitely lights on ahead. As they drew closer, Mallory realized that the light was coming from the hospital. "How do they have power?" She wondered out loud. As much as she hated going to the hospital with her various and inventive injuries, she had to admit that the lights looked welcoming.

"The hospital and the other city management buildings all have their own generators," Caleb said. Mallory was always shocked at the things she was unaware of in the city. The management of the city was something that the Governor and the guild leaders tended to, not necessarily something the Matriarch or the Administrator had to worry about, so she and Alex were often ignorant to things Caleb spent hours learning in detail, along with all the words to control every aspect of the city. Days like today, where Caleb got to come out and relax with his friends were rare. Mallory knew that those days were only allowed to strengthen the bond of the family Triad; it would be hard to lead the city if the three of them were strangers when they began their terms of leadership. Still, Caleb never complained of the burden, and he never talked about it. He was always just happy to be free with his friends for awhile. And here he was again spending time with his friends, though the circumstances were not great.

Caleb and Mallory grew silent as they drew near to the hospital. It was five stories tall and full of glass windows— almost half of them with lights on in them. The exterior was white-washed stucco, and a large red cross was painted on a white sign hanging over the door. Spotlights among the shrubs in the landscaping shone up from the ground, illuminating the sign, and it was the most wonderful thing Mallory had seen all day. It looked normal.

Caleb seemed to perk up at the hospital's light as well and picked up his pace with the cart considerably so that Mallory had trouble keeping up with him. When they finally reached the entrance, they stood outside the Dikaió double glass doors waiting for them to slide open.

Nothing happened.

Mallory walked forward and held her good hand up to her forehead to shade her eyes from the lights around them, pressing against the glass to cut the glare and get a better look. The burn on her head exploded in pain, and Mallory drew her head back slightly from her hand, hovering centimeters from physical contact. After closing her eyes and taking a deep breath to calm the pain, she opened her eyes again and could see a reception desk inside. There was a nurse standing behind it, yelling at somebody. Mallory banged on the glass of the door.

The nurse turned and looked at the door, and her eyes got wide. She ran up to the door, pointed to her left, and yelled, "Go to the East side. The door seems to be working there." Then she took off running in the direction she had just pointed toward.

Mallory looked at Caleb, and he lowered his head and pivoted the cart toward the East. The trio made their way slowly to the East side of the hospital and found a service door standing open. The nurse was standing there, a silhouetted angel standing in a bright white rectangle leading into a hallway of white tile, white walls, and bright white fluorescent lights. She looked at each of them with concern, and then looked down into the cart at Alex. Her concern turned to alarm. "Oh my! I don't think that cart is going to fit through the door." There was a folded wheelchair resting against the wall next to her, and she grabbed it and expertly popped it open. "Can you lift her into the chair?"

Caleb nodded and picked Alex up again, minding her burned spots as best he could. While she was mid-transfer, Alex woke up and began to yell, "Mal, the book! We have to get the book!" Caleb startled and nearly dropped her into the chair, but he managed to lower her gently. "The book! Where is the book?"

"Alex," Mallory called.

Alex looked through her at first, and then her eyes came into focus. "Mallory, did you get the book?"

"No, Alex. The book is gone. I'm sorry."

Alex looked stricken and then slumped in defeat. The nurse maneuvered the wheelchair around and rushed off down the hall, leaving Caleb and Mallory standing outside the doorway without a word. The two looked at each other, and then followed the nurse trying to keep up. She quickly turned a corner, and when Caleb and Mallory reached the turn, they found it branched off in three different directions, and there was no way to tell which way the nurse had gone.

"This place is a labyrinth," Caleb lamented.

"Should we split up?" Mallory asked.

"I don't know." Caleb said with frustration. He stood for a moment looking down the halls and thinking, rubbing his reddened hands tenderly; his fingers were already forming blisters from the weight and friction of the cart.

Decisively, Caleb turned back to Mallory: "Someone is taking care of Alex now. There's probably not much we can do but get in the way. Let's see if we can get someone to help with your arm and your burns."

Mallory's adrenaline had all but forgotten about her injuries again, but once Caleb pointed them out, they all started to hurt at once. She nodded and they headed down the hallway that led to the West, hoping to find the nurses' station or whoever the nurse had been yelling at. The hospital was very quiet, which made their footsteps all the louder.

The hallway changed very little as they walked; attempts to break up its monotony could be found in various pieces of artwork and unlabeled doors, but the effect of these just created a disjointed sameness that made Mallory feel claustrophobic. The hallway finally exited into the lobby, and Mallory felt instant relief to be in an open space.

The lobby was a large room with a wall of windows to

the left, and two double doors, the main entrance to the hospital. These were the doors that usually opened automatically, but would not open for Mallory and Caleb when they first arrived. There were several blue couches and some tall, planted trees tastefully set around to make the place seem inviting.

Voices were coming from their right. Two people were yelling commands, and then there was a crash and a roar of rage. The voices seemed to be coming from a door behind the reception desk.

Mallory and Caleb took off running toward the sounds of distress. They sprinted around the desk and opened the door: Inside, a stocky nurse with brown hair was standing on a round table that was barely supporting her, swinging a metal tray wildly at a medic sprite that was going about its nightly routine of loading medications into paper cups. Every time it would get a round of doses loaded, the nurse on the table would knock them out of its grasp with her metal tray. Another nurse was on the ground wrestling with a second medic sprite, and he was losing the fight, as it dragged itself slowly toward the medication dispenser. Mallory felt hope begin to fade—the Dikaió was gone here, too. There would be no magic cures tonight.

$\mathcal{C}$aleb crossed the room to the stocky woman with the brown hair atop the table and stood between her and the medic sprite. Her wild eyes did not even blink as she turned her attention toward him and swiftly brought the metal tray across his cropped blonde head. Caleb roared and stumbled back falling over the medic sprite that had finally succeeded in loading some medications into paper cups. It was heading toward Mallory and the door when Caleb stumbled over it, sending a rainbow of various-sized, colorful pills into an arc through the air. As the pills scattered across the floor, Mallory rushed to try and stabilize Caleb, but she had trouble finding traction as her feet rolled across the pills. Her legs were trying to go different directions when Caleb's weight landed solidly on her outstretched arms. Electric pain rocketed up her broken arm, and she screamed in agony. Caleb's momentum finished off the work the pills had started, and Mallory found herself knocked off her feet for the third time that night. Both teenagers tumbled to the floor in an awkward pile.

The commotion of flailing, screaming teenagers broke the trance the nurses were under. The woman on the table blinked several times, and the man on the floor let his opponent loose. Both sprites momentarily free from their human adversaries righted themselves and headed quickly toward the medication dispenser, once again measuring and adding doses to paper cups. A cleaning sprite swept into the room and began to vacuum up the loose pills around the room. The two nurses clamored past the sprites, and they both spoke at the same time as they helped the teens to their feet, "Do you know what's happening? What happened to the Dikaió? Are you okay?"

Caleb shook off the nurses and spoke with a power and authority Mallory had never seen. He was intimidating even while dabbing away a spot of blood rolling down his forehead, "The Dikaió is out all over the city. The Matriarch's daughter has burns and a broken arm that need to be treated. You'll have to work without your sprites. I assume you're trained for emergencies, if needed."

The male nurse replied, "Well, we've had training, but we've never had to…" he trailed off, noticing Mallory's burns for the first time.

Caleb spoke soothingly, "Tonight, you'll use all your training," he leaned in to look at the nurse's name tag. "Jerry,

time is of the essence, and we are counting on you. The
Matriarch's daughter and the Administrator's granddaughter
may have the key to restoring the Dikaió, so we need to
get them back to our parents as quickly as possible. Do you
understand?"

"Yes, sir!" Jerry nodded and left to find a wheelchair.

Mallory had never heard the word 'sir' to address Caleb
before. She was certainly not ignorant to the ways they were
all becoming more like adults than children now—but after
watching adults treat Caleb not just as an equal, but as a
superior, she might not ever be able to recapture the image of
him as her childhood friend. Nevertheless, he was someone
she could trust, and he always looked out for her.

The female nurse turned to look at Mallory's burns and
arm, measuring the wounds, asking questions about the
smoke and how long ago the burns occurred. Mallory didn't
answer, feeling dazed. Maybe she was hungry.

"Sir?" Jerry asked Caleb as he returned with a wheelchair
for Mallory. "Can I look at your head? That wound doesn't
look good."

Caleb brushed away more blood that was starting to run
freely down his head and stared at it incredulously, but he
replied with the same air of authority: "I need you to look
after Mal first. She is to be your prior— . . ." His sentence
trailed off, and his face grew pale. Caleb passed out, falling
into the male nurse's arms, nearly bowling him over. Jerry
lowered him carefully to the floor and began examining the
head wound.

Mallory pushed past the female nurse feeling panic rise,

"Caleb!" Her voice caught and her lungs and throat ached from the shout.

Jerry turned and stood up in her path holding up his hands, "Mallory, please."

Caleb got 'sir,' and she got the familiar first name. True, the staff at the hospital were pretty familiar with her at this point, as her lack of Dikaió and various inventions to compensate had resulted in multiple hospital visits over the years. Mallory knew some of the doctors, but she had never taken the time to learn the nurses' names. Still, she was the Matriarch's daughter. Should she not get a 'ma'am' at least? The male nurse continued, "We'll make sure he's taken care of, but my orders are to look after you, too."

"You probably killed him!" Mallory yelled and ducked past the nurse in her path and knelt beside Caleb. She put her hand on his chest, it rose and fell in shallow motions. He was breathing, thank goodness.

"Ma'am?" The female nurse seemed to respect her position at least. She knelt down beside Mallory and looked her in the eyes. "I'm sorry—but we can help him. Please let us help you, too." Mallory met the woman's gaze with what she hoped was a withering ocular response. Stocky and strong, Mallory noticed the nurse was young and quite pretty with large eyes and a light brown complexion like tea and milk, just slightly lighter than Mallory's own—but that could have just been a result of working nights at the hospital. Mallory did not recall seeing this nurse at the hospital before; she must be new since Mallory's last visit. There was no familiarity then with Mallory as a patient, though she seemed to know who she was based on the respectful title.

"Ma'am?" The woman said again and reached out and touched Mallory's good arm compassionately.

Mallory recoiled from her touch but stood up and nodded at the woman: "Okay, I'll go with you." She looked at the male nurse: "You see to him; I don't want this one near him. She's done enough." Mallory eyed the woman suspiciously as though checking to see that she was no longer armed with a metal tray before sitting down in the waiting wheelchair. These were the same people who said she would feel a "little poke" before drawing sword-like needles and stabbing them into her—she did not trust anyone wearing white in a hospital, especially someone who could knock out a behemoth like Caleb Aiworth.

A cloud passed over the female nurse's face, but she pushed Mallory's wheelchair slowly out of the office and toward another set of double doors on the right side of the lobby. The doors swung open of their own accord without a Dikaió command. They apparently knew the nurse well enough to open for her with the old magic. Two large-shouldered men in white uniforms were on the other side of the doors leaning against the wall. They were watching some medic sprites with curiosity as the sprites continued their nightly duties as if nothing was wrong whatsoever. The men seemed totally unphased by the loss of Dikaió or at least amused by it. The female nurse paused and addressed the nonchalant duo, "Jerry needs a gurney in reception. There's a patient there with a head injury who is unconscious."

"A head injury you gave him," Mallory added with venom.

The two men's eyebrows arched, and they looked at the female nurse expectantly for more details. She rolled her eyes and said, "Just get the gurney, okay?"

They both smiled wolfishly and pretended to cower away from her like she was going to hit them. The nurse huffed and puffed then turned her back on them, stamping down the hall, muttering under her breath, "I'd like to give all of you some strong meds to keep you quiet for the night." The two men laughed, then ran off to find a gurney for Caleb. Mallory did not appreciate their flirtatious humor at Caleb's expense, and she certainly did not appreciate this vicious nurse's inappropriate comments. The woman had nearly killed Caleb even if it was just an accident. If she could have used both arms, Mallory might have knocked her upside the head with her own medication tray if the opportunity had presented itself. In her present condition though, she was going to have to suck up the indignity of being treated by this woman. She closed her eyes and clutched the sides of the wheelchair, while the nurse nearly ran down the hall in heavy, thudding steps. She took two turns, and then opened a door to an examination room.

As soon as they entered into the room, a medic sprite burst through the door carrying a sky-blue paper gown.

The nurse raised her hands in amazement: "Stop," she commanded, but the sprite continued into the room and lay the gown on the examination table. The nurse started to get agitated and reached for a clipboard on the wall, never taking her eyes off the sprite. It was clear that she intended to beat the poor thing into submission.

"It won't do any good," Mallory said standing and walking toward the examination table. "They seem to be indestructible. I've seen people all over town beating them, and nothing happens. They just keep working."

The nurse plucked the clipboard off the wall but looked away from the medic sprite and focused her attention on Mallory, "What happened tonight?"

"I ran into a burning building to save the Administrator's granddaughter."

"I mean what happened to the sprites . . . the Dikaió?"

Mallory stood in front of the exam table and repositioned the gown on the table. She started trying to pull off her shirt, but the pain in her arm and the burns all over hurt too much to do more than raise her shirt above her belly button. Mallory looked at the nurse suspiciously, weighing what to tell a citizen about what had happened that night. She settled on a guarded version of the truth. "It was a careless word. One of the ones they're always warning about . . . Look, I'm going to need some help here."

"Oh right, sorry." The nurse immediately transitioned from a curious person into a human medic sprite; she was all business. She opened a drawer in the small desk and pulled out a pair of crooked scissors, and she started to cut a line up the entire back of Mallory's jacket and shirt.

"Whoa! Whoa! What are you doing?" Mallory tried to turn away.

"You're never going to be able to raise your arm to get these off, and there are parts of your clothing that that are fused to skin where the burns are." The nurse pointed to a few patches in her jacket and shirt where the fire had burned through. Tiny strips of blackened thread intertwined with white blisters and red puffy skin, and when Mallory shifted her body in any direction, those threads pulled tight. Their tips were inside her like tiny flexible hooks.

Mallory felt her stomach heave. Having noticed the wounds, it was impossible to ignore them, and then pain again broke through the adrenaline of the night. "I think I need to sit down," she said, and the nurse helped her onto the examination table and continued to cut off her clothing. It was a slow and painful process. Once the big cut up the back was made, the nurse cut down along the sleeves of the jacket and shirt. When she got to a point where the fabric was fused, the nurse had to cut slowly, gently pulling around the area, leaving bits of fabric around every burn. The nurse's tailoring was agonizing, and Mallory felt like her skin was on fire again, but she bit her lip and tried to tune out the pain, staring thoughtfully at her silver reflection in the medic sprite that had frozen in place in the corner while the nurse worked. Mallory tried to ignore the snipping scissors and searing pain by focusing her attention on how they might go about fixing the Dikaió.

She bit her lip and tilted her head in thought. Clearly the Dikaió's magic was not completely gone. So far, she had noted that the sprites were still doing their tasks. Some of the doors were still opening. It might be useful to figure out what in the city was still working, but the major issue was the one that Mallory understood all too well: The gift of the christening seemed to be gone. No one was able to command

the Dikaió with their voice anymore. Everyone was as helpless as she had been as a child. If it were not for her rebellious
determinism and the books she had read, Mallory would have
gone crazy.

That made her think of the Dikaió Chorus her grandmother knew—he had survived with his books as well.
Perhaps books were not the problem; maybe books were
the key. If the Dikaió could not be fixed, they would need
someone to teach them how to live like her, and that meant
teaching every citizen how to read, how to learn to rely on
themselves rather than magic.

The nurse was kneeling on the floor, and she began to cut
Mallory's pant leg.

"Really?" Mallory protested.

"Would you ever wear them again?"

Mallory looked at the muddy, torn, fire-singed pants
and shrugged, "No, I suppose not." She bit her lip again and
looked thoughtfully at the nurse. "Can I ask you something?"

The nurse did not look up and kept cutting up Mallory's
pant leg toward her thigh, but she said, "Sure."

"Do you know how to read?"

The nurse paused and looked up at Mallory, "No, of
course not."

"Isn't it hard to remember everything you have to do here
in the hospital without reading? Medications, treatments,
patient's names?"

"Well, we do have to rely on the medic sprites quite a bit
to keep things straight."

"Are the medic sprites answering questions about those

things now?"

The nurse turned to the sprite standing in the corner: "What is this patient's name, sprite?" The medic sprite remained silent and still. "What is the patient's name in room 231, sprite?" No answer. "What medication was prescribed for Harry Botain in room 231, sprite?" Nothing.

The nurse put her face in her hand and began to cry with frustration. "What are we going to do, ma'am?"

Mallory was put back by the nurse's tears. She had been looking at her as another citizen and not a particularly good one after what she did to Caleb, but now Mallory saw her as she was: a young girl, barely older than Mallory, who had been christened and raised for the job of helping others here at the hospital but had no real understanding of how to do that without the Dikaió. On the other hand, she was performing the job of helping Mallory out of her clothes with a lot of care without any Dikaió at all.

"The Governor's son asked if you had any emergency training, yes?"

The nurse wiped her tears and shook her head. "No, some of us have had emergency training in case someone needs help outside the hospital without the use of the medic sprites. There is a team of emergency doctors, nurses, and sprites that handle most of those calls. I've never had to do anything like that and would not be expected to, so I haven't had much of that sort of training."

"This job that you're doing now, helping me out of my clothes, isn't that emergency training? Wouldn't a sprite normally do that?"

The nurse snapped back to her task and started cutting again when Mallory brought it up, but she spoke while she worked: "No, some things the sprites can't do."

"I guess, for now—to answer your question—you should stick to those things the sprites can't do and whatever emergency skills you know from what the sprites used to do, at least until we figure out what they'll still do without commands."

The nurse got to a patch of pants on Mallory's thigh that had burned through and began to cut carefully around it. Mallory inhaled sharply as the fibers tugged at the burn on her leg, but she clenched her jaw and gripped the bed to keep from crying out. The second pantleg had managed to avoid the fire and went much faster until Mallory was completely loose. The nurse helped her into the paper gown, not tying it so it would rest loosely over her injured skin until all of her wounds were cleansed and dressed.

Mallory touched the nurse on the shoulder, "We're going to get through this, okay?"

The nurse nodded, "I'm going to go find a doctor to see what we can do for your arm and burns." Then she left, taking Mallory's ruined clothing in heaps with her.

As soon as the door closed behind the nurse, the medic sprite came to life; it pulled a glass thermometer off the wall, held it up, and Mallory allowed it to place it in her mouth. Then it grabbed an oximeter out of a drawer and placed it on Mallory's finger to check her heartbeat and oxygen levels. While the meters were checking their levels, the sprite grabbed a blood pressure cuff. It moved toward Mallory's broken arm. "No, no," Mallory said, "This one." She waved her good arm at the sprite. She had spent her whole life being ignored by the sprites, and yet in a moment of need, she fell into the same expectations everyone else had tonight, thinking the sprites understood what she said without the magic of the Dikaió translating.

The sprite whipped the cuff across her broken arm and inflated it before Mallory could pull away. It squeezed against burned spots, and she felt her bone shift beneath her skin; the broken edges first grating against each other then snapping loose. The pain was excruciating, and she held her breath until she finally released a scream while the cuff deflated and her bone shifted against her injured flesh again.

The oximeter sounded an alarm as her heart raced, and her oxygen levels dropped. The medic sprite swirled to the counter and pushed a red button on the wall, and a red light above the door began to flash. It ripped open a drawer producing a clear plastic facemask connected to a large rubber balloon. As it turned back toward Mallory, the sprite sprouted two new arms, for a total of four, and came rushing toward her. With two arms, it pushed Mallory backward onto the bed, with another it pulled the thermometer loose, and with its fourth arm, it fitted the mask over her nose and mouth. Then it began to pump the balloon. Mallory felt air rush into her mouth and nose, violently inflating her lungs. It almost hurt more than the smoke she had inhaled at City Hall. She coughed and squirmed, trying to get away from the sprite, but its strong silver arms pinned her into place. The oximeter alarm grew louder and more urgent as Mallory struggled to get away, her heart rate increasing. She tried to shake the device off, hoping that the lack of alarm would calm the sprite, but the sprite seemed to sprout a fifth arm and gently pinned her arm with the oximeter to the table. Mallory felt like she could not get a good breath, and the room was getting fuzzy around the edges. She wasn't sure how much longer she could hold out against the sprite.

Then a metal chair clanged against the side of the sprite. The young nurse had returned, and she was back to beating the sprite, trying to get it off Mallory. Another woman was with her, wearing a white lab coat. The other woman ducked under the chair as the nurse swung it again at the sprite. She reached up from her crouching stance and removed the oximeter from Mallory's finger. The alarm ceased, and the sprite stopped pumping the rubber ball and searched for the oximeter. The ducking woman pulled the cord off and dropped the device in her white coat pocket just out of the sprite's reach while Mallory gasped for air, panting wildly.

The crouching woman spoke calmly near her ear, so Mallory could hear above the clanging of the metal chair hitting the sprite, "Slow down, take deep breaths, or you'll hyperventilate."

Mallory held her breath a moment and tried to count her breaths slowly as the haze on the outskirts of her vision began to recede. The woman in the white coat crouched patiently while the nurse continued to flail on the sprite. The sprite remained utterly unphased by the beating and continued to search for the oximeter, holding the disconnected cord. After a while, the sprite left to search for a new oximeter to attach to Mallory's finger.

"Next time, don't hold your breath," the crouching woman said. "It needs to see a normal oxygen reading to register that you do not need emergency resuscitation. Breathe deeply and calmly, or it will start pumping the mask again."

Nodding, Mallory breathed deeply and calmly, allowing the returning sprite to attach a fresh oximeter to her finger. After a short time, the sprite pulled away all the medical equipment, including the blood pressure cuff still wrapped around Mallory's arm. Mallory reeled in pain as the fool thing callously ripped it off, but she kept breathing normally for fear it might try to save her life again.

The nurse continued to wail on the sprite with the metal chair with rage and frustration while it returned the supplies to their various homes in the examination room. She followed it to its place in the corner of the room pounding out a beat that would rival the Dikaió musicians during the christenings.

The crouching woman yelled at the nurse, "Please, stop! It's done."

The nurse looked wildly at the crouching woman, and Mallory warned, "Watch out, she's dangerous!"

"I can see that," the crouching woman replied. "That's why I'm still down here out of her reach."

The nurse blinked, the wildness cleared from her eyes, and she looked sheepishly at the floor. "Sorry," she mumbled.

The crouching woman stood up then and looked at Mallory but spoke to the nurse, "Quite alright, Jennifer. What are we looking at here?"

"Oh yes, she has several partial-thickness burns,

particularly affecting her left arm. Her jacket was missing a sleeve on that side, so the skin was likely more exposed—"

"I used my sleeve to cover my nose and mouth, trying to keep out the smoke." Mallory interrupted.

"Clever," the now-standing woman said then motioned for the nurse to continue.

Mallory was non-plussed to be dismissed and said through gritted teeth, "Yes, it was rather clever. Thank you."

The nurse rolled her eyes and continued her report, "Besides the smoke inhalation, there are multiple contusions, and the right arm appears to be broken."

The now-standing woman moved around to the other side of the examination table to look at Mallory's arm. She pulled on a pair of gloves and felt along the forearm up to her shoulder. Mallory hissed as she felt bone scrape against bone again just from the woman's touch. She noted that there was a small protrusion of skin in her forearm when her arm was in this position. The torturer in the white coat noticed it too and began to bend Mallory's arm to a sling position. This time Mallory cried out from the pain, "Ahh, you're as bad as the Sprite. Please tell me you're not a doctor!"

The woman's eyebrows lifted, but she seemed otherwise unphased by Mallory's comment. "I am Doctor Navarro. We're going to have to do surgery to set your arm, and properly debride and dress these burns."

Mallory knew very well who the woman was. Doctor Navarro had treated her for at least six different injuries in her life, including a broken leg two years previous, but she never remembered any of her patients. Mallory looked at her sideways: "Can you do surgery without the Dikaió and the sprites helping?"

Doctor Navarro nodded. "Yes. Of course. Well, not me, but the surgeon can. It's more difficult to be sure, but doctors are required to spend a semester working Dikaió free in medical school, just in case of emergencies. You have nothing to worry about." The doctor turned to the nurse, "Take her to pre-op, and tell them to get started as soon as—" she paused and turned to Mallory and asked, "When did you eat last?"

Mallory's stomach rolled. She had missed out on the party feast that night because of all the commotion, which meant the last time she had eaten was a quick bite in the late morning at the Farmer's Market just before she started shopping. Alex, Caleb, and Mallory had stopped at their favorite Dikaió chef's stall for chaffles: Chef Adam filled a waffle iron with shredded cheese, eggs, and roasted veggies. The waffle iron turned the cheese and egg into a salty waffle that was crispy on the outside and fluffy on the inside. He served it with a sweet and spicy sriracha sauce. It was delicious. It was divine. Her mouth watered. She was starving. "This morning. Why? What are you offering? Hospital food I suppose."

The doctor looked back at the nurse, "Let's get started as soon as possible. Fasting until post-op clears her, okay?"

"Fasting?!" Mallory shouted. "You're a monster! I'm starving!"

The doctor smiled at her. "You can eat whatever you want when you're out of surgery. Doctor's honor." She raised two fingers in a Dikaió scout's salute. Mallory dropped her head backwards against the soft examination table and sighed in defeat.

"I'll be back," Jennifer the nurse said as she walked out the door with the doctor, and a few minutes later she was. She motioned toward a hospital bed in the hallway being pushed by one of the flirtatious orderlies they had encountered earlier.

Mallory walked over and climbed up on it. "Has anyone let my parents know I'm here?"

"Of course. Your mother authorized whatever treatment you need."

"Are my parents coming?"

"I don't know. I haven't heard anything about that. Just that we're supposed to get you to surgery right away."

Mallory laid backward and watched the rectangular Dikaió lights in the ceiling tiles float by like clouds in a stiff wind as the bed was rolled down the hallways. The regularity of the flashing lights made her mind slow, and the events of the night began to fade into meaninglessness. She was incredibly sleepy. She woke briefly in the operating room to an anesthesiologist placing another face mask over her nose and mouth. The man noticed she was awake, and his eyes twinkled with a smile. "It's okay. It's just a little silly gas to make you laugh."

Mallory did not feel comforted in the least with another mask on her face. Some motion to her side caught her eye, and she saw a medic sprite carrying a tray of shiny, sharp scalpels, scissors, saws, and other nasty looking instruments toward her. The sprite set the tray on a table and picked up a scalpel. A bodiless voice from somewhere outside her field of vision yelled, "No, no, I'll do it! Stop!"

Mallory was sure that she was in mortal danger, but she could not seem to move her arms and legs. And for some reason, she found the whole situation quite silly. She laughed out loud and kept laughing as the room faded slowly into darkness.

Mallory's mother and father were sitting at the dining room table when Mallory got home. Her mother was sitting in the high-backed chair at the foot of the table planning another party for that night. She was dressed in her best blue ball gown, and her hair was steamed straight, neatly pinned into place by invisible barrettes and bobby pins, and her hair was sprayed into a fortress of perfectly tight lines. She was wearing eyeliner with a strip of blue eyeshadow that matched her dress. Her father was dressed in a casual twill shirt with blue jeans, and he was wearing work boots like the Manager of the Dikaió City Services. His hair was a mess, and his face was covered in a thick stubble like he hadn't shaved in days. The room smelled thickly of smoke and was warmer than usual. Something must be burning in the kitchen, but before Mallory could walk away and check, her father leaned back in his chair and swung his boots up on the table; they were caked with mud that splattered across the white linen. "How many guests do you think will come tonight, dear?"

"I guess it will depend on how many survive the fire our daughter decided to start at City Hall. We're only hosting this event to apologize for her poor behavior."

Mallory's father looked uncomfortable and turned toward Mallory, "Sorry, Mallory, my little pumpkin, your mother has a point this time. I can't defend every bad decision you make, no matter how much I love you."

Mallory had not actually started the fire or caused the light to go out over the city—that was from the storm. She was about to defend herself when a kitchen sprite whirled into the room. It was carrying a smoking serving tray full of blackened vegetables. "Oh yes, those look lovely," her mother called. The sprite sidled over to her, so she could taste them. As she picked up a fork and reached for them, the sprite poured them into her lap. Her mother's blue gown was covered in black smudges and burnt vegetables. She plunged her fork into what used to be a carrot on her lap and brought it up to her lips. She chewed thoughtfully, as black saliva ran down her chin. Finally, she swallowed and said, "Delicious! But perhaps a garnish of cilantro?" The sprite whirled backward around her mother's chair and took a running charge through the wall separating the dining room and the kitchen. Her father laughed heartily at the sprite's antics.

Then a slit of light flashed in the middle of the room, and

in it, Mallory could see what appeared to be another universe. There was a woman dressed like a nurse sitting in a bright room very close to the tear in the universe. She seemed to notice Mallory looking at her and stood up, walking toward her. Mallory quickly shut her eyes. She did not like how strangely her parents were acting in this universe, but she was sure that the universe where that nurse existed was worse. A woman's voice called out, "It's okay, love. It's just the anesthesia wearing off. You'll feel fine in a few minutes."

Mallory opened her eyes, and her mother and father were gone along with her house and the silly wall-smashing sprite. The smell of burning was joined with the antiseptic smell of a hospital room, though it still lingered in the room. It was probably coming from her; the smell of the fire at City Hall clinging to her nostrils. Tiny beeps of a monitor sounded regularly somewhere near her. Interestingly, when she moved, all the pain from the night was gone, though she could not seem to move her right arm, and she wondered if that was a residual of the anesthesia. She had not been able to move in the operating room either.

The operating room!

Mallory's eyes flashed open. Where was the sprite with the scalpels and saws? What had it done to her arm? She began to thrash in her bed, trying to see if she were still in one piece.

The nurse moved quickly, trying to hold her down. "It's okay! It's okay!" Then the nurse turned toward the curtain and called out, "I'm going to need some help in here!"

Mallory scratched and clawed to get free from the nurse's grip. There could be a homicidal sprite coming for her at any moment. Then there were six arms holding her down. Mallory began to hyperventilate in fear. The sprite had her, and it really was going to finish her off.

A familiar voice began to coo, "Remember, deep breaths. Deep breaths." It was Doctor Navarro.

The other sets of arms belonged to her and a male orderly, not a sprite. Mallory took deep breaths and began to calm down, and as she did, she was able to get her bearings. There were no sprites in the room at all, just the doctor, the nurse, and the orderly. She breathed deeply, and then looked at her right arm that still could not move. It was wrapped in a white plaster cast. Mallory rasped in a whisper, "Oh great, there go my plans for the weekend."

Dr. Navarro laughed, "She'll be fine. I think she's ready to head up to her room."

"Food?" Mallory croaked.

Dr. Navarro laughed again, "In a little while, let's let the anesthesia wear off all the way before you fill your belly."

"You said there'd be food?" she croaked pleadingly. Her lips were dry and her tongue was cracked and swollen.

Dr. Navarro chuckled again and then walked away while the orderly and the nurse unlocked the wheels on her bed. While the orderly pushed her carefully out of the room, the nurse walked beside the bed on the left, rolling an IV pump with a large plastic bag full of clear liquid hanging from a hook on the pole. Mallory noted that there was plastic tubing running from her left hand over the bed rail up to a small plastic bag where a clear liquid that looked like water dripped down at regular intervals.

"What's that?" She asked the nurse as they walked.

"Oh, that's just some extra fluid. You were severely dehydrated from being in the heat, and your body is going to be using a lot of moisture while it heals your burns . . . And there's a bit of medicine in there to help with the pain."

Mallory studied her left arm, which was not broken, and noted bulky layers of gauze on the burns all the way up to her shoulder. She was a mess, she was still a bit woozy, but mostly she was hungry.

"How long until I get to eat?"

The nurse laughed, "If you ate right now, it would probably come right back up. Let's get you settled in your room and see how you're doing in fifteen minutes or so."

Eternity was never so long as the trip to her room. She lay watching the lights in the ceiling slide by, and they had the same hypnotic effect as they went by overhead. She felt like she was floating backwards, prone on an uncomfortable bed, but still having some trouble concentrating and staying awake as she floated. She probably would have fallen asleep, but the hospital was cold—colder than she remembered it being last night—and she wished they had at least thought to put another blanket on her. She shivered and wanted to pull her arms and legs closer into her core, but the broken arm would not respond, and when she moved her other arm, the IV tugged on her skin, reminding her of its presence. Her legs were free, but when she pulled them up, she felt a draft move up the back of her legs, and she remembered that all she was wearing was a hospital gown that was open in the back. Embarrassment warmed her a bit, but she still put her legs down, conscious of the presence of strangers around her.

The hallways were fuller and noisier than they were during her first trip on the stretcher. A lot of people were walking with nurses, doctors, orderlies, even citizens in everyday clothing were helping these wounded people around. A lot of the wounded sported gauze dressings much like Mallory's on their arms, legs, and even faces. Some were in wheelchairs with oxygen tanks being wheeled behind them.

Mallory recognized more than a few of them as the leaders of the City Council and their families. She desperately wanted to search their faces to see if her mother and father were okay, but then she caught a wicked glance from a short fat man in a wheelchair. It was the head of the Dikaió Smith guild. His hair was half burned off his head, and he had gauze taped to his ear and cheek on the same side of his head where his hair was missing. His nose and mouth were covered by a respiration mask, and his usual well-quaffed mustache drooped out the bottom of the mask in sad, uneven burnt strands. Above the mask, vessels had burst in both his eyes, which had turned their whites an angry red color and made the green of his irises stand out in a horrible contrast. He rolled slowly by and tried to kill Mallory with his gaze.

She wanted to be angry with him, and the way he had acted toward her that night. The things he had said to her were horrible, and he deserved her spite, but seeing him here, paying the price for her attempt to undo the curse of her life, made her feel sorry for him. Sorry for all these people stumbling through the Dikaió-free city. How many more would be injured because of her folly? How many would die in this curse she and Alex inadvertently placed on them? How many died last night because of the fire? That question made her wretch a little, and the nurse pulled a plastic bag like magic out of thin air for her to vomit into. There wasn't anything in her stomach to heave out, so she tried to spit, but the glands in her jaw just swelled, and no moisture came out. There wasn't enough liquid in her body to produce saliva.

What a miserable existence she had brought down on herself and her beloved city, friends, and family. She was not the Matriarchal Chorus that would save the city. She was its damnation. She closed her eyes for the rest of the trip, not being able to bear the stares of those she had cursed.

Finally, they wheeled her into an antiseptic-smelling double room. The place for her stretcher was empty, and the orderly expertly whipped her into place and locked the wheels on the stretcher and IV pump. The nurse pushed a couple of buttons on the pump, and then leaned over Mallory and shone a penlight in her eyes. She nodded and put two fingers on Mallory's wrist while looking at her watch. Then she placed her stethoscope on Mallory's chest and asked her to take deep breaths. Finally, she checked the IV site once more.

The nurse looked at Mallory thoughtfully and asked, "Do you still want something to eat?"

"I don't think I'm fit to have dinner," Mallory moaned and her stomach lurched inside out at the thought of food.

"It's morning and time for breakfast," the nurse replied cheerfully, clearly not interested in Mallory's self-flagellation.

"Am I fit for breakfast?" She closed her eyes grumpily and turned away.

"Oh, that little nausea in the hallway? That could just be the pain medicine giving you trouble on an empty stomach. I think you need a little something to settle it. Let me see what I can scrounge up." The nurse turned and walked out of the room muttering something under her breath about the fickleness of teenagers.

Mallory could not tell if the nurse was purposefully ignoring her moral suffering, or if she was being genuine in her dismissal and really thought food would help settle the roiling waves tossing in her belly. She laid there miserably looking at the ceiling for a while, willing her stomach to settle down. She had been in trouble too often to feel sorry for herself for long. She figured that even though she may have caused the trouble, she was the only one in the city that knew how to do anything without the Dikaió—well, except for these people at the hospital; they were surprisingly capable, and she was secretly grateful. She wondered how many other professions in the city had trained in their work without the Dikaió and how many would need to learn to read and have access to books to survive without it.

As Mallory's mind wandered, she started visually exploring the room. The ceiling was drop-in Styrofoam, and there was a bright rectangular Dikaió light above her bed and one above her neighbor's bed. The white curtain on her neighbor's bed was drawn completely closed, so Mallory could not see who her roommate was. The window was on her roommate's side of the room, and light shone through the curtain, casting a silhouette of her neighbor's bed. The chest of the silhouette moved mechanically up and down, and there was the faint hum of a machine moving in sync with the motion.

Mallory had had a few hospital roommates over the years, but they had rarely talked or made lasting connections despite sharing some of the most painful and vulnerable times of their lives. But she could remember the names of everyone that she had shared mischievous secrets with, no matter how long ago. Life's memories are funny that way, lasting and endearing in the joyous times and almost imperceptibly fleeting in the worst of times—yet people spent more time talking about regret and pain than joy. She supposed it was not so much the memories, but the people themselves that chose to hold onto those memories and were oddly focused on every bad thing that happened to them. The day City Hall burned down would almost certainly be a day burned in the memories of the city, but would anyone remember the doctors, nurses, or sick roommates they shared the aftermath of the event with? Probably not.

She thought about calling out to her neighbor and learning their story, but she shook her head and looked away from the bed, continuing to explore what she could see of her room. On the wall across from the beds, there were two pine armoires separated by a long bench with storage alcoves below it that were about two feet by two feet. Above that was a large white board with a solid black line drawn down the middle of it. Her name and her current nurse's name, Sandra, were written in marker on one side. On the other side was her roommate's nurse's name, Talia, and her roommate's name: Alexandria Nelson. Mallory's eyebrows raised, and she looked sharply to her right over her broken arm at the drawn white curtain. "Alex?" she called.

There was no reply.

She pulled at the bed railings, trying to figure out how to lower them, so she could go and see her friend. She desperately needed Alex to be okay. She found a lever that seemed to lower the railing, and she was in the process of swinging her legs out of bed while keeping her IV from ripping out of her arm when the nurse walked in wheeling a stainless-steel cart with a brick-colored plastic serving plate and matching cloche atop it, and what looked to be a glass of apple juice and a glass of milk on the side.

"Where do you think you're going?"

Mallory froze half in, half out of bed, tangled in her IV line.

The nurse wheeled quickly around the bed and stepped out from behind the cart. She helped to untangle Mallory and picked up her legs, gently pushing them back atop the mattress. The nurse covered her with a blanket and muttered, "teenagers" under her breath, then addressed Mallory more directly, "Why don't you try to eat something and heal a bit before jumping up and getting back to whatever mischief you were planning?"

Mallory scowled at the nurse, sizing her up. She was a short woman about her mother's age. Even with the broken arm, if Mallory wanted to leave, she was pretty sure the nurse could not stop her. Still, if she were going to have any chance of the citizens listening to her later, she needed to stop being such a fiery rebel and start behaving more like the Matriarch she knew she could be. Plus, she needed to know if Alex was okay.

"Listen," she glanced at the whiteboard quickly and then back to her nurse, "Sandra. My friend's name is listed up on the whiteboard as my roommate. I tried calling her name, and when there was no answer, I wanted to go and see her." Mallory felt tears well-up and trickle down her cheeks. "I want to know if she's okay."

The nurse softened immediately. "Oh, sweetie! I'm sorry." She walked over and drew the curtain. Inside was just an empty bed with a pillow. Whatever Mallory had thought she had seen and heard behind the curtain was just her mind playing tricks on her. The nurse continued. "The other patient isn't out of surgery yet. I'll tell you what, why don't you sit up and eat some breakfast, and I'll go and see if there's any sort of ETA for her, okay?"

Mallory nodded. She would take an estimated time of arrival over nothing, and her stomach had just noticed the smell of whatever was beneath that cloche. It smelled like eggs and toast, but Mallory knew after spending enough time in the hospital that it would just be an approximation of those things. Still, she was back to being hungry enough to devour anything edible. The nurse pulled the cloche off the plate, and a bit of steam wafted into the air. The plastic plate was divided by partitions into three sections: one was filled with a clumpy yellow puddle of curds, in the other was a slice of toast cut into triangles, and in the third there were six orange slices so thick with fibrous pith that they looked white with veins of orange rather than the other way around. She picked up the metal fork and dove heartily into the puddle of eggs. They were completely unseasoned, but Mallory did not take time to taste them. Next, she started in on the bread, which was unbuttered, but, like the eggs, she did not linger long enough to notice the taste. The oranges, juice, and milk went down just as quickly. The nurse had barely turned around and started walking toward the door, when Mallory pushed the plate away from her and called, "I'm finished, thank you."

The nurse turned back, eyes wide and walked back to Mallory's bedside. She examined the empty plate and glasses and shook her head, chuckling. As she rolled the cart out of the room, Mallory heard her mutter once more, "teenagers," and then she was gone.

Mallory wondered if the food the nurse had brought her had been laced with medicine because as soon as her belly was full, a shadow of tiredness swept down on her like a bird on its prey. Her head fell back against the barely stuffed pillow; she stared absently at the light above her for a few moments, eyes fluttering; and then she fell into a dreamless sleep.

"Mallory?" Her mother's voice called from somewhere in the distance. Oh, no! She thought. The last time her mother woke her, she had to face the City Council, then a storm, then a burning building, and she had not had a full sleep in who knows how long.

"Mallory, dear!" Mallory's eyes fluttered angrily open, and she found both her parents sitting beside her bed in padded wooden chairs. They were smiling, but they were a mess. Her mother's hair was a tangle of stray curls sticking out in random directions, her father's clothes were torn, and they were both covered in black soot from the fire. Just over their shoulder in the doorway, Mallory could see one of the magistrates standing in his blue uniform leaning up against the doorframe. Her father leaned over into her vision and blocked the view of the doorway momentarily with his concerned smile. He was saying something that she could not quite make out, but she pushed up further on the bed to see past him into the hall. The magistrate was gone.

"Is this another nightmare?" Mallory asked blinking in confusion at her parents.

Her mother sat back in her chair, "No, it is not. Do you often have nightmares about us?"

Her father laughed and pointed at his wife, "Well, it's no wonder she should think so, love. You should see yourself— it's terrifying!"

Her mother tilted her head at her father incredulously, "You're no picnic yourself, Roger!"

Her father hooted with laughter, and Mallory felt herself smile and then chuckle as well. Soon her mother joined in laughing with them both. They sounded like a cackle of hyenas, hooting and yelping together. Soon a nurse ran into the room and yelled at them: "Shush! Your neighbor is still sleeping!"

Mallory stopped laughing immediately and looked

toward the other bed. The curtain was open, and a middle-aged woman with bright-red hair lay there asleep with a mask and tubes running from her face to a beeping machine. Her arms and neck were covered in gauze bandages. Mallory looked at the board, and instead of Alex's name, the patient's name read "Reddy Lamarr." It was the Sprite Master.

"Where's, Alex?" Mallory almost cried in panic.

Her mother touched her hand. "Alex needs a bit more attention from the doctors and nurses for awhile, so they've moved her to a wing with fewer patients and more staff to look after her."

"Can I go visit her?"

"Oh, I'm sure in time," her father nodded, "but for now we'll let the doctors do their work so she can get better. Besides, you need your rest, too. If the two of you were in here together, who knows what kind of trouble you would get into." Her dad chuckled at the thought of his mischievous daughter and her friend, and then stopped when he saw his wife looking at him eyes wide. Mallory had turned her head away and started to cry.

"Well . . . well . . .," he stammered, "I wasn't trying to imply anything about the trouble you're currently in. It's just that you two are always doing something mischievous, but nobody's ever been seriously hurt before—well, not before City Hall and this whole end-of-the-world Dikaió business."

"Roger," the Matriarch reprimanded, as Mallory moaned and choked back a sob then sniffled loudly.

He reached an outstretched hand toward his daughter, who did not notice, and then he turned awkwardly toward his wife, hand still outstretched questioningly. She grunted and crossed her legs. He shrugged and twitched his shoulders rhythmically for a moment then said, "Hmmm . . . yes, well, perhaps I'll just wait outside?"

"That would be helpful, thank you, Roger." The Matriarch nodded, and he backed slowly out of the room, his shoulders hunched slightly.

Mallory turned to look at her mother, tears still streaming down her face. "I never meant for this to happen, you know."

"Of course not, Mallory." Her mother patted her hand, being mindful of the dressings.

"Do you know if Caleb is okay?"

"Oh yes, he's already home with some stitches and a mild concussion. He'll be fine." Her mother waved her hand impatiently, a sign that she had something to discuss and had grown tired of pleasantries. "Mallory, do you know where the book is that Alex used to remove the christening of the Dikaió? We've looked everywhere we can think of and can't find it anywhere."

Mallory's eyes widened. They did not know the book was gone? How could they really? The only one that knew was Caleb. "Caleb didn't tell you?" Mallory asked. Deep down she was hoping this was one of her mother's rhetorical questions, trying to get her to 'fess up to something her mother knew full well she had done. She did not want to be the one to have to disappoint her mother or the whole city again.

Her mother looked perplexed, "I haven't seen Caleb directly. I was just informed about his status during a briefing with the hospital director."

Mallory tried to sink farther into her mattress and closed her eyes, hoping to fall asleep, but there was not any point in hiding the truth or giving anyone false hope. She spoke with her eyes still closed, "Alex had the book with her in the fire. When the beams fell, and I tried to pull her out, it fell out of her jacket. We couldn't get it out. It's gone."

Mallory lay there for a long time with her eyes closed, waiting for some sort of reaction from her mother, but all she got was awkward silence. Her mother was the queen of saying only what needed to be said, and apparently the doom of the city and the end of life as they knew it did not need words to commemorate the moment, not even now when her daughter needed solace to ease her fears.

The empty silence continued, interrupted only by the maddening blips of the hospital equipment in the room. Soon it became a struggle of wills for which of the women would speak first, the mother or the daughter. Mallory dug in her proverbial heels, squeezing her eyes closed even tighter, silently demanding that her mother comfort her, forgive her for the mess she made, absolve her of the consequences of her actions. She felt like a helpless child again, and she wanted her mother to tell her everything was okay.

"Mom?" She finally caved in and opened her eyes. The only other person in the room was the silent Sprite Master in the other bed. Her mother had left without a word; without so much as an "I love you." Mallory's chest caved in on her heart with crushing grief, and all the fluid that had been pumping into her veins from her IV surged out as tears onto her cheeks and rolled back onto the pillow below her head, drenching her hair and her bed. She had been utterly abandoned.

10

Mallory's arm itched, and there was little she could
do to alleviate the sensation. It felt like she had a brood of
mosquitos living under her cast. Of course, this was not
the case, but still the description seemed apt for the arm's
constant demand for the taste of a nail scraping skin. All the
city was bemoaning the lack of luxury in using the Dikaió,
but Mallory just wanted to scratch the persistent itch just out
of reach. It is the little pleasures in life that get missed most
when they are gone.

Over the last six weeks, she had tried to scratch away
the itching in a multitude of ways. First, she tried to lever
her other hand's fingers down the chasm of the cast, but
she could not get further than the bottom of the nailbed.

Then she had wrangled silverware away from the kitchen sprites and wiggled forks and knives down inside her cast, which managed to reach down about four inches or so into the cast and at least rub the itchy spots, but it was not as effective as she had hoped, and she had trouble gripping the edge of the silverware the further down she went. She had lost a butter knife into her cast at one point and spent an hour dancing around her room shaking her broken arm like a monkey trying to dislodge it. Finally, she had tried using sticks dropped from the massive oaks in her front yard. These proved the most effective at getting down into the cast and scratching away the irritation. They were not smooth like the silverware, and the friction created by the rough bark was near enough to a fingernail that Mallory had achieved a modicum of relief. While she knew she ought to be figuring out a solution to bring back magic, Mallory had become more and more distracted by the itch in her cast, and she was spending most of her time sitting on her porch scratching her arm with twigs, which she felt were quite a bit like magic in terms of the relief she felt in using them. She had put together a varied collection of these sticks, each with a different arc and degree of bumps and crevices that could reach specific parts of her arm in the caverns of the cast, and with them, she drove back the insanity by fighting off the itch.

She wished she had her sticks with her right then. It was a hot day, and she could feel sweat inside the cast, trickling down her arm toward her hand. The sweat drops' slow crawl tickled the nerve endings in her skin, causing the dreaded itch to rear up. She did not have access to her sticks because she was trekking up Main Street toward the hospital. On the positive side of the issue, this was the day she would get the cursed cast cut off her arm. On the negative side of the issue, the more her arm itched the slower the trek seemed to take. And worse, it was not just the itching that slowed her progress; it was market day again, and the whole city was out gathering groceries.

Main Street was lined with citizens buying food from the vendors. Grocery boxes hovered above their families waiting patiently for the citizens to deposit fruits, vegetables, milk, cheese, and all the usual assortment of edible necessities. Mallory thought that it would be easy to assume it was just a normal day at the market, the same as it always was, if the place was not so eerily quiet: No merchants were calling out for customers. No customers were haggling over price. Everyone on the street kept their head low, and their mouths shut. Mallory's explanation to the nurse six weeks ago that someone had used the Dikaió carelessly had spread through the city, and that a slip of the tongue had brought this curse on them all resulted in a city in silence. It was better that everyone said as little as possible; words could hurt others. A few looked hatefully at Mallory as she passed by, knowing that she was involved somehow, but no one dared to say anything. Instead, they picked up their produce, paid vendors, and went down the line in brooding silence.

Another oddity that stood out as being different from the days of the Dikaió was that, while the grocery boxes were hovering in place about three feet above their families as usual, the boxes refused to come down and collect the groceries that had been purchased. On the first market day after the Dikaió ended, the head of the Dikaió Cultures Co-op had climbed up on one of the stalls and jumped up to grab his family's grocery box. It shot up into the air, hauling the man upward six more feet before he fell. When he landed on the street, he shattered his left ankle, and while he screamed, the grocery box floated back down to hover three feet above him again. The grocery boxes apparently wanted to keep their distance, and no one tried to wrangle them out of the sky again. All the families carried their groceries home in their arms that week, and many ran out of food before the next market day came.

Foreseeing the issue, Caleb had Mallory come to his house to show him how to build one of her carts. All of her tools had been fashioned out of images in the books, and since he had to do most of the work with Mallory's arm out of commission, most of the time was spent teaching him how to use a hammer and a saw. Once he understood the concepts, Caleb took to craftsmanship like a bird to air. He quickly added the two legs Mallory had wanted to add to the first model, so it stayed up when it was set down, balancing on the wheel up front and the two legs in the back, and he marveled at the improvement the addition had made.

The next day he came back with fifty men and women from the city and showed them the cart.

"Thank you all for coming," he said. "You remember Miss Knenne's grocery cart?"

The crowd all squirmed silently, afraid to say anything,

but looking from the cart to Mallory with trepidation and confusion. Caleb had referred to her formally instead of using her first name as he usually did. Mallory was not sure what to think about that, but for the moment, she decided not to dwell on it. The Sprite Master, Reddy, had recovered quite quickly after being Mallory's hospital roommate, but found herself without a lot to do after leaving the hospital. She broke the silence, "Yes, we remember it. Why wouldn't we? It was an evil omen of what was coming that day."

Caleb was undaunted. "Well, if we want to make sure people are able to take enough food home with them during the market days, we need to use Miss Knenne's old magic to make one of these carts for every family in the city."

The small crowd gasped when they realized what he was suggesting. There were roughly 500,000 people in the city, and the average family had five or six people living in their home. So, Caleb was suggesting that they needed roughly 100,000 carts. Another member of the crowd, a middle-aged citizen that Mallory thought was a baker or a café owner yelled, "Even if we wanted to do what you ask, there's so few of us." He looked around the crowd and then marveled, "Plus, none of us are qualified as Dikaió builders. Well, except the Dikaió Sprite Master here."

"There isn't any more magic to craft with, Louis," Caleb retorted. "None of you currently have a job within the city without the Dikaió to aid in your work. But at least for now the culture sprites are continuing in their day-to-day farming duties, so the food production is still running. If we can get this food delivery system up and running, then at least one of the city's basic needs will be met, and then we can figure out how to use the old magic to get your vocations back into working order."

"Why aren't you spending your time figuring out how to get the Dikaió back?" Someone questioned from the back.

Caleb nodded solemnly. "Restoring the Dikaió is an important priority, which is why the City Council is working toward that end, except for the Sprite Master. We're going to need her help with this project. I've been assigned the task to make sure the city gets enough to eat. Now, let me show you how to build one of these things."

Caleb gave a brief description of the tools and the concept of the cart, and he set a few of the citizens to hammering and sawing lumber he'd pulled out of some abandoned sheds on the Governor's property. When he seemed confident that the group knew what they were doing, Mallory pulled him aside. "We're going to need more than wood, Caleb." Mallory picked up a rusty bolt out of a small pile near her foot. "It took me years to find these materials, scrounging through junk piles and old sheds around the city. In order to make so many carts, you're going to need tens of thousands of wheels, bolts, and nails. Where are we going to find those?"

Caleb smiled and called to the Sprite Master, "Reddy, can you come here for a moment?" Caleb held up a wheel, a nail, and a bolt for her to see. "Since we don't need more sprites at the moment, do you think your guild could make these?"

The Sprite Master brushed a few loose red hairs out of her eyes and took the nail and bolt from Caleb, turning them over and over in her hands, studying their design carefully.

"Well, I have not been to the Sprite Rookery since we lost the Dikaió because of my injuries, but without the Dikaió, I am sure it is a mess." She looked coldly at Mallory and then addressed Caleb when continuing, "I think we could make wax molds out of these then slip by the forge sprites that are still keeping the fires hot, syphon off some of the molten steel, and set up a manual assembly line for them." She picked up one of the wheels, "Wheels, we have a lot of. There are a lot of unjoined sprite wheels laying around. You are welcome to them."

"We're going to need tens of thousands," Mallory chimed in.

The Sprite Master looked her in the eye and then shrugged in reply, holding her hands out wide in a half-curtsy: "You're welcome to all we have."

Mallory could not quite tell if she was mocking her or actually being courteous, but she was pretty certain it was the former and not the latter. She was puffing up her chest to say something she would likely regret, but Caleb started barking orders, interrupting the near confrontation between the women: "Okay, Reddy, you and Miss Knenne and four men come with me. We're going to go see if we can fetch some wheels." He looked around the crowd. "I need twenty of you to head out around the city and collect as many useable, intact boards like these that you can find." He pointed at the stack of wood he'd hauled out for the construction project. "Meanwhile, the rest of you need some more of these tools constructed, and you should start putting together as many carts as you can with the materials we've got here."

The Sprite Master looked at the tools and said, "We could probably scrap some of the sprite parts at the Rookery and build some of these rudimentary tools as well."

Caleb nodded, "That would be very helpful. Thank you, Reddy. Okay, folks. Let's get to work. Market day is fast approaching, and I would like to get as many of these carts into the hands of families in the city as we can."

Caleb, Mallory, and the group heading to the Rookery took the two finished carts and started out. It was a long hike to the Rookery; it was just past the hospital at the edge of the city, near the pastureland where the Dikaió Cultures kept the cattle and the sheep. Mallory was walking behind the group, the pain in her arm was significant with all the jostling of a long hike, and even though it was daylight, this walk up Main Street dragged up memories of that night hauling Alex to the hospital. She tried to distract herself by making a mental list of how much material they were going to need to construct a cart for every family in town. "I don't think these carts will hold enough wheels," she called ahead to the group.

No one acknowledged her or even looked in her direction. When she thought about it, almost no one had spoken to her since she had left the hospital. She could understand the regular citizens that were afraid of careless words, but even those that knew what had really happened and that their words were no longer dangerous without the Dikaió were ignoring her. Her own mother and father had barely uttered four words to her since she came home from the hospital. They were both very busy trying to keep the city running, but there were certainly times in the morning when they were getting ready that they could have stopped to check on her. It seemed to Mallory that her father wanted to, but his rule was to always choose his wife's side over his daughter's in any argument, whether he really agreed with the Matriarch or not.

"Mallory," he would say, "one day, you're going to grow up, find some boy to marry, and leave us, and then all your mother and I will have left is each other. We need to be a united front all the time, so we can stay united in our old age. Do you understand?"

Mallory did not.

In fact, Caleb was the only one talking to her regularly at all, but at that moment, he was too busy talking logistics with Reddy at the head of the procession to hear her comment, which she thought was important—certainly more important than whatever that impertinent Sprite Master was talking to him about. Mallory felt irritated and half-walked, half-ran, trying to keep her broken arm from jostling too much but still wanting to catch up with Caleb. She finally caught up to him just as the Sprite Master was saying, "I'm not sure these two carts will hold enough wheels to be much use." Mallory slowed to a walk and glared daggers at the redheaded woman.

Caleb shrugged in the carefree way he always had about him and replied, "Well, sure I don't expect to fill these two carts with 10,000 wheels. I figure we'll fit as many as we can to complete the carts the others are working on, then maybe we'll come back with twenty carts, and then two-hundred, etcetera—a sort of exponential collection of materials if you will."

"Wouldn't it be better to just move all the production into the Rookery?" Mallory asked.

Caleb glanced over his shoulder and smiled, "I thought about that, but if the Dikaió does come back, there's a lot of damage that's been inflicted by its absence that could use sprites for repair, so I think leaving the Rookery ready for that influx is the best strategy."

The Sprite Master nodded in agreement.

But Mallory bit her lip and thought a moment before responding, "And if the Dikaió doesn't return, we'll have wasted hours of labor and resources trekking across the city for materials."

Caleb shrugged again, "Maybe, but for now that's the plan, Ms. Knenne. If we need to change it later, we will."

"Who's plan?" Mallory was feeling irritated being left out of the city's discussions, and the more Caleb called her 'Ms. Knenne,' the more she wanted to punch him in the eye. At least for now, she was still heir to the Matriarchy.

Caleb paused and turned around to reply to Mallory, so Reddy stopped and turned too. The Sprite Master looked nearly as red as her hair and looked like she was ready to strangle Mallory. Caleb's deep blue eyes were downcast. "Look," he said. "It's nothing personal, but—"

His sentence was cut off by one of the four citizens that had come with them urgently whispering, "What is that?"

Mallory looked back at the citizens behind them. One was pointing off to the right, and she followed his gaze. He was looking at the Rookery, which they had managed to get within one-hundred and fifty yards of while they were talking. Behind the building, just beyond the pastures, and towering over the horizon, was one of the most amazing things Mallory had ever seen: A canopy of trees as tall as any of the skyscrapers in the city center, bigger around then the oaks in the Matriarch's front yard, had sprung up around the city where the light used to shine.

Mallory had been to the outskirts of the city before. She, Caleb, and Alex had often played at the edge of the light when they were children, much as all the children in the city did. They would toss bits of grass or sticks or really any little thing into the light and watch it sizzle into vapor. The boys used to dare each other to touch it, but of course no one went through with such foolish challenges. The light protected the city from what lay beyond, but it was dangerous, and they all knew it. Yet, they could all see what was beyond the light. It was just more pastureland, which is why the cattle and the sheep were still fenced in lest they run through the light looking for greener pastures and get vaporized.

But now all those pasturelands beyond the light had been vaporized and replaced by monstrous trees. Their branches were trimmed into an arc, tracing the curvature of where the light used to shine. Mallory's eyes followed the branches reaching into the sky down to the base of the trunks. No light shown below the trees. It was dark, and the darkness seemed alive and dangerous. All the childhood stories of what lay beyond the light flooded back into her memory. And somehow Mallory knew that the trees had always been there, the pasturelands in the light were never real—just a projected illusion—another protection from what lay beyond the city.

Then Mallory noticed that the sheep and the cattle were thronged up against the fence opposite the forest. Their eyes were fixed on the trees, and they were all making wavering calls in their own animal tongues. The animals seemed to be afraid of the forest as well, and they wanted to get away from it. A shiver ran down Mallory's body causing the hairs on her arms to stand on end. Using her good arm, she grabbed Caleb's hand and pulled herself close to him. Caleb did not pull away but instead wrapped his other arm protectively around her, holding her tightly. Mallory could feel his heart beating rapidly in his chest through her shoulder. She looked up into his eyes, hoping for some reassurance, but his eyes were fixed on the forest, pupils dilated, and quickly scanning back and forth looking for danger.

A murder of crows lifted off from the trees suddenly, cawing loudly. Caleb spoke with some urgency, but his voice was low and authoritative. "Let's get inside and get what we need quickly. I need to get back and tell my father about this."

The group nearly ran the rest of the distance to the Sprite Rookery, never really taking their eyes off the dark forest and remaining utterly silent. The doors of the Rookery opened for the Sprite Master when she approached them, and when the group of seven made it through the entrance, the group breathed a sigh of relief. Their relief was short lived, as the Rookery was nearly as dark as the undergrowth below the distant forest.

The interior of the building looked like a large warehouse with brick walls and a concrete floor. Rows upon rows of industrial shelving spread out endlessly before them loaded with pieces of sprites not yet joined together and birthed by the Dikaió. The shelves loomed four stories high, and somewhere up in the gloom there were Dikaió lights that were not shining. With the destruction of the generators below City Hall, the City Services Manager had been stringing wires across the city, trying to tie together all the emergency generators in the city in order to provide some semblance of Dikaió power to the citizens. Of course, these services were being provided on an essential basis, which meant the government and City Council members first, then the clothing and shelter industries, and so on. Most citizens were still living without power, and non-essential services like the Sprite Rookery were still in the dark. The only light in the building came in from some windows high above the Rookery floor, and an eerie, undulating red glow that seemed to be emanating from the far end of the long rows of the shelves. The group stood looking at the light with wide eyes, trying to make out what could be making such a wicked-looking glow.

"The steel vats are downstairs, and in the dark their light shines all the way upstairs," the Sprite Master said, breaking some of the tension in the group.

Caleb got down to business. "Where are the wheels? And let's grab some of those parts that can be used as tools while we're here."

"The wheels are in aisle D-17," the Sprite Master pointed to her left. There were large signs on the shelves near the front with alpha-numeric designations. "And the parts I'm thinking of are scattered about in different areas."

"Okay, Ms. Knenne and you two bring one cart and come

with me to get the wheels. The rest of you go with Reddy with the other cart. Let's meet back here in ten minutes tops, alright?"

Caleb started walking toward the aisle labeled D-1, and Mallory followed him, though she was uneasy about walking deep into the darkness of the row. Two men followed behind her cautiously wheeling the cart with wide eyes. The shelves were divided into a grid; each crosswalk between shelves would start a new number: D-2; D-3, etc. The parts housed in each shelf seemed entirely unrelated to each other, at least so far as Mallory could tell. There were piles of red-wire mesh sitting next to stacks of copper disks next to plates of silver metal. It was a wonder that the Sprite Master could find anything in this mess, but Mallory supposed she did not usually need to since most of the work was done by the Dikaió rook sprites anyway.

They had just passed D-12 when there was a sharp noise of metal scraping against metal to their right. The whole group jumped, and Mallory felt herself once again in Caleb's embrace looking for protection. She was getting tired of feeling so afraid, but the scraping metal did not make her feel like leaving Caleb's arms anytime soon either. The scraping noise stopped, and a large shadowy figure crossed in front of them. It had a multitude of arms and was holding a huge sheet of metal in the air. It turned and rambled down the labyrinth of shelving toward the glowing red light. It was one of the rook sprites rushing off to the forges to continue joining new sprites for the city. The group shook off the shock of meeting the sprite in the dark and continued down the aisle.

Section D-17 was the final section of aisle D, and the light of the windows barely reached this far into the depths of the building, but there were three large doors glowing red from the forges below that not only provided light but a withering heat from the fires below the building, melting the sheets of metal dragged into their depths into red-hot liquid. The red glow from the doors provided enough illumination that Mallory could see there were piles of sprite wheels stacked on the shelves, falling off the shelves, and in piles along the back wall. She was not sure if there were one-hundred thousand wheels here, but there were certainly thousands of them. The men stopped and began loading wheels into the cart. Mallory tried to help, but her broken arm only allowed her to pick up one wheel at a time, and she found herself getting in the way more than being of service, so she stepped back and wandered over to the doors to the forge. Through the two outer doors there were ramps for the rook sprites to go up and down, and through the center was a stairway that descended into the forge. Smoke was billowing up the ceilings of the stairways and ramps, and when Mallory looked up, she could make out a vast cloud of smoke gathering in the rafters of the Rookery. The ventilation fans were probably not working without the Dikaió to power them. It would not be long before the whole building was filled with smoke.

Still, Mallory was curious about what was below and started cautiously walking down the staircase. She had never seen the process of sprite birthing, but she knew from her leadership studies that it was very similar to the christening for citizens. Once a sprite had been joined together, the Sprite Master would assign it a Dikaió purpose and a citizen to serve in its purpose. If the rook sprites were continuing to join the pieces of the sprites together, Mallory wondered what purpose the sprites were serving without the Dikaió. It did not take her long to discover the answer to her question: The floor of the forge was scattered with the empty husks of oblong silver sprites, all seemingly glowing red in the light of the forges' fires. Rook sprites were busily molding and hammering in the creation of new sprites all over the room and when a sprite's body was finished, it was placed in a bin, already heaped high enough over the top of its sides that the sprite would roll down the pile and spill onto the floor. The piles of sprites were getting high enough that they were starting to make their way up the stairs.

Mallory was startled by a voice behind her, "One thing is for sure, if the Dikaió ever comes back, the Sprite Master is going to have her hands full." Caleb laughed, and then coughed a little. The fumes of the molten metal were pretty strong and getting stronger.

"C'mon, Mal. We've got what we need. Let's get out of here."

She noted that he had reverted to his pet name for her when the others were not around, and she made a note to ask him about what was going on when they had more time alone, away from others' ears. When they got back to the entrance of the Rookery, the rest of the group was waiting with two carts full of materials. The sun was setting, and none of them wanted to be anywhere near the dark woods at night, so they all rushed back to the Governor's house to deliver the materials for the carts.

Now as Mallory was walking to the hospital to get her cast taken off, the cart construction had been going on for four weeks, and Mallory marveled at the change the Farmer's Market had made in that time. While the grocery boxes all still hovered over their respective families, nearly one-in-ten families was pushing what had come to be known as a Chorus cart to haul home their groceries. Most of the families had joined together in packs, carrying each other's lighter items and putting the heavier items for all the families in the cart. Cooperation had always been one of the city's highest imperatives, but Mallory had never seen the city come together in such camaraderie in her lifetime. Still, the citizens' hateful looks at her were often followed by a disgusted look at their Chorus carts, and Mallory knew they would be only too happy to ditch those carts if the Dikaió returned.

She felt a sense of relief when she got out of the market area, but that relief was short-lived because as she climbed the gentle slope of Main Street nearing the hospital, she could see the tops of the dark forest rising higher above the horizon with every step. Scouts had gone round the pasture-lands surrounding the city over the last month and found that the forest completely encircled the city. No one had dared to venture within two-hundred yards of the forest, but it was there, looming and dangerous.

Mallory found that every inch nearer to the forest increased her anxiety just a little. By the time the hospital was in view, she was sprinting for the safety of the building. Her eyes darted from the hospital to the distant, dark trees, and back again as she ran. She swung through the open door on the side of the building in what she felt was the nick of time and was caught up short by a hand that grabbed her shoulder.

"What's the rush, Mal?" She looked into Caleb's blue eyes, and Mallory felt her anxiety fade away. He had been waiting there for her.

Mallory was surprised to see Caleb at the hospital. He had been very busy, not just with the Chorus-cart project, but his father had appointed him to oversee other projects around the city. It was odd what the sprites wanted to maintain and what they did not. For example, the Culture Co-op sprites wheeled around and continued to mow the grass in every yard and park in the city on the same schedule they always had since any of the citizens could remember. However, these same sprites previously maintained the flower gardens and the hedges with the direction of a member of the Culture Co-op, but these more aesthetic duties were completely discarded without the Dikaió. The flower gardens and hedges, being heavily watered from the recent storm, quickly overgrew their boundaries, and weeds sprouted up amongst the flowers. The Culture Co-op guild tried to compensate for the lack of mechanical help by using their hands, yanking out weeds and trying to prune the out-of-control flowers with their fingernails, but the work was slow and the plants, good and bad, were out-pacing them.

The City Council declared gardening an essential service and added it to the list of projects Caleb would oversee as heir to the Governorship. Their reason was that as the plants grew wilder, mosquitoes and other pests began to take up residency in them. However, the state of the wealthiest citizens' prized flower gardens suggested that pride was more at the heart of the decree. However, the Council did tie Caleb's hands somewhat in telling him that the Culture Co-op's first responsibility was food production atop the skyscrapers downtown, so he could only have twenty members of the guild to get the flower gardens into shape. They were out every day with small silver scissors cutting branches and stems and pieces of old leaves, digging out the prolific weeds.

Another issue the City Council thought was important was getting the hydrant sprites to be more functional in case of another fire in the city. The loss of City Hall was devastating, and the city could not sustain more building losses. Ultimately, they hoped to figure out how to build structures again—their ancestors were able to, so they should be able to manage—but for now, maintaining what the city had was the goal. Caleb had come to Mallory's house to ask her for help with that task.

He smiled in his usual 'Caleb' way at her door when he

asked, but she was still confused about the way he had acted at the Sprite Rookery, and she was not sure she wanted to help him with any more of his projects.

"What do you want me to do, Caleb? I'm stuck in this cast." She raised her incapacitated arm, so he could see it.

He just smiled, shrugged, and then held up his hands, palms facing her. "We'll do it just like the carts, Mal. You tell me what to do, and I'll be your hands."

She wanted to tell him to use his hands to smack himself in the mouth, that annoying but charming mouth. Instead, she sighed, and said, "Okay, let's see what we can find in my workshop."

Caleb smiled sheepishly as Mallory took him back to a dilapidated shed behind the Matriarch's house where she kept the various construction supplies that she found around town, which usually consisted of rusted hunks of metal and scrap wood. The occasional nail and screw were like gold, but the shed was mostly filled with junk. The doorframe to the shed was warped with age and wedged up against the doorjamb, so she usually had to use both arms and her entire body leaning back as a counterweight to tug it open. Since she was incapacitated, Caleb had to pull the door open for her, which he managed with one hand and a quick yank. She found his physical strength both impressive and deeply irritating. He held the door for her like a gentleman, so she gave him a smile anyway and entered the shed in front of him.

Inside, she was surprised to find all her construction supplies were gone—not a single rusty nail was left—but the shed was not empty. Someone had filled it with shiny silver sprite parts of all shapes and sizes. Mallory was set back for a moment and then asked, "Where did this come from?"

"We've got to learn how to live without the Dikaió, Mal, and while I can get people to do things, I can't figure out how to join things together and use the old magic to make them do what I need. You've been an old-magic user your whole life, so I had your workshop here filled with supplies. Look at these," Caleb pulled her over to the bench and desk. "Reddy managed to design some tools for you with the sprite steel they syphoned off for bolts and screws for the carts."

Mallory picked up a silver-colored hammer in her hand—it was light as a feather. There was also a saw, a screwdriver, pliers, and a few wrenches that could fit different sized bolts. Caleb took the hammer and pounded it on the desktop: "They're super durable like the sprites. Pretty much indestructible."

Mallory did not say anything. She was overcome by an emotion she could not quite place. On the one hand, she was excited to use all the new equipment, but on the other hand, the loss of the old equipment felt like part of her childhood had passed away. She looked around the room at all the sprite parts and then her eye fell on something useful. She rushed over and pulled out a conical-shaped piece of metal. It might have been joined to a kitchen sprite for cooking, but it also looked similar to the nozzles on the end of the hose-like arms of the hydrant sprites. Then she grabbed some rubber tubing lying nearby. "Look," Mallory called. She held the tube up to the narrow end of the conical steel. "If you were to attach this tubing to the hydrant sprite's nozzle like so, and then make another nozzle on this side like so." She moved the cone to the other side of the hose with the wide end on top. "Then you could redirect the water from the hydrant sprites wherever you wanted it to go." She waved the makeshift nozzle back and forth making water noises, "shhhh shhhh shhhh."

"Awesome, Mal! This will be perfect! How do we make a nozzle?"

Mallory laughed, "Well, you want a lot of water going in one end, and a smaller amount coming out this side—that way there's pressure. The smaller the hole on this side, the more pressure. And the hydrant sprites are already supplying a lot of force behind the water, so I don't think it has to be perfect to redirect the flow—just a tight fit. Let's see," she scanned all the parts and found some rubber gaskets in a small pail. She stretched them out and then put one on the hose, then the cone, and then another gasket, which cinched the end of the hose a bit tighter. "Yeah, something like this. I'd have to fiddle with it a bit. You might not even need the cone, just a gasket on the hose connected to a hydrant sprite's nozzle."

"There might be a couple of inactive hydrant sprites in the piles of un-birthed sprites at the Rookery. Maybe Reddy could find us some joined nozzles that we could cut off and attach to your hose?"

Mallory frowned, "Why do you call the Sprite Master by her first name?"

Caleb smiled, "Why? Are you jealous? Now what about my idea with the nozzles?"

Mallory shook her head. "The woman's twice your age.

What do I have to be jealous of?"

Caleb's smile grew bigger. "We're not going to talk about the nozzle anymore are we?"

"C'mon, Caleb. What's the reason? It's not normal for children to call adults by their name and not their title."

Caleb's smile faded, and he turned serious. "Mal, I'm eighteen. The Council appointed me to lead all these projects, and my father told me I should start to act like an adult, or no one will take me seriously. That means calling other adults by their first names."

"Is that why you're calling me 'Ms. Knenne' in front of others? To show off how grown-up you are?"

He paused and looked her in the eye. "Me growing up and taking my place among the city's leaders also means I need to start thinking about getting married and starting a family. You know the customs, Mal. I'll be expected to announce my choice for the Governess by my twentieth birthday, and my father says that with the Dikaió gone we need to hold to the old customs even more. The people can only handle so much crisis . . ." He paused when Mallory winced at the word crisis. ". . . I mean so much change. He's been talking to your mother about uniting our houses with you or your sister; whoever is not going to be the Matriarch." Then he reached down and took Mallory's hand. "If I could, I would choose you, Mallory."

"Would the old customs allow it?" Mallory pulled away, reeling from a conflict of emotions. "The Matriarch and the Governor enjoined? The balance of power would be upset."

"Not if you let your sister be Matriarch. I mean, with the

Dikaió gone, what difference would it make?"

Mallory stood up straighter and turned away slightly. "I feel like we've talked about this already, Caleb. With the Dikaió gone, I could be Matriarch as a Chorus just like my grandmother foresaw. The City Council can't even argue that I shouldn't be, as my sister won't be a Syntec either. You'll just have to wait until my sister comes of age for a wife, I guess."

Caleb deflated and ended the conversation. He was not there to argue with her. "Thanks for your time, Mal. I may need some more help later. Would it be okay if I stopped by when the next crisis needs a solution?"

Mallory winced again. He'd switched back to 'crisis' on purpose, but she was not going to bite: "Of course, I'm always happy to help the heir to the Governorship." Two could wage a war of words. She felt even more irritated with Caleb than when they were in the Sprite Rookery. Maybe it was frustration with his dismissal, or tradition, or her grandmother's prophecy. Maybe it was that the confusing old dilemma was rearing up once again: duty or love. She wished she had someone to talk to about her emotions—someone who had faced this dilemma before her. But Caleb was right that the city and its citizens loved their traditions, and it was impossible to find any empathy. Everyone here chose duty; love was always an afterthought.

Caleb left the shed without another word, carrying off the rubber tubing and cone. He had not called on her again since. In fact, she did not see him again until he surprised her and caught her arm inside the hospital entryway. She was even more surprised by how happy she felt in seeing him. Maybe love was stronger than duty.

"Caleb, what are you doing here?"

Caleb laughed, "You didn't think I would miss out on the day you got your arm back, did you? Besides, once you're free of this," he tapped her cast, "I have something amazing to show you!"

He was so frustrating. Was he really standing there flirting without even a hint of acknowledging their last discussion? Did he still intend on convincing her to marry him? Part of her wished he would, and she did not want him to leave; the other part was still anguishing over the sense of purpose her grandmother's prophecy had given her.

"What is it? Some more carts? Sprites that need alterations? Does the Culture guild need me to fashion spades and shears for them?" She loved the thought of a fresh project with two free hands.

"Spades and what?" Caleb shook his head with genuine mirth. "No, none of that. No more guessing. You're not going to ruin my surprise. C'mon, let's go get your arm free."

He pulled Mallory down the corridor to the lobby and the reception desk. Silver sprites were running in and out of the medication room behind the desk, carting off little cups of pills on trays. An older nurse with a pixie cut of gray hair and bifocals sat at the desk, smiling and completely ignoring the sprites just like the staff used to in the days of the Dikaió.

The nurse looked at Caleb and Mallory and said, "Hello! What can I help you with?"

Mallory watched a sprite carrying a tray of medication cups run over to a pair of double doors that opened for it and disappear in the labyrinth of the hospital. Mallory asked, "So are the hospital sprites working properly again?"

The nurse looked at a sprite bringing its empty tray back to the medication room and shook her head, "Oh, heavens no—they seem to be fulfilling the same orders they were given on the night the magic ended. They carry those pills up to empty rooms, feed them to empty beds, and come back down here for more. We've got a whole team of orderlies who are just collecting the pills and bringing them back here for a pharmacist to sort out." She huffed and looked over the rims of her glasses at them, "But that's confidential, you know? Now, how can I help you two?"

Caleb grabbed Mallory's cast and held up her arm nearly toppling her over with the shift in her center of gravity. "She's ready for someone to take this thing off!"

"Name?" the nurse asked.

"Mallory Knenne," Mallory answered.

The nurse pushed her glasses up the bridge of her nose, so she could get a closer look at who she was talking to. "Hmmm . . . so, you're the one who caused all this trouble? You've been a real pain in the neck for me, you know that?"

Mallory and Caleb inhaled sharply.

"What?!" the nurse asked. "Afraid of some words, are you? If the Dikaió is really, truly gone, I can say whatever I want, and I'll tell you something," she pointed a withered finger at them, "I've never felt so free in all my life. I've had a lot going on up here," she touched her head meaningfully and then touched her mouth, "that I could never let out here. It's not such a big sacrifice if you ask me to give up a little convenience to say what you think. Not a big sacrifice at all."

Mallory smiled. She liked this nurse. "Yes, I completely agree!"

"Don't get friendly with me, Miss! That doesn't mean I think you aren't a troublemaker, putting the city in peril like you have. Just that I'm pleased to tell you as much. That's all. Now, if you'll come with me, I'll lead you to the doctor to get that cast off, and I'll mind you not to get too chatty on the way. I can't have the rest of the staff thinking we're chummy or anything, you know?"

Mallory hid her smile and pretended to button her lips. She looked at Caleb; he was staring at the old woman with his mouth agape. Mallory was probably the only other person he had heard speak her mind in his life. Mallory elbowed him gently in the ribs, and as if a spell had broken, he looked down at her. When he saw her hidden smile, his face broke into a grin, and his blue eyes twinkled. The nurse set off at a slow, hobbling pace to the same double doors they had wheeled Alex through six weeks ago.

Alex.

Mallory had wondered about how her friend was doing constantly since that night, but she had not heard any word on her condition since then. She cleared her throat and asked, "Is Alexandria Nelson out of the ICU yet?"

The old nurse answered without turning around, "That girl had a lot of troubles, but they managed to stabilize her a couple of weeks ago, sure enough. Going to have scars for life, but she'll live. Just this week she was downgraded to a regular room . . . 220 on the second floor, if memory serves. Probably won't be long now until she gets checked out of this place. Of course, that's confidential information, you know?"

Mallory and Caleb smiled at each other. Their relief was palpable. Alex was going to be okay.

"Okay, son," the old nurse said. "You'll have to wait over there in the waiting room for your girlfriend here." She pointed toward a small alcove with some uncomfortable looking rust-brown and khaki-plaid couches.

Mallory watched Caleb walk toward the room and thought he would likely be quite comfortable over there on the couches. It would be just like the old couch in the Book Club. The Book Club was something Mallory had thought a lot about over the last few weeks. With the city needing more old magic, she had desperately wanted to go to the Administrator's attic to raid the collection of books locked away up there, but under what pretense could she go? The general sentiment of being anti-book had likely intensified among the City Council and the ruling class after another book had been to blame for the current crisis facing the city. She was still certain that if they knew there were at least a hundred volumes hidden away, they would take them out and destroy them—even if they held the keys to keeping the city alive. Now that she knew Alex was going to be getting out of the hospital soon, there was a chance to get to the books again, and together maybe the three of them could figure out some solutions to the new problems that losing the Dikaió had created.

The nurse pulled Mallory through a door, breaking her train of thought slightly. They entered a bright, artificially-lit hallway full of doors and no windows. Doctor Navarro was just walking out of a door on the left, her jacket and stethoscope swinging in the speed of her exit. She spotted Mallory and the old nurse and yelled, "Oh, you're ready to get that cast off, are you?"

Mallory nodded.

"Put her in 17. I'll be there in just a minute. I need to get a saw."

Mallory's eyebrows raised. "A saw?"

The nurse herded her toward the room with a smile. "'Course, honey! How do you think casts come off? Used to be the sprites would handle the sawing. They have little spinning blades. But we wouldn't trust them not to take your arm with it, so now the doctors are sawing things themselves. Don't worry, there've only been a few nicks. Nothing serious. And besides, if the doctor does cut too deep, you're in a hospital—we'll fix it right up!"

Mallory's eyes widened to match her raised eyebrows, but there did not turn out to be much to worry about. Doctor Navarro appeared with a small handsaw and hacked the cast off with no muss. A cleaning sprite appeared out of nowhere and vacuumed up the pieces of cast, chips of bark, a butter knife, and plaster powder off the floor then disappeared just as quickly. She looked at her right arm, and a stranger's arm was in its place. The arm was pale white and slightly shriveled. She wiggled her fingers and marveled that the wiggling mass of flesh was even attached to her. Then pins and needles rushed through her hand. She squirmed and shook her fingers trying to get rid of the sensation.

Doctor Navarro nodded, "You might notice a bit of tingling as more blood flow reaches your fingers. Make sure you get some sun, but not too much, because you don't want a burn. Before you know it, you won't be able to tell the difference. Also, please wash that arm now. There's a sink and soap right over there." She plugged her nose and waved her hand in front of her face.

Mallory lifted her newly-freed right arm to her nose, and it smelled a bit like a piece of musty old cheese. She jumped up and ran to the sink and started washing, and washing, and washing. Even with the hospital's antiseptic soap, it was hard to get the musty smell off her arm, but eventually her arm at least smelled more like soap than a dirty sock. When she turned around, Doctor Navarro was gone, and the old nurse was standing impatiently by the door. Mallory quickly wiped around the sink, and the nurse led Mallory back to the waiting room and Caleb.

Caleb was sitting in the plaid chair, slumping with his shoulders hunched up by his ears and his legs spread out. His hands were clasped on top of his chest, and he was staring at the Dikaió ceiling light intently. Mallory looked up and saw the object of Caleb's interest. A green and blue dragonfly had slipped inside the hospital, and it was perched upside down on the light. The girl and the dragonfly regarded one another for a moment; its small globular eyes tracking her movements, gauging the threat she might pose. Mallory's eyes traced the feathery veins in the dragonfly's wings in fascination. Her chest tightened, and she thought of her grandmother and about the curse she had put on her, which was now the whole city's curse. She wished she were a child again without the burden of duty, when love ruled every moment of the day, and her dreams were more real than life.

Caleb looked up then and noticed Mallory standing in the room. "Ewww! Your arm's all white and shriveled. It looks like a snakeskin!" he yelled.

Her eyes met his, and she smiled. "You want to touch it?" She reached out with her shriveled hand and flexed her fingers.

"No way!" He waved his hands to ward her off.

"It wants to touch you, Caleb Aiworth!" She ran for him, arm outstretched. He tried to melt out of the chair and roll away from her, but she pinned him with her knee in an instant, rubbing her white arm up and down his face while he squealed and squirmed. She laughed triumphantly, and soon his squeals turned into laughter too. Then Mallory sat up, still pinning Caleb with her knee, both of them laughing hysterically.

The old nurse cleared her throat behind them. Mallory had forgotten she had walked her to the waiting room and looked back at the nurse, flushing. The old woman was standing in the doorway with her arms crossed; her eyebrows were furrowed and her upper lip was curled in disgust. Mallory looked back down at Caleb, expecting even more amusement on his part. He always enjoyed making adults feel uncomfortable. Bright red color had blushed up through his cheeks, and there was embarrassment in his eyes. With a quick twist of his core and a shrug of his shoulders, he brushed Mallory off him. She felt her center of balance shift twice as Caleb bucked, and she spun through the air, landing sprawled out on the floor.

"Oof!" she exclaimed and just lay there looking up at the Dikaió light. The dragonfly was still there staring down at her; its perch unperturbed by the commotion below. Her grandmother's winged messenger looked down at her with the same disgust the old nurse had on her face. It brushed its arms on its mouth and seemed to whisper the word 'duty' to the girl on the floor. Mallory's eyebrows furrowed, and she stuck her tongue out at the dragonfly.

Meanwhile, Caleb jumped up, dusting himself off, and then he offered Mallory a hand to help her off the floor. His eyes were focused on the corner of the room to avoid the eyes of both the nurse and the girl he loved. Mallory looked from the dragonfly to Caleb's hand and back again. She felt the decision before she made it, and she grabbed his hand with her shriveled white one and started to pull herself up. Her weight made Caleb look down at her momentarily, and when he saw which arm he was holding, he closed his eyes and sighed heavily. Mallory smirked at the snoopy, old nurse still staring down at the two of them. The nurse rolled her eyes, and then walked away leaving Mallory and Caleb alone in the waiting room.

When Mallory was right-side up, Caleb took back his hand and wiped it on his pants. "There's something I wanted to show you," he said without the earlier enthusiasm.

Mallory nodded but said, "First, I want to stop by and see Alex."

"I don't have a lot of time, Mal. There's a lot to get done

around the city. Can you see Alex another time?"

"Have you seen her since that night, Caleb?"

"No, I haven't had time."

"We're her friends. Besides, she's still the heir to the Administration. The Triad must remain united, right? Could the city really stand a crisis of future leadership after the crisis it just faced?"

Caleb looked down at his shoes, clearly uncomfortable to have his father's words thrown back at him. "Okay, Mal. Let's go see her."

The Dikaió elevators were still running at the hospital, so they were able to rapidly reach the second floor and room 220. The door was open, but Mallory still knocked quietly. There was no answer. Mallory poked her head into the room. It looked very similar to the room she had been in just six weeks ago, but the furniture was flipped and situated on opposite sides of the room. Mallory glanced at the whiteboard and confirmed that Alex's name was listed as the patient in residence. The other half of the board was blank, so Alex had the room to herself. Mallory walked cautiously into the room. The bed nearest the door was empty, and the curtain separating the beds was drawn. "Alex?" Mallory called as she stepped around the curtain to see her friend.

Alex startled at Mallory's voice. She clearly had not heard the soft knock on the door, and she quickly grabbed a white knit blanket and threw it over her arm, but not before Mallory saw the white and red welts that ran like intertwined rivers up and down her forearm and onto the top of her hand. Otherwise, she looked good. Her face and her other arm were spared from any lasting marring from the fire. Her legs were covered by another knit blanket, so it was impossible to know if Alex had sustained any other scarring, but it looked like it was mostly the arm that had been trapped under the burning debris. Mallory's gaze moved up Alex's body until she was looking at her friend's face, and her friend looked back at her with embarrassment. It was nearly the same look Caleb had given the old nurse in the waiting room.

Mallory's chest tightened, and tears sprang into her eyes. "Oh, Alex! I'm so glad you're okay!" She ran to the side of the bed with Alex's good arm and fell on her friend in an unabashed embrace. Alex began to cry, and the two girls held each other for awhile, communicating without words.

Caleb cleared his throat and kicked at some imaginary dirt on the floor. "I'm glad you're okay, too. Any room for another friend in this hug?"

Alex nodded, knocking off her knitted blanket as she reached for Caleb with her scarred arm. Then she realized what she'd done and tried to get it back beneath the blanket.

Caleb laughed, "I already had to touch Mallory's creepy arm, I don't mind getting hugged by yours, too."

"What?" Alex looked perplexed, and then looked at Mallory's white arm draped across her chest. "Gross, Mallory! Why?" She squirmed a bit like she was trying to get away, and Caleb laughed again. Then he grabbed Alex's scarred arm and threw it around his neck, and the future of the city embraced in the hospital bed together for a time, swearing their fidelity to one another, imperfections and all, without speaking a single word.

While the friends embraced, a medic sprite whirred into the room carrying a silver tray with three paper cups of medication on it. They watched as it sidled up next to the vacant bed in the room. A long silver arm with a pincer extended out from its back, grasped the paper cup, and held it gingerly up to the bed waiting for the nonexistent patient to open its invisible mouth, which the sprite promptly dumped the pills into. The pills landed softly on the pillow, and the sprite zipped over to the door, dropped the paper cup into the waste bin, and left the room. Immediately a female orderly dressed in white walked briskly into the room. She nodded at the three friends, who were locked in an embrace and staring at her wide-eyed. She scooped up the medication, dropped it into a small box that she was carrying and ran back out the door, chasing the medic sprite.

The three friends fell apart from each other laughing. Caleb clutched his sides and guffawed himself off the bed onto the floor. Mallory stood up, wheezing and trying desperately to catch her breath and stop the giggling. Alex laid in the bed nearly screaming with laughter. Just as they were starting to calm down, Caleb crawled over to the empty bed, got up on his knees and pretended to throw medication at the pillow. The teens fell into fits of laughter again.

Time seemed to slow down for the old friends as they laughed, but soon the laughter died down, and the room dimmed with the gravity of the situation. Those medic sprites used to help people, and now they were not only useless, they were a nuisance—dangerous even. If one gave the wrong medication to the wrong patient, it could be lethal.

Alex began to cry again. "I worried that no one would ever come to see me at all after what we did," she said through sniffles and tears. "My grandfather came once when I got out of the ICU. He wanted to know if we'd really dropped the book into the fire. Once he knew for sure, he left. I called after him. I wanted to know if my parents were coming to see me. He turned around and looked at me as if I were a monster for even asking. Oh Mal, I'll never forget the look in his eyes. I think he hates me. I think my parents hate me. Maybe the whole city hates me!"

Mallory lowered herself back to the bed and took hold of her hand. She wanted to say it was not true, but she had been out there in the streets and seen the hate directed toward her.

It was impossible to know how many were aware of Alex's involvement, but if they knew, they probably did hate her.

Caleb stood behind Mallory and said, "Alex . . .", but that was as far as he got. Mallory knew him well enough to know that he was too honest to lie, even to comfort his friends. He had no doubt overheard people talking: the City Council, his parents, their parents.

"Well," Mallory demanded. "What are they saying about us, Caleb? You might as well tell us; we'll find out soon enough anyway."

Caleb shifted uncomfortably. "No one hates you, not so much anyway. They're just scared. My father says that when people get scared, they say and do things they don't mean."

"What do they say, Caleb?" Mallory pressed.

Caleb sighed. "I'm not going to repeat it, Mallory. They don't mean it."

"Are you scared? Have you said things you don't mean?" Mallory's gray eyes flashed as she stared Caleb down.

Caleb met her gaze with a strength of his own. He was the only person besides Mallory's grandmother who had never tried to change her and was completely at ease with both her curse and the indomitable force of her will that she had developed in compensation. The corner of his mouth turned up in a half-grin. "I've never said anything I didn't mean, Mal. And I still want what I want."

Alex's voice sounded uncomfortable, "What is happening?"

Caleb looked past Mallory, still half-grinning. "Mallory and I are getting married."

Alex laughed nervously, looking up at Mallory, "What?"

Mallory shrugged and plopped down on the side of Alex's bed. She flicked her curly brown hair haughtily, "Caleb proposed a couple of weeks ago, but I turned him down."

"I find that hard to believe," Alex said.

Mallory crossed her legs and put both hands on her knee and made a pouting face at Caleb. "What? That Caleb would propose?"

"No, that you would turn him down!" Alex pushed herself up farther in the bed and stared wide-eyed at the two of them. "Why would you do that? I thought you wanted to marry him?"

"I never said that!"

Alex shrugged, "Well, you sure didn't want your new sister to marry him!"

Caleb clapped, "I knew it! Why do you have to play hard to get, Mallory?"

Mallory jumped off the bed and yelled, "I'm not playing!" She ran past Caleb toward the door. Just before she left, she turned and said, "Sometimes things aren't meant to be. I wish you both would just leave it alone." She could not remember which way the elevators were, and she could hear Caleb calling her name in the room, so she ran to her right without looking back. She burst through a pair of double doors at the end of the hallway. The elevators were not this way, but she really did not want to go back to all the questions she could not answer, so she wandered deeper into the labyrinth of the hospital corridors searching for a stairwell.

Every hallway looked the same: pale Dikaió lights,

white-tiled floors, wooden-paneled doors, various pieces of equipment littering the hallways, men and women dressed in identical hospital scrubs scurrying about, popping in and out of doors. It was all a blur. Then she heard a familiar voice say her name, and she slowed her pace and looked around. The old nurse that had led her to the room to get her cast taken off was standing at a nurse's station talking with two other female nurses, a woman in a suit with her hair pinned tight in a bun, and an older, well-dressed man. The man she recognized immediately; it was Alex's grandfather, the Administrator. They had not noticed her, so she pulled herself up against the wall and listened.

The old nurse's mouth was running: "... those two love birds came to get Miss Knenne's cast cut off. They were laughing and getting very personal with each other, the way young'uns do when they're sweet on each other. I took her back to one of the rooms, the doctor cut her arm loose, and then the next thing I know they were tussling in the waiting room. Miss Knenne was on top of the Governor's boy and just before they started kissin', I made sure they knew I was still there watchin' the whole thing. I don't mind young love, but this ain't the place for it. And I don't mind sayin' that just because the Dikaió's broken, don't mean I want to see the Triad taken over by two houses, which is why I called the Chief Medical Officer here to send for you, your Honor. Seems like the Administrator's house would be worse off with a match like that."

Mallory's cheeks flushed. That old bat had the nerve to gossip about the heirs of the Triad? She was ready to go tell her exactly where she could go when the Administrator responded, and Mallory froze in place: "I thank you, Ma'am. You were right to call. I agree that Ms. Knenne and Mr. Aiworth should not be matched, though I do not think my house would be weakened for such a pairing. Strengthened, I should think."

"Well, you certainly can say that again," the old nurse laughed. "That Knenne girl is a walking disaster. The whole city had been dreading her being the next Matriarch. She's just as likely to curse us than christen us."

A woman's voice Mallory could not place as one of the nurses or the hospital's Chief Medical Officer chimed in with a musical voice, "She's already done that, hasn't she?"

The group sounded a solemn agreement.

The old nurse addressed the Administrator, "And what of that, sir? Where's the justice for the Knenne girl? Isn't that your department? If it were one of us who'd done all this, your magistrates would have put us in stocks in the city jail, though there ain't been need for that since I was a wee girl, when those boys built that fire sprite that destroyed part of the city. Seems to me we got another arsonist with what happened to City Hall. Beggin' your pardon, sir, but why ain't the magistrates dragging her off for a trial yet?"

The Administrator responded, "I won't address the Council's business here, but rest assured, plans for redressing Miss Knenne's crimes are being discussed in earnest."

The old nurse laughed: "I suppose the Matriarch's holdin' up that process. I wouldn't want my daughter to face your justice neither. No sir, I would not."

Mallory could not listen anymore and headed back the way she had come. Eventually, she found the elevators, and absent-mindedly pushed the down button. What did the Administrator intend to do with her? Would Alex face the same punishment? The Administrator's family were probably arguing against punishing her just like Mallory's mother for Mallory. How much of this did Caleb know? Was that why he was pushing marriage now? Was it a way to protect her from justice? Did she deserve protection?

The doors to the elevator opened, and Mallory stumbled inside. She pushed up against the wood paneling on the far wall of the elevator, and leaned her head back against the cool surface, closing her eyes. In the thirty seconds that the elevator dropped to the first floor, her mind took another dark turn. Was Caleb so desperate to marry her all of a sudden because he knew what the Council was discussing? And if so, was the Administrator right in his estimation that their union would be a weakness, Dikaió or not?

Caleb would be better off without her, it would be better to let him know, but as the doors opened and she opened her eyes, the first thing she was confronted with was Caleb leaning up against the wall watching the elevator, waiting for her. Just the sight of him made her reconsider everything about their relationship and his awkward proposal again. What was wrong with her?

Caleb clearly had no useful answers for her. He smiled that lop-sided grin of his and sort of leaned his way off the wall toward her. He had the most elegantly lazy way of moving: completely carefree in every motion. She stepped off the elevator, and he sidled up beside her, near enough that she felt a quick warm breeze wave off him, but not close enough to touch her. He leaned his head down in a conspiratorial tone.

"Thought you could duck me, did you? When I found the elevator was not on the first floor, I knew you'd come down at some point."

Mallory walked down the hallway and into the lobby. "I'm really not in the mood to talk about our relationship right now, Caleb."

"That's fine," he said walking beside her. "I wanted to show you something. Remember?"

"I just want to go home. Please! Just leave me alone."

Caleb stepped forward two large steps and stood directly in Mallory's path. "You'll want to see this, Mal. It's in the dark woods."

Mallory froze and stared at him. Her mouth was agape, and she blinked several times trying to process what she had just heard. "What?" she finally managed.

"The dark woods. C'mon, I'll show you."

He turned around and started walking quickly across the lobby of the hospital toward the hallway with the only working exit. Mallory watched Caleb walking away, but she was a statue. Her mind's eye traced the shadows of the dark woods, and she imagined all the horrors they held, and fear spread like ice in her veins. Her arms and legs were stiff, wanting very much not to lead their host into an encounter with anything that required the light to keep it out of the city.

Then that portion of her mind that had always caused her

the most trouble reared up and breathed warm life into her stationary limbs. Curiosity drove her forward, first shuffling one foot after another, then running to catch up with Caleb, who had not once looked back to see if she would follow him. He knew her too well to wonder.

Mallory caught up with Caleb outside the hospital. He was heading toward the pastureland and beyond that to something he had found in the Dark Woods—something beyond the light.

"What is it, Caleb? What's out there?"

"You'll have to see it for yourself, Mallory. It's hard to believe. It really is."

They reached the fence of the pastureland, which was made of wooden beams set between wooden pillars, constructed in the time before the city's memory, like most things in the city. Over time, a few beams had rotted through, and since carpentry was a discarded art, they had been replaced by sprite steel, which did not break down or rot. Mallory wondered why they had not just replaced the whole fence, but she supposed that it would take too much steel since the pasturelands surrounded the entire circumference of the city. She looked across the pasturelands to the dark forest, and then looked to see if the herds were still staying away from the dreaded place. They had been clustering up by the fence closest to the city, but they were not there now.

About twenty cows were a couple hundred yards away from them, standing in a circle with their heads facing out. The circle was shrinking as the cows backed up towards its center. They were bellowing and waving their heads wildly.

The sharp white horns they brandished, moving back and forth tracking something in the grass around them.

Mallory felt the hairs raise on her neck when she saw them: There were silver-haired four-legged animals running on all fours around the cows, herding them into the circle with yelps and snarling. There were six of them. They had long, bushy gray tails that were all pointed upward toward the sky. Their ears were also pointed and moved about tracking the sounds of the herd. She figured they were roughly the height of a sheep, judging by their proportion compared to the cows. Whenever a cow got too close with her horns to one of the creatures, they jumped nimbly away with the speed of a rabbit, and the hair on their body bristled. They snapped at the cows with their mouths, which were also like rabbits' mouths but longer and more pronounced. Mallory could see even at this distance that their mouths were full of wickedly sharp teeth. Their incisors were especially long and curled their lips in a snarl, even when their mouths were closed. They made guttural growling noises that carried on the wind in between the fearful lowing of the cows.

Seeing a break in the snapping creatures from the dark woods, one of the cows broke ranks and started running full sprint across the pastureland. The rest of the herd took her lead, and they all started running frantically in the same direction. Mallory looked in the direction of the cows' path and saw that they were running toward a wooden pen separated from the rest of the pasture. Inside the pen stood a massive bull. He was watching his herd with fury rippling through his muscles. He paced back and forth, tossing his head, desperate to plow into the creatures.

An older cow lagged behind the fleeing herd, and the creatures from the dark woods swarmed her. Two nipped at her hind legs on either side, and two ran in front of her, steering her away from the herd with snarls and bites. The other two made a wide arc, and in a coordinated moment, the ones on her heels sank their teeth into the cow's hind quarters, and the flanking creatures converged, leaping into the air and hitting the lowing animal at caddy-corner angles, causing her to spin slightly. They latched onto her with their vicious teeth, and her front legs buckled in opposite directions under the weight of their diametric momentum. The two that had been shepherding her away from the pack dashed forward and slashed at the old girl's neck while she bellowed in terror.

Mallory bit her lip and grabbed Caleb's arm, "We have to help her!" she screamed.

Caleb looked at her wide-eyed. "What would we do? We'll get killed if we go in there!"

Mallory looked at the herd who had reached the bull, crowding up against his pen, though it offered no protection as the bull could not cross the barrier to come to their aid if he wanted to. Tears sprang to Mallory's eyes. "We've got to do something! We can't just stand here and watch."

"Look!" Caleb pointed.

Flying across the pastureland toward the suffering heifer were two silver culture sprites. Their silver arms began to lengthen as they drew nearer, and two of the dark-woods creatures spun around, growling; their fangs barred; red drool dripping from their chins. They were guarding their prize from the silver intruders in the pastureland. The sprites' arms were now several feet long and trailing behind them in the grass. They stopped in front of the creatures. Then, in a synchronized gesture, they each raised one of their long arms, which arched up in the air and back down like a limp rope. The sprites brought their arms down lightning fast, and the silver-rope arms whipped out at the creatures almost faster than Mallory's eyes could track. It took a second at this distance for the sound to reach Mallory and Caleb, but their motion was followed by a crack like thunder and a sputtering of half-yelps. Bits of gray fur puffed up from the path of the sprites' whips. The creatures tried to turn and run, but within two steps they had fallen over in the grass, dead.

The other four creatures that had been biting at the wounded heifer sat up at the sound and watched their comrades fall before the sprites. They hunched down and growled but began to walk backwards slowly keeping their eyes trained on the sprites. The sprites circled around the injured animal, and then raised all four of their whip-like arms and flew quickly toward the remaining creatures. The growling creatures turned and started running back toward the dark woods, yelping to each other—but they were not faster than the sprites that cut them down within ten feet of the wounded heifer. The sprites then seemed to scan the area, turning this way and that, and then they turned around to the animal on the ground: It was no longer calling out in pain, but just lying there in the grass.

"I've never seen the culture sprites kill an animal before,"

Caleb whispered.

"C'mon," Mallory called, climbing over the fence and running toward the wounded cow.

"Wait, Mallory!" Caleb yelled after her. It was not any use to try and stop Mallory once she was in motion, and she knew that Caleb would be right behind her when she got to the injured animal.

The sprites' arms had shortened to their normal length. One of them was spraying something on the cow's wounds, and the other had a needle and thread and was stitching up some of the worst injuries. It only took a few moments, and they had closed up the open wounds, and pushed the animal back to her feet. She was unsteady, but they pushed her along toward the herd that was still clustered around the bull's pen, looking wild-eyed.

Mallory walked along beside them, not sure what she would do if the cow fell back down, but she desperately wanted to help. When they reached the herd, the injured cow pushed herself into the comfort of the herd that parted for her, and the sprites then prodded some of the other cows to move in and close the gaps around her protectively, shutting Mallory out. She pushed through the herd anyway, being jostled and lowed at angrily, but she was determined to check on the cow that had been attacked.

She got through to the bull's pen and still did not see the cow or the sprites. She stood in the midst of the jostling herd, nearly overwhelmed by their caustic smell like a mix of hay, multivitamins, and just a hint of something sweet like coconut. Their breath was heavy and hot around her, and everywhere she turned were horns, hides, and wild eyes. Suddenly, she had a deep sense of claustrophobia, and she needed to get out of the middle of these animals, so she ducked through the wooden railings of the pen in front of her.

She took a deep breath of the open air. Another deep breath sounded near her that had not originated from her, and it was followed by a loud snort and a thud. She turned to see the massive bull just a few yards away from her in the pen. Its muscles looked like someone had stuffed too many pillows inside a single pillowcase, and they shuddered under taut skin as if they wanted to break out and kill Mallory themselves. The bull's horns were much larger than the cows, and they were twisted forward for spearing. Its body heaved with fits of ragged, angry breaths. The bull's eyes were rolling in their sockets, bloodshot with murderous intent, but they were rolling in Mallory's general direction. Mallory felt herself freeze, just like when she was on the operating table, but there was no crazy laughter around her. The bull roared and charged.

Mallory felt someone grab her by the shoulder and the scruff of her shirt, yanking her hard under the beams of the pen's fence. The bull's horns scraped across the wooden beams, showering splinters where she had just been standing. Its body pressed against the fence, and Mallory could see the beams bend under its weight. She was getting pulled backward farther and farther away from the fence and the danger of the bull, back into the thick of the herd. Part of her logical mind knew what happened next was crazy, but when she was back in the midst of the herd, the same claustrophobia she had felt before hit her, and she began frantically clawing back toward the bull's pen, but she could not break free of her rescuer's grip.

When she was finally pulled free into the open space of the pastureland, she took a deep breath and felt her fears settle down. She turned around expecting to see Caleb behind her, but instead she found one of the silver culture sprites. It had saved her from the bull's charge. The other one was holding Caleb back from running into the herd of cows. His face was full of panic, and he was batting at the thing with his fists and screaming, "Mallory? Mallory?"

It felt good to know he intended to risk his life to save her, but she felt better letting him know she was safe before he got past the sprite and tried to fight a bull for no reason.

"Caleb!" she called.

He turned his head toward her voice, and the moment he saw her, his body relaxed with relief. He backed up, and shook loose from the sprite, which seemed to understand that he was not going to try to fight the bull anymore and let him go.

"Mallory!" he called. "Are you okay?"

"Yes, I think so." She looked down at herself and could find nothing amiss, save a bit of mud from the pastureland caking her shoes. Well, she hoped it was mud anyway. "I'm fine."

Caleb crossed the distance between them in what seemed like two steps and pulled her into an embrace. Mallory tensed for a moment, wanting to pull back and define their relationship once and for all, but it did feel good to know with such certainty that he genuinely cared for her. She had not felt this feeling for weeks: the feeling of being in the arms of family.

Caleb pulled back and looked into her eyes. "You sure you're okay?"

"Yes, I'm fine!"

"Okay, let's get you home then." He turned toward the city and started to take a step.

Mallory grabbed his arm and pulled him to a stop. "Isn't there something you wanted to show me? In the dark woods?" She pointed toward the woods.

"That was before I knew there were creatures like these lurking in there. I think it's better to take you back."

"The creatures are dead, Caleb." Mallory walked over to one of the bodies of the dead monsters. It lay motionless. Its gray fur was stained with blood, and a long red tongue lolled over its teeth and out of its mouth.

"Mallory, be careful!"

Mallory laughed, "You're not my mother, Caleb Aiworth! Now, come here and look at this thing." Caleb moved in for a closer look. "See?" Mallory motioned. "It's just an animal, not a monster."

"It's a monstrous animal," Caleb corrected.

"Maybe, but they're dead now. C'mon, show me what we came all the way out here for, so we didn't make this trip for nothing."

Caleb stretched his head slowly to the side until his neck cracked. "Fine! If I found what I think I found, these things just prove how much we need them."

Caleb ran toward the dark woods, and Mallory ran after

him. The shadows of the trees were growing longer as the day descended into the evening hours, so they hit darkness before they came to the tree line. The temperature around them dropped ten degrees in the shade, and Mallory, even though she was hot from running, felt the hairs on her neck rise again as the chill ran over her body. There was a red strip of fabric tied to a broken tree branch laid up against one of the massive trees, and Caleb was running toward it. He must have marked the place where whatever he wanted to show her lay inside the dark woods. He slowed down when he got to the branch and waited for Mallory to catch up.

"It's not far inside the forest: just a few feet actually," he said in hushed tones.

They walked around the tree that Caleb had marked, and Mallory marveled at the diameter of its trunk. If she were to hug one side of the tree and Caleb the other, she was not sure they could reach each other's hands. Maybe with Alex they could encircle the tree, but she was doubtful. The next tree they encountered was about eight feet away, and it was just as big as the first. Mallory looked up into the canopy and was fascinated to find that the trees' branches were not entangled in one another. Between the leaves that traced through the top of the forest, there were clear lines of sky showing like grout between the cobblestones of the outer walls of the Matriarch's house. The trees seemed to respect each other's space, and Mallory worried how they might feel about her and Caleb trespassing in their domain.

Caleb stopped and said, "Here it is!"

Mallory looked down from the canopy and found herself

confronted by a sprite. It was old. It had begun to rust, and holes had broken through its exterior in places, but bits of silver sprite steel still shone through the rust. Compared to the trees, it was miniscule, but compared to Caleb and Mallory, it was gigantic. Mallory figured the old sprite must be twelve feet high, at least.

Caleb ran over and pointed at the rusted holes. "Looks like they're not indestructible after all, right? Also check out the top; this one has a head and eyes."

Mallory had noticed. It looked agitated, annoyed. Forever angry about some distant past. Its arms were quite large with nozzles for hands, and hoses ran from the nozzles to large packs on its back. "For water, do you think, or . . .?"

"Fire," Caleb said matter-of-factly. "I've looked through the fire sprite book in the Book Club. It's nearly identical."

"What's it doing out here?" Mallory asked walking around the sprite, looking into holes in its armor, and picking out bits of plant life that had grown into it over the years.

"I wondered that too. Protection, I think, and now that I've seen the kinds of creatures living in this forest, I wonder if our ancestors used it to burn back the forest before the light was invented to keep the city safe. Once the light was built, they wouldn't need it anymore, so they left it out here to rust."

Mallory bit her lip and tilted her head, considering Caleb's idea. Then she turned to face him and smiled deviously. "Why Caleb Aiworth, you've had a logical idea. I think you may be embracing the role of Dikaió Chorus after all!"

The corners of Caleb's eyes crinkled as his face brightened in a lop-sided grin. "Does that mean you'll marry me?"

Mallory laughed heartily, "I don't know about that, but I'll help you figure out how to get this sprite up and running again to protect the city from those animals in the forest."

Caleb nodded, more solemn now. He looked up at the fire sprite, shadows encompassing its rusty hull as the sun set, and said, "That's what I hoped you'd say."

Caleb and Mallory strained under the weight of the fire sprite. They had broken it into pieces and divided it into two Chorus carts that they were hauling across the open pastureland. Mallory felt her heart racing, partly because of the labor, but mostly she felt nervous turning her back to the dark woods—especially at this hour as the sun began to sink behind the tree canopy, and the forest's long shadows reached out for them across the pastureland. She could feel the temperature drop as the darkness overtook them, and she glanced furtively behind her, half expecting a pack of gray creatures to be bounding after them, fangs bared. There was nothing behind them except a single silver culture sprite standing guard. Another was spaced five-hundred feet to the

North, and another five-hundred feet beyond that, all the way around the city. The Culture Co-op had no way of controlling the sprites to take these positions, but after the attack on the herds, the sprites had just headed to the pastureland and taken up guard positions on their own. Only about half the culture sprites were left in the city for agricultural purposes, and they were struggling to keep up with food production and grooming services like lawn care. The City Council had voted to impose rationing at the Farmer's Market, and the entire city was now living on sustenance rations only. Apparently, the culture sprites' duty to protect the cattle was a higher priority in the Dikaió than feeding the citizens.

Mallory's stomach growled and then seemed to flip over in her abdomen at the thought of food. She had never known what real hunger was in her entire life. There had always been food available in her house and in the market, and she was surprised at the effects of the feeling on her: At times, she felt utterly exhausted like she could sleep forever, and at other times she felt irritated at the slightest offense. Just minutes before they started trekking across the pastureland, Caleb had told her to be careful in lifting the fire sprite's nozzle into her cart, and she had yelled, "Shut up! I'm not incapable, no matter what you think!"

He had just stood there blinking like he had looked into the sun for a second too long, and then turned back to loading some more sprite pieces into his cart, murmuring under his breath, "Okay, crazy lady."

Mallory roared at him and threw the nozzle into the cart hard enough to crack a bit of its tip off. Caleb sucked in his breath hard, and Mallory looked away from him, peering deeper into the dark woods. That's when she saw it: There was a glint of metal that she could see by one of the trees in the distance. She started walking toward it, and Caleb was by her side in an instant with his hand on her arm. "Mal, I'm sorry. I didn't mean it. Please, don't go deeper into the forest. We're too far from the culture sprites already. C'mon back."

She brushed his hand off her arm and said, "I know, but look." She pointed in the direction of the metallic object.

He saw it too, and he picked up a large piece of sprite steel to use as a club, if needed. "C'mon. Stay close beside me."

Mallory grabbed her own piece of sprite steel and walked close to Caleb. They picked their way through the undergrowth of the forest, swinging their sprite steel like machetes to get through particularly dense sections. Then the metal took shape: Yet another giant fire sprite stood in the midst of the trees, nearly identical to the one they had just finished dismantling. Rust had punctured holes in its sprite steel, and the forest had grown in and around it as if it had been sitting there for centuries. While Caleb rooted around this fire sprite, Mallory peered farther into the forest, and she spotted another one—though that one was laying on the ground under a fallen tree. The tree looked to have gotten the better of the rusted fire sprite as bits of the sprite were scattered all over the forest floor. Beyond that, she could barely make out another metal something, and she assumed it was another fire sprite. Each fire sprite was about five-hundred feet from the next. She could tell that they were that far apart because when Mallory narrowed her eyes and looked out of the dark woods toward the pastureland, she could see that they were lined up perfectly with the culture sprites.

"Caleb," she pulled him away from his investigation and showed him the other fire sprites, and then pointed to the culture sprites in the pastureland behind them. "They look like they're facing each other."

"Huh?" Caleb scratched his head, glancing from the fire sprites to the culture sprites and back again. "I wonder why."

Mallory bit her lip and tilted her head in thought. "Maybe the culture sprites are trying to make up for the lack of fire sprites in pushing the dark woods back? Maybe that's why they're lined up where the fire sprites should be standing. I guess they could use their spinning blades to trim back any dark trees that try to root themselves in the pastureland?"

Caleb scratched his head some more and then shrugged. "That could be, I suppose. It's odd that the fire sprites are facing the city, though. Why wouldn't they be facing the woods?"

Mallory did not have time to process the question as Caleb let loose a hoot and a whistle. "Look, this one has a nozzle that you haven't broken yet!"

Mallory glared at him. "What!?"

"Well, uh, I mean, if we're missing parts on one, we can come and get them off another. Maybe between a few of them we can get a couple up and running."

Mallory answered him with a glare, and Caleb squirmed nervously before her icy gaze until finally he shrugged helplessly and laughed. Mallory felt her rage subside momentarily, and she finally chuckled, too. Then they had pulled the nozzle off the second fire sprite and walked back to their carts.

Now, in the pastureland as they breathed heavily, hauling their carts toward the city, Mallory's joviality had passed. They had spent too much time looking at the ruins of the fire sprites, and the sun was sinking fast. The sky was turning purple, and the reddish-orange rays of the sun barely shone out from behind the trees at their backs. Trudging over the pastureland struggling with the weight of her cart had ignited the hunger in Mallory's stomach once more. She felt both scared and angry, and if she was honest with herself, she wished that things could go back to normal. She was tired of living life without the Dikaió. Even if she could not use it, everything had been easier when there were others around her that could. She thought of how Alex was always trying to fix her problems with a little magic, and she understood Alex so much better now. Mallory's desire to know the power of the Dikaió was even greater now that there were so many people who were helpless without it. She wished she could just say a word and fix the city's problems quickly without so much hard labor.

To his credit, Caleb seemed to be thriving in the hard work of the Dikaió-free environment. He seemed to really enjoy rolling up his sleeves and getting lost in a project, using just his intellect and brawn. The boy who used to slough off even the hint of work—back when work was as easy as learning the right words—seemed to be quietly enjoying physical labor. In this outdoor classroom, he appeared to be growing bigger and more imposing both in body and mind every day beneath the weight of this new Dikaió-free educa-tion. He trudged across the pastureland, one foot in front of the other, never looking from the right to the left, absorbed in his single-minded determination.

"What are you thinking about?" Mallory asked.

"Hmmm . . . ?" Caleb muttered.

"What are you thinking about?" Mallory repeated.

"Oh, I was just remembering my grandfather telling me stories when I was little," he said.

Mallory waited for him to continue, but he seemed to have fallen back into deep contemplation. Finally, when it seemed he really was not going to elaborate, she said, "My grandmother used to tell me stories about the old days too. Even some about your grandfather."

Caleb looked at her now. "Like what?"

"Like how he stopped a fire sprite from destroying the city when she was a little girl."

Caleb tilted his head to the left a little, and his eyes drifted up toward the sky as if he were watching the scenes of his childhood play out on the backdrop of the evening's crimson clouds. "Yeah, he told me that one too."

"My grandmother said he was amazing—fearless even—confronting the sprite even though he might have died."

"That's not the way my grandfather told the story."

"What do you mean?"

"Sometimes when I was little and I got scared, I would go find my grandfather and talk to him. He used to sit in the big recliner by the fireplace in the Governor's house, pull me up on his lap, put his hand on my shoulder and look right into my eyes. Then he would say, 'Caleb, I remember being scared when I was your age. There are a lot of things that are unknown in this world when you're young. The older you get, the more you know, and the less you have to be scared of—but that doesn't mean there isn't anything to be scared of when you're old.'

"'Like the fire sprite?' I asked.

"My grandfather smiled, but then his eyes drifted to the fireplace. The fire burned in his irises, a reflection of those houses burning on that distant day. As the blaze in his eyes deepened, his grip on my shoulder tightened—not enough to hurt—but enough to be uncomfortable. His mouth worked wordlessly, and his tongue dampened his dry lips. Long, worn worry lines deepened, and his shoulders slumped; he seemed to wither like a stalk of grass without water. Then he spoke, 'It must have been twelve-foot tall, at least tall enough to reach the tops of the houses. It glowed like the embers in the fireplace,' he pointed at red-hot coals below the logs and then continued, 'Fire sprayed from the spouts on its arms in bright arcs, like a rainbow after a storm. Droplets of fire fell from the arcs into the street, running in raging rivulets down toward the gutters. I could feel the heat from their streams mixed with the heat from the burning houses rolling over me in waves.'

"He broke out in a sweat despite the chill in the room. His eyes darted around the fireplace tracking the fiery phantoms. His voice quivered as he continued, 'The crowds were growing as the city gathered around. The smoke had drawn them, and the giant sprite spraying hot death all around it kept them there—transfixed. They had their own heat, pressing forward on every side. As more came, they pushed against each other, vying for a glimpse of what had caused the commotion. Children clung to their parents' legs. Some were crying. Some were screaming. No one turned away. Even the City Council with the Matriarch and the Administrator were there—our entire city's leadership drawn to danger like moths.

"'I could not blame them. Fire is an ancient magic that preexisted even the old magic still in the city, and that sort of power mesmerizes us. Its heat and light provide much of what we need to live, but fire can quickly extinguish that same life. We can barely contain it much less control it. Yet, that sprite wielded the ancient magic like a child's toy, haphazardly burning everything around it. I tell you, Caleb, there was intent in that sprite: It burned those houses on purpose, and it did not care if there were people left inside them or not. I don't know how I could tell, but I could just sense an aura of evil about the thing.'

"He shuddered and then lifted his withered hands, palms facing each other, trembling slightly, then he started moving them together slowly as if about to clap. 'The sprite continued to move toward the crowd, and the crowd thronged toward the sprite; the citizens in front were pushed forward by the curiosity behind them. I could see that eventually the two were going to meet in a fiery collision, and that a lot of citizens would not be able to get away alive.

"'I yelled for them to get back, to run away—but the crowd was so loud already, the fires were roaring, and then there were the shrieks of the sprite every time it sprayed fire into the sky, like metal slowly scraping across metal. The Administrator signaled to his magistrates, and they aimed their weapons at the monstrosity. I could see the flashes in their muzzles, and some tiny sparks flashed on the hull of the sprite, but even the normally loud booms of the magistrates' weapons were washed out by the din of the crowd and the sprite. If it noticed the projectiles, it did not indicate concern. Instead, it continued its onslaught of the neighborhood, slowly advancing toward the crowd.

"'I could tell that the people needed something to get their attention—some way to quiet their shouts—so they could hear my warnings. I stepped a few feet toward the sprite. I figured my foolishness would make them hush, and it did. The noise of the crowd ended immediately. I intended to turn around then and repeat my orders, but--.' His hands froze in place, and he looked from one to the other. His eyes were wide. His dry, cracked lips parted slightly, and he licked them, but it did not seem to relieve them. 'The sprite noticed me. It locked me in its horrible gaze. That blazing countenance measuring my fear: the same fear that now froze me in place, face-to-face with blazing death.'

"I shifted my weight on his leg and leaned toward him, 'And that's when you said the words?'

"He nodded, 'Yes, I said the words.'

"I jumped off his lap then and pointed at the inferno in the fireplace: 'DIKAIÓ FIRE CEASE!' My voice echoed through the house, but the fire continued to crackle softly.

"My grandfather grabbed me from behind and turned

me around violently. His eyes were wild. 'Stop it!' he yelled. 'I said the words and the fire sprite stopped, but if it hadn't . . .' His wild eyes turned slowly toward the fire. 'If it hadn't, none of us would have survived. How could we have stopped it? How could we? The old magic has been lost for so long, and those boys summoned what ought not to have existed. We destroyed it in the molten depths of the Rookery. Every evil piece of it. But if we hadn't; if it hadn't stopped--.' Tears flowed down his cheeks, and he let go of me to cover his face with his hands.

"I stumbled backward, looking up at my hero—the city's hero—and feeling uncomfortably embarrassed. I was embarrassed because he made me think I had done something wrong in celebrating his victory, but also embarrassed for him, old and cowering before a distant memory. No, my grandfather was no hero. He feared even the memory of the fire sprite."

Mallory had been growing more and more uneasy as Caleb told his story. They were near to the relative safety of the city, but she stopped pushing her cart and whistled to Caleb to stop. It took him a moment to break free of the memory, but he turned to look at her. "What?"

"What do you mean 'what'? You're telling me that your heroic grandfather was terrified of these things, and you want to go put them together?"

Caleb set his Chorus cart down. He pointed back toward the dark woods, the details of which were now completely obfuscated by the darkness of night. "Those woods are the threat now. Those monsters that tried to kill the cow are the threat. I am not my grandfather. I've—We've been through fire. The loss of City Hall shows what kind of danger we're in without the light—without the Dikaió. I am not my grandfather, Mallory. Fire can be controlled."

Mallory fidgeted, and she glanced back at the woods. She felt them return her gaze, but was it the woods or the giant sprites in them that were watching her?

"What if you're wrong, Caleb? What if we're making the same mistake those boys made all those years ago? What if, without the Dikaió, they can't be stopped?"

"That's a lot of 'what ifs,' Mal. Here's one for you: What if those creatures come in the night and start attacking children instead of cows?"

"The culture sprites will stop them."

"What if they don't? These are things we need to be thinking about as the future leaders of the city. As the Governor's heir, I'm going to put together this fire sprite to protect the city, not to harm it. Are you with me, Mal?"

Mallory bit her lip and tucked her curly locks behind her ear. There was more that Caleb was not telling her. She had known him long enough to know when he was keeping secrets. Still, the sprite parts in the Chorus cart called to her, and when she looked down at them, she could see how they might connect together. Caleb's challenge merged with the puzzle of the work, and Mallory felt herself giving into the magnetic draw of both. Whether Caleb was right or wrong, deep down, she wanted to build a fire sprite and bring it to life.

"We're going to need the book from the Book Club."

Caleb nodded and picked up his cart and started walking toward the city again. "Alex got out of the hospital today. We'll stop buy and pick it up tomorrow."

"Alex is out of the hospital? Why didn't you tell me that earlier?" She grabbed her cart and hurried after him. "Let's go see her now."

"We can't. Her family is with her now."

"So?"

"The Administrator is with her."

"So what? I've been with Alex when the Administrator is around."

"Things are different now, Mal."

Mallory thought about the conversation she had over-heard in the hospital hallway. "Because he wants me to pay the price for the loss of the Dikaió?"

"And the fire at City Hall, but it will never happen. The Matriarchy holds as much sway over the City Council as the Administrator, so long as there's hope for . . ." Caleb trailed off.

"Hope for what?" Mallory demanded.

Caleb spoke quietly, "The return of the Dikaió."

Understanding began to dawn on Mallory. "Without it and the christening, there's no need for the Matriarchy? Is that what you're saying?"

"I'm not saying it, Mal. But it is being said. Your mother is a tough one, though. She's put the Administrator and my father through the paces. I've heard them go round after round arguing about what to do with you."

"And what does my mother want to do with me? Does

she want me to be Matriarch?" Caleb was silent, and his silence was all the answer she needed. The City Council, the Governor, the Administrator, and now her own mother had decided that her unborn sister would be the Matriarch, and even without the Dikaió, that decision was not being reconsidered. Mallory asked another question, "Does she want me to marry you?"

"My father says it will protect the traditions if we marry; it will protect the Matriarchy. He thinks the Administrator is planning on using the crisis to consolidate the power of their house and edge out the Triad. He does control the magistrates, and there would not be much we could do to stop him," Caleb said.

Mallory bit her lip, tilted her head slightly, and looked at the parts in her cart with a dawning understanding. Then she said, "But a fire sprite could stop him if it came to that."

Caleb's shoulders tensed and his voice was low and menacing: "Yes, yes it could."

The Dikaió City Services Manager had added emergency power to the Governor's district, though most of the city still remained in darkness even all these weeks later. However, without the ability to control the Dikaió—much like the hospital and the municipal buildings—the lights could not be turned off. Sleeping was a nightmare, and they had all taken to tying pieces of clothing around their eyes to keep the light out at night. Caleb had convinced the City Services Manager to run a line out to Mallory's workshop and install a Dikaió light, so the workshop was full of Dikaió light even late at night.

A small moth circled the Dikaió light above. Mallory only barely noticed the small insect in the periphery of her vision because she was preoccupied with Caleb, who was acting strange. Every time he set down an armful of parts, he would turn to Mallory, spread his arms wide, open his mouth like he either wanted to begin a speech, or needed air like a fish out of water—she could not tell which—then he would shake his head and walk outside for another load. Mallory could tell he wanted to continue their conversation from the pastureland and was struggling to find the words, but she nearly giggled out loud every time he made the wild gestures.

He reminded her of a little male robin she had sat and watched one spring. The bird was helping his mate build a nest in the eaves of the Matriarch's roof. He would land on the edge of a board near the nest, carrying a piece of grass or thread, then the female would hop out of the nest over to her husband. With her unmoving eyes fixed on his offering, she bobbed her head to the left then cocked it to the right, inspecting the building materials for quality. If she was satisfied with his selection, she would pull it away from him and hop back to their nest for installation. The male bird would then turn around, spread his wings wide, and squawk wildly, yelling, "Look at me, world! Look what I've done! My lover has accepted my gift, and soon we will have a family. Squawk! Squawk! Squawk!" Then he would fly away with his chest puffed out in search of another worthy gift for his beloved. When Caleb spread his arms wide after dropping parts onto the floor, Mallory desperately wanted to fill in his lack of speech with a "Squawk! Squawk! Squawk!" However, she buried the amusement and maintained a stone-like expression. Caleb might take her laughter as an invitation to say what was on his mind, and right now, Mallory wanted him to stay quiet; she had other plans, and they required that Caleb go home sooner rather than later.

Finally, the carts were unloaded and Caleb hovered in the workshop. His eyes met Mallory's, and their blue irises reflected hers for a moment: A gray storm hovering over a blue sea, and the combination seemed to bring order to his thoughts. His pupils constricted with new courage, and he opened his mouth, but before he could start, Mallory cut him off: "Well, I'm exhausted." She yawned and stretched her arms wide. "I'm ready to call it a night, Caleb."

Caleb blinked and stumbled backwards like he had been slapped. "I . . . um . . . yeah. I guess it has been a hard day. Well . . . I guess I'll go then."

Mallory bounded past him to the door, flashing him a flirtatious smile. "Okay! See you tomorrow?"

Caleb's confusion disappeared seeing her smile, and he nodded and flirted back with his own sheepish grin. "Yeah, sure. Of course!" He stumbled out of the workshop after her. She started up toward her house, and he turned toward the Governor's house. As he started walking, he paused and turned back, "Mallory?"

"Bye!" She yelled and kept moving. She made it to her backdoor and through its welcoming entrance before looking back over her shoulder. Caleb was on his way home, spreading his arms and bobbing his head, no doubt rehearsing the conversation he wanted to have with her in the workshop. When he made it to his house, Mallory saw him stand in the Dikaió light and turn to look back at the Matriarch's house.

She hugged the beam of the door, hiding out of sight, but still peeking out at him from the window. For a moment, she thought he saw her watching him. Finally, he went through his door and disappeared inside. Mallory waited as long as she could bear it and then ran out into the night toward the Administrator's house to see Alex.

The Dikaió lights were permanently on at her house as well, and Mallory stood on tiptoes to peek through the large picture window into the main room. Alex's parents were on the couch nearest to the window facing away from her. Alex was sitting on a chaise lounge; her back was pressed up against the single raised side, and her knees were pulled up to her chest with her arms wrapped around them. She was wearing dark blue pants and a long-sleeved shirt with arm-length gloves to cover her scars. Tears were streaming down her face. Mallory's heart rate quickened. What was going on in there? Her eyes scanned to the right. The Administrator and his wife were sitting in two overstuffed leather recliners across the room from the window she was looking through. The Administrator's wife was wiping away tears with the back of her hand, and the Administrator himself was scowling and looking directly at Mallory.

Mallory dropped to the ground. Their eyes had met for an instant; of that, she was sure. However, she was not sure what her next step should be. Should she just go home? Should she knock on the door? Ultimately, she wanted to see her friend. That was why she was here. She steeled her nerves and stood up to go knock on the door, but when she turned back toward the door, she found herself standing face-to-face with the

Administrator.

"Eek!" She involuntarily squeaked in fear.

"Miss Knenne," the Administrator said in a low, angry voice. "What can I help you with?"

Mallory stammered, "I . . . I wanted to see Alex. I heard she was home from the hospital."

The Administrator's expression did not change. "We've always encouraged the heirs of the Triad to be friends with one another." He rolled his hands into small fists, pulling the words out with some difficulty. "In your case, that may have been a mistake. What you did to the city demands justice. And I will see that you receive it." His voice quivered slightly, whether in anger or sadness Mallory could not quite determine. "What you did to my granddaughter is unforgivable. Even if it takes my dying breath, I will see that you pay for her scars." He took a menacing step toward her. He was not a tall man—at least not as tall as her father or Caleb—but his presence made up for his stature. Mallory was frightened. "You are not welcome here, Miss Knenne," he said, and then without a hint of change in demeanor, he turned to the side making a space for her to pass. "Please, leave!"

Mallory wanted to say something, wanted to run past him and into the house to Alex, but she was not sure what the Administrator would do if she tried it. She walked slowly past him looking at the ground.

"And Miss Knenne," he said, making her turn back to face him once more. "Never speak to Alex again, or so help me, I'll . . . I'll . . ." Even in the dark, Mallory could see the veins in his forehead throbbing as his face bloomed bright red. His fists curled tighter, and his torso shifted slightly to the side as if he were ready to swing one of those tight fists directly at her. She took her cue and ran as fast as her feet would carry her.

Tears blinded her vision as she ran. Her heart was still beating fast. She could not quite label the emotions she felt: fear, shame, anger, grief? Her feelings were similar to how she felt when the leader of the Smith Guild confronted her the night the Dikaió was lost, so it was definitely anger. On the other hand, the Administrator was a different animal altogether from the portly leader of the Smith Guild. Like the beasts of the Dark Forest, the Administrator had teeth. If he chose to charge her with a crime, she could be imprisoned; judging by the way he had looked at her and spoke to her tonight, she wondered if the judgment would not be harsher.

She ran blindly, turning corners and looking back, hoping that the Administrator had not changed his mind and decided to pursue her with a team of magistrates after all. From her Matriarchal training with her mother and grandmother, she knew that there were certainly worse judgments that could be passed according to city law, up to and including death. Her grandmother said that the two boys who had built the fire sprite might have received that harsh punishment if they had not been the fire sprite's first victims. There was no more atrocious crime in the city than harming another citizen—even if it were accidental.

Perhaps Mallory was both angry and afraid of the Administrator because she knew that he would not be unjust in calling for capital punishment for what she and Alex had done. And perhaps that is what Caleb was worrying about when he spoke of the conversations amongst the Triad, and needing the fire sprites to stave off a power grab by the Administrator and his family. He may intend to kill her. A shiver ran down Mallory's spine, and she slowed her run to a walk. With her thoughts collected with new understanding, she became aware of her surroundings. The night air was cold; cold enough for a coat, and she had left hers at home. She rubbed her arms vigorously to warm them up. She looked around to figure out exactly where she was, and that is when she realized that it was very, very dark.

In her blind run, she had apparently left the Governor's district, and without the city's light or even Dikaió lights on the doors of the houses, she had a hard time getting her bearings. The only light she could make out was the moon, and it was just a sliver of a new moon partly covered by clouds. Then she noticed a flickering glow farther up ahead up the street from around the corner of a small, modest house. She must be in one of the citizens' districts, though it was still impossible to tell which one it was. The streets leading to the citizens' districts all ran like spokes in a wheel toward the city center and the Governor's district, with crisscrossing avenues like the thread of a spider's web. At the outer edges, the districts ended in walled cul-de-sacs. If she went the wrong direction, she would end up having to backtrack out of a dead-end, or even worse, across the pastureland near the Dark Forest, which was not a pleasant prospect in this thick curtain of night. She decided that she would find out where the flickering light was coming from and see if there was someone that could give her directions or at least a street name that she would recognize and be able to follow back home.

She was unprepared for the site she found when she turned the corner. Down the avenue several bonfires had been lit in the middle of the street on each block, and hundreds of citizens were clustered around them. Mothers sat on the pavement with their children, wrapped in comforters and blankets, and the men were hauling furniture and other belongings out of their houses and tossing them onto the fires to keep them roaring. Mallory shivered in the cold air and found herself drawn to the fire's warmth. As she approached, she began to notice the faces of the people around her, especially the children. Their eyes were sunken, and their cheek bones protruded too far against tight, nearly translucent skin. The men's faces were drawn as they carried the heavy furniture, and their mouths hung open while they breathed hard. Their gums were receding up over their teeth unnaturally. She had never seen a malnourished person, but she instinctively knew that these people had not been eating enough.

Then the smell of the street washed over her: There was a pungent odor of sweat, sewage, and filth—a smell her own sweaty body no doubt added to, having just finished hauling sprite parts all day and not having showered yet—but there was also an acrid odor in the air with a hint of what smelled almost like sweet wine. The smoke of the fires masked it somewhat, but Mallory could not get away from it as she walked amongst the crowd. As she followed the trajectory of the odor, she realized that it was the heavy breath of the people around her; something about it did not smell right.

For the most part, the people were quiet. There were some soft conversations here and there, and Mallory could hear the wordless hymns of the mothers comforting their children. She would almost expect this scene of human suffering to be full of sadness, but all of them bore empty expressions. They seemed to be feeling nothing. Hungry lethargy so encompassed the citizens that many could not raise their hands to bat away the flies landing on the watery corners of their eyes. She felt like she was stumbling through a nightmare.

Suddenly, a man's voice called out, "It's the Matriarch's daughter!"

Mallory looked toward the sound of the voice and saw a tall man with a stocking cap and loose-fitting clothes pointing at her. The crowd around him was looking in her direction as well. Their empty expressions began to shift: Some eyes widened, and the corners of their mouths ticked in hopeful expectation. The eyebrows of the tall man who pointed at her were furrowed, his mouth twisted in anger— no, it was deeper than anger. Disgust? Maybe Rage? Others around him bore the same twisted look.

As the crowd's attention turned toward her, their bodies began to move toward her as well. Listless children cowered from her while their mothers crawled toward her, their empty eyes locked on her. The angry group of men moved faster than the rest, and their clenched fists suggested they harbored the same intentions as the Administrator.

While Mallory tried to register what was happening, she stumbled backward to get away from the crowd, but her own reactions were dulled somewhat by hunger and confusion, and she found herself caught by strong hands that locked tightly on her arms and shoulders on the dark street. Suddenly, someone had a handful of her hair and was tugging at it. Sweet-foul breath bloomed in her face, and sweaty, hungry faces began to drag her toward the nearest fire. Murmurs of "witch" crackled in the air, and everywhere she looked she saw dirt-smeared faces, blood-shot eyes, and yellow-stained teeth. She was no longer moving her legs; her rubber-soled shoes dragged on the pavement if they touched it at all. The crowd's motion was now her own. She knew that she should be screaming, but the crowd's voice was now her own as well; their stifling proximity sucking away whatever air she might have used to call out. The claustrophobia she had experienced inside the herd of cows reared up, but the only way out of the crowd was the fire, and it was drawing nearer with every step.

An explosion sounded from somewhere outside her jumbled prison of humanity, and a man to her right yelped loudly. He shook his head, and blood began to run from the top of his ear, which seemed slightly shorter than the other. Another man to her left had gone limp and then fell to the ground. The cluster of men tripped over him, and the crowd toppled, taking Mallory with it. Legs and arms were swinging wildly, and Mallory felt a boot connect with the bottom of her chin. Warm saltiness flooded her mouth, but she hardly had time to notice as the surrealness of the moment had ended, and her survival mode kicked in. She bit and scratched wildly; wiggled and kicked; punched and clawed; fighting her way out and over the sprawling bodies of the men, all fighting to get untangled from one another.

"Get up and disperse," a woman's voice called. "By the authority of the Administrator and the magistrates, step away from the Matriarch's daughter."

The men looked in the direction of the voice as though in a haze and pulled themselves to their feet groggily. She was an average build, but she was wearing the blue uniform of a magistrate, which looked almost black in the darkness of the night. She had arm-length black leather gloves and knee-high leather boots to match. Her head was covered with a helmet and face shield, which reflected the dance of the bonfire in its mirrored surface. She was pointing her weapon at them, and a thin tendril of smoke trailed from its barrel. The men's rage turned to solemn confusion. They looked at each other and then back in the direction of the voice, and then one of them shrugged and turned away. Soon most of them were walking away dejectedly, picking up the furniture they had dropped to add the fuel to the fire. Two of the men picked up the man who had stumbled and caused the rest to fall. The injured man groaned, lucky to have survived the magistrate's shot. Most of the men dispersed as ordered, but some just stood staring at Mallory with concentrated hatred. Their shoulders rocked back and forth, and they shuffled wearily from foot to foot. Whatever rage had compelled them before had not been completely dissuaded by the appearance of the magistrate and her weapon.

"Mallory, come with me now!" the woman hissed.

Mallory did not hesitate. The magistrate walked quickly and purposefully away from the crowd without looking back.

Mallory followed, trying to keep pace, but she kept looking back to see if they were being pursued. Some of the men were following them, but once they turned onto the Dikaió-lighted paths of Main Street, Mallory did not see them again. The magistrate did not slow down though, and Mallory found herself quickly running out of breath following this law-keeper.

"Can we slow down? I think you lost them!" Mallory called.

The magistrate stopped cold and swiveled toward Mallory. She closed the gap between them in two steps and loomed over her in silence with her hand on her weapon. Mallory thought of the Administrator's threats, and suddenly, she felt like she might be in as much danger now as she had been when she was in the hands of the angry men. Mallory lifted her hands defensively as the magistrate reached up suddenly. Rather than strike her, the magistrate unstrapped her helmet and pulled it off. Mallory's eyes widened as Alex's face emerged from beneath the magistrate's helmet.

Alex seemed like she was about to say something, when Mallory pounced on her and wrapped her in the tightest hug she could manage. "Alex! I'm so happy to see you. I thought that we'd never be able to see each other again."

Alex patted Mallory awkwardly on the back, barely able to move her arms. "Yes, yes, well okay! C'mon, Mallory, get off me." She squirmed and wriggled out of Mallory's embrace. "That's partly why I came after you—to talk to you about my grandfather's plans, and partly to save you from that mess." She gestured toward the darkened part of the city with her gloved hand.

"How did you know I would need saving?" Mallory wondered out loud.

"You were out at night. Clearly, you were not obeying the Administrator's warning for the wealthy and the ruling class to not go out after dark, and why were you out? Surely, your parents have warned you? My parents and grandfather have been in my hospital room updating me on the deterioration of the city and the mobilization of the magistrates for days now, preparing me for what to expect when I was discharged. Honestly, Mallory, what were you doing?"

"No one told me anything about . . . that!" She waved her hand in the same direction that Alex had gestured. "I'm out because I wanted to see you, Alex! But your grandfather—"

"I know. He blames you for all of this."

Mallory dropped her head. "And he's right; the citizens do deserve justice."

Alex grabbed her friend's shoulder, "Not any more than I do. I told him I was the one who read the words. I was the one that destroyed the Dikaió! But he won't hear it, Mallory!" She let go and turned her head away. "He doesn't want justice; he wants to see you executed. He wants to see the Matriarchy and the Governorship abolished. He thinks a city without the Dikaió can only be ruled by the justice of an Administrator. My father and the magistrates are with him, and they expect me to join them. That's why I'm wearing this uniform. When my grandfather excused himself and went out the front door, I went to the window and saw him yelling at you. When you ran away, I said I had to use the restroom, and

I slipped out the window to find you." Alex looked down at the darkened street below them, then jerked her head back to Mallory with fire in her eyes. "I can't be part of what they're doing, Mallory—especially not after what I've done. Mal, they're planning a coup."

"My mother and the Governor will stop them."

"How? Maybe with the Dikaió that would have been true, but without it?" Alex pulled her weapon from its holster. "How will they compete with these? You saw what it did to that citizen. They have hundreds of these and enough ammunition to subdue the city." She paused and looked at the weapon with glazed eyes.

Mallory bit her lip, weighing how much of her recent activities she ought to share. Alex was her friend, but she was also an heir of the Administrator. Still, she would not be here if she could not be trusted. Her grandfather had made it very clear that he did not want the two of them talking, and Mallory decided to trust her.

"Caleb knows about their plans, and we've been working on a solution."

Alex's eyes refocused, surprise written on her face. "What do you mean?"

"We found fire sprites in the dark woods, and we're rebuilding them to fight the magistrates if it comes to that."

Alex shuddered and then shouted at her, "You're doing what!? Do you know how crazy that sounds?"

Mallory raised her hands in frustration. "Not any crazier than using the magistrates to take over the city. Like you said, without the Dikaió, we can't fight back. The citizens starving to death down in the dark streets certainly can't fight back. What choice do we have?"

Alex began to pace. "But without the Dikaió how will you stop the fire sprites if they start burning the city?"

"Caleb is convinced that they can be controlled. He thinks they were part of the city's defense against the dark forest and were discarded when the light was constructed. If they can be controlled by some type of old magic, they'll protect us from the magistrates and the dangers of the dark forest."

Alex lowered her head at an angle, considering the possibility. "I was going to suggest running away, but this could be a better option—assuming Caleb is right and the fire sprites can be controlled. It's a terrible risk though, Mallory."

"So is doing nothing."

Mallory watched her friend's lips tense as her jaw clenched, straining the muscles in her neck as she seemed to consider the devastation of the past against the threats of the impending coup.

"The Governor and the Matriarch are on board with this plan, then?"

"I don't know. My mother hasn't been speaking to me, and Caleb has been keeping me busy with projects and speaking very little about the affairs of state. The only thing he's let slip is that it's been decided that my sister will be Matriarch, regardless of what happens with the Dikaió, and that our parents want us to get married to strengthen our families' position in the city."

Alex laughed, "Well, you've at least got to be happy about

that, right?"

Mallory frowned. "I think we can deal with that particular issue once we ensure that the city will still have a Governor and Matriarch, and that I survive your grandfather's plans for justice."

"Why do you do that?"

"What?"

"Demure and deflect when the topic of you and Caleb comes up?"

Mallory's frown deepened. "What do you want from me, Alex? My whole life, I've been the heir of the Matriarch. The night I found out that's changed; we destroyed the Dikaió. You nearly died. The city is in shambles. Now, your grandfather wants to kill me and stage a coup. There's a forest with killer creatures in it, and we're building fire sprites in my shed to fight them—and apparently the magistrates as well. Forgive me if I think talking about Caleb and me living happily ever after is a waste of time. Besides, I'm just seventeen-years old. Even if we were going to be married, it wouldn't be for a few more years, and that is only if I'm not in prison or dead."

Alex smirked. "So, you're saying you want to marry him."

Mallory rolled her eyes in reply.

Alex's demeanor shifted then, "Fine, let's talk about survival for you and the city leadership. What's your next step for building the fire sprites?"

"We need that sprite book from the Book Club."

Alex's expression fell. "We can't get it."

Mallory felt her muscles tighten instinctively. "Did your

grandfather find out about Book Club?"

"No! That's not it." Alex reached up and unbuttoned the top two buttons on her uniform. Her upper chest was pale white in the Dikaió streetlights, but there, where the key to Book Club used to hang, was a pink and white scar the exact shape of the key. Alex was looking down at her chest, but she couldn't quite position her head in a way to see the scar. The tips of her index fingers traced it tenderly. "The key got so hot in the City Hall fire that the metal left its mark."

"Oh! Alex!" Mallory felt her own chest tighten in empathetic suffering for her friend. "I'm so sorry. Where's the key now?"

Alex shook her head. "I don't know."

Mallory's sleep was fitful that night. Her dreams were strings of incoherent scenarios interwoven in a chaotic tapestry. In one moment, she was older and happily married to Caleb. They sat nestled together on a couch, sipping hot drinks from mugs while their children played with wooden blocks at their feet, and a fire roared in the fireplace. Mallory was watching the fire, and in the fire she could see the city burning: The buildings turned to ash as tiny fire sprites walked along stacked logs, streams of fire arcing from the nozzles on their arms. The sound of scraping metal filled the cozy room, and the family laughed. Outside the picture window of the house, she could see the light ebbed and sparked, shielding them from all the ills of the outside world, but it did not project an endless prairie as the city light once had—instead, she could see through it to what was being kept at bay. Her parents were out there, standing with the Governor and the Administrator, and behind them stood an army of blue-clad magistrates. They were all holding weapons and firing their barrels at their cozy house. The light sizzled and cracked as it absorbed every shot.

She smiled and lightly brushed the hairs on the back of Caleb's neck. He squirmed under the rising goosebumps. Out of the corner of her eye, she saw one of the kids get up and run to the door. "We've got to let Grandpa and Grandma in," the child squealed in delight. Mallory tried to get up and stop the child, but Caleb was in a playful mood now and held her firmly in place, trying to tickle her back. The cushions of the loveseat had become quicksand and were pulling her and Caleb down into their depths even as he continued to tickle her. Their child had made it to the front door and was turning the knob. As the door opened, Alex walked into the house. On her chest, the outline of a key glowed in yellow light. Another of the children laughed and ran up to her. "Auntie Alex," she squealed. "Look, they match!" The child held up one of the wooden toys: a key carved in the exact shape of the glowing one on Alex's chest. Alex smiled and bent down to the little girl, who touched the toy to her chest. When the keys collided, the light that protected the outside of the dream house suddenly vanished, and the Administrator's face contorted in a wicked grin. He pointed his weapon directly at Mallory and squeezed the trigger.

Mallory's eyes shot open, and she saw nothing but

darkness. She was blind. She could feel that her hands were up in a defensive posture, but she could see nothing. She patted at her eyes and found that they were bound with a piece of cloth. It was just the sleep mask to keep out the Dikaió lights that could not be shut off. She pulled down the mask as she breathed a sigh of relief and squinted in the brightness of the light above her bed. That confirmed it; she was alive and in her own childhood room. The dream family was just that and nothing more. She pressed her hands into the bed to push herself up and found that her bedsheets were cold to the touch; they were drenched in sweat. When she was sitting up, she wiped away trickles of sweat on her brow. Her hair was quite damp from the night terrors.

She stepped into her bathroom and turned on the water. As she washed away the sweat from her face and hair with cold water, she thought of her grandmother. The old Matriarch had often said, "Dreams are just the Dikaió's way of sorting out life for us. The answers are often there in front of us all along; it just takes a bit of magic for us to see them clearly." So, what was this dream trying to tell her? That she was supposed to marry Caleb, or that doing so would turn the city against them and mean the death of them all? Just then, cold water trickled down the front of her nightgown, and she tensed with the shock of it. Her eyes squeezed tightly shut, and her hands clenched in fists; the picture of a wooden key filled her mind's eye. Suddenly, her eyes popped open, and she raced out of the bathroom to get dressed. The purpose of the dream was instantly clear.

She dressed quickly and ran down the stairs to the dining

room. Her parents were not there, though a small plate of cold fruit and oats were sitting in her spot at the table. This is how every morning had been since the fire at City Hall. The mornings of having a breakfast as a family were becoming more of a memory than an expectation. Her heart ached in her parents' absence. She felt homesick in her own home. Despite those feelings, she could not ignore the deep, empty hole in her belly. She sat down at the table and looked at the small plate and bowl. The fruit smelled a little bit over-ripe, and its taste and texture was sweet but mushy. The oats had been made with too much water to make the bowl look fuller than it really was, which helped their weekly food storage last longer. Before they lost the Dikaió, breakfast used to consist of eggs, toast, butter, juice, yogurt, fresh fruit, oats, granola, and occasional bacon or sausage on special occasions. Most of the time, they threw away more food than they ate. Now, there was barely enough to curb the gnawing hunger of breaking the nighttime fast.

As she sat and slowly ate the meager meal, she thought of the people she had seen in the streets last night. If the governing class were barely eating enough to survive, those people were starving. She had seen the hunger in their faces and their demeanor, and she knew that she was the cause of their misery. They knew it too; the men that grabbed hold of her last night wanted to kill her. Apparently, the Administrator wanted to kill her too, and maybe they were all right. Maybe justice demanded that she pay that ultimate price. However, justice would not solve the lack of food in the city due to the preoccupied culture sprites, and the Administrator wanted more than justice—he wanted complete control over the city. The fire sprites Caleb wanted to build could solve both those issues. They would give the Matriarch and the Governor the means to oppose the Administrator, and they would relieve the culture sprites, so they could return to the culture farms atop the skyscrapers on Main Street.

Mallory finished breakfast and stood up. A kitchen sprite automatically rushed in and cleared away her dirty dishes, nearly knocking her over in the process. She pirouetted clumsily out of the way to regain her footing then ran through the kitchen and out the back door into the sunlight. As her eyes adjusted, she could see Caleb standing beside the bush near her workshop. He was plucking leaves off the bush and tossing them in the air, looking quite impatient. "How long have you been waiting there?" Mallory called.

Caleb brightened considerably when he saw her. "Long enough, Mal. I was starting to wonder if you'd ever wake up. It's nearly lunch time for goodness sake, and we haven't even started."

"And how are we going to start without the book?" A voice called from behind the bush. Caleb nearly fell over himself wheeling backwards away from the intruder. Alex stepped out. She was dressed neatly in her magistrate uniform without a single wrinkle. Light glinted off the brass buttons that closed the jacket and the brass belt buckle at her waist. The belt was black as night, as was the holster and the handle of her weapon.

Caleb gained control over himself and stepped between

the two girls, facing Alex and protecting Mallory from a perceived threat. "We don't want any trouble, Alex."

Mallory bounded past Caleb and hugged her friend. "It's okay, Caleb. Alex and I talked last night. She's with us."

Caleb looked unconvinced. "Why would she go against her family? How can we trust her?"

Alex looked pained, and Mallory turned on Caleb. "Alex and I have been best friends since before either of us can remember. Why would either of us want to fight the other?"

Alex nodded. "I do love Mallory like a sister, but that's not the only reason I want to help. What my grandfather is doing is wrong, and it's not the worst thing he's ever done—if anyone should pay for his crimes, it's the Administrator."

Caleb raised the palms of his hands and asked in confusion, "Hold on—What did you say?"

Alex nodded toward the workshop. "Let's go inside. There are too many eyes and ears in the Governor's District."

The trio moved inside where the Dikaió light shone bright, and a vent in the ceiling blew cool air making the small space feel frigid cold. The room was not large, so after a few moments, the teenagers' body heat began to compensate for the cold. Alex pulled herself up on a clear spot of the table and sat with her gloved hands in her lap. Mallory sat on her workbench, and Caleb plopped nonchalantly on the floor, with one leg stretched out and the other bent up so that he could rest an arm on his knee.

"Okay, we're alone; what are you talking about, Alex?" Caleb asked.

Alex sighed and shifted uncomfortably. "I went home last

night and had gone to bed, but I woke up in the late hours of the night, and I heard my father and grandfather talking downstairs. Since I was thirsty, I thought I would slip down and grab a drink of water and maybe sit with them by the fireplace for awhile. I paused on the stairs when I heard my father ask my grandfather about the fire sprite. I'm not sure what made him bring up the fire sprite, but given my talk with Mallory, I was afraid they were on to your plot, so I slipped back behind a corner and listened closely. It turned out to be unrelated to all this," Alex pointed at the mess of the fire sprite parts sprawled throughout the workshop, "but it was so much worse."

Mallory was eager to tell them about her epiphany this morning and wasn't interested in hearing another story about the old fire sprite if it was unrelated to their plans, so she interrupted Alex. "My grandmother used to tell me about that day, and Caleb's grandfather told him what he saw too. We know that story pretty well."

Alex nodded, "But did they tell you about the third boy who helped build the fire sprite? The one who didn't die when the sprite was birthed by the Dikaió?"

Both Caleb and Mallory sat up straighter and leaned their heads forward.

Alex nodded, "That's because the third boy was my grandfather."

Caleb coughed and again exclaimed, "Wait, what?!"

Mallory swiveled in her chair, "But our grandparents said that he was there on the street with all the rest of the people."

Alex nodded again, "That's what my father said last night

too. My grandfather smiled and said, 'Yes, I was there with the rest of the city leadership: The Governor; the Matriarch; my grandfather, the Administrator; all their heirs; and the entire City Council were there looking on like buffoons, putting the whole city in danger of being entirely without real leadership. My presence amidst them was part of the plan.'

"'The plan?' my father asked.

"'Yes, the plan, Daniel. The plan to take control of the city and save it from itself.'

"'Save it from itself? I don't understand.'

"'My grandfather sighed and settled back in his chair. 'Where do I start? There was a man that lived in one of the houses that burned down on Manuel Avenue. Like the Matriarch's girl, he was a Dikaió Chorus. Unlike her, he did not cause much trouble. He kept to himself for the most part, but he was friendly enough when approached. However, he did not seem to have a productive job in the city, and yet, he did not go without. I began to grow suspicious that he was stealing. I started watching him covertly, trying to gather evidence that I could present to the Chief Magistrate, my father.

"'Over the course of the next few weeks, I noted that he never paid for his groceries, but kitchen sprites would work together with a grocery box and collect a share of supplies for him and deliver it to his house. It was the oddest thing to watch the sprites at the market—everyone acted as if they did not see them. The kitchen sprite would weave in and out of the crowd and grab shares off the owner's tables, putting them in a grocery box, and no one—not even the owners—noticed the food being taken. It was as if the oddity was so out of the ordinary, that they purposefully ignored it. One day, I confronted the kitchen sprite at the market and began to take the groceries out of the grocery boxes, putting them back on the tables. The kitchen sprite went back and recollected the produce and extended its arms upwards to add its ill-gotten gains to the grocery box, which gained enough altitude to be outside my reach. I hollered for a magistrate to help me, and the fool just stood there, unable to comprehend the idea of using sprites to steal.

"'I followed the sprites back to the Dikaió Chorus's house and confronted the old man on his porch. "What do you mean stealing groceries from the Dikaió Culture Guild?"

"'His dark, wrinkled face smiled back at me, exposing a mouth with more than one missing tooth. "Mornin' to you, young sir. 'Fraid I didn't quite follow the direction of your comments. I'm gettin' on in years and can be a little slow. Want to give 'er another go?"

"'I am the heir of the Administration, son of the Chief Magistrate, and I demand to know why your sprites are collecting groceries at the market without paying for them! It's theft of the highest order."

"'"Ah, I see. Well, if that's all, come in and sit a spell. I'll tell you all about it."

"'I hesitated, but I could tell the old man was not a threat, so I followed him into his house. Daniel, you should have seen the books in that house—hundreds, maybe thousands of them, stacked in every nook and cranny, on the floor, on shelves, on the stairs—the danger of the knowledge contained in that house was staggering—though the city had not quite begun to understand the dangers of reading at that point. I stood with my back to his front door and awaited an explanation.

""""Care for some tea?" he asked, ambling toward the kitchen.

""""Only if you can prove that it's rightfully yours to offer," I shot back.

""""Oh, well, okay then." He stopped and lowered himself down onto a pile of books. "What proof should I offer you?"

"'That was a question I had not considered. Was there a way to prove that he had paid for the groceries? "Any proof will do. Do you have any money to pay for them?"

""""No, can't say that I do."

""""So you admit that you haven't paid for the food those sprites are putting away in your kitchen now?" I could see the commotion of the kitchen sprite and the grocery box in the other rooms.

""""Oh, yes. Those aren't even my sprites, young sir."

""""Aren't your sprites? They're right there in your kitchen. I can see them with my own eyes."

""""Oh, there's nothing wrong with your eyes. They're in there putting away groceries all right. Same as they do every week, and when they're done, they'll leave."

""""Leave?"

""""Surely. Not all of us can afford our own kitchen sprites like the rich folks up on Governor's hill. Least that's what my mother used to say before she left."

""""No one in the city is without a grocery box or a sprite,"

I retorted. "It's a right of the Dikaió."

""'True, it is, but a Dikaió Chorus wields a different magic." He gestured around him at the books. "An ancient magic."

"'I looked down to my right and saw a book called Birthing Sprites.'"

Caleb and Mallory both pricked up their ears.

"That's the book in Book Club. The one with the instructions for making the fire sprite," Alex continued.

Mallory nodded enthusiastically. "You mean that book came from the Dikaió Chorus? My grandmother knew him and used to spend afternoons reading books with him. She never told me about that book, though."

Alex shrugged. "I suppose not, and you'll know why if you let me finish."

Caleb and Mallory both settled back and indicated that she should continue.

"Okay then, let's see. My grandfather picked it up and thumbed through it. As you know, there were hundreds of familiar sprites in the book, showing how they were birthed in the Rookery, and there were schematics showing how their inner parts worked together to do different things. And of course, there were some unfamiliar sprites in the book as well that surprised him—at least that is what he told my father: 'I closed the book and tapped its binding against the palm of my hand and said, 'I'm not sure what you're talking about, but it seems you owe the Dikaió Culture some compensation for the groceries you're eating, or you need to tell the sprites to stop bringing them to you.

"'The old man threw his head back and cackled loudly. "Alright then, young sir." He turned toward the kitchen. "Hey you, sprites. Stop putting those groceries away and come here." Nothing happened, and the sprites continued unloading groceries into the cupboards. The old man shrugged and said, "Perhaps you'd like a go at it?"

"'His incompetence made me angry, and I yelled, "Kitchen sprite, Dikaió kitchen sprite, cease." The sprite paid me no heed either. I marched past the old man and yelled again, "Kitchen sprite cease." Still the sprite continued in its tasks. I turned on the old man, sure of some trick, "Why doesn't it hear me?"

"'The old man shrugged. "Some magic is older than me, young one. My parents might've been able to answer your question, but I was just a little one when they left, and whatever makes the city work the way it does 'tis long forgotten. I've spent my life readin' these books, tryin' to understand, and there's nothing here that helps. That book you're holding is the nearest I've found, but it still doesn't explain nothin' useful—just how to make a sprite if you want, but not how the Dikaió makes them work."

"'I looked down at the book with curiosity. I do not know why, but I suddenly wanted to have the book and learn its secrets like the old man had. I looked him directly in the eye and said, "No one in the city should be able to just take whatever they want without payment. As heir to the Administration, I judge that this book should be payment enough to cover your crimes, so I will take it with me."

"'The old man raised an eyebrow and then shrugged.

"Quite alright with me, young sir, there ain't a book in this house that I ain't committed to memory anyway. Take whatever you like."

""'This book is sufficient for now, but I may be back should the need arise. Take care to keep yourself out of trouble."

"'The old man cackled again as I turned to leave. "Oh, that I will, young sir. That I will."

"'I walked slowly home, thumbing through the pages of the book. When I got to the section on the fire sprite, I sat down and studied the thing in detail. What would the city do if one of these sprites were set loose? Could it overcome a challenge like this? The magistrates were not trained to deal with this sort of disaster. What if there was a food shortage? A power shortage? No running water? No one in the Triad or the City Council was planning for anything other than continued excess. I do not know what made me worry about things that had never happened at that young age, but I could tell even then that the city was one crisis away from chaos.

"'I had two friends who shared my concerns, and I decided to call on them that afternoon to discuss a plan that was forming in my head to at least get the city to consider changing course and start planning for a safer tomorrow— like a planned test of the city's services. Jacob LaMarr and Dillon Silvana, heirs to the Sprite Master and the Smith Guild, lived in the market district not far from our home. I stopped in to see them, and we slipped away to our secret meeting place in the Sprite Rookery. We had cleaned out a small supply closet on the lower level of the Rookery near the forge. People rarely go downstairs because of the heat, but Jacob had discovered that the little room was insulated from the heat and had a vent that pumped in cool, fresh air. When the supply shelves were in the room, there was just a small aisle, but once we cleared everything out, we found we could comfortably stow a table and three chairs in the space. We sat around the table, and I placed the book I had secured from the Dikaió Chorus in the center.

"Jacob, recognizing the mark of the Rookery on the cover, grabbed it and started flipping through the pages. "This is fascinating, Will! Wherever did you find it?"

""The old Chorus had it and many others. There's a particular sprite I want to show you." I reached for the book, and Jacob handed it over reluctantly but was soon satisfied when I handed it back just as quickly with my finger stuck between the pages to mark the spot. It pinched when he grasped hold of the book, but he opened the pages and relieved the pressure.

""It's a fire sprite," I intoned, pointing toward the diagram that showed fire spewing out of the nozzles.

""What would we do with it?" Dillon asked.

""Exactly what we talked about. Make the city leaders understand that things happen and that we need some contingency plans in place to keep the city safe. Dillon could provide the raw materials from the Smith guild, and Jacob could birth it as the heir to the Sprite Master."

""And then what? We'd let it spray fire all over? What if someone got hurt?" Dillon was always the pragmatist.

"Jacob answered, "We could stop it before that happened.

It's just a sprite."

"'You have guessed by now that we could not stop it before it hurt someone. It was my idea to birth it on Manuel Avenue near the Dikaió Chorus's house. I knew that we could make it look like the old man and his books had been the cause if anything went wrong. Jacob and Dillon were supposed to say the words, and I would get my father, the magistrates, the City Services Manager, and the firefighters to come and stop it. But I was still running down the street to gather everyone when they said the birthing words. The sound it made when the Dikaió entered it was terrifying—like a metallic, high-pitched scream. I did not look back, but I could feel the heat of the fire at my back as I ran. The whole way I was yelling, "My father! Someone call my father and the magistrates!"

"'Of course, we couldn't very well blame the Dikaió Chorus because they found Jacob and Dillon's bodies near where the fire sprite was activated. They did not even have time to back up before the sprite turned on them, and the Dikaió Chorus was in his house when it burned, as were several other people on Manuel Avenue.' He turned and looked at my father with tears in his eyes. 'I've never shared this story with anyone, son. Not my parents. Not even your mother.'

"My father looked away from him; his lip curled in disgust. 'Why are you telling me now? Have I made a mistake throwing in my lot with you and your plans for the city?'

"My grandfather stood up and began to pace with his hands folded behind his back. 'No, son. That's why I'm telling you all of this. What we did that day wasn't wrong; it was just ill-conceived in the ignorance of youth. That day has haunted me, and I had almost convinced myself that it had all been a mistake. Nearly forty years have gone by. I was ready to retire and live my life out in the peaceful tranquility of a city without want or need, where nothing ever went wrong like I used to think it would. Even my grandfather's choice to ban reading for all but the Triad didn't seem to make anything worse in the city, though I thought an ignorant populace would almost certainly bring destruction on us all. Everything seemed to support the utopian vision, but then that witch's curse proved my youthful foresight was correct all along. The city did need a backup plan. We were ill-prepared for this disaster—but mostly the Triad was unwilling to prepare.

"'I have been calling for a solution to the Mallory-Knenne issue ever since her witch of a grandmother cursed her to be a Chorus . . . and then to find out she used a book to trick an heir to the Administration into bringing about that catastrophe? It sounded so much like my own childhood mistakes. I see myself in Alex so much. There is something unnatural in the magic of the Choruses.'

"'Yes, I see your point,' my father allowed. 'Alex wasn't responsible for her actions, and I agree she should not be punished. Perhaps the Chorus did the same to you all those years ago?'

"'Exactly! I fear that Alex may find herself drawn back into the Triad, so we should move quickly to initiate our plans.'"

Alex sighed and looked at her friends. "We don't have

much time now—the magistrates will make their move soon."

Mallory jumped off her stool. "Well, let's not sit around telling stories then. We're going to need that book if we're going to build these things."

Alex deflated, "But I don't have the key, Mallory!"

Caleb was trying to pull himself off the floor while patting at one of his legs, which must have fallen asleep. He nearly toppled back down when Alex said she did not have the key. "What do you mean you don't have the key?"

Mallory stepped between them holding a bottle of black ink and a piece of paper. "Actually, you do have the key, Alex. It left its shape on you. If we apply some ink to the scar and press this paper to it, I can make an outline that we can use to carve a wooden replica."

Alex's eyes got wide as she asked, "Do you really think that will work?"

"It has to—all we can do is try, right?"

Alex unbuttoned the top two buttons of her magistrate's uniform, and Mallory began to carefully paint black ink on the key-shaped scar. Caleb was hunting through the piles of parts looking for a piece of wood around the right size for a key, and respectfully trying not to look toward the girls. He found a piece that might work under a pile of wooden handles for the Chorus carts. "How about this one?" he said turning slightly to show it to Mallory.

The wood was plucked out of his hand before he had finished turning.

"Thank you!" Mallory giggled on her way to the work bench. She pressed the paper to the wood and made the imprint of a key on the block. She worked fast with an awl and chisel, splintering out pieces of wood and used a sharp knife to whittle down other parts. Alex and Caleb watched her progress in amazement, and within thirty minutes she had a fairly decent approximation of the key to Book Club.

"What do you think?" she asked holding it up so her friends could inspect her work.

"Amazing," Caleb said taking the key. "Do you think it will work?"

"There's only one way to find out," Alex was already moving toward the door. "My family is out meeting with the Captains of the magistrates until lunch. If we hurry, we can be in and out before they even notice."

The trio were running together again, though their expressions no longer bore the careless joy of youth like they once did. Now their expressions were weighed down with the experience of pain and responsibility. The streets in the Governor's District were empty. Before the city lost the Dikaió and City Hall, they would have been bustling at this time of the day with business owners and bureaucrats bantering about policies and taxes, but now the silence was an uncomfortable reminder of how much had changed. Today, it was a reminder of the urgency of their quest as well. This silence could be filled with sounds that would be so much worse if they were unsuccessful and the Administrator actually managed to start a one-sided war in his coup d'état against the Triad government.

They reached the Administrator's house quickly and piled up the stairwell to Book Club. Caleb handed the wooden key to Alex, and she slowly inserted it into the keyhole. She turned the key.

The door remained closed.

"Let me try," Caleb pushed past the girls and took back the key. He tried to turn the wooden key in the lock. It still did not move, so he applied some muscle. The extra torque did not unlock the door, but it did cause a loud crack. Caleb carefully pulled the key from the keyhole, brushing wooden splinters off what was left as it came out in pieces.

"Oh, man, there goes that idea," he sighed.

The trio walked morosely back down the stairs. They exited into the hall of the Administrator portraits, and Mallory felt their heavy gaze staring down at her again. How were they going to stop this current Administrator from undoing all their work? How could they save the city without the book? And how could they get the book without the key?

"Maybe we could break down the door?" she thought out loud.

"We won't have to," Alex chirped. "Look!"

Mallory and Caleb followed the direction of her pointing finger and saw a gleam of bronze on top the mantel of the fireplace: It was Alex's key.

Alex rushed across the sitting room and grabbed the key. "I was so caught up in all the drama since I got home, I just never noticed it."

Caleb turned back toward the stairs. "Quickly, let's get the book and get out of here."

The trio bounded back up the stairs. Alex inserted the bronze key, and the door to Book Club swung open.

Alex and Caleb set out into the forest with Chorus carts to bring back as many of the remaining fire sprites as they could, and Mallory set to work repairing the old fire sprite she and Caleb had already collected as soon as she got back to the workshop. She bit her lip, studied the diagrams in the book, and then looked over the fire sprite, mentally labeling each part she found that corresponded with the diagram in the book. While the hulking exteriors of the fire sprites had no equivalent in the city, the innards of the ancient dark-forest sprites were surprisingly made of nearly identical parts as those listed in Birthing Sprites—the very parts that Caleb had filled her workshop with could form the base of either a culture sprite to water plants, or a defensive fire sprite.

When Alex had said that her grandfather had worked with the heirs to the Sprite Master and the Smith guild so that they could gather materials and make the parts needed, Mallory had worried that she might need specialized parts that were unavailable—but so far, it seemed that the only component that was forged from scratch would have been the shell—and those they had in spades, even if they were some-what rusted from years of exposure in the forest. The size of the fire sprite was a bit challenging as well: At twelve-feet tall fully extended, they would have been too tall to stand in the shed, but Mallory found that the legs were triple-jointed so that they could fold over themselves. Once folded, she could lower the sprite down to about seven-feet tall, which was low enough to work on the topmost parts with just a small stool to provide a boost.

As she studied the book, Mallory found it amusing that over the hundreds of years that separated the history of the city erecting the light, the printing of the book, and the current birthing of the city sprites, nothing about the make-up of a sprite had changed. The parts were just assem-bled in a different order, depending on the function of the sprite, but there was some aesthetic variation in the inner parts, if not the design.

As she scrubbed and oiled down the rust, she noticed that the ancient sprites had strange markings stamped into them that were different than the ones marking the city's sprite parts. The marking looked like a crescent moon inside a large star and four smaller stars that were symmetrical to the curve of the moon, whereas the familiar city marking used the shape of a heater shield with a solid W-shaped top and stripes at the pointed bottom. Mallory knew that the symbols were probably family crests because of the portraits of the line of Administrators in Alex's grandfather's house. The earliest Administrators in the portraits were wearing family crests, but that practice had been discarded generations ago as the families of the city mixed, and lineage became cloudy. Since that practice was no longer used in the houses of the Triad, she found it intriguing that Reddy LaMarr was still using a family crest on new sprites as the current Sprite Master—and even more interesting that these older symbols suggested Reddy's family may not have always been Sprite Masters. She wondered to which of the city's families this ancient crest belonged. Knowing that Reddy LaMarr was not a direct descendant of the oldest guild families in the city made Mallory feel joyful despite her station now.

While she worked, she began to whistle old hymns her parents had sung when she was small. When Mallory was nearly three-quarters of the way through repairing the sprite, she took a break and went inside to grab a bite to eat. She scrubbed her greasy hands in the sink with soap and water and marveled at how long it took to get the grease off. She never could quite get it out from under her fingernails. She grabbed a plate and cut off a hunk of bread and then grabbed an apple.

While she chewed her food, she thought about the work she had completed so far. If the book was accurate—even with what she had managed so far—she was pretty sure the

Dikaió command in the book could birth the sprite into working order. The most interesting part was the way the fire sprite ignited its stream of fuel. The sound of metal scraping on metal that their grandparents had told them about was made by two large metal discs inside the sprite with a layer of rough coating on them. One would spin one way, and the other would spin opposite, and the rough coating of the discs grinding against each other created sparks. The propulsion system for the fuel operated almost exactly like the hydrant sprites, and Mallory wished she had been able to read the book when Caleb had asked for ideas about redirecting the water; seeing how the sprites worked would have made that a much easier task. Perhaps when this business with the Administrator and the magistrates was finished, she could return to that problem. As far as the fire sprite went, she figured the remaining work was mostly cosmetic, patching up the rusted holes in the shell. She was sure that she could finish the next one even faster; they really were not that hard to put together.

"Mallory?" Caleb's voice called into the house.

She swallowed a hunk of apple before she had fully chewed it, and it moved slowly and painfully down her esophagus. There was a moment when she was worried it would not go down all the way, and she grabbed her glass of water to wash it along, which sent her into a fit of sputtering. Finally, the apple cleared, and she yelled back, "I'm in the kitchen, having a bite to eat."

Alex and Caleb came in dirty, covered with sweat, and smelling of manual labor. "You have food?" Caleb asked. "Is it okay if we have some?"

Mallory waved toward the nearly bare pantry. "Tomorrow's market day. We should finish off what's there, so it doesn't go bad. Help yourselves." The pair accepted her invitation. Alex pulled off her long gloves to wash her hands, and Caleb started to open the pantry.

"Ahem," Mallory huffed.

Caleb turned, confused, and Mallory pointed toward Alex. "We may be going through hard times Caleb Aiworth, but we're not riffraff. Wash your hands, please."

Caleb laughed heartily. "You do a great impression of my mother, Mallory Knenne."

Alex laughed at them both and moved over so Caleb could get in and wash his hands too, but she moved quickly to pull her glove over her scarred hand before the others could see it. Then they rummaged in the pantry looking for something to eat. Alex came back with an over-ripe pear and some crackers. Caleb found some dried bananas, the rest of the bread, and a bottle of honey. He proceeded to pour honey over the bread and nibble at it, savoring every crumb. Mallory laughed. "Not long ago, Caleb would have eaten that loaf in two bites."

Caleb looked up, licking the honey on his lips like a bear after dipping into a beehive. "Not long ago, there were six loaves three times the size of this one in your pantry."

Mallory's mirth faded. "I think I've got the fire sprite ready except for a few minor cosmetic issues."

Alex's eyebrows raised. "Already?" she asked before nibbling a bit of cracker.

"Yeah, sprites are not that complicated once you see how they fit together—well, at least not mechanically anyway. The parts that the Dikaió controls are hard to understand, though. They're like these tiny boxes with tendrils that plug into different parts." Mallory made tendrils by squiggling her fingers on one hand. She used her other hand to make a fist then plugged one of her finger tendrils into the hole created by her thumb and forefinger. She looked up at Caleb. "Do you think the Sprite Master would know much about them?"

Caleb shrugged. "I doubt it. She told me she just says the words to birth the sprites. The Dikaió of the Rookery does all the work assembling them. Why do you think I came to you for help with the hydrant sprites?"

Mallory blushed but shot back, "So, even in fixing problems, I'm your second choice."

Caleb smiled, his lips covered with honey again, "First, second, you're the only one who actually seems to be able to do anything without the Dikaió, so that makes you number one in the city, right?"

Alex huffed, "Well, my grandfather seems to be doing alright without the Dikaió, which is why we're here, right?"

Caleb licked his lips some more. "Right! I think we've got a whole other fire sprite in our carts, Mal. The process is moving a lot faster now that we've done one, and I know how to pull them apart."

"And?" Alex prodded.

"And . . . Alex had the idea of pulling the parts out, loading the hull, and then piling the parts back into the hull. The load is a lot harder to push, a lot harder," Caleb whined rubbing the muscles of his arm, "but we managed a whole sprite in one trip instead of two. I think we can get another one back here before dusk if we hurry."

Mallory's head spun. "I don't know why, but I thought putting these together would have taken us days, if not weeks."

Alex shrugged, "It's just as well. We have that long before my grandfather takes action."

"How long do we have?" Mallory asked.

Caleb stood up and began to pace. "The City Council is meeting this morning at my house. My father has been using our entryway as a temporary City Hall until they can find a more permanent location."

Alex chimed in, "We think my grandfather will say something there that will put his plan into motion."

"What do you think he'll say?" Mallory bit her lip, wondering if she really wanted to know the answer.

Caleb and Alex looked at each other and shrugged. Caleb mused, "Probably something about the Matriarchy being unnecessary, you needing justice—who knows? Maybe he'll call for the immediate surrender of the city."

Alex stood up and shoved the last bit of cracker into her mouth. The dryness of the cracker made her cough, and she stammered, "Whatever it is, we should go get what we can and let Mallory get back to work. We want to be ready for him, not trying to play catch up."

The three parted ways with fresh focus, and Mallory walked quickly back to her workshop. She grabbed hold of the handle and yanked. Sharp pain spread up her tricep and shoulder as her arm moved, but the door was stuck again. She pulled hard again at a different angle. Still no luck. She stepped out from behind the hedge, hoping Caleb was still within shouting range, but she could see his and Alex's forms disappearing down the hill pushing their Chorus carts in diagonal zig-zags like Mallory had shown them. There was no way they would hear her call. Mallory huffed and walked back toward the door of the workshop. She planted her feet in line with her shoulders, bent her knees, and grabbed hold of the handle with both hands. Then, using her whole body, she pulled on the door.

With that technique, the workshop's door swung open much easier than she thought it would, and she stumbled backward into the grass, which had grown longer than she ever remembered it being. She lay there for a moment looking up at the tall grass that had sprouted. Several gnats and mosquitos had been disturbed by her fall and were swarming above her in the warm afternoon air. Suddenly, several dragonflies entered the mix, darting this way and that, eating their way through the swarm. Mallory watched them in curious amazement. When the dragonflies were sitting still, their translucent wings were an intricate maze of windowpanes; in motion, their wings were just a blur, pounding the air to keep their living fuselage airborne. Mallory imagined what it would take to make a sprite that could fly like that. The book had some flying sprites in it, but they all hovered with propulsion units or propellors, but adding wings that could move like these dragonflies would add speed and height to the sprites' movements. She added the thought to the mental list of things she'd like to explore after the business with the Administrator was finished.

Mallory dragged herself up out of the grass, brushing off bits of green blades and swatting happily feasting mosquitoes off her as she stood. Those bites were going to be annoyingly itchy later. She had noticed that the mosquitoes had gotten worse lately, but she honestly could not tell if the mosquito issue had sprung up after the city light went down or after the culture sprites took up their defensive positions around the city and let the grass get too long. Either way, she'd have to apply some honey to the bites to stop them from itching when she thought of it next—if Caleb had not eaten it all with his bread. A few of the bites were bleeding since she had brushed the bugs off before they had sealed their work with their coagulating serum. She wiped absently at the blood as she walked into the workshop.

She paused at the entryway and blinked in the Dikaió light. Caleb and Alex had piled the next fire sprite just inside the doorway, and she had to step cautiously over and around the rusted metal heap. Caleb's presence in the workshop explained the wedged door. The boy was a hulking beast these days, though Mallory had to admit he was not all brawn with no brain. After all, this was his plan. One day, he would make an amazing Governor of the city, and the way things were going, she would be his Governess. The thought brought a smile to her lips, and she realized that, for the first time, she felt at peace with the idea of not being the City Matriarch. She was a fighter, and now that she had something other than her station to fight for, she did not mind losing that station to her unborn sister. Working with Caleb like this was actually very fulfilling, and without the Dikaió as an issue, she felt that she could be a very good Governess.

Of course, she would have to survive the Administrator's plot, and in order to do that, she'd have to finish these fire sprites. Once she skirted the heap of fire sprite parts on the floor, she inspected her work on the nearly completed specimen that she had been working on all day. Checking the current step in the book, she quickly checked off and squared up what she saw in her own model—only one thing was off. One of the Dikaió box's tendrils were not connected to the black metal panels on the sprite's shoulder. She was not entirely sure what the panels were for, but she snaked the tendril up behind the gears and pistons, being careful not to get it tangled in the moving parts. The tendrils had small arrowheads on them that collapsed slightly when pressed, and when they were plugged into a corresponding slot on a sprite, the tips of the arrow would spring out with a click, and the tendril would not come back out unless the tips were depressed with a flat instrument. Mallory had suffered a few finger injuries trying to get the things back out of the wrong slot, so she double-checked the book before shoving this tendril's arrow into the corresponding slot in the black panels. Confident that this was the right course, she slid the tip into place.

As soon as the edges of the arrow clicked, a red light began to blink on the Dikaió box. Mallory laughed out loud, "Will you look at that?" She sat back and watched the blinking light, mesmerized by its syncopated blip, a little sino-atrial node in the heart of a giant that had sparked to life. She looked at the other parts of the fire sprite to see if anything else had changed. Nothing had changed as far as she could tell—just that one hopeful, blinking light.

She shrugged and went back to work. The tanks that would hold the accelerant on the back of the fire sprite seemed pretty solid. When she and Caleb had pulled them off in the dark forest, they were full of old rainwater, so she was certain they could hold the accelerant. They'd decided to use the same fuel they had used for the old magic lamp in the Book Club and had borrowed three fifty-gallon barrels of paraffin from the Culture guild. However, the rubber hoses that ran to the nozzles were full of holes and would need to be replaced, so she ripped those off and grabbed some of the hydrant-sprite hoses that Caleb had provided. They were about half the length of the fire sprite's hoses, so somehow, she was going to need to splice two of them together, and that splice would need to be waterproof to keep the paraffin from leaking all over.

She bit her lip absent-mindedly and started digging through the parts from the Sprite Rookery, hoping for the mechanical muse to strike. Eventually, she spotted a tub of rubber gaskets that seemed like the right size for the ends of the two hoses to fit inside. She grabbed some wire and used a knife to notch it then bent it back and forth to break off a piece that was roughly twice as long as the diameter of the gasket. She inserted a hose into one side of the gasket and wrapped the wire around it, twisting the wire around itself like a bread tie. With each turn, the gasket began to shrink, and soon she could not pull the tubing back out of the gasket. She gave the wire a few more twists just to be sure the hose was not coming back out. She repeated the process with the other hose and then connected the new hosing to the fire sprite's tank and nozzles.

At that point, as near as she could tell, everything that was left really was cosmetic. She sanded at a bit of the rust on the front of the hole and ended up making a bigger hole in the sprite steel. Mallory frowned at the fire sprite. "Well, I guess you're not going to be a pretty sprite, are you?"

She pulled a board toward her that sat on small wheels about an inch off the ground—it was another tool she had invented with the abundance of wheels now available in her shop, and she used it to move heavy things without lifting so much. She pushed against the fire sprite's top and tipped it upward slightly, then she kicked the rolling board under it. She rocked the sprite back and forth until she had managed to leverage it atop her board. Then she rolled the entire sprite over to the side where it could rest out of the way. It was time to start working on the next mess of a sprite that Caleb and Alex had dragged in.

She found herself looking at the book much less often with the second sprite, and she replaced and clicked the Dikaió box's tendrils in much earlier on this one. Sure enough, the red light began blinking just like the first. She looked back and forth at the two red lights. At first, they were blinking at different rates, and then after about a minute, they seemed to sync with each other. Mallory moved to the other side of the room, so she could see them at the same time, and noted that the two lights were blinking at the exact same frequency.

"Curiouser and curiouser," Mallory mused, and then started back to work, polishing and repairing the hose on the second fire sprite.

She had not gotten very far, when the door to the workshop was ripped open. She let out a scream and spun around half-expecting to see magistrates bursting in to arrest her. It was just a hot, sweaty, and very stinky Caleb. His body odor hit her like a wall. "Oh my gosh, Caleb!" she yelled waving her hand in front of her nose.

He looked at her incredulously, breathing hard. "Are you kidding me? I've been out busting my butt all day, and the first thing you're going to say is that I stink?"

Alex yelled from behind, "It's horrible. I've got little pinecones shoved up my nose, and I still can't get away from it."

Caleb burst into laughter and looked over his shoulder, "You just wait; I'll get some bigger pinecones for your nose, Nelson!"

Mallory laughed too. "Put some up mine while you're at it!" She kept waving her hand in front of her nose while her eyes watered.

"Laugh it up, you two! You know what? You all can unload this last sprite by yourselves while I go shower if it's that bad. How about that?"

Mallory jumped off her chair and rushed over to him. "No, no! Okay you win. You smell like roses."

Alex, who still had not been able to get into the workshop because Caleb was standing right in the doorway, shouted from behind him again. "That's fine. The stink under your arms is stronger than the muscles in them anyway!"

Caleb spun around and ran out of the door. "Oh, yeah!?"

Mallory ran out after him into surprising darkness. She had no idea that she had been working until after sunset, but the moon was a quarter of the way into the sky surrounded by stars that were already twinkling. Alex was behind one of the Chorus carts, leaning slightly to the right, then to the left, getting ready to run in the opposite direction of whichever way Caleb decided to move. He was faking right and left, trying to get her to bolt before committing to going around the cart.

Mallory laughed at the sight of her friends playing just like they had when they were kids. It was funny to think of the three of them as children. It had not really been that long since they were, and now the heaviness of change and tragedy had shifted them to adult responsibilities. Yet, they were planning an armed defense to an armed revolution, and she was not sure the adults were even aware of any of the plans taking shape.

She bit her lip and tilted her head a bit. No, that was not completely true. No one had tried to stop them from building fire sprites. She was pretty sure the adults were oblivious to their plans—they were probably knee-deep in their own plans for how to handle the Administrator. Besides, why would anyone suspect that the trio was up to anything mischievous? If one of the adults were to check in on them, they would see them engaged in a harmless game of tag in the Matriarch's backyard.

Just then Caleb reached out over the Chorus cart and grabbed Alex's glove. She squealed in glee and pulled away, leaving Caleb holding just the glove and laughing. Mallory inhaled sharply. Alex's scarred hand hovered between her and Caleb; its fingers flexing and unflexing, stretching for the glove. Caleb was still laughing, but slowly the realization that he was the only one dawned on him. He looked at Alex's face, and then over his shoulder at Mallory. Mallory could not take her eyes off Alex's arm. In the hospital, they had bonded over their disfigured arms, but Mallory's disfigurement had been temporary. Once the cast was off, it had only taken a few days before it was difficult to tell that her arm had ever been shriveled, white, and stinky. Alex's arm retained all the scars of the fire, and it would never heal—it was a reminder that their childhood really had ended. This momentary relapse into innocent play was just flippant fantasy—a covering over the scars of their sin, of which Alex would forever bear the mark.

Caleb averted his eyes from her scars and handed Alex back the glove, and she solemnly covered her hand. "I'm sorry . . ." he started to say.

"I should be getting back," Alex interrupted. "My mother and father will be anxious to know where I've been."

Caleb shrugged. "I guess I should be going as well."

Mallory felt a tug of something bottomless in her heart and said nothing until her two friends started to walk away from each other in opposite directions toward their respective houses.

"Wait!" She shouted. "You haven't seen what I've done." Caleb and Alex both turned around.

"Done?" Alex asked.

"Yeah! I've got one of them finished."

"Finished?" Caleb murmured. "Already?"

"Yes, come and see!" Mallory ran back into the workshop followed by her friends. She showed them the finished fire sprite up against the far wall. "Ta-da!" She motioned her hands like a magician showing off a trick.

"It doesn't look done," Alex said, walking over and picking off a piece of rust from a gaping hole in the hull.

"Well, unless we have a Sprite Master and a Smith guild expert fashioning a new shell, this is really as good as it gets. But the insides are all together—and look!" Mallory pointed to the blinking light on the Dikaió box. "It's doing something."

"What does it mean?" Caleb asked.

Mallory paused and looked back at the blinking light. She shrugged and waved her hands in circles like her father did when her mother asked impossible questions. "Something!"

Caleb looked confused, and then nodded acceptingly. "Something."

Alex picked up the book sitting on Mallory's worktable. "Let's try the words."

Mallory's head snapped toward her friend. "Right now? I mean the others aren't done, and without the Dikaió, we don't know if the words will even work."

Alex shrugged. "And we never will unless we try the words."

She did not wait for their approval but began reading the birthing words in the book: "Dikaió ignus flamma asprueto."

Mallory thought that the little blinking light flickered for a moment, but then it continued its slow pulse unabated. The fire sprite did not move an inch, and the three friends' shoulders sagged in defeat. Mallory turned to Caleb and asked, "so, what now?"

His brow furrowed. "Are you sure you put it together, right? I mean you did it awfully fast, Mal."

"You're welcome to check my work, Caleb, but I'm pretty sure it's right."

Alex put the book back on the table and said, "It's late. We can all take another look tomorrow. I think we still have some time, but while we work on them tomorrow, let's think about alternatives if the fire sprites don't pan out, okay?"

Caleb shook his head unbelievingly. "Not pan out?"

Alex put a gloved hand on his shoulder. "This isn't our only option, Caleb. Failure is just an opportunity to try again. It's not the end of the story, okay?"

He sighed heavily and said, "okay."

This time the friends did part ways; each heading to their parents' homes, heads hung in defeat. Mallory mentally retraced the schematics of the fire sprite in the mental image of the book she had built in her mind's eye. Nothing was out of place physically, but she knew, just like Caleb and Alex knew, that the problem was not likely a mechanical one. The problem was that Mallory and Alex had destroyed everyone's ability to control magic, and without the Dikaió, they could no more birth a fire sprite than they could command a kitchen sprite to get them a drink of water from the tap inside their homes. She could think of no way to combat the

Administrator and his magistrates, nor prevent him from enacting whatever he deemed appropriate in punishing her.

She walked into the backdoor of her house, and the house was as brightly lit as ever with all the Dikaió lights forever shining in every room. She made her way slowly through the kitchen and thought briefly that she should eat, but even though there was a gnawing pain of hunger in her stomach, the thought of eating after her failure made her feel nauseous. She passed through the kitchen and dining room and began to ascend the stairs to her bedroom, when her father's voice surprised her from the sitting room: "Mallory?" It had been a long time since she had heard her father's voice, and its sound made her heart roll over in her chest. Tears sprang immediately to her eyes, and she ran back down the few stairs she had climbed into the sitting room.

Her mother and father were sitting on opposite ends of the large plush couch under the picture window, and they had left a space between them for her to sit. She bounded over and sat down. Her parents both embraced her, enfolding her betwixt them. Mallory's tears became rivers. Her body heaved in sobs, and she clung desperately at their arms, hoping that they would never pull away from her again. Her mother began to hum the wordless hymns of Mallory's childhood, and the family swayed in rhythmic coziness. Mallory could always sense that whatever the words to these old hymns were, they contained a powerful Dikaió magic—maybe even more ancient than the Dikaió; some kind of powerful magic that, if it could be accessed, could make everything that was wrong in the world right again.

After a long time of holding each other, her father pulled back and said, "You know then? I'm so sorry, Mallory, my dearest girl. Your mother tried so hard to change their minds."

Mallory shook loose from their embrace. "Know what?" Her voice squeaked through tears and dust.

Her father's eyes grew wide. "I thought that's why you were upset."

Mallory shook her head, "I was upset because you two haven't talked to me in weeks, but then you called me in, and I thought . . . I thought . . . I don't know." She sat up suddenly as they edged back to their corners on the couch. "What is going on?"

Her mother's face hardened with the undeniable look of duty. Now the Matriarch, her face still streaked with the tears of a mother as she looked at her daughter and said, "The City Council and the other two members of the Triad have called for a trial."

So that was it. They were out of time. The fire sprites had failed and there was no longer time to invent a device or come up with a plan. All she could do was pay the price and let her friends and family try to carry on without her. Mallory nodded and answered quietly, "Oh, I see. And the Administrator is calling for the death penalty?"

Her parents' eyes widened, and they glanced at each other with hurt in their eyes. "We tried to protect you from their attacks. We thought it would be best to keep these discussions from you," her mother was defending herself, talking through the reasons why she had not spoken to her daughter.

"I'm not so ignorant, you know. I have my own connections to the inner workings of the city. I am the Matriarch's daughter," Mallory said, trying to appear confident. "And if my fate is to die for my sins, I'll do it with dignity."

Mallory's mother's face fell, and her voice rose several decibels. "I tried to stop them. I tried with all my influence, Mallory, but without the Dikaió . . . without the Dikaió—I'm sorry, Mallory. I'm so sorry." Tears choked her words again as Matriarch and mother converged in sadness.

Mallory sat back between her parents once more, and they fell on her in an embrace, both of them sobbing now. But Mallory's eyes were dry. She could not bring herself to grieve her own death, and she felt happy that her parents had at least fought for her, even though she had been partly to blame. She was not even upset if she should pay the price for the trouble and save Alex—at least her friend would still be alive. She did not even feel the sting of defeat in failing to birth the fire sprites to fight the Administrator anymore. At this point, she felt a magnificent emptiness.

"When is the trial then?" she asked, her voice dull and emotionless.

Her father shuddered in sobs. "Tomorrow, my sweet girl. Tomorrow and we will never see you again."

Mallory sat with her parents late into the night. None of them said anything, they just clutched tightly to one another in their grief. Eventually though, sleep's inevitable call pulled them apart. Mallory trudged with blurred eyes to her room, neglecting all her bedtime rituals, and collapsed into her bed. She half expected her sleep to be fitful and full of nightmares, but with the exception of being briefly awakened by the loud noise of a storm that night, she slept soundly. She slept so soundly that, when her eyes finally did open, the sun was shining brightly through the dragonfly stained glass of her window, casting its green and purple light across the room, rippling like tiny dancers on the floor and walls. The only thing that was missing was music for the dancers to move to. Mallory's eyebrows raised. She had not heard music beyond the wordless hymns of the human instrument since the Dikaió disappeared. The joyous musicians that used to play at the christenings and on market day were silent. She had not seen their glowing instruments dancing around them in all that time either. She supposed that without the Dikaió, there was no means to call the instruments. She had killed music.

Mallory sighed as the memories of the night swept over her, and now she would have to face the music as the old saying went. She climbed out of bed and cleaned herself up. She put on her most royal-blue dress; she did her makeup, highlighting her eyes with a matching mascara; she pulled her hair back into a bun, taking the time to tame the wild curls into straight lines like the stems of a bouquet, and finally, she added a spritz of glitter. She looked like her mother, ready to go to a ball rather than an Administrative trial that would undoubtedly end in her death. Still, if they meant to kill her, she wanted to be sure they saw her, not as a troublesome girl that needed to be dealt with, but as an heir of the Triad who stood in the way of the Administrator and his family's coup d'état. She wanted them to know that Mallory Knenne was not afraid.

She walked down the stairs and found her parents sitting at the table eating breakfast. Her father burst into fresh tears when she turned the corner.

"My girl," he sobbed. "You're beautiful."

Her mother, whose hair was also pinned tight and straight for business, wiped at her eyes with her napkin and nodded approvingly. "You always were wise beyond your years, Mallory."

Mallory sat down to her place. There was a spread of all her favorite breakfast foods on multiple plates: eggs, bacon, toast, orange juice, cinnamon rolls, a chocolate éclair, dates, oatmeal, strawberries; there seemed to be no end of food. She looked askance at her mother. "But how? Why so much?"

"The City Council thought it appropriate to not deprive you from your favorite foods this morning."

"But how many people are going hungry because of me?"

Her mother paused, looking sideways at her, but did not answer.

Mallory caught her meaning without pressing for an answer: All the people were going hungry because of her.

Her mother changed the subject.

"Did anyone else hear the thunder last night? It was so loud and awful, I think the wind was knocking things over."

Her father, still weeping a bit, said, "I would have slept through it if you hadn't woken me up."

Mallory spoke around a mouthful of chocolate éclair. "I heard it too, but I fell back asleep."

"Mallory, finish chewing before speaking, please!" Her mother demanded.

Mallory laughed and took a huge bite before saying in a muffled chew, "Mother, if this is to be my last meal, I don't see how manners are going to make a bit of difference."

Her mother rolled her eyes and waved her hand dismissively. "Fine, but if the Matriarch has anything to say about it, it will hardly be your last meal, and then won't you wish you'd used your manners like I asked?"

The whole family burst into laughter. Mallory felt good to laugh with her parents again. She knew that her mother would fight until the end, and even though she might not live through the day, it did feel good to be a happy family again. The laughter was short-lived, though, as a knock sounded abruptly at the backdoor.

Mallory's mother shot up from the table, "No! They're early! The trial is not supposed to start until one o'clock this afternoon. They said they would give us the morning."

Mallory's father stood up and stepped in front of her protectively, blocking the way to her from the kitchen. "And so they shall! So they shall!"

Alex's voice called through the kitchen. "Mallory? Are you home?"

"It's just, Alex. It's alright," Mallory said starting to stand up.

Her mother shouted, "It's too soon! Go and tell your grandfather the trial is not until one o'clock."

Alex stepped around the corner from the kitchen, wearing her magistrate blues. Mallory's father stepped forward and folded his arms, looking down at Alex.

"She won't be going with you until the time comes. We get the morning with her. It was decided."

Alex looked at the floor timidly. "I'm sorry, Mister Knenne. I wasn't sent here by my grandfather. I came to talk to Mallory as a friend, not as a magistrate, or as an heir of the Administrator—but that's not why I burst ...."

Mallory's mother huffed and interrupted her. "I don't care

what capacity you've come in; we were given the morning to prepare our daughter for the trial and to spend time with her should the worst case be decided, and . . . and you . . .." The Matriarch turned red and the tenor of her voice began to rise. "You of all people have the audacity to call her your friend? You're just as guilty in all this as she is—why are you not standing trial as well? With a friend like you, who could ask for enemies?"

Alex nodded. "You'll get no argument from me. I demanded that I stand trial beside her. My grandfather has forbidden it, and he's forbidden me from attending. I didn't even know the trial was today until this morning. But I can tell you this—I intend to testify at that trial, and I'll demand from the City Council whatever fate they give to Mallory. I don't care what my grandfather says."

Mallory's mother softened. Suddenly, tears began to flow freely down her face. "At least my daughter has made better allies than I have within the Triad. You are welcome to stay, Alex Nelson."

Alex shook her head. "Thank you, but it's like I was trying to say, that's not why I burst in and interrupted your morning." She turned to Mallory. "Mallory, where are the fire sprites?"

Mallory cocked her head in confusion. "In the shed. Where else would they be?"

"They're not there. I checked just now before coming up to the house. Caleb and I were going to go over the schematics like we talked about to be sure you didn't miss anything."

Mallory's father tilted his head in confusion, nearly a mirror of his daughter. "Did you say, 'fire sprites'?"

Mallory turned to her father. "They were going to be our contingency plan against the Administrator's coup d'état."

The Matriarch covered her mouth, and then quickly folded her arms, trying to grasp the situation. "Honestly, Mallory, fire sprites? As if you had not done enough to turn the city against you, and now you're building fire sprites?" She began to pace, speaking with her hands as much as her mouth, "I thought maybe I could save you from the trial today—that the City Council could be reasoned with, that the Administrator could be reasoned with—but if you're building fire sprites, how do I convince them that you're not a threat to the city? I'm not even sure I believe it anymore." She stopped in front of Mallory and clasped her hands pleadingly, "Why couldn't you just keep your head down? Why do you have to be so much like your grandmother? The Administrator never did like her, you know. And if you remind me of her, it's no wonder he's out to get you."

She paused for a moment and then looked at Alex who was awkwardly trying to avoid her gaze during the uncomfortable family moment. Then she looked back at Mallory with narrowed eyes, "What's all this about a coup d'état?"

Alex answered, "You mean you don't know? Caleb said that you and the Governor were aware of my grandfather's plans . . . well, he implied it anyway."

"This is the first that I am hearing about this. I don't believe it for an instant." Mallory's mother looked at her husband and made a 'what are we going to do with these children' gesture.

"My grandfather is mobilizing the magistrates to take control of the city. We're not sure when, but quite soon."

"The magistrates?" the Matriarch's tenor rose higher. "And the Governor is aware of this?"

"My father is quite aware of the Administrator's plans, and we've been devising counter strategies for weeks," Caleb chimed in, just now walking into both the house and the conversation like he lived there. He had already snagged some of the unfinished bacon off Mallory's plate at the table and shoved a whole strip into his mouth. "You don't mind, do you?" He raised the bacon in his hand questioningly. Mallory smiled and shrugged, but the Matriarch did not seem to notice at all and sat down roughly. Her mouth hung open, her shoulders slumped, and she looked one way and then the other in shocked disbelief. Mallory's father rushed to her side and began to ineffectively fan her with a limp, folded napkin.

Caleb shrugged, turned to Mallory, and asked, "And speaking of counter strategies, what did you do with the fire sprites, Mal?"

"I didn't do anything with them. They were in my workshop when I went to bed last night."

Mallory's mother asked, "What workshop?"

"The old shed, Mother—where I build my inventions." Mallory wished her mother would keep up.

Her mother nodded but stared past them with shock at the Administrator's betrayal. "Oh yes, the shed."

Mallory's father jumped in now, "Do you suppose something happened to them in the storm last night?"

"What storm? There wasn't any storm last night—the grass is dry." Caleb folded his arms and addressed Alex. "Do you suppose your grandfather is on to us and dragged the fire sprites out in the night?"

Alex shrugged. "I honestly don't know. It's certainly possible. I mean, we had to cart the parts through the city; it would be weird if the magistrates hadn't noticed us. Maybe one of them followed us?"

Caleb shook his head. "I watched for followers; I didn't see anyone."

Mallory chimed in then, "We're not going to figure it out here. Let's go see if we can find any clues." Caleb, Alex, and her parents piled out the back door. Mallory cocked her head as they walked outside. The wind was roaring loudly through the trees, but it must have been blowing at an angle that was shielded on this side of the house because the air was perfectly still where they stood. They all walked back behind the trees and shrubs to Mallory's workshop.

The door to the shop was wide open, and its hinges were slightly bent; the wooden frame around the doorway was cracked in several places as well. Mallory ran her hand over the shattered wooden planks. That must have been the thunder they had heard in the night: the door being ripped off the shed. She looked inside, and all three fire sprites were gone: the complete fire sprite, the partially completed one, and the one that she hadn't even started to fix. Sprite parts from the Rookery were scattered all around the floor. There was a sharp odor in the air that stung her nose, and that was when she noticed something very strange: "The barrels of paraffin are empty." She pointed at the three fifty-gallon barrels that were laying on the floor, nearly bone dry. Alex and Caleb rushed past her to inspect them.

Caleb set one of the barrels upright and checked the floor around it. "There doesn't seem to be a single drop spilled."

Alex turned slowly in confusion. "If the magistrates were going to take the fire sprites and the paraffin, why wouldn't they just load the barrels and cart them in a Chorus cart like we did? It's not like they could carry the liquid around without a container."

Caleb grabbed Alex's arm. "Come on, let's give the Knenne's their morning, and we'll go investigate."

Alex nodded, and the two of them hustled out the door. Mallory walked over and looked inside the empty barrel. She started to reach in, and her mother yelled, "Mallory!"

"What?" Mallory spun around half expecting a battalion of magistrates at the door.

Her mother pointed at her with concern. "It's your good dress!"

Mallory looked down at herself and laughed, "Oh, right." She stepped carefully away from the barrel. "You know, if the trial doesn't go our way, the dress isn't going to matter much."

Her mother scowled and scolded, "Well, it certainly won't go our way if you walk in covered in sprite grease and smelling like nail polish." She waved her hand at the barrels. "What was in that barrel anyway?"

Her father spoke this time. "It smells like the stuff the Culture guild uses to keep the bugs away."

"Paraffin," Mallory said, moving towards the door. "It's

also highly flammable."

The Matriarch inspected the room with her hands folded behind her back like a military general. "So, that's what you've been using this room for? Building weapons?"

"Well, that's what I've been building recently. It started out just as a tinkering shop, then Caleb co-opted me into building solutions for the city's problems."

Her mother's eyebrows raised. "Like what?"

"The Chorus carts, the hoses for the hydrant sprites, amongst others. Surely you've heard about it? He said his father and the City Council put him in charge of the projects."

"Caleb's father has done no such thing. All three of you have been barred from any official discussions in the City Council meetings ever since the City Hall fire."

Mallory shook her head. "But Reddy Lamarr, the Sprite Master, helped him with the Chorus Carts. She's on the City Council—surely they knew about it?"

The Matriarch looked confused. "Are you sure?"

"She was standing not five feet from this shed, getting her directions from Caleb Aiworth acting as the Heir of the Governor."

The Matriarch's eyes narrowed, and she looked at her husband with rage. "Have they all turned against me, then? Have I truly become such a social pariah in this city? They've shut me out just as much as they've shut out my daughter." Tears began to roll down her cheeks, "Roger, what are we going to do? Either the Administrator takes the city by force, or the Governor takes the city by fiat. Without the Dikaió, we've got no hope of standing against either of them."

Her father just stepped forward and held his wife in his arms silently.

"What about marriage?" Mallory ventured.

Her mother sniffed and looked at her. "What do you mean?"

"Caleb said that you and his father have talked about us getting married, uniting the houses."

Her mother nodded. "We've discussed it. You're abundantly aware that the Council has already decided that your sister will be Matriarch, and you marrying the Governor's son seemed the most likely choice before the Dikaió was lost, but who knows if that is even still on the table?"

Mallory nodded. "But if it were, as Governess, I'd at least have the influence to keep our family's place on the Council, even if it were my sister sitting there instead of me."

The Matriarch broke loose from her husband's embrace and looked thoughtfully at Mallory, who could see her mother's political wheels turning. "I honestly hadn't considered that aspect. I was just thinking about finding you an appropriate match, but you're right. Installing you as Governess would solidify our family's place in the government, even in the new order of things."

Her father, on the other hand, looked very concerned and said, "I'm not about to sell my daughter like so much cattle to a suitor for political gain. You don't need to make a sacrifice for us, Mallory. The Knennes have more dignity than that."

"Daddy," Mallory blushed. "It's not a sacrifice. I love Caleb Aiworth, and he loves me. I've been torn between love and duty for a long time—but if love can be duty, then it's the best of both worlds. Don't you think?"

Her mother bounded over to her, full of enthusiasm. "Is that true, Mallory? You and Caleb love each other?"

"Yes, I think so. I mean, well, I love him, and he keeps talking about marriage, so I assume . . . ?"

Her mother slammed her fist in her hand. "Then we need to push that at the trial. If the Governor also joins the push for leniency because of a marriage, then perhaps we can tie the Administrator's hands."

Her father laughed and said, "Well, that is a good plan, my loves. Come on, ladies. Let's go enjoy our morning while we have it, shall we?"

They all headed back into the house and resumed their same position on the couch as the night before; parents cozying their daughter in the middle. In the old days, they used to call this the Mallory Cozy Sandwich. This time, though, they were not waiting for the night to carry them off to sleep, but for the magistrates to carry Mallory off to trial—a fight that they were more prepared for now than before Caleb and Alex had arrived.

Still, when the knock came at the door, Mallory knew that time had gone by too fast. She had not said everything she wanted to say, and she hesitated on the couch. Her parents apparently felt the same way because they clutched Mallory uncomfortably tight, and she hoped beyond hope that it would be enough to not be lost.

The Chief Magistrate called from the back door, "It's time. Sarai, please don't make us come in and get her."

The Matriarch let go of her daughter, stood up, and straightened her dress. She tucked a few loose hairs neatly into place, and Mallory wondered how she could know that they were loose without a mirror. Mallory pulled gently away from her father and stood up facing her mother.

"How do I look?" She asked.

Her mother smiled, and quickly tamed the stray hairs on Mallory's head as well. "You're beautiful as ever, Mallory Knenne. Now, head up! Let's show them what the Matriarchs are made of."

Her father leapt up and shouted, "Quite right!"

Outside stood the Chief Magistrate with ten magistrates phalanxed out behind him. The Matriarch scoffed at the site of the uniformed accompaniment. "Really, Daniel? She's no common criminal to be paraded by all this." She waved her hand dismissively at the guards.

"Your opinion has been noted, Matriarch, but a common criminal could have not done all this." The Chief Magistrate waved his hand out toward the city and then toward City Hall. "So, I agree that your daughter is no common criminal, and we will take every precaution accordingly."

Mallory laughed at that. "I'm a super-criminal then? And what of your daughter, Mister Nelson? She's the one who said the words, not me."

The Chief Magistrate bared his teeth and hissed. "Save your arguments for the Council, Miss Knenne. My job is only to escort you to the trial."

"I know all about what your job is, Mister Nelson. I know all about the plans you and your father have for the city, and I know what he did to the city when he was young."

The Chief Magistrate moved quickly before anyone realized what he was about to do. Using the back of his hand, he cuffed Mallory across the mouth. "Be quiet, witch!" He yelled.

Mallory's head whipped back on her neck. Her vision swam, and she stumbled a little on her feet. The metallic tinge of iron filled her mouth, and she spat blood in the grass. She did not fall all the way down, but the work it took to stay upright was significant. The Matriarch pulled herself up to her full height and stepped between the Chief Magistrate and her daughter. "How dare you strike the family of the Matriarchy! You'll be on trial next if I have anything to say about it, you weasel!"

His sneer slid into a wicked grin. "Well, you'll not have anything to say about it, Matriarch—I can assure you of that. Now, come with me peaceably, or there'll be more of this." He motioned his hand in striking motion, and then used his other hand to make an "after you" gesture toward the Governor's house.

The Matriarch did not make one step toward the Governor's house, nor did she move out of the Chief Magistrate's path. She stood like a stone monument; her eyes glaring down at him in an expression that Mallory called her "mom glare." That look had always been enough to get someone to stop and apologize for anything they were doing; the mom glare even worked on Alex and Caleb when they were younger. It was a withering expression of will, and the Chief Magistrate's eyes momentarily looked to the ground uncomfortably before it. Then, again moving quickly before anyone could have guessed it was coming, he struck out with the back of his hand.

The Matriarch wheeled away beneath the force of the blow and rolled across the ground a couple of times. Mallory's father barely let his breath out before he'd hit the Chief Magistrate in the jaw with a right cross. The Chief Magistrate stumbled sideways, and Mallory's father began moving his hands in small circles like Mallory had often seen him do when he was thinking. The Chief Magistrate righted himself and then swung hard at Mallory's father and one of her father's circles moved up, easily pushing the magistrate's fist away from his face. Then Mallory's father returned the swing with his other hand and sent the Chief Magistrate sprawling onto the lawn. "You never were that good at hand-to-hand combat, Daniel—even when we trained together as magistrate cadets."

Mallory gasped. Her father was a magistrate? She did not have time to internalize the thought because the Chief Magistrate propped himself up on his elbows and barked, "Take them!"

The ten magistrates drew their weapons and leveled them on the Knenne family. Mallory and her father quickly raised their hands, and the Matriarch stood slowly and regally up off the ground. She drew herself up to her full height once again and wiped blood from her lip. "We'll go peacefully, but if you intend to lead us to trial brandishing those at us, you'll be carrying us there instead. You can let the Governor and the Council see your evil machinations out in the light of day, as well as the rest of the city."

The Chief Magistrate stood and motioned to the ten magistrates who were with him to lower their weapons. He smiled callously, "Very well, Matriarch. I think we'd all like this trial to go civilly. There's been enough pain and heart-ache already." He bowed slightly and made the "after-you" motion toward the Governor's house once more. This time the Knenne family fell in line and began the march across the Governor's district. The magistrates filed in beside them, five on either side, and the Chief Magistrate took point at the front of the procession.

They could see the back of the Governor's house from the back door from where they started in the Matriarch's yard, but it quickly became clear that the Chief Magistrate did not intend to take them on the most direct path. They walked around to the front of the Matriarch's house where the two oaks stood, and Mallory gasped. Thousands of people stood in the Governor's district.

The roar Mallory had heard, and assumed was the wind, was actually the voice of multitudes. Apparently, the news of the trial of the Matriarch's daughter had spread through the city, and throngs of citizens had filled the streets. The Chief Magistrate clearly intended to parade the Knenne family through the crowd. Mallory bit her bloodied lip thoughtfully. It was a brilliant political move. She knew from her night in the lower parts of the city that the average citizen blamed her for what happened to the Dikaió, and many of them wanted to see justice satisfied at the cost of her life. The City Council would more likely rule in the Administrator's favor out of fear of the mob tearing the Governor's district apart if they did not satisfy their cries for justice.

When the processional entered the throng, Mallory was suddenly glad that the Chief Magistrate had brought ten magistrates to escort them. In fact, she wondered if they would be enough to hold the crowd at bay. People pressed in from every side; their faces blurring in a tapestry of rage and disgust all around them. The crowd jostled the magistrates, who more than once bounced roughly into the Knenne family before pushing the mob back. The walk to the Governor's house was a relatively short distance. Mallory had run to Caleb's door throughout her life, and it never took more than a minute or two at the longest. But this trip seemed to take hours: Every two steps they pressed forward in the throng, they were pushed back one. It seemed like they might be lost to the mob forever, but eventually they arrived at their destination.

As the new acting City Hall, the front of the Governor's house had been transformed: The single-door entryway had been extended into a massive double-door, and all the outdoor furniture that used to sit on the wrap-around porch had been removed, revealing the cold gray stones and beams beneath. The gothic windows were all propped open, so that the proceedings that occurred inside could be shared with the curious crowd outside. The processional solemnly climbed the stairs, and as they did, the magistrates took up positions on the steps and turned to face the crowd to keep them from following. When they reached the porch, the Chief Magistrate opened both double doors, and then stepped out of the way, so they could enter.

The Governor's House was a marvel of architecture, and the entryway had always taken Mallory's breath away. It was nearly as large as the Matriarch's entire first floor, and it was nothing but open space. A chandelier with one hundred Dikaió lights hung in the center of the room above a mosaic of the city's seal set amongst the white-tiled floor. Two curved, symmetrical stairways with mahogany banisters started on opposite sides of the seal and led to a walkway on the second floor, the mahogany banister continuing seamlessly across the walkway. The whole setup seemed to float in the space in front of three stained-glass cathedral-style windows. Each window depicted an idealized member of the Triad: on the right, a Governor holding a sword and shield; on the left, an Administrator holding a projectile weapon and the scroll of law; and in the center, holding a bowl full of water being poured over a child while dragonflies flew over her head in a wreath, a Matriarch clothed in a blue gown, much like the one that Mallory now wore. She drew in a deep breath amidst the cold, gray background, straightened her posture, and focused her eyes on the confidence and grace of the Matriarch looking down on her from the window.

Then Mallory looked down and saw that the entryway itself had been transformed as well, for now on the seal of the city sat a U-shaped table, around which sat the City Council. The Governor and the Administrator sat at the center of the table, each sitting below their avatar in the stained glass. The center seat was empty, and the Governor motioned toward it and said, "Sarai, take your seat, please, so we can begin."

Mallory's mother squeezed her daughter's hand, and

Mallory shuddered to think that it might be for the last time. Then the Matriarch walked around the right side of the table and took her place, head straight and shoulders squared.

The Administrator stood up and spoke loudly, "And so begins the trial of Mallory Knenne, daughter of the Matriarch, Chorus-christened, and destroyer of the Dikaió. The Administration intends to prove that through her actions she has brought irreparable harm to this city—"

A murmur erupted from the crowd outside as the Administrator's words were relayed among the throngs. Mallory knew that the very idea that the leadership saw the loss of the Dikaió as "irreparable" confirmed the citizens' worst fears: The Dikaió was not coming back.

The Administrator shouted to finish his opening statement, "—and as such, her actions are deserving of the city's harshest punishment: Death."

The crowd cheered, and Mallory steeled herself, stepping forward into the center of the City Seal to face the judgement of the Council.

The Administrator sneered at her and said, "No one on this Council is unaware of the crimes this girl has perpetrated. We've all felt the harm in our homes, in our businesses, even in our bodies as we tighten our belts due to hunger. Our protection from the light is gone. Even last night some of the beasts of the dark forest managed to evade the sprites and kill one of the cows in the pasturelands. Is there any reason we should not vote immediately to decide her fate?"

Suddenly the Chief Magistrate and a blue-uniformed magistrate burst into the entryway breathing hard:

"Administrator!" the Chief Magistrate yelled.

The Administrator's veins bulged in his forehead. "What is it, Daniel?"

"I'm sorry to interrupt, father, but the market is on fire!"

The Administrator glared at the Chief Magistrate then looked at Mallory, then the Matriarch, and back at the Magistrate. He put one hand on the table and ran the other hand through his hair. The Administrator hesitated in that position for a moment more and sat down hard in his chair, looking at the ceiling. He sighed deeply before looking back at the Magistrate. The whole room was watching him. Only the Administrator could adjourn a trial once it had begun, and Mallory wondered if he would. Were his plans for usurping power more important than attending to the news of a fire? Then she began to wonder what had started the fire—had Alex and Caleb been able to activate the fire sprites? Or had someone else?

She could hear the murmuring crowd behind her, and the repetition of the word "fire" burning through their ranks. The murmuring grew to become like thunder, and she knew that the crowd was leaving the Governor's District to see what was happening in the market. She desperately wanted to run back out the double doors and follow them, but she kept her curiosity in check and kept her eyes on the Administrator.

The Chief Magistrate stepped up beside Mallory then. "Father," he implored. "I know it's not ideal, but members of this Council are needed in the market."

The City Services Manager began to stand, and the Administrator shot up out of his chair. "Sit down, Jake Carpenter! No one has excused you!" The big man fell back into his seat, nearly toppling over backwards in the process.

The Governor stood up then and yelled at the Administrator over the head of the Matriarch, "James, what are you doing? We have to go; the city needs us."

The Administrator squirmed and sneered. "No, the city needs to see justice served!"

"What good is it to see justice served if the marketplace is burning? If it spreads to the crops on top of the skyscrapers, well . . . " The Governor narrowed his ice-blue eyes. "We will take a recess; we'll come back and hear the matter after the fire is resolved."

The Administrator was not so easily cowed into following orders. "No, we must finish what we've started! The trial is in motion." He sat down heavily at the head of the table.

The Matriarch burst up out of her chair and shoved her finger down into the Administrator's seated chest, "You mean to say that your coup d'état is in motion! What is this trial meant to distract the Council from, James?"

The Governor put his hand on her shoulder, "Sarai, please!"

She swiveled on him, "Don't 'please' me, William! How long have you known about his plans, and how long have you been conspiring?" She turned in a wide arc around to the Council. "And how many of you have staked your claim on one side of these two or the other? They're about to destroy what's left of the city, Dikaió or not: magistrates on one side," she pointed at the Administrator, "and fire sprites on the other," she said pointing at the Governor, who looked down with a pained expression.

The Administrator jumped to his feet and raised his hand in the air, knocking over his chair and causing the Matriarch to step back. He seemed ready to strike her, but after noticing the eyes around him, he pointed at Mallory instead. "Your daughter already wrought the very destruction you are now accusing us of." He looked at the Council. "How can we let this stand? The city demands justice, and it demands it today!" He slammed his fist hard on the table.

The Matriarch laughed. "So that's where your son gets it. He struck both me and my daughter on the way here. Neither of you understands justice, hitting unarmed women and trying to excise the Triad and the City Council for your own selfish gains. You care nothing for the integrity of the Dikaió!"

The Administrator sneered, "The Dikaió is gone, and you're just a priestess serving a dead god, Matriarch."

The Sprite Master raised her hand timidly to interrupt the heated exchange, and all three members of the Triad glared at her. "Excuse me, I'm sorry to interrupt. As necessary as these conversations are, I just want to know—did I hear something about fire sprites?"

The Administrator was again frozen, hunched over and blinking with his fist still solidly planted on the table, staring daggers at the Sprite Master.

The Governor looked from the Sprite Master to the Matriarch. "Yes, what was that part about fire sprites when you pointed at me?"

Mallory spoke then, "Caleb and I found the fire sprites in the dark woods. At first, we thought they might be able to help fight back the woods, but then Caleb told us about the Administrator's takeover, and we thought they could help with that too. Alex helped us get the sprite book that shows how to build them from the Administrator's house."

"My house?" The Administrator reeled; fear registering in his eyes. "How was that cursed book at my . . ." He steeled himself again and shouted across the room, "This trial is in recess! Daniel, call all the magistrates to the city marketplace. Bring all available weapons and ammunition."

He walked briskly around the table toward the door, and then paused. He turned back and in the same tone he had used at his house the night Mallory came to visit Alex, he said, "Mallory Knenne, there is no punishment worthy of the evil you've inflicted on this city." Then more broadly, he addressed the Council, "None of you are competent to run this city. When this fire has been subdued, this trial will extend to the lot of you!" With that he ran out the door, followed by the Chief Magistrate.

The Governor watched him leave and said darkly, "Caleb received no direction from me to build fire sprites. This is the first that I've heard of them, but if that's what is starting fires in the city, we all need to get down there and try to stop them."

Mallory shook her head, "I don't see how it could be the fire sprites. Without the Dikaió, we could not birth them. However, the accelerant we were going to use in them was all missing this morning, so someone may have used it to start the fires."

The Governor walked around the table, "Whatever it is, we need to take action now. Jake, are the hydrant sprites ready?"

The City Services Manager nodded and stood up, "Yes, I'll get them to the site right away."

The Governor spoke to the Culture Master then, "Andrew, the Culture Guild has quite a bit of water on top of the buildings in the marketplace, right? Is there a way to get the hydrant sprites up to the top, so they have an easy way to reload?"

The Culture Master looked up at the ceiling as though weighing the hydrant sprites in his mind. "We've had to rejig the grain elevators to run on a pulley system. It takes quite a few of us to lower crops down and raise an empty elevator back up to the top. Depending on how heavy the sprites are, we could probably get them to the top if the City Services men were working together with us. Otherwise, it would be the stairs—and that's going to be a lot more work."

The Governor nodded, "You and Jake see what you can do. The rest of us know what worked well, and what did not, with City Hall. Let's activate the bucket brigade, and we'll all meet in the marketplace."

The Matriarch ran around the table and grabbed Mallory's arm. "C'mon, Mallory. Let's go get some buckets at the house."

The Governor's District was deserted when they ran out of the Governor's house. Mallory looked toward the marketplace, and there above the houses and the tree line was a column of black smoke roiling into the sky. The size of the plume concerned her—what if the fire was too big to be put out? Could this fire threaten the entire city? Was this all part of the Administrator's plan? To set a fire and blame it on her for building the fire sprites? She had all but admitted her guilt on that front, but she had implicated both the Governor's son and the Administrator's granddaughter in their construction. Surely, the old usurper would spare his own granddaughter from the trouble that would come from constructing fire sprites?

And where were Alex and Caleb? They had left her house hours ago in search of the fire sprites, and they had not attended the trial. Alex had said she would be there to testify on her behalf or suffer the same consequences whatever they might be. Mallory began to run through possibilities of why they might not have come, and none of those reasons were comforting: They might have run across the magistrates and been detained, or worse; they might have been caught in the fires that were now raging; they might have been part of the conspiracy of both their families to usurp the city for the Governor or the Administrator, respectively. And really, was her mother right in pointing a finger at the Governor for doing the same thing as the Administrator? And had members of the City Council chosen sides? And if they had, why had no one chosen the Matriarch's side? Was the Matriarch really just a priestess in want of a deity?

The Knenne family ran to the side of the Matriarch's house and began to fill silver-colored buckets from the water spigot on the side wall. The buckets were one of the Governor's recent initiatives after City Hall burned. He had suggested that, in addition to the modifications to the hydrant sprites, the city should have a bucket brigade, so every household could bring water to help extinguish fires if the need arose. They had been cast from sprite steel at the Rookery and delivered to every residence, one for every hand.

When all the buckets were full, Mallory and her parents began the trek to the marketplace. At first, the buckets were not too hard to carry, but by the time they got to the end of the yard, the muscles in Mallory's arms screamed at her to put the heavy things down. The Governor and his wife met them at the intersection with Silver Street, and they all began the steep decline toward Main Street and the marketplace. The pillar of smoke to her right continued to rise high into the sky, and at this time of day, the sun was on the other side of it, casting an eerie red glow over this part of the city. Black and gray pieces of ash were floating in the air like gray snow, and it was getting harder to breathe.

Mallory's muscles continued to burn, and the worse they got, the more she noticed that the incline of the street and her awkward steps caused the water to slosh out of the bucket. The adults around her seemed to be able to keep the water in their buckets while they walked, but her water continued to slop out onto the street. She wondered how much water she would even have left once she got to the bottom of the street. She looked down at her feet and realized part of the problem was that she was still wearing the sparkly heels that went so well with her blue dress, which she was also still wearing. She quickly slipped off the shoes and continued down the hill, much more stable with her buckets now, though losing the shoes did little to alleviate the muscles aching in her arms. Fighting a fire in her fancy blue dress was going to ruin it, just like her clothes that night in City Hall. The thought of City Hall made her heart beat fast, and her breathing picked up, making her cough slightly in the ash-filled air. The thought of facing another fire in such close proximity was nearly unbearable; she felt like dropping the water buckets and running away.

Then somewhere in her rational mind the thought occurred to her that building fire sprites was bound to result in fires. It did not make any sense to be so scared of getting burned when she had literally been playing with fire for days. The dark humor in this dichotomy made her chuckle out loud, and all four of the adults looked back at her with some weird mixture of fear and disgust—she recognized the familiar disapproval that adults often give teenagers, especially the boys when they were being rambunctious—but the girls got the disapproving looks often enough for her to recognize it.

The anxiety about facing a fire faded, but as the fear faded, the urge to run away intensified. When these fires had been burned out or put out, they would go back to the trial, where she would very likely be sentenced to execution. Even if Alex went through with her plan, she would join her in death, not pardon. Mallory realized that the fires presented the perfect opportunity to run away. No criminal had ever run away from the Administrator before—where could one go to hide in the city? The light had made sure that no one could get beyond its borders, and eventually the criminal would be found, so everyone just accepted the Administrator's judgments without question. But without the light, Mallory could leave the city—and who would be able to find her? And maybe leaving would be the best option anyway; she did not want to make her parents and friends have to deal with her death. She did not want Alex to join her in that outcome either. But if she could find a way to survive in the dark forest, she would at least have a chance for life, and her family and friends could keep some hope not knowing whether she was alive or dead. She thought it was a pretty good solution.

Then her grandmother's voice sounded in her head: "You are the Matriarch who is a Chorus that will save the city."

Mallory growled and spoke back to the voice in her head defiantly, "Some savior I turned out to be." She stared at the smoke plume ahead. "Looks like I'm doing a pretty good job destroying the city. The Administrator may not be a good man, but he's certainly right about one thing—your curse was the worst thing that ever happened to this city. I am the worst thing that ever happened to this city."

Mallory felt like her grandmother's voice in her head had a response to her argument, but as the voice was just Mallory's own, Mallory muffled it. She had spent so much of her life trying to live up to that prophecy, and all it had ever done was cause everyone around her pain. She was done trying to save the city. With saviors like her, who needed destroyers?

Suddenly, Mallory's self-deprecating thoughts came to a screeching halt. She heard them before the group rounded the corner and saw them: the sound of large, metal discs scraping against each other.

It was impossible. How could they have been birthed without the Dikaió? Yet, when the Knennes and Aiworths turned onto Main Street with their buckets of water, there in the street were the unmistakable shapes of three fire sprites spraying hot death all around them. The three sprites were quite far down the street, and if they were not twelve feet tall, they would have been hard to make out. Between them and the fire sprites stood the crowd of citizens from the Governor's District.

The Governor walked into the crowd with his buckets of water, screaming at the top of his lungs, "What are you all doing? Go! Get your water buckets! Let's put out these fires!"

Mallory followed behind him, every thought of escape forgotten with the weight of what she had unleashed on the city. At first, she did not want to meet the eyes of the citizens while she weaved between them in the Governor's wake, but then she began to be curious why none of them seem to be responding to his orders. She looked around her, and she saw the same blank, gaunt faces from the night they had tried to throw her into the bonfire: They did not have the energy to care that giant sprites were destroying their city. Instead, they stared ahead at the fire sprites, watching with dull eyes and limp hands. They were no longer brown-eyed, blue-eyed, and green-eyed citizens—all that was left were empty husks of orange-eyed humanity, the fire of their own demise reflecting in their corneas.

Mallory could not bear looking at these people any longer, so instead, she looked up at the skyscrapers where the remainder of the city's food was located. So far, the fires did not seem to be taking to the glass and steel structures, but if it did, the populace would starve completely. Somehow, these monstrosities needed to be stopped.

Then she saw two tiny streams of water began to spray off the top of one of the skyscrapers. Mallory could only just make out two firefighters holding the nozzles of a hydrant sprite, directing the streams of water just like she had imagined it working. Against the fire sprites' onslaught, the hydrant sprite seemed almost completely ineffectual—at least, Mallory could not see the streams of water extinguishing any of the flames.

On the other skyscrapers, she saw small platforms slowly ascending the buildings: Ropes on the sides of each platform were being pulled by four men, and in the center of the platform stood a hydrant sprite. She did a quick count, and there were about eight platforms ascending. She was not sure how many hydrant sprites there were in the city, but she could tell they would be little help against the fire sprites. She could feel the water in her buckets sloshing onto her bare legs, and she knew these buckets of water would do little to help, either. If they could just stop new fires from forming, maybe then they would have a chance to put out the existing ones.

As they got closer, they could see a line of magistrates firing their weapons at the fire sprites. Just like the stories that their grandparents had told, the magistrates' weapons seemed to be having no effect on them. At this distance, Mallory could see that the sprites were in nearly the same state of repair as when she had left them. The one she had completed was moving along quickly, spraying fire in steady, accurate streams. The half-completed one was a bit more haphazard, but still causing plenty of destruction. The third one had just been piles of parts yesterday, and it did not look like much more than that now. It lumbered along in uneven steps, trying to spray fire out of rotted hoses and rusted nozzles, which were just dripping the fire down on itself so that it looked more like a bumbling ball of fire than a fire sprite. There was a trickle of fire coming from its nozzles that was catching bits of odds and ends on fire, but most of the destruction it was causing was from crashing into things, destroying them with the force of its weight and momentum while simultaneously catching them on fire.

They were about halfway through the crowd when the bumbling sprite bounced off the corner of one of the skyscrapers and went stumbling through the line of magistrates and into the crowd. Suddenly, the orange-eyed masses dissolved into multi-colored terror. The crowd turned and began to push back against itself. Mallory was jostled to the left and right. She tried desperately to cling to her buckets of water, but she dropped both of them when, in a moment of self-preservation, her body decided that clinging to useless buckets was less important than staying upright in the mad rush of the crowd. Her body also seemed to decide that pushing forward against the crowd would not work, and that going backwards was not an option either, so through much mashing and shoving, she managed to make it inside a skyscraper to her left.

Mallory turned to watch the crowd scramble past the buildings. Her adrenaline was pumping, but as it subsided a little, she felt some stinging pain in her feet. Her feet were still bare, and her toes were covered in blood. The toenails had been cracked and broken by the boots of the mob as they scrambled past her. Her dress was torn in several places as well. Mallory was not sure exactly what to do about all of it. Should she run back up to her house and change clothes and get some shoes? In the midst of this thought, a lumbering pile of fire smashed against the windows in front of her: It was the animated jumble of sprite parts.

She was surprised that it could move at all. The parts were barely connected; wires dangled, balls moved in and out of sockets, and toothless gears spun pointlessly inside the rusted holes in its hull. The thing looked almost as if it had been roughly pushed together rather than connected by skilled hands, and Mallory wondered if it was possible that this abomination was the handiwork of the other two fire sprites.

She did not have time to wonder long because the sprite backed up, and then ran hard into the skyscraper again. The windows shattered as their steel frames bent. That's when Mallory determined that the fire sprite was not ambling aimlessly: Its red, glowing eyes were set on her. It lowered both nozzles in her direction, and the sound of metal scraping metal enveloped the air around her. She could see the sparks of the flint wheels inside the fire sprite, and she could see the mechanism inside the pumps leading to the nozzles begin to move: It was going to spray her with liquid fire.

She stepped backwards and felt glass slide into the bottom of her foot. She squeaked quietly but knew there was no time to deal with pain; it would be better to have her feet cut to ribbons than be roasted alive by this homicidal sprite.

Then out of nowhere a silver flash hit the top of the sprite, and Mallory watched as the rusted bits of the fire sprite collapsed in on the moving parts. The flint discs went topsy turvy, and the sprite's arms bounced up just as the accelerant pumped out of the nozzles. Paraffin shot into the air above the fire sprite, and it collapsed on the ground. As the liquid fuel ignited, the fire sprite's tanks exploded, knocking Mallory backwards onto the glass-strewn floor.

Mallory lay there on the floor blinking, staring at the ceiling of the first floor of the skyscraper through smoke wafting in from the street. Copper ceiling tiles with alternating lilies and fluers-de-lis stretched across the room above her. The reflection of the fire flickering on the copper artwork amongst trails of smoke was surprisingly beautiful, like light-dragons dancing in cloudy skies. Her mind took her back to that night at City Hall when the backdraft had knocked her into the grass with Caleb. She could almost feel his protective weight again. She suddenly wondered how she had managed to live her entire life without being blown up, and now at seventeen, she had been blown up twice. She imagined the stained-glass Matriarch wearing non-flammable bubble-wrap armor over her gown, and Mallory reached out to pinch one of the bubbles and feel its satisfying pop. Her fingers closed over empty space.

She blinked. Hot, dry smoke filled with the stench of paraffin enveloped her as her eyes adjusted once more to the fiery reality around her. She pulled herself to her feet, trying to shake off the pain and disorientation of the explosion—but when she was fully upright, she felt herself gasping for air and quite dizzy. Her head throbbed every time she coughed. The walls in front of her were on fire now, and smoke had filled the air. She felt the fabric of her dress, thinking she would make a mask of it, but the dress was made of chiffon and was too porous to keep the smoke out. She considered crawling her way out, but the floor was littered with glass shards, and that same blue chiffon dress would offer little protection for her hands or knees. Walking seemed to be the only way to survive, and her bare, bloody feet ran the risk of further injury.

She bent down and began to tear strips of blue fabric from around the hem of her already torn dress. Then she tied the fabric around her feet like bandages, hoping that the delicate dress material would at least provide some cushion between her bare skin and the glass on the floor. Once her feet were covered, she waited for what seemed like an eternity—blinking, trying to clear her vision—before carefully picking her way forward to avoid more glass. She peered through the broken windows, trying to figure out what had hit the fire sprite, and she saw the glint of shiny silver steel amidst the flames: a hydrant sprite. The unstable fire sprite must have knocked it loose from the platform that was making its way to the top of the building. When the hydrant sprite fell, the nigh-indestructible sprite steel had gone through the fire sprite's older, rusty steel like butter. It looked like the fall had ruined the hydrant sprite as well, as pieces of shiny, new sprite steel were sprinkled about, and its silver hull was now a mangled mess. She narrowed her eyes and thought to herself, "They can be broken after all."

Limping gingerly out into the street, she was relieved that most of the crowd was gone, but there were still some people laying in the street. Mallory limped painfully over to the nearest woman to see if she was okay.

The woman had her face to the ground, and her hands were covering her head. Dark, deep burns traced up her arms and legs, and parts of her scalp were showing through her singed blond hair. Her yellow dress was now mostly black and smoldering. Mallory bent down and gingerly touched the woman's back. The woman did not respond. Mallory pushed a little harder, and said, "Miss, are you okay?" There was still no response. Mallory shoved her hands under one side of the woman's torso and pushed, starting to turn the woman over. As the woman's face became visible, Mallory realized by the glazed eyes and gray color that the woman would never respond to anything in this life again.

Mallory dropped her and scrambled backwards as shooting pain radiated up from her feet. She wheeled backwards and nearly tripped over the limp form of a magistrate laying behind her.

Mallory spun around slowly; the streets were sprinkled with citizens that did not get away from the fire sprite fast enough. When her grandmother died, it looked nothing like this.

She felt sick to her stomach.

The fire sprites she created were busy setting fire to whatever they could further up Main Street, and there were still some magistrates struggling behind them, ineffectually firing at them. She watched one of the fire sprites take aim at a magistrate that was too close, and the grinding metal noise carried across the wind, drowning out his scream. She turned away in horror, stumbling away from the fire sprites and bodies, limping hopelessly away from the destruction. Her eyes burned from smoke and the images of death. Her head throbbed. Her feet were full of glass spikes that pulsed into her legs like an electrical current. Her grandmother was wrong. Mallory was no Matriarchal savior. She was the mother of damnation, and she had birthed the death of the city and christened it with fire.

Mallory nearly fell onto Silver Street, trying to shuffle up the big hill, dizzy and without thought; she felt empty inside. Her feet screamed in protest, and she slipped from the oozing blood that seeped through her makeshift bandages. The world was swimming in and out of focus—but what did it matter? She took deep breaths for the first time since the explosion. She coughed, sputtering on the taste of chemical smoke. After she coughed, the dizziness felt a bit better, though her head still throbbed. She found herself thinking that if she could just get home, everything would be okay—like when she would wake up from a nightmare to dragonfly lights dancing on her ceiling.

On the other hand, if she did not make it home, it would

at least be hard to execute her if she were already dead. Alex's grandfather had been so reluctant to end the trial even when the city was on fire. Perhaps without the public spectacle of humiliating the Matriarch's house, he might not be able to initiate the next phase of his plan. The fear on his face when she mentioned the book at his house revealed how terrified he was that the truth would come out, and she had all but told the Chief Magistrate she was willing to unveil the secret. Considering his history with fire sprites, and now with three fire sprites attacking the city, the Administrator's plans were at least on pause if not ruined. Of course, the heirs' plans were not exactly working out either: How were the fire sprites birthed without the Dikaió? And even more importantly, could they be stopped?

Her view of the street ahead turned slowly sideways then, and she felt herself falling over some obstacle in the road. She willed herself to stay upright, but it was no use against the dizziness that was creeping up her neck and face. She briefly saw blue sky with white cumulus clouds drifting quietly in the expanse ahead of her, and then she saw gray pavement and a sparkly shoe some careless girl had left in the road. Blue sky and gray pavement blurred together in her vision again; she was rolling backwards down the hill. There may have been pain, but her consciousness was so blurred, she could not say where for certain. She came to a hard stop at the bottom of the hill, staring up at the sky with too much shock to register where she was or what had happened. The blue was still there, and the clouds, but there was black smoke at the periphery of her vision. The sound of scraping metal echoed down the wall of skyscrapers, reverberating fiery destruction. Mallory closed her eyes, but the noise could not be blocked out, and even in the darkness, she could hear the scream of fire.

Somewhere outside the screech of metal, she heard running footsteps; someone was close, maybe more than one. Frightened, she forced her eyes halfway open and looked up into crystal-blue eyes. Was it Caleb or the Governor? Or was it a blue-eyed citizen? She forced her eyes farther open. There was a female magistrate beside Blue Eyes. It was Alex and Caleb. They were both covered in soot and ash. Caleb began to rip the bottom of his shirt, and Alex knelt down and began to unwrap Mallory's feet. Another pair of feet stepped into Mallory's vision along with the wheel of a Chorus Cart. She turned her head and saw that it was her father. He started to tear strips off his shirt as well. The blur of her mother ran past him and knelt beside Alex to help unwrap the other foot.

The women used the strips of the men's shirts to rewrap Mallory's feet, and her mother pulled tight on the one with the lacerations to stop the bleeding. Caleb and her father carefully picked her up and laid her in the cart. Her mother shouted over the sound of the fire sprites, "Take her to the house so we can tend those wounds."

Caleb did not hesitate and picked up the handles.

Mallory had wanted to get home, but she felt like home had come to her. Tears stung in her dry, aching eyes but she fought them back. She looked down at herself in the Chorus cart and wondered if they should take her to the hospital instead, even as Caleb maneuvered the Chorus cart toward her house. As he turned around to get a good position to go up Silver Street's hill, Mallory got a brief view down Main Street. There was not much chance of getting to the hospital anyway. The partially completed fire sprite was busy working over one of the skyscrapers with flame. The completed one was missing. Mallory scanned the street quickly, and then she spotted it: The fire sprite was climbing down one of the skyscrapers, balancing a huge plastic barrel full of liquid. Mallory knew at once that it was paraffin.

She sat up unsteadily in the cart, throwing Caleb to the side as he grasped the handles, and pointed. "They're reloading!"

Caleb stopped the cart with a thud, and Mallory could feel the breath of his "No!" whisp through her hair more than she could hear it.

The Matriarch yelled, "There's nothing we can do about it right now! Let's get Mallory to the house and regroup!"

Mallory laid back and stared in horror as the completed fire sprite began to refill its compatriot's fuel tanks. Fire danced all around them, raging in places and sputtering in others, even as water rained down from the hydrant sprites on the roofs. There were two or three hydrant sprites on each roof now, and the makeshift elevators were still pulling more hydrant sprites up to fight the fires. The water was slowly putting out fires, but if the fire sprites could refill their tanks from the Culture Co-op's stores of paraffin on top of the buildings, there would be no way to extinguish all the fires they were starting.

As Caleb moved uphill toward the Governor's district with the Chorus cart, the last thing she saw on Main Street before her view disappeared behind the wall of the last down-town building was the burning heap of the fire sprite that had been crushed by the falling hydrant sprite.

"That's it!" Mallory yelled and sat up again.

Caleb, who had been just powering through going up the hill instead of using the zig-zag method that made the trip up easier, nearly dropped the cart with Mallory's motion. Mallory did not seem to notice and was trying to climb out of the cart. Caleb strained under his wiggling passenger but managed to wheel the cart sideways and set it down.

"Good grief, Mal. What are you trying to do to me?" He asked, rubbing his forearms and triceps.

Mallory did not seem to notice and was trying desper-ately to get out of the cart. The Matriarch, who had been a few steps behind, caught up and grabbed her daughter's shoulders.

"What is it, Mallory? What can't wait until you're prop-erly bandaged?"

Mallory stopped struggling and looked into her mother's eyes, "I know how to stop them!"

Her mother shook her head, "The Dikaió didn't work, Mallory. The Administrator tried to use the words to stop them. When he said 'Dikaió fire cease,' they turned on him, and . . ." The Matriarch shook her head.

Mallory let the news of the Administrator's death sink in. She looked at Alex, and Alex looked away.

Mallory looked back at her mother with fresh determi-nation. "No, Mother. We don't need the Dikaió. We can stop them another way."

Caleb leaned into the conversation and asked with intensity, "How?"

"We'll push the hydrant sprites down on them. The fire sprite's steel is old, rusted; it's much more brittle than the new sprite steel—that's what happened to the one that exploded. A hydrant sprite fell when the fire sprite rammed the building." She closed her fist and opened it quickly wiggling her fingers while mouthing the sound of the explosion.

Caleb scratched his head, "That makes sense; the hydrant sprites are indestructible, so—"

Mallory shook her head, "The fall or the explosion destroyed the hydrant sprite, too, so they're not completely indestructible."

Her father asked, "What if we push the hydrant sprites, and they miss, or don't stop the fire sprites with one shot?"

"There are lots of hydrant sprites on the buildings. We'll push as many as needed to stop them."

Her father's eyebrows went up. "Then how will we put the fires out afterwards?"

Mallory hesitated at that. Her father was right; the hydrant sprites had another purpose. If they used them as falling missiles, the city would continue to burn. Down in the marketplace below the Governor's District, the buildings were built a lot closer together, and the proximity of the houses on the streets behind them were also very close—nearly touching each other. If the wind picked up, it would not be like the City Hall fire; the inferno could quickly spread through the whole city if it was not stopped here. The hydrant sprites could not be sacrificed so easily.

Caleb spoke rapidly then, clenching his fists like he was ready for a fight: "If we could get to the Rookery, there are hundreds of un-birthed sprites in the basement forges. We could drop those off the buildings."

Mallory's mother shook her head with disappointment, "The only way to the Rookery is up Main Street."

"Are there no other side streets through the city that go around Main Street?" Mallory asked.

Caleb shook his head. "No, it's all dead ends and cul-de-sacs in the neighborhoods; the city flows to Main Street. We'd have to go out the South side and walk through the pastureland all the way around the city."

Then Alex spoke for the first time: "There is another way to get to the Rookery."

They all looked at her with their eyebrows raised. Alex pointed at a manhole cover in the center of the street. "The sewers run under every street, including below Main Street all the way to the hospital and Rookery. If we went through them, we could get there safely."

The Matriarch nodded, "That could work. How do we get the un-birthed sprites back here?"

"We don't have to," Mallory said. "The fire sprites are working their way up Main Street, not back this way. We just need to get to the skyscrapers on the other side of them."

"Sprites are heavy," her father said. "How are we going to carry them out?"

Mallory grinned and slapped the sides of her beloved Chorus cart. "With these!"

The Matriarch nodded, "Okay! Roger, you and Alex go

find as many people as you can to get through the sewers to the other side of the fire sprites. Have them gather Chorus carts and then carry as many of the un-birthed sprites as you can manage. Caleb, I need you to help me get Mallory up to the house."

Mallory shouted, "No, I want to help!"

Her mother smiled, "You have helped, sweetheart, but if we don't bandage your feet and stop that bleeding, you'll be falling on the fire sprites yourself—and I doubt you'll do enough damage," she teased. She motioned to Caleb that he should continue up the hill. He lifted the handles of the Chorus cart, and Mallory fell unceremoniously backwards into it. She watched longingly as her father and Alex rushed back down the hill, yelling at the top of their lungs for help.

Mallory was unhappy about getting left out of the plan. In her mind's eye, she could see herself trapesing through the sewers toward the Rookery. Of course, her mental vision of what a sewer looked like was a bit hazy, considering she had never seen the inside of one. Still, the idea of missing out on her own idea was clouding her mood as surely as the black billows of smoke that were spreading over the city. They finally had some shred of hope, but the daylight filtering through the hazy sky was starting to acquire an odd, dark-reddish tint—almost as if it was evening—though it was still afternoon. The city had grown eerily quiet—even the birds and insects had stopped chirping. The only sound that could be heard was the distant sound of grinding metal.

At the Matriarch's house, Caleb lifted her out of the Chorus cart and carried her into the kitchen. Her mother pushed everything off the counter, causing kitchen sprites to burst into the room and start cleaning things off the floor. The people danced and weaved between the kitchen sprites, now quite accustomed to their obnoxious presence.

"Put her here," the Matriarch said, "with her feet in the sink, so we can clean those wounds." Her mother unwrapped her feet carefully, and then turned on the tap on the kitchen sink. Cold water hit Mallory's feet, and the temperature shocked her. She squirmed beneath the sting of water entering her wounds and pushing out the glass and dirt. Caleb was leaning on the counter, and she clawed at his arm to hold back a scream desperately working its way up her windpipe.

Caleb seemed to find her scream in his own windpipe, and he yelped. "Ow!" He pulled back from her claws, held his hand to his chest, and looked at her with big puppy-dog eyes full of betrayal.

She laughed out loud at him, and the pain in her feet subsided, at least until her mother poured antiseptic on them. Then Mallory took her scream back, "Yow! Mother! Must you do that?"

Her mother looked at her sternly. "Your whole life I've told you the worst thing about a cut is the potential for infection. So yes, I must do this, Mallory!"

"My whole life, you've been pouring that wicked stuff on me. I've been burned by real fire, and it didn't hurt so bad," she answered grumpily.

"And for your whole life, you've never had an infection. You're welcome! Now let's see. It doesn't look like these cuts are too deep. I think we can just bandage them, and you'll be fine. But I want you to stay off them, so they can heal."

Mallory looked wide-eyed at her mother. "Fire sprites are destroying the city, Mother. I don't think laying around the house is the best thing I could be doing right now."

Her mother replied, "And what would you do that the rest of the city can't, Mallory?"

"Were you not just there on the hill? Who had the idea of smashing them with the other sprites? I can help if I'm out there."

Her mother shook her head and said, "No, I think you've done enough, Mallory. Stay here and heal."

Caleb spoke up then. "Mrs. Knenne, Matriarch, I believe you're making a mistake."

The Matriarch stood up straighter. "I think I know what's best for my daughter."

"I'll have to agree with my wife," Mallory's father entered the kitchen.

"Roger?!" her mother shouted. "I thought you were rounding up people to go to the Rookery."

"I was, and I did. We ran into the Governor and the Chief Magistrate. When Alex explained the plan to them, they took over organizing the people, and I came home to check on Mallory. I agree that going out there is not what is best for her."

Caleb shook his head. "We're not talking about what's best for your daughter right now. We're talking about what's best for the city. I've never seen anyone who can solve problems the way Mallory does. Even my father says she is a brilliant strategist, though he disapproves of many of her actions. If there are problems executing her plans down there, we need someone capable of making effective decisions and pivoting in the moment. She has lived this way her entire life, solving problems in the moment and recovering from injuries when they happen. We need Mallory there to help."

Mallory's mother squirmed and pointed at her daughter's feet. "She can't go into the sewers with her feet like that. They'd be infected for certain."

Caleb nodded. "I'll concede that. We do need a way to get her past the fire sprites to help organize our counterattack though."

The Matriarch straightened and pulled her shoulders back, "She cannot walk on those feet. They need to heal. I won't allow it."

Caleb looked down at the woman, his blue eyes flashing. "With all due respect, Matriarch, if Mallory does not help us stop those fire sprites, her hurt feet will be the last of her issues . . . all of our issues. They're aiming to wipe out this city."

"And who's fault is that, Caleb Aiworth? Wasn't this your idea?"

Caleb's blue eyes did not blink, "Yes, I made a mistake. What's happening is my doing, and I'll take full responsibility—after we stop these monsters. But I need Mallory with me to stop them; I don't think it can be done without her."

The Matriarch turned her gaze away, and Mallory's mother withered into the arms of her husband. "Why is everyone so intent on taking my daughter away from me, today?" She whispered into his chest.

"Mother!" Mallory choked on tears. Seeing her mother show such weakness made her heart swell. "Mother, I'll be okay. I promise."

Caleb nodded, "I'll carry her in a Chorus cart and protect her feet—and her life—with my own if needed."

Mallory's father shook his head. "And what if you both lose your lives in the fire?"

"Mother, you've given your life to this city in service. It's something I was never going to be able to do—but I can do this—and if it costs me my life, so be it." Mallory reached out for her mother's hand. "Life is more than just existing."

Her mother took Mallory's outstretched hand and said, "Your grandmother was fond of that saying, but existing is better than dying, Mallory."

"Birth and death are just a part of life," Mallory pulled her mother into an embrace. "I very nearly died earlier today without fulfilling my purpose. My decisions have cost a lot of other people their lives, but I still have a chance to save the ones who are left. Today, Grandmother's prophecy will be fulfilled; this is the day a Matriarch who is a Dikaió Chorus saves the city."

Her mother breathed deeply. "Fine, but we're going with you two."

Her father nodded vigorously and added, "Quite right!"

Caleb worked carefully with Mallory's father to lift her off the counter and back into the Chorus cart. The Matriarch still looked uneasy about the whole ordeal, but she came along quietly.

Back on Main Street, the small group rounded the corner to see if there was a way to skirt the fire sprites. Mallory's parents stayed behind the cover of a wall and peeked their heads out. Caleb and Mallory had to go out into the street for Mallory to see because the Chorus cart could not be angled more stealthily. She desperately wished she had one of the wheelchairs from the hospital; the Chorus carts were very uncomfortable. Mallory did her best to ignore her discomfort, as she surveyed the battlefield.

Two skyscrapers on the left side of the street were engulfed in flames. The hydrant sprites and the firefighters on top of the buildings were trying desperately to keep the fires at bay, but the half-completed sprite was standing at the corners of the buildings and adding flames to both. The flames were slowly winning the fight. Across the street, the fully completed sprite was concentrating its fire on another building. The steel beams of the building were growing red as the flames climbed; soon it would be engulfed in flames like the other two. Mallory could barely see beyond the fire sprites: Multiple figures covered in muck were pushing carts full of silver sprite steel. Platforms carrying empty sprite husks were being raised quickly by fresh arms, but she saw that they could not get sprites to the skyscrapers that were on fire, nor save the firefighters on top of those buildings.

The Matriarch covered her mouth with her hand and said quietly, "Those poor people."

Caleb shook his head. "I don't know how we can save them; we have to focus on the plan."

Mallory had decided that enough people had died today

because of her poor choices. She looked around. There were three skyscrapers between them and the ones that were on fire. She pointed up at the skyscraper next to the one the fire sprites were torching. "If we could pull the elevator platform all the way up and onto the roof of that building," then she pointed to the one on fire, "and we could get the ropes across to the fire fighters on that one, then we could use the four sets of ropes and the pullies to make a horizontal elevator of sorts."

"What?" her mother, father, and Caleb asked in unison.

"I wish I had something to draw it on. Give me your hand, Caleb. Look, Caleb's hand is the platform. You can see that the platforms are already connected at the four corners via pulleys." She pulled up Caleb's fingers, so his hand made a cup shape. She touched his fingertips with her pointer finger. "After the rope is across, we can run it through each of these pulleys. The platform can dangle from the ropes like a carriage. We can use another unthreaded rope to pull ourselves across to the other building." She made a motion of pulling on a rope, as if she were in a tug-of-war game. The trio around her nodded uncertainly.

"How are we going to get the ropes across to the building that's on fire? Or tell the firefighters over there what to do?" Caleb asked.

Mallory bit her lip. That was a tough question. There was really no way into the building with the fire sprite blasting away at the entrance. Some of the ash that was floating in the air nearly landed in her eye, and she batted it away. The ash swirled and danced in the air following the current of her hand and then floated away. That gave her the idea, "Now, we really do need some paper and a pencil. The firefighters will likely not know how to read, so I'll draw a picture of the directions on the paper, and then we can fold it like the paper birds we used to make as kids. The paper birds will float over to the firefighters, and they can tie the ropes themselves."

"And how do we get the ropes over?"

Mallory looked around the street. It was not market day, so all of the Dikaió Culture's market tables were folded and packed away. Grocery boxes were sitting neatly stacked on top of them.

"Caleb, what happens if you throw one of the grocery boxes in the air?" Caleb grabbed a grocery box and flung it into the air. The propellors under the box immediately kicked in and brought it down to a safe landing.

"That's what I thought," Mallory nodded. "Now try throwing it across the street." Caleb threw the grocery box as hard as he could, and once again the propellers engaged and slowly brought the box down, but it maintained its forward momentum and trajectory, landing the box several feet away from them.

Caleb smiled, "Do you think it will make it across the gap between buildings?"

The Matriarch said, "It's going to have to."

Caleb nodded, "Okay, Mister Knenne, can you help me load Mallory on the platform with some of these grocery boxes, and the two of us will pull them up the building? Matriarch, I'm sure one of these floors has an office of some sort with paper and pencils. If you take the stairs, you should be able to find some and meet us on the roof. Grab enough to send over multiple messages—the updraft between these buildings might blow some of them off target."

The Matriarch looked up at the twelve-story building and breathed in heavily. "Okay," she said with a quiver in her voice, putting a hand on her stomach. Mallory had completely forgotten that she was also carrying her tiny, little sister, and she would have to carry them both up all those stairs. The Matriarch reached up and pinned some stray hairs into place, pulled her shoulders back and then ripped open the double-doors and hurried inside in search of paper and a stairwell.

Caleb and Mallory's father began pulling on the ropes to lower the elevator platform on the side of the building, and Mallory sat and watched the twelve-foot sprites work over the buildings with fire. They seemed to be learning as they went, testing points of integrity in the buildings, seeing what would burn and what would not. They had been at this awhile, and only managed to set these three buildings on fire. So far, any time they let up, the hydrant sprites were still able to beat down the fires.

Mallory thought about the ancient magic possessed by the people who constructed these buildings generations ago. Unlike City Hall and the houses on Manuel Street, these buildings seemed like they were designed to withstand fire. She had a real urge to get out of the cart and go investigate the buildings that were on fire, to understand what kept them from being consumed. Her hands grasped the sides of the cart, and she was just starting to lift herself up when she felt the cart lurch: Caleb was behind her. "Okay, Mal," he said, picking up the handles. "Here we go!"

The street shrunk below them as Caleb and Mallory's father pulled the ropes through the pulleys, and the platform ascended the side of the skyscraper. The two men had to pull the ropes in sync as the platform was tenuously balanced on the pulleys. The citizens had quickly set-up the pulley system given all the issues the city had faced after the loss of the Dikaió, and little attention had been paid to the safety of the platform.

Mallory looked out over the edge and wished desperately for even a simple rope to act as a guard-rail. If one of the men should pull even slightly higher than the other, the platform would tilt sideways, and they'd all slide off. The smoke billowing out of the building next door was wafting along the breeze in their direction and into Mallory's eyes. Tears sprouted up, and her vision blurred once again. She looked at her father and could see the same tears and irritation in his reddened eyes, but he dared not let go of the ropes and overturn the platform.

Caleb was in the same predicament but seemed less capable of ignoring the irritant. He tried to wipe at his eyes with his bicep, but his grip on the rope slipped slightly. The whole platform shook, and Mallory felt her Chorus cart tip slightly backward as she gripped the edges with her hands. Caleb quickly clamped down hard on the rope and pulled his end level with her father's.

"Careful, Caleb," her father called. "Close your eyes if you need to; I'll call out the strokes until we're at the top." Caleb nodded, and stroke-by-stroke they rose to the top of the building.

At the top, the two men wrapped the ropes around cross-sections of metal crossbeams and tied it off to secure the platform. The wind was cold and vicious at that height, and Mallory wished she had taken the time to change clothes. She was still in her formerly elegant blue formal, which was now tattered, burned, and torn up. Her arms were bare and covered in goose pimples prickled by the cold gusts of the updraft.

The platform was a step below the lip of the roof, so the two men picked up Mallory first and heaved her up over the lip. For a moment, while her back was pressed up against Caleb, Mallory warmed up slightly from his body heat—then they dumped her onto the roof and the cold blasts hit her again. Caleb lifted the Chorus cart onto the roof, and her father passed up the grocery boxes. Once the men were on the roof, they lifted her back into the cart and pushed her away from the edge over to a small square building on the rooftop with a door to the stairway.

The rooftop gardens of the Culture Co-op were a thing to behold. Mallory had been on a few tours as part of her schooling as an heir to the Triad. Crops were organized in terracotta pots on tiered shelves ascending toward the center. Green plant stems rose above the terracotta tiers, and below them, glass fish tanks held the roots, so the Culture Co-op could monitor their health. The tallest tier was about ten feet off the ground, and behind it, in the center of it all, was the orchard with fruit and nut trees; the glass bowls for their roots were roughly the size of a large swimming pool and extended below the surface of the roof. The city's fresh-water aquariums flowed into these with fish that fed on and cleaned the roots. Across the terracotta tiers, medium-sized plants like corn and beans grew near the treetops, and smaller plants like strawberries and root vegetables spread out across the bottom terracotta tiers. Hydroponic pipes pumped aerated water and nutrients through each level.

Past the Culture tiers, there were four firefighters with two hydrant sprites at the edge of the building facing the burning skyscrapers. The four men were each holding a redesigned hose that had been haphazardly attached to the old nozzles of the hydrant sprites, just like Mallory had designed. They were pointing the new nozzles where the water needed to go, while the hydrant sprites sat there and sprayed. Mallory wished she had been able to make the attachment more secure; a lot of water was spraying out of leaky connections—but water was at least going where it needed to go now—unlike the fire at City Hall. Caleb and her father walked over to the firefighters and tapped two of the men on their shoulders.

The firefighters nearly jumped off the edge of the building, clearly surprised that more people had been able to get to the top of the building without them noticing. Mallory could see the men all gather into a circle and begin talking. Caleb was talking with his hands, tying and untying invisible knots to help the firefighters understand the plan. Her father would wave his hands in little circles when he added something, and the firefighters would listen politely and then turn back to Caleb for explanation. She smiled watching the interaction. Soon, the men all walked over and began the more difficult task of pulling the platform onto the roof, untying the ropes, and decoupling the pulleys.

Mallory's attention strayed over to the other building that was on fire. There were four firefighters on that building, too, who were spraying water down at the fire that was threatening to consume them. She knew firefighting could be a dangerous job—one of the most dangerous jobs in the city—but these men had no idea there were plans in place to rescue them. For all they knew, they were staring down at the very flames that would eventually consume them. Yet, they showed no panic; they just continued bravely doing their duty and putting down water where it needed to go. The city needed more men like that. And maybe it was already full of men like that.

Mallory looked past the firefighters to the buildings toward the hospital in the north. She could make out the forms of people on the roofs, and the shiny silver steel of un-birthed sprite husks being set up against the sides of the roofs, ready to deploy against the fire sprites. She wished that she could see the fire sprites below her in the street to see what they were doing. In order for their plan to work, they would need to get the fire sprites to move to the building they were occupying, so they could drop the sprite husks on them, but they seemed intent on destroying these three buildings before continuing down the row.

In her head, she imagined that taking the firefighters away from the burning building would also mean that their hydrant sprites would stop extinguishing the fire, which would speed up the fire sprite's progress. Now that she was on top of the building next to the fire sprites, she wondered what would happen if they moved to her building instead of further down Main Street toward the hospital. They needed to get some of those sprite husks over to the building already on fire and stop the sprites there.

Mallory called to the men busily working to carry out her plan, but the wind on top of the building carried her voice away from them. Frustration rose up in her chest, and she beat at the sides of the Chorus cart. No one paid her any attention. She could see no way around it: She was going to have to disobey her mother's wishes, get out of the cart, and walk over to the men to relay her idea. However, when she tried to push herself up out of the cart, she found that the sides were too steep to just vault over. She was going to have to pull her feet into the cart, putting pressure on them, and try to climb out over the side.

Mallory had just started the process when the stairway door swung open, and her mother walked onto the roof carrying a ream of paper and a handful of pencils. Mallory yelled out to her, "Mom!"

Her mother turned and said, "Mallory, what are you doing? Get off your feet; you're going split those wounds wide open again!"

Mallory sunk back into the Chorus cart. "Mother, they can't hear me. We need to adjust the plan."

Her mother nodded. "Okay, I'll get them. You stay here."

"Where would I go?" Mallory yelled and threw up her hands.

Soon, the men were gathered around her cart. Mallory felt strange encircled by all the adults looking down at her. She craned her neck to look into their eyes as she spoke, "The fire sprites are going to keep working on the buildings that they're at until they burn down, so we need to hit the first fire sprite from that building." She pointed at the building currently on fire, "which means, we'll have to use the carriage to get over there, and then make another carriage to send over for the sprite husks. And we'll have to do the same thing for those two buildings across the street."

"Do we really have time for that?" Caleb asked.

"I think we have to. Besides, what happens if the fire sprite comes this way instead of going that way?"

All of their eyes grew larger, and they nodded,

understanding that only having one carriage meant only having one exit that could be cut off by a fire sprite's attack.

Her father asked, "How do we help those guys across the street?"

"Let's get the horizontal elevator set up here, and then you can split up. Two head across the street, and two head across to tell the firefighters nearest to us how to build their own horizontal elevators to get the sprite husks across. Mother, I'll start drawing the directions, and you fold the paper birds. We'll make enough to send across the street."

Everyone went back to work. Mallory drew rudimentary pictures of men tying knots in rope, and she hoped it would be clear enough for the firefighters across the way. The men worked much faster than Mallory had expected them to; she found the firefighters were quite adept at tying knots and threading pulleys. Soon they had secured the two support lines on this building and tied them into the pillars of the terracotta tiers. They were ready to send over the other ends of the ropes in the grocery carts. Caleb came over and wheeled Mallory closer to the edge, so she could see what was happening in case any adjustments needed to be made.

Mallory called to her mother, "Do you have some paper birds ready?" Her mother had about four birds folded, and she walked over to the edge of the building and threw one over. The paper bird fell initially, and then it was caught in the updraft between the tall buildings and spiraled up, and then fell back onto their own roof. Her mother tried another bird, and it followed an identical trajectory.

Mallory shook her head. "Mother, stop. That's not going

to work. Let's see if one of the grocery boxes with the rope will get across."

Caleb smiled. He had apparently been waiting for this. He grabbed one of the boxes with the rope tied to the top slot, backed up to the Culture tiers, and took a running start before throwing it over the edge of the building as hard as he could. The box soared out into the open air. After it had gone about a foot, it got caught in the updraft just like the paper birds. The box drifted upwards. Mallory held her breath, waiting for it to upturn or fly back onto their roof, but the propellers engaged, and the box maintained its forward motion, slowly floating across the space of the two buildings, landing perfectly on the other roof.

Mallory immediately shouted, "Put the directions in the next box and weigh them down with one of those broken pieces of terracotta."

With the directions secured, Caleb sent the next box sailing across the expanse. Mallory was not sure how the distant firefighter across the way saw the second box floating onto their rooftop, but he set down his hose, walked around the terracotta tiers on his rooftop, and met the box while it was still in the air. He watched the box land gently on the rooftop and retrieved Mallory's directions out of the box. He studied them for a moment and looked across the expanse at them.

Mallory and the rest of the group began to point at the rope tied to the tiers on their side. The distant firefighter gave a thumbs-up sign, and soon Caleb, her father, and the two firemen were slowly crossing between the buildings on her horizontal elevator. When they reached the other side, Mallory and her mother both cheered.

The two firefighters from the first building walked away with the others, but her father and Caleb started pulling their way back over to the building on which Mallory and her mother were waiting. When they got back to their roof, Caleb jumped off and said, "I don't think there's enough room for all of us and the Chorus cart, but we're going to need you both over there. Mal, are you okay sitting on the ground?"

Her mother jumped between them. "What do you need her for now? What's wrong?"

Her father moved his hands in small circles then stiffly through his hair. "The platform on that building is on fire down below. We're going to have to send this platform over on the other side for the sprites. You may not have any way off this roof if the fire sprites move to this building. I'm not okay leaving either of you here without a way out. At least over there, we can still get you to safety depending on which way they turn, either north toward the hospital or south toward the Governor's District."

The Matriarch shook her head. "We can just go down the stairs now and get out of harm's way."

Her husband pointed at Mallory's feet. "What about her injuries?"

The Matriarch processed this information then nodded.

Caleb lifted Mallory out of the Chorus cart and lowered her carefully down to the platform. She could not help but land on her feet a little, but she tried to keep her weight off the worst foot. The last thing she wanted to do was lose her balance at this height, so she readjusted her weight onto both feet, even though the pain was excruciating. She squared her jaw with determination and managed to lower herself down to a sitting position off her feet.

Mallory's father helped the Matriarch down, and then the men climbed aboard as well. The support lines were connected to four corners on the platform as it dangled between the buildings, which made this horizontal elevator more stable than the vertical version with only two connections at the top. As the men pulled away from the edge across the expanse, the platform bucked wildly in the updraft. Mallory grabbed the ropes leading to the supports and laid down as low as she could. Her eyes drifted over the edge of the platform: The updraft hit her face, carrying heat and smoke formed by what looked like a river of fire and smoke below them. The fire sprite itself was barely visible despite its massive size. They were going to need remarkable aim to hit it from this height.

The fire itself was climbing quickly up the building without the hydrant sprites working to hold it back. Mallory could tell that they were working against the clock to get what they needed done, and there was a good chance this building would not be saved. The platform touched the side of the building. The firemen stabilized the cart, helping the passengers up. Mallory crawled on hands and knees, and two of them lifted her up over the ledge and carried her out of the way. The men quickly pulled the platform over the side and started untying it from the ropes and pulleys, so they could get the platform to the other side of the building and send it over for the sprite husks.

Mallory was sitting near the grocery boxes, and she had a sudden inspiration. "Did you bring a pencil with you, Mother?" she asked. Her mother tapped her vest pockets and pulled out three pencils. "Perfect, thanks." She took one of the sheets with the knot-tying directions and flipped it over. She bit the corner of her lip and began to draw a new set of directions for the people on the other building. When she finished, she looked up and found the men were gone, likely on the other side of the roof, getting the platform ready to send across to the other building. Her mother was still sitting quietly beside her, staring up at the smoke-filled sky, lost in thought. "Here, give this to Caleb," Mallory said, breaking her mother's trance.

The Matriarch looked down at the drawing, and her eyes widened. "Will this work?"

Mallory said, "I think so." She tapped the boxes. "They carry a lot of weight in groceries."

Her mother nodded thoughtfully and walked off to find Caleb.

All alone now, Mallory looked up in the direction her mother had been gazing. Dark rivulets of smoke filled the sky. The sun was getting lower, and Mallory could not tell how much of the red sky was from the smoke or from the nearness of sunset. For the first time, she wondered if she would die up here, roasted alive on a rooftop. Oddly, she wondered if the crops would smell good while they cooked, and she realized that she had not eaten since breakfast. All of a sudden, the smell of the smoke reminded her of summer barbecues and her stomach rolled in protest and neglect. She rolled her eyes at her body's poor sense of timing.

A lot of time had passed and Mallory started to wonder if they had all forgotten her. She could not see past the terracotta tiers of the rooftop crops to what the group was doing, or if her new plan was working. Waiting was absolutely maddening, so she pulled herself up onto her hands and knees again. She kept her feet elevated off the rooftop, focusing all her weight on her kneecaps. It was not easy crawling in that position, but she made it to the edge of the terracotta tiers and peeked around them to see what the group was up to.

Two firefighters were pulling a grocery box over the edge, and inside it was the silver husk of an un-birthed sprite. The plan had worked. There was no need to send a platform across; they could use the grocery boxes to accomplish the same task. She could see that they had tied the support lines anyway: They now had a means of escape from the building on both sides.

Caleb turned around and started running toward the terracotta tiers. He stopped short and laughed when he saw her peeking around them. "Mal! I should have known you couldn't stay put. Did you see? It worked!"

Mallory nodded and smiled as another sprite husk arrived via grocery cart from the neighboring building to the north. "Can you see across the street? Are they watching what we're doing? They can do the same thing!"

Caleb ran to the western edge of the roof and held his hand up to his eyes to look over to the other buildings. He nodded approvingly and came back to Mallory. "It looks like they saw. They've got an elevator climbing one of the buildings, and it's full of grocery boxes."

Mallory sat back on her haunches. "Great! Let's throw one and see if we can kill one of those things!"

Caleb clapped his hands, "Now, you're talking!"

He ran over to the group of adults and started talking to them animatedly. The sprite husks were fairly heavy, and it took two firefighters to carry one over to the edge. Mallory watched as they positioned it. Caleb directed them to the left and to the right then he held up his fist, waiting in anticipation. His hand lowered quickly, and his shout was lost in the wind gusts atop the skyscrapers, but the firemen were close enough to hear, and they pushed the sprite husk over the edge of the building. Caleb and the three men leaned out over the lip of the rooftop, tracking the descent of the husk.

Their countenances all fell at the same moment, and Mallory knew that they had missed their target. Caleb walked over to her and said, "The fire sprite is standing too far back from the building. We need to be about this much farther out." He held up his thumb and forefinger just slightly apart to demonstrate the slight adjustment that needed to be made. "But the sprites are too heavy; we'll never be able to throw them out farther over the edge."

Mallory bit her lip and thought about the problem. She looked around the rooftop gardens: There were various gardening tools, including shears, spades, and hoses—even a couple of long-handled fruit baskets for picking fruit off the tall trees. "What if we balanced a sprite on two grocery boxes, like so?" She made a V with two fingers and placed the forefinger of her other hand across the top. "We'll tie ropes to the boxes and push them off the roof, so the propellors engage. We can use those fruit pickers to position them over the fire sprite, and then spread the grocery boxes away from each other to drop the sprite."

"That could work!" Caleb said. "What were the ropes for, though?"

"If we miss, we'll need to reel-in the baskets to try again."

"Righ—"

An explosion shook the building under their feet and cut Caleb's agreement short. He lost his footing and fell over backwards. Mallory looked toward the adults, and those who had not been near something to hold onto had fallen to the rooftop as well. Caleb pulled himself up and ran to the edge of the building to see what had happened. He did a double-take and then jumped up and down cheering. The other adults collected themselves and ran over to see too. Soon they were all cheering. Mallory quickly assumed the uncomfortable hands-and-knees crawling position and slowly made her way to the edge of the building. She pulled herself up and peered over.

Across the street, she could see that the half-completed sprite was on the ground in a pile of flames. On the rooftop corner, she saw firefighters, a magistrate, and a blond-haired man, who were all jumping up and down and cheering. It was the Chief Magistrate and the Governor, and they had managed to drop their sprite husk directly on top of the half-completed fire sprite, putting it out of commission.

Mallory felt her heart leap inside her chest. "Yes!" She screamed, starting to pull herself to her feet to join their cheers. Her mother caught her arm, and even though she was laughing quite giddily, she shook her head and pointed down. Mallory laughed and sank back to the ground, clapping her hands instead of leaping up and down on her injured feet.

Suddenly a groan sounded out above the cheering, and the building lurched about six inches to the south. One of the firefighters stumbled forward and fell over the edge—if it had not been for the quick hands of his compatriots, he would have surely fallen to his doom. Mallory pulled herself up onto her knees again, just high enough to look over the lip. She thought for sure he would have screamed when he went over the edge, but instead he was just dangling upside down, anchored to the building only by the hands of two firefighters holding his feet, looking bewildered. They slowly pulled him back on top of the roof. Mallory looked down into the street after the firefighter was safe. The last fire sprite was still busy spraying fire. The south-side corner of the building looked warped, and the metal beams were bending outward through the flames. Everyone was so elated that they almost forgot about the sprite burning the building they were standing on—and they did not have much time.

"Get those boxes and prepare a sprite!" Caleb barked. "Let's end this, so we can get off this building."

Two firefighters ran off to grab a sprite husk, two others grabbed ropes and poles, and Caleb and Mallory's father grabbed the grocery boxes. Caleb and her father dropped the grocery boxes on the roof, and just before they touched the rooftop, the propellors engaged and the boxes began to slowly lower toward the ground. Just before they could land, the fire-fighters slid the poles into slats on the sides of the carts and pulled them gently back up. Mallory was satisfied to see that the propellors stayed engaged. The firefighters with the sprite husk set it on top the two boxes, half on one and half on the other. The boxes dipped toward the center a bit as the sprite steadied on top of them, but they stayed afloat when the firefighters applied some leverage with the poles. Caleb and Mallory's father ran the rope through the slots and around the poles, and the firefighters with available hands tied quick knots, securing the ropes to the floating boxes.

"It's perfect!" Mallory shouted.

The firefighters with the poles began walking toward the western lip of the building, pushing the hovering boxes with the sprite before them. Everyone else ran to the edge, and Mallory pulled herself up on her knees again to see over the lip. Caleb shouted, "Good, another foot or so should do it."

Mallory yelled, "No, it's further. Look at where the first sprite landed. The fire sprite is now about ten feet behind that spot. Those poles are only about twelve feet long, so they need to be all the way to the edge before they drop it."

Caleb looked down, and then back at the firefighters. "You heard her. All the way to the edge." He pointed to the other firefighters. "You men go and help them. The poles are dipping a bit up front. They need more leverage on the back end."

Soon, all four firefighters were at the edge of the building, holding onto the poles. Mallory yelled, "It looks right. Pull the poles apart." The firefighters pulled as instructed, and slowly the boxes holding the sprite husk began to move away from each other. The sprite husk teetered backwards and fell off the backside of the boxes. Mallory had hoped the sprite husk would fall directly between them. She desperately watched the silver football fall, hoping it would hit its mark on the fire sprite's head. End-over-end it tumbled: down, down, down. The closer it got to the fire sprite, the more Mallory worried that the trajectory was off. She was just about to yell to the firefighters to load another one when the sprite husk made contact with the fire sprite—or at least part of it. The sprite husk was a little behind Mallory's target, so instead of hitting the fire sprite's head, the husk smashed through one of the accelerant tanks on its back. There was a split second where the fire sprite was tipping backwards, paraffin mushrooming upward like the splash of a stone breaking the surface of a stream, and then the accelerant touched the flames coming out of the fire sprite's nozzle. The explosion was brilliant.

Mallory's vision blurred as the concussion hit the building: The entire structure tilted nearly a foot to the south. Mallory lost her balance and fell to the rooftop. Everyone else fell over on top of her, and then they were all rolling toward what was now the lower edge of the building. Mallory hit the lip first, and the others hit her. They lay there in a jumble for a moment, and then they began to cautiously stand.

"We need to get off this building," one of the firefighters yelled. "Now!"

The horizontal elevator was on the north side of the

building, opposite where the lilt had tossed them. Everyone began to climb the angled hill that the rooftop had become; the adults walking, and Mallory crawling on hands and knees. It was not a steep incline—only about a fifteen-degree angle—but any incline at that height is worrisome.

Water from the terracotta tiers flushed over the tops of the fishbowls and splashed across the tarred surface of the rooftop—it was so slippery, it might as well have been oil. Their feet slipped this way and that, and what was left of Mallory's blue dress was quickly soaked as she fell into the flow more than once. They were not far in their climb when they heard a terrifying noise coming from just over the western edge of the building: the sound of metal scraping against metal.

There were two or three crashes as windows shattered, and then a flaming sprite head appeared over the top of the lip. The fire sprite was climbing to the rooftop, and it was covered in burning paraffin. One of its tanks was crushed, but the other one looked okay. Mallory shouted, "It needs to reload. It's going for the paraffin!"

The tanks of paraffin that the Culture Co-op used to ward off insects were on the other side of the building from where the sprite was climbing up. They had to stop it from getting more fuel, but Mallory was not sure how. She had run out of ideas.

Suddenly, one of the grocery boxes that were attached to the poles smashed into the fire sprite's head. Mallory followed the pole to see who was wielding it and was surprised to see her mother on the other end. The Matriarch let lose a primal scream that rivaled the fire sprite's screeching metal flints, and she ran forward, pushing the fire sprite hard like a knight with a lance. The fire sprite did not look like it was moving at first, but then its flaming head disappeared from view.

The group ran to the lip of the building. Mallory forgot her injured feet in the rush of adrenaline coursing through her body, and she jumped to her feet and followed them. She got there just in time to see the fire sprite land face-down at the bottom of the building.

The fire sprite lay there for a time, and they all waited for it to explode or show some sign of being destroyed—but then, unfathomably, it started to push itself up off the ground. It was clearly damaged and fell back down several times, but it continued to push up again.

The Matriarch screamed again, and Mallory turned to see her push one of the hydrant sprites off the edge of the building. They all watched the hydrant sprite fall, cart-wheeling water trails all the way down. This time the dropped sprite found its target, and the fire sprite crumpled. An instant later, it exploded. They instinctively grabbed the lip of the building, just before the concussion hit.

The skyscraper groaned as if it were a living animal, then it squirmed in agony. The rooftop buckled and shifted below their feet, and the angle to the other side of the building increased to twenty-five percent. "Let's go!" screamed Mallory's father, waving his arms in clockwise circles toward their only exit.

They all began to run up the rooftop hill. Plants in the gardens let loose, and Mallory watched an apple tree fly past them over the edge of the building, swept along on a river of water from its basin. Fish flopped around, gasping for breath across the rooftop surface. Then a pear tree broke loose, and a walnut tree, followed by an orange tree. If the group had not moved closer to the street-side edge to see what happened to the fire sprite, they would have been directly in the flying orchard's path. They trudged upward past the terracotta tiers until they could see the ropes for the elevator. The ropes were taut as guitar strings and hummed an eerie high C note as they resonated in the updraft.

One of the firefighters said, "The Matriarch, her husband, and the heirs will go first."

Mallory shook her head. "No, there's no time. The ropes are about to break. We all need to go, now!"

The firefighter shook his head, "There's not room for eight people. We'll stay; you go."

Mallory blinked and bit her lip. Her mother cupped her face in both hands. "Mallory, there's not time to argue." She turned to her husband and Caleb. "Get her on the platform, now!"

The two men picked Mallory up, and she did not struggle. Her mother was right; there was not time for a plan B, nor time to argue. When the four of them were on the platform, Caleb and her father began to pull them toward the other building, which Mallory noted was oddly quite a few feet below them. She looked back at the skyscraper they were leaving and could see why: The edge they had just climbed off was several feet higher and seemed to be going higher as she watched it. This side of the building was angling up as the other descended. She looked at the support ropes they were crossing. Frayed bits of rope were starting to stand up along the length of it as the pulleys worked their way down.

"Faster!" she yelled. "The rope is going to break."

Caleb and her father started pulling as fast as they could, and they reached the other building, climbing off quickly. They picked up Mallory and set her down on the rooftop while the waiting firefighters helped the Matriarch off.

The humming of the ropes was climbing the musical scale as the ropes pulled more and more taut. Caleb started climbing back onto the platform. The Matriarch grabbed his arm, "What are you doing?"

"I'm going back for those men!" Caleb shouted at her.

"No!" The Matriarch shot back. "One of the firefighters here will go. You have other duties." Caleb stepped down reluctantly, and a firefighter stepped forward to take his place.

Before he could swing his foot over the lip down onto the platform, there was a rumbling explosion, then another, and another. The building next to them began to sink downward, and they watched with horror as the windows on each floor started bursting outward and the floors collapsed on them-selves in dusty eruptions. The support ropes on the horizontal elevator went limp, then taut again, and then the platform slid off their frayed ends and tumbled into the fiery chasm below.

Nearly a month had passed since the fire sprites had terrorized the city. Mallory had spent a few days in the hospital for stitches, and then two weeks on crutches while her foot healed. Her mother and father invited Caleb and Alex to dinner for her eighteenth birthday, but it was not a joyous occasion; both of her parents cried. This should have been the day she ascended to her matriarchal apprenticeship with her mother, but of course, that was never really a possibility with Mallory's curse, and even less so with everything that had happened over the preceding months. Just as in the days after the Dikaió was lost, she did not see her parents often, though this time they did not keep her completely in the dark. The City Council had been meeting daily to decide what should be done regarding the heirs of the Triad. The trial had been swift and certain, and the heirs were not offered the chance to present their side of the story; the verdict and the sentence having been decided before they ever entered the Governor's house.

Now the time had come for the Council to announce its decision to the general public. The entire city stood in the Governor's District facing the Governor's House. Mallory stood, wearing jeans, calf-high boots, a long sleeve button-up shirt under a thick jacket and a backpack. Her curly hair was tied back in a bushy ponytail that was tucked beneath a wide-brimmed canvas hat. Caleb and Alex stood on either side of her, similarly attired. The Matriarch stood at the top of the stairs with the Governor at one side and Alex's father—now, the Administrator—at the other. The City Council flanked out to the sides of them, and the three teenage heirs stood three steps below them all facing up toward the Triad.

The Governor spoke, "The Council has reached a decision in the trial, as well as an appropriate sentence. First, we have two orders to communicate to the city:

"Number one, this day shall forever be remembered as a day of memorial to those who lost their lives in the fire-sprite attack. We have commissioned the guilds to work together to build an appropriate memorial from the rubble of the building that fell. Should we find the remains of those brave firefighters who stayed atop the roof to save the Matriarch, they shall be entombed there and forever remembered.

"Second, the number of citizen representatives on the City Council will now be equal to the representation of both the guilds and the Triad. We have heard the outcry of the city, and without the Dikaió, we all stand equal as little more than Dikaió Choruses. As such, the citizenry must have more power in the decisions of the Council. Furthermore, the Triad will, from this point forward, submit itself to the vote of the City Council. We no longer stand above you by right of birth, but among you as equals."

Murmuring trickled through the crowd, as the citizens digested the information.

Someone yelled from the crowd, "And what of the heirs who built the fire sprites? What will come to the traitors?"

Another voice echoed the word "traitors" and then another. Soon the whole crowd was chanting the word in unison, and Mallory felt her blood run cold.

The Governor held up his hand for silence, and the mob ignored him for a time, but slowly the chant puttered out, and he was able to speak again. "The Council has weighed their crime and its consequences: the destruction by fire, the loss of life, the treasonous disregard of our laws on one side of the scales of justice; on the other side, their bravery in stopping their creations, for without their ingenuity we could never have stopped the fire sprites. Unfortunately, we would not have had to deal with fire sprites at all if that same ingenuity had not birthed them. For the act of building the fire sprites, the Council has voted that the heirs be executed according to our laws—for the act of bravery, they have voted for a stay of execution and mercy."

The crowd erupted in anger. Shouts of "No!" "Favoritism!" "Injustice!" rang out across the Governor's District.

The Governor yelled now as well, "Please! Please! I am not finished!" The crowd slowly calmed, but Mallory looked over her shoulder, and she could see angry eyes darting around. Spittle was wet on their lips, and their hands were clenched into tight fists. If what the Governor said next did not satisfy them, they were liable to riot and tear them all to pieces.

"However," the Governor yelled, "the Council recognizes that we cannot abide such a danger among us."

Mallory grabbed hold of Caleb and Alex's hands in anticipation of the Governor's next words. The trial had been closed to the public this time, but the three of them knew exactly what was coming. They were given one day to prepare for it, and Mallory only hoped that she had anticipated enough eventualities in packing to survive the Council's decree.

The Governor pronounced the sentence: "Henceforth, Mallory Knenne, Caleb Aiworth, and Alexandria Nelson shall be banished from this City, forever exiled to the dark forest at our borders. Should they return, the Council's mercy shall be ended, and the initial judgment shall be carried out: The heirs shall be immediately put to death in accordance with our laws."

The crowd murmured amongst themselves, and then voices began to signal assent. "Exile! Exile! Exile!" the chant began.

The Governor again waved for silence and then continued. "The memorial in the marketplace will list their names among the deceased, as they will be lost to us forever.

They are to leave us today carrying only what they selected for their life outside the City. However, since no one has left the City in any of our generations, or for eons before, the guilds will now present gifts of their trade to help them on their journey."

He stepped back, and the short Smith guild master stepped forward. "The Smith guild offers you a reminder of your houses." He handed them each an ornamental broach of their house's symbol: Caleb received a shield, Mallory a dragonfly, and Alex a scroll of law.

The Manager of City Services stepped up next and handed them each a flask of water and explained, "There are filters on the lids of these flasks that will remove the impurities and bacteria from any water source you find in the dark forest."

The head of the Mercantile guild stepped forward. She presented them each with a heavy woolen cloak and full-length leather gloves. "Should the days turn cold, you'll need these to keep you warm."

The Head of the Science guild followed her sister and presented Alex with a compass, "so you can find your way when you need it." To Mallory, she gave a miniature tool kit, "for whatever new inventions you may make." To Caleb, she gave a flint and striker, "for the one who likes starting fires," she said with a wink.

The Sprite Master walked up next and handed them each several feet of rope. "I wish I could offer you a sprite, but this may prove more handy when you need it." She paused in front of Caleb and looked deep into his blue eyes. He stared back, and Mallory wondered what secret message passed between them, but then the Sprite Master returned to her place.

The Culture guild came next. He handed them knapsacks full of nuts, dried fruits and various jerkies. "You'll be hungry at some point, no doubt. Should you find open land, you may also need these." He handed Mallory several packs of seeds. "I've written the directions for tending the crops on the packets."

The Governor then stepped forward. He presented them each with two blades: a long-serrated knife and a short sword. "May these help you in times of need, whatever that may be." He reached his hand up and cupped his son's shoulder. There were tears in his eyes, but he blinked them away quickly and stepped back to his place.

Alex's father, the new Administrator, stepped forward now, looking anywhere but at his daughter and the other heirs. "For the exiled heirs, I offer the protection of the magistrates' armory in their exile." Mallory's father stepped forward, wearing the uniform of the Chief Magistrate. A member of the familial Triad was required to hold the role, and he was the only one who had training as a magistrate. The City Council had agreed that he would hold the title for as long as an heir to the Administration was absent, or until the Matriarch's daughter was old enough to hold the role of Matriarch. Then Mallory's mother would join her husband as the wife of the Chief Magistrate. He stood in front of the former heirs, holding holstered belts with magistrate weapons and three pouches of spare ammunition. "Whatever dangers are out there in the dark forest; may these weapons protect you." The pair of fathers hugged their respective daughters and then stepped quickly back to their places.

Finally, the Matriarch stepped forward. Tears choked back her words, but she took Mallory's hand, and then reached out and took Caleb's and said, "As my gift to you, and with the power granted to me as Matriarch and the voice of the Dikaió, I give you marriage—if you'll have each other." She paused and waited for their responses.

Caleb looked at Mallory and said, "I will."

Mallory's heart beat fast, and her mouth went dry. She thought that she should take time to consider what was happening, but while her mind was occupied, her heart spoke of its own accord, and she said, "I will."

The Matriarch smiled. "Then it is so. Let it be recorded that Caleb Aiworth and Mallory Knenne were bound one to the other before they were lost from the city." She nodded to Caleb, who reached gently for Mallory. Drawing her close, he whispered, "I love you, Mallory Aiworth" and kissed her.

Mallory looked up into his clear, blue eyes and answered his warm embrace with a smile, "I love you, too, Caleb Aiworth."

The Matriarch turned to Alex, who had lost her composure and was crying profusely. "Dearest, Alex. I wish there was something equivalent that I could give you, but to you I give the charge to protect the future of this pair. Children are the life of the city, and they will be your life beyond its borders. Will you accept this charge?"

Alex wiped her eyes and nodded, "I will."

"Then, while you will no longer be present with us, if you cherish these sacred promises, the city will be with you wherever you might go."

The Matriarch turned to the citizenry then. "The Triad has committed to giving you new heirs to replace these that were lost. You can see that I carry a child; she will be the Matriarchal heir. The tradition of the city will continue through her; the city will continue through us and through our children. Though the loss of the Dikaió has left us all equal as Choruses, still the city will live."

The crowd shouted in agreement. "The city will live!"

The Matriarch looked again toward the former heirs, "And now you must leave. I love you, my daughter." She smiled at Caleb. "And my son. A mother should never outlive her children. I will remember you forever."

The three teens descended the stairs, and the crowd parted in front of them. They walked down Silver Street, leaving the Governor's District behind them for the last time. The crowd followed behind them. Musicians worked their way to the front. They had cobbled together rough instruments in workshops that resembled the ones that the Dikaió used to make out of light: One had a stringed guitar made of a sprite's un-birthed husk and wires, one had drums made of silver sprite heads, one held a flute whittled from a tree branch, and the last played a violin made from what looked to be an old chair, some dried leather, and a cow-hair bow. The music was not as clean as the Dikaió's, but the imperfection of the sound imbibed the music with more emotion than Mallory had ever heard before. As they turned onto Main

Street, the crowd's footsteps began to fall in tempo to the beat. Children ran beside them as they walked, laughing and dancing, and in another less somber circumstance, Mallory might have joined them. It felt a lot like they were walking in a Christening procession.

Mallory bit her lip and tilted her head as a thought struck her: Her mother was a Matriarch who was a Chorus now. She was the one who had defeated the final fire sprite and saved the city. She had fulfilled the Dikaió's prophecy when Mallory could not.

Mallory smiled.

It seemed fitting that her mother, who embodied the Matriarchy so well should be the hero the city needed. Even now, in bearing a new Matriarch, she was giving herself in service in a way Mallory never would. Whatever children she and Caleb had would never be heirs of the City. Mallory's destiny suddenly looked much like the forest they were approaching: dark and mysterious. Oddly enough, Mallory felt as if a weight had been lifted off her shoulders.

Suddenly, a swarm of dragonflies flitted past her, spinning and darting amongst the dancing children. She took hold of Caleb's hand, squeezed it hard, gave him a smile, and laughed heartily. As she laughed, she let the music take hold of her, and ran ahead with the children and dragonflies, dancing into the unknown.

The darkness was nearly impenetrable at that time of night in the forest. The moon and stars barely shone through the thick canopy above them, and when it was cloudy, like it was that night, their eyes could not adjust to the dark. Caleb was striking the flint behind Mallory and cursing under his breath. She and Alex stood close to one another, sensing each other's warmth in the cold of the night more than seeing each other.

They had their magistrate weapons out, but it was impossible to get a bead on the noises in the woods. Leaves rustled, and grunts and growls moved among the undergrowth. The four-legged beasts of the dark forest had surrounded their little clearing every night for the last three weeks since they set up camp there. The creatures would stay away if they kept the fire going, so they had been sleeping in shifts to continue tending the flames. It was Caleb's shift to tend the fire, and Mallory was not sure what had happened, but when he called for help, both she and Alex had sprung out of light sleep and grabbed their weapons. Now, they were standing in the dark trying to figure out what to fire at.

"Caleb," Mallory hissed. "Hurry up!"

"I'm trying," Caleb hissed back. Then a spark caught in the kindling, and Caleb blew it to life. The flame slowly climbed up through the smaller sticks. The tiny blaze was reflected in multiple pairs of eyes. The beasts had left the underbrush and were slowly making their way toward them from every side.

An explosion tore through the tense silence as Alex opened fire and hit one of the animals directly between the eyes. It winced and dropped dead. The rest of the pack hesitated then, and one nuzzled its fallen companion curiously. When the dead animal gave no response, the beast looked up at Alex with menace and leapt for her. She fired again, and the beast fell at her feet.

Mallory followed suit then and began firing haphazardly at the pack. She had not trained in using the magistrates' weapons like Alex had, and she missed her targets until the beasts charging her were within a stone's throw—then she hit one, but two more were closing in quickly behind it. Immediately, Caleb was beside her with his magistrate weapon in one hand, and his short sword in the other. He fired at one beast and stabbed the other as it lunged. As the beast's weight thrust against the sword, it knocked him off balance, and he stumbled backwards.

Just as he fell, Alex yelled, "I need help!"

Mallory turned to see four of the creatures creeping toward her. Alex fired at one, and it fell. Mallory fired at another and grazed it. However, she knew that they would never be able to stop what was coming. Caleb reached up and grabbed Mallory's hand, and she braced for whatever death and suffering these creatures had in store for them.

Without warning, a white light illuminated the clearing. Mallory's eyes were blinded in the brilliance, and she squeezed them tightly closed. The certain death Mallory thought they were going to face never materialized. Soon, behind her eyelids, her pupils adjusted to the light, and she cautiously peaked out at the campsite. The rest of the beasts lay on the ground dead—they had been torn apart just like the ones that had attacked the cattle when the light went down in the city. The white light was emanating from two small orbs floating in the darkness. Then they vanished, and Mallory's eyes had to once again adjust to the change in luminescence. The small campfire had a comparably dimmer glow, which gradually revealed a strange little bronze sprite.

The sprite looked like it was made of clockwork parts; gears and springs ticked and clicked as it moved toward them. Caleb was still holding Mallory's hand, and he squeezed it tighter now. After all the trouble they had faced with sprites, seeing a strange one in the dark forest at night was unsettling. Seeing what it had done to the creatures of the dark forest did not help. If it chose to attack them in a similar fashion, they would be helpless against it. They would have stood more of a chance fighting off the fangs and claws of a pack of beasts than the unforgiving, nigh-indestructible power of sprite steel.

The sprite stood between them and the fire now, and it eyed them—the dimly-lit orbs focused and refocused on them. Then it came slowly forward, and reached out for Alex's scarred hand, which she had not covered with a glove as she usually did because of the confusion. Its eyes focused on the arm, then moved back from them and in a metallic voice asked, "You are from the Lost City?"

The three friends looked at each other with their eyebrows raised. Then Caleb answered, "We are from the city, yes."

The sprite ticked and clicked, and its eyes scanned over their campsite, their weapons, their broaches, and when it seemed satisfied with what it saw, it said, "You bear the symbols of the Triad of leadership. The Dikaió Archivist requests the city leaders to send a Chorus, that they may study the ancient ways."

Mallory spoke then, "Our lineage is of the Triad, but I am a Chorus." She paused and looked at Alex and Caleb, felt a tinge of guilt, and continued, "We are all Dikaió Choruses."

The sprite responded, "Will you answer the Archivist's call?"

Caleb and Alex huddled around Mallory.

"What do you think?" Caleb asked.

Alex shook her head, "I don't know. I've never heard of a Dikaió Archivist."

Mallory laughed a little and asked, "You'd rather stay out here with these things?" She nodded at the dead creatures around them.

Caleb nodded, "I say we take our chances with the sprite and whoever this Archivist is."

Alex considered their argument, and somewhere out in the darkness a four-legged creature howled. Alex's eyes rolled toward the sound, and she nodded, "Fair enough."

Mallory turned toward the sprite, "Will the Archivist accept three Choruses?"

The sprite responded immediately, "I believe she will. She was quite adamant that I not return without one. Three is better than one."

"Then we accept."

The sprite turned toward the dark forest. "Very well, you should sleep. I will keep watch, and we shall leave in the morning. It is a long journey to the Library."

Acknowledgements

We thank God for calling us to finish this project: We owe sincere gratitude to You not only for providing constant inspiration and real joy in the process, but also for hounding us with conviction when we were distracted, discouraged, and ready to quit. We are thankful that You gave us this idea, that You turned our hearts toward our children and their needs, that You blessed our marriage with times of creative bonding, while guarding our words so that we would not mislead or cause harm in the process.

To our parents, thanks for helping us obtain library cards and supporting our creativity. Thanks to Stephen's father, Dale Porter, for exhilarating overnight adventures at the TV studio and encouraging his education. Thanks to Stephen's mother, Terry Porter, for providing his first dictionary and encyclopedia sets. Thanks to Gayle's father, John Gustafson, for trips to the library and teaching her how to operate the micro-fiche machine and use the Dewey decimal system. Thanks to Gayle's mother, Marjorie Gustafson, for teaching her that girls can learn anything if they are willing to work hard. Thanks to all our parents for giving us a good sense of humor, and for showing us beautiful places to remind us that God is the creative genius who made this vast, gorgeous world.

To our dear friends, Brad and Joy Kroes, and Ken and Donna Stucki, thank you for encouraging us and never telling us that we were making a huge mistake to become writers. We are grateful for your faithful friendship, for laughter and good food, and for your indelible patience with our incessant puns and sarcasm.

We also thank August, Anne, William and Abigail Thurmer; Brandon and Kaylee Gustafson; and our church family for patiently cheering us on during this endeavor.

Finally, thank you to our readers who give purpose and fresh perspective to our writing. May you be inspired by our words, as you have inspired us to write.